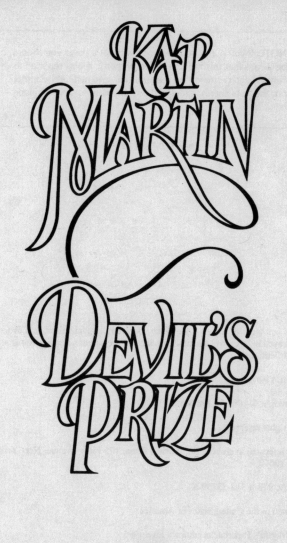

KAT MARTIN

DEVIL'S PRIZE

St. Martin's Paperbacks

This is a work of fiction. All of the characters, organizations, and events portrayed in this novel are either products of the author's imagination or are used fictitiously.

DEVIL'S PRIZE

Copyright © 1995 by Kat Martin.

For information address St. Martin's Press, 175 Fifth Avenue, New York, NY 10010.

ISBN: 978-0-312-53259-8

Printed in the United States of America

St. Martin's Paperbacks edition / June 1995

St. Martin's Paperbacks are published by St. Martin's Press, 175 Fifth Avenue, New York, NY 10010.

15   14   13   12   11   10   9

To my editor, Jennifer Weis, for her hard work and support, and to Sally Richardson, for taking a chance on me—and making me feel like a star.

A special thanks to Roger Cooper, whose energy and enthusiasm make him so much fun to work for; to Jen Richards and all of the St. Martin's staff. You guys are terrific! The sky is the limit!

A thing of beauty is a joy forever:
  Its loveliness increases; it will never
Pass into nothingness; but still will keep
A bower quiet for us, and a sleep
Full of sweet dreams, and health, and quiet
    breathing

John Keats

Chapter One

London, England, 1809

CAT AND MOUSE, DAMIEN SCOFFED. *MORE LIKE SEASONED PANTHER AND WARY YOUNG DOE.* HE WATCHED HER through the french doors leading into the main salon of Lord Dorring's town house. Gowned in emerald silk the same shade as her eyes, laughing softly with one of her beaux, she led the young man onto the dance floor.

It was crowded in the sumptuous high-ceilinged room, a crush of London's finest. Men in tailcoats and brocade waistcoats, ladies in silks and satins, some of them more richly gowned than she, but none of them nearly as lovely. She crossed the inlaid marble floor, all elegance and grace, a slender white-gloved hand resting lightly on her suitor's arm. For an instant her glance veered toward the terrace.

She knew he was out there.

Just as he had been watching her, she had been watching him.

Damien Falon, sixth earl of Falon, propped one wide shoulder against a rough brick wall of the town house. He had made it a point to discover the balls and soirees, house parties and musicales the young woman would be attending. The Season had begun, and the fashionable elite had arrived in London—Alexa Garrick among them.

He assessed her now, dancing a roundel, her pretty face flushed with exertion, fiery auburn hair shimmering softly beside her cheeks, then she and her partner left the dance floor. He was a thin man, the young Duke of Roxbury, but there was a presence about him, and he was obviously enchanted by the lady at his side. He pressed her for another dance, but Alexa shook her head. The duke bowed somewhat stiffly and left her near the door.

Damien raised the snifter he cradled in a dark, long-fingered hand and took a sip of his brandy. She was walking toward the terrace, tall and regal, looking neither right nor left, making her way through the French doors. Careful to avoid the place where he stood in the shadows, she crossed the terrace and paused at the opposite end, her gaze going out to the garden. The faint glow of torches lit the manicured oyster-shell paths, and moonlight glistened on bubbling fountains of water.

Smiling faintly, Damien set his brandy glass down on a small ornate pedestal and made his way across the brickwork to the woman at the opposite end.

She turned at his approach and something flickered in her eyes. He couldn't decide if it was interest—or anger. It didn't really matter. Already he had achieved his first objective.

"Good evening . . . Alexa."

Surprise flared in her clear green eyes, which ran

over his black tailcoat and white cravat, taking in the fashionable cut, the impeccable fit, seeming to approve, though the use of her name had caught her a little off guard.

"I'm sorry," she said, "I don't believe we have been introduced."

"We haven't. But I know who you are . . . and I think you know who I am."

Her head came up a fraction. She wasn't accustomed to a man who challenged her. It was the key, he had discovered, the way to intrigue the lady, to capture her attention and lure her into his web.

"You're Falon." Her tone said she had heard the stories about him, most of which were true. Still, it was obvious she had no idea who he really was.

"Damien," he corrected, moving closer. Another woman might have walked away. He was betting Alexa would not.

"You've been watching me. I noticed you last week and the week before that. What is it that you want?"

"Nothing every other man here doesn't want. You're a beautiful woman, Alexa." He stood close enough to smell her perfume, the soft scent of lilac, to catch the hint of uncertainty in the depths of her pretty green eyes. "The truth is, you intrigue me. That hasn't happened to me in a very long time."

She said nothing for a moment. "I'm sorry, Lord Falon, I don't know what it is you expect of me, but I assure you it isn't worth all of this trouble."

A corner of his mouth curved up. "No? Perhaps it will be . . . if you let it."

She stared at him, wary, yet her interest had been piqued. She glanced out into the shadows and nervously moistened her lips. "I-It's late," she said with a slight hesitation. "They'll be looking for me soon. I had better be going back in."

He could ruffle her a little. Good. From what he had

observed, it wasn't that easy to do. "Why would you want to go in when it's far more pleasant out here?"

She stiffened a bit, throwing the lines of her face into shadow. "And far more dangerous, I should think. I know who you are, Lord Falon. I know you're a rogue with a despicable reputation. I know you're a rake of the very worst sort."

He smiled. "So you've been asking about me. I suppose that's a start." A delicate indentation marked her chin, he saw, as she thrust it forward.

"You flatter yourself, my lord."

"What else have you heard?"

"Not much. You're hardly a favorite topic of dinner conversation."

"But the consensus is that I'm off limits to innocent young girls."

"You're very well aware that it is."

"You don't think a man like me could change?"

Her eyes surveyed his face. There was nothing timid in that look, nothing shy or demure. He hadn't expected there would be.

"I didn't say that. How could I? My brother was an even worse rogue than you—if that's possible. Now he's a happily married man."

"So you see, there's hope for me yet."

Again she said nothing, sizing him up, studying him from beneath her thick, dark lashes. "I really have to go." She turned and started walking.

"Will you be at the soiree at Lady Bingham's on Saturday?"

She paused but did not turn. Beneath the torches her burnished red hair blazed brighter than the flickering flames. "I'll be there," she said, and then she was gone.

Damien smiled into the darkness, but his hands balled into fists. How easily she could make a man's blood heat up, his loins grow thick and heavy. Half the young bucks in London had begged for her hand, but she had refused them. Instead she merely toyed with their affections, leading them on, flirting outrageously, moving from one poor besotted fool to the next.

A dozen had offered her marriage.

She should have accepted when she had the chance.

"Alexa! We've been looking all over. Where on earth have you been?" Lady Jane Thornhill, a small, round-faced girl of two and twenty walked toward her. Gowned in a tunic dress of aqua silk ornately embroidered in gold, Jane was the daughter of the Duke of Dandridge. She was also Alexa's best friend.

"I was only out on the terrace." Alexa plucked at a button on her long white glove. "It's so very warm in here."

"The terrace? But surely you haven't forgotten Lord Perry? Faith, he's one of the most eligible bachelors in London. And so handsome . . ."

"Lord Perry, yes . . . I'm sorry, Jane. As I said, it was just so warm."

Jane eyed her shrewdly, soft brown eyes taking in the heightened color in her cheeks. She glanced toward the French doors leading out to the terrace just as Lord Falon walked in.

"Dear God, Alexa, surely you weren't out there with *him*!"

Alexa shrugged. "We spoke briefly, that was all."

"But he's—he's— Why, you haven't even been introduced."

"No, and we probably never will be."

"You've the right of it there. Your brother would probably cock up his toes if he knew that man was anywhere near you."

"I don't see what's so awful about him. Lots of men have affairs with married women."

"There aren't many who've killed three husbands fighting duels over them."

"My brother has certainly fought duels. And it's hardly a secret that Rayne carried on with Lady Campden. Why, he was—"

"Rayne is reformed. Lord Falon is not and probably never will be."

She toyed with a strand of her dark auburn hair. "I don't remember seeing him before, not until this Season."

"He's been out of the country for the past several years. Italy, I believe, or perhaps it was Spain." She glanced back toward the earl. "At any rate, he isn't much for Society. And they aren't much for him."

"Then why do you suppose he's here?"

"I can't imagine." They watched him cross the main salon, turning more than one head as he passed, moving with masculine grace toward the ornate doors leading out to the street. He was taller than most of the men in the room, lean but broad-shouldered, with wavy black hair and dark skin, high carved cheekbones, and incredible bright blue eyes. In a word, he was one of the handsomest men Alexa had ever seen.

"Do you think he's a fortune hunter?" she asked, almost reluctant to hear the answer. At present, she was unmarried and one of the wealthiest young heiresses in London.

"To be honest, I don't think so. From what I've heard, Lord Falon's estate has dwindled, but he isn't really poor—and he isn't in the marriage mart. If he were, there are at least a dozen wealthy young ladies who would marry him despite his reputation. To say nothing of a number of the eligible widows who are his usual cup of tea."

"What else do you know about him?"

"Not much, really. He lives in some dreary old castle on the coast. At one time there were rumors that he was mixed up in smuggling. Another time there was gossip that he was sympathetic to the French."

"The French!" Her brother, Chris, had been killed by the French. She loathed Napoleon and his endless bloody war.

"He's part French on his mother's side," Jane said. "That's where he gets those dark good looks."

Alexa sighed. "A rake, a smuggler—perhaps even worse. There isn't much to recommend him." She frowned at the thought, a little uncertain why the dark earl so intrigued her. Then she smiled more brightly than she had in a very long time. "Still, he *is* incredibly handsome. And those eyes—as blue as the sea after a storm."

"Yes, and just as unfathomable. You may rest assured, that man means nothing but trouble."

Alexa merely shrugged. Already she was counting the days until Saturday next.

Though the week seemed to drag for Alexa, for Lady Jane Thornhill the days swiftly passed. Standing next to a long white-clothed table at Lady Bingham's, beside an ornate punch bowl lit by a silver branch of candles, Jane watched her friend walking toward her on the arm of the handsome Lord Perry. Alexa was smiling, listening politely as she always did, just as bored as she had been since the start of the Season.

She had returned to London from Marden, not far from Jane's father's estate at Dandridge, where the two of them had met. For the Season, Alexa was staying with her brother and his wife at Stoneleigh, the viscount's mansion on Hampstead Heath. They had insisted she return to London this year, forcing her back into Society, hoping at last she would choose a proper husband. If it hadn't been for Peter and the tragedy that occurred, Jane was certain Lord Stoneleigh would have pressed his sister long before this.

Instead he had indulged her, knowing she had taken her young friend's death too hard, knowing she felt responsible, allowing her to remain closed up at Marden for the past two years.

But Alexa had finally returned, and within the first few weeks of the Season was just as sought after as she had been that very first year. She was just as beautiful—more so now that her features had matured—just as charming, just as warm. But inside she was different. She was no longer the carefree young innocent who selfishly basked in the male adoration lavished upon her. She was no longer willful, no longer spoiled.

Alexa was a woman now, in every way but one. The loss of her friend had cost her youth, and along with it some inner part of herself. It was almost as if she held herself back, as if some tiny spark of life inside her had died that day along with Peter.

Jane wished Alexa could be more like the rest of the girls her age. Caught up in the adoration of her young male admirers, having a difficult time choosing from the long list of suitors vying for her hand.

But Alexa wanted none of them.

"They're all just little boys," she'd once said. "I want someone who will make my heart pound. I want someone I can respect, someone I can talk to. I want a man, and I don't intend to settle for anything less."

Jane had laughed at the time, admiring her friend for being so outspoken, and knowing that was part of the reason they were such good friends.

And Jane had always understood her. Alexa's mother had died when she was young, just as Jane's had, leaving her friend in the care of a father and two older brothers nearly twice her age. It was hardly surprising that Alexa was attracted to more mature men. Unfortunately, most of those who pursued her seemed to hold as little appeal as all the rest.

Except for Lord Falon.

Of all the men her friend could choose, this one was the worst. True, he was mysterious and intriguing. He was also volatile and dangerous, perhaps even criminal. Any interest he had in Alexa must surely be dishonorable—though Jane had to admit she had never heard it said he had deliberately seduced an innocent young girl. His wealth was far less than Alexa's, and even if they fell madly in love, the viscount would never approve the marriage.

And yet there had been that spark in Alexa's eyes, missing for so very long.

Beneath the flickering lights of a crystal chandelier, Jane watched her friend moving gracefully among the fashionably garbed men and women of the ton, her pasted-on smile fooling all of them but Jane. Perhaps Lord Falon would be good for her. Perhaps he could rekindle the flame of life that had all but died inside her.

Perhaps the danger would be worth it.

Lady Jane Thornhill smiled. If Alexa was careful, what could it hurt?

She glanced toward the door leading out to the garden. The handsome Lord Falon had not yet arrived, but Jane didn't doubt that he would.

What would it hurt if Alexa flirted with the man just a little? What would it hurt if she even went so far as to kiss him?

There had never been a man Alexa couldn't handle. Perhaps it was time she met one who left her a little bit uncertain, challenged her in some way, sparked that hidden flame.

Perhaps, she thought—but she wasn't really so sure.

He was here; she could feel it. And he was watching her. Alexa laughed brightly at something her companion, the sandy-haired, slightly pudgy Admiral Lord Cawley had said, determined to disguise how nervous she felt. The admiral was speaking of the war, regaling his several-years-past victory at Trafalgar for at least the dozenth time.

Alexa's mind strayed from his droning nasal voice, and out of the corner of her eye she saw the earl enter the ballroom, tall and lean yet powerfully built. It made her stomach flutter just to watch the way he moved, sparsely, smoothly, with an innate self-assurance she found lacking in other men.

Pausing only briefly to exchange a word now and then, he made his way toward the doors leading out to the garden. How long would he wait? she wondered, unwilling to approach him too soon.

For hours, she decided, as the time ticked away. It appeared the earl was a very patient man.

She went to him just after supper, finding it easy to break away, grateful Rayne and Jocelyn had grown weary and left to return to Stoneleigh, an hour's carriage ride away. Thankful her brother had allowed her to spend the week with Jane.

"I've spoken to the duke," her handsome brother had said with an affectionate smile. Jocelyn stood beside him, one of them slender and elegant, the other massive and strong. "His grace is not yet ready to leave. You and Jane may stay until he is. Behave yourself, have a good time, and I'll send round a carriage on Monday." With his thick, dark, coffee-brown hair, masculine features, and rough male charm, her brother had always had a way with the ladies.

"Thank you, Rayne." She leaned over and kissed his cheek, thinking oddly that though her brother was more stoutly built, he was the only man she knew as tall as Damien Falon.

"Have a good time, dear." Jocelyn smiled and hugged her. Two years older, Jo was tall and slim, matching Alexa in size. She was dark-haired, pretty, and intelligent. In the years since her marriage to Rayne, she and Alexa had become close friends.

"I promise I shall dance every dance." That wasn't the truth, but it made Jo happy to think she was enjoying herself. In truth, until Lord Falon had made an appearance this Season, she would rather have been back at Marden.

She waited for her brother and his wife to leave, then summoned her courage and made her way toward the rear of the house, a two-story brick affair done in the French motif. Crossing the last few paces to the door, she smoothed the front of her high-waisted gold silk gown, pressing the sheer tulle back into place, straightening the deep vee neckline that showed a great deal of her bosom, a style, thanks to Jocelyn, her brother had at last grudgingly accepted.

The Birminghams' garden was smaller than the one at Lord Dorring's, where she had last seen the earl, with only a single ornate fountain. Insects hummed in the darkness and the smell of damp leaves hung in the air.

Alexa glanced round the neat hedgerows and sweet-scented flowers. Crocus and tulips bloomed, and there were ceramic pots heavy with pink geraniums, but there was no sign of Lord Falon.

Perhaps he had not been so patient after all.

Still, she walked down the steps and off toward the high stone wall at the rear. She heard him before she saw him, his shoes crunching softly on the dimly lit path.

"I hoped you would come," he said in a deep male voice reminiscent of brandy dashed with a hint of cream. The odd combination of rough and smooth sent a ripple of heat through her body.

Her hand came up to her throat, where a necklace of topaz glinted in the light of the moon. Several more of the deep amber stones were fastened in her hair, which was coiled in a dark auburn wreath above her head. "I shouldn't have."

"No . . ." he said, "you shouldn't have. Why did you?" He blended into the shadows, his skin dark and swarthy, yet his teeth were white, his eyes unmistakably blue.

"Perhaps . . . you intrigue me."

He smiled then, apparently recalling he had said those words to her. It made him look younger, his face a little less harsh. "Perhaps it's the danger you find attractive, doing something your brother would forbid."

"My brother gave up trying to run my life some time ago. It's true he's a little too protective, but that's only because he loves me."

"It must be nice," he said, "having someone who cares that much."

"Is there no one who cares for you that much?"

A corner of his mouth curved up. It was a hard mouth, she saw, yet it was decidedly male and remarkably attractive. "Not really. There was someone once I cared a great deal about, someone whose happiness meant more than my own."

"A woman?"

"No."

Strangely, she felt relieved. She wanted to press him, to know whom it was he had cared for, but she could see by his eyes he would not answer. "Why have you come to London? Obviously it isn't to mingle with the social elite."

"I had business to attend. I meant only to stay for a week. Then I saw you—at the opera—and I decided to postpone my return."

Something fluttered in her stomach. It was an odd sensation that made her heart speed up and her palms grow damp. "Why are you—"

"No more questions, Alexa. We don't have that kind of time." In an instant she was pressed against him, his arm around her waist, his long legs intimately brushing against her thighs. His eyes held hers the instant before he took her lips, his mouth slanting down in a fiery kiss. She gasped at the feel of it, hard and soft at the same time, hot and tingling and incredibly male. He used the moment to his advantage, sliding his tongue inside, sending shivers of heat through her body. He was tasting her, drinking in the desire he sparked, taking her breath away. He cupped her face in his hands and deepened the kiss, spawning whirlwinds of heat inside her, stroking her with his tongue, claiming her in a way no man ever had.

Alexa made a sound of protest in her throat—or was it one of longing?

In seconds she was clinging to him, unsure what was happening, fearful of this tall dark man and the things he made her feel, more afraid of herself.

Dear God what am I doing? Trembling all over, her legs unsteady and threatening to give way completely, she tore herself free and took a shaky step backward. As the heat burned into her cheeks, reminding her of what she had done, Alexa drew back and slapped him, the sound echoing loudly across the garden. She turned to leave, but he caught her arm.

"Alexa."

"Let go of me."

Slowly, he released her. "I'm sorry. I know I shouldn't have done that."

"That doesn't alter the fact that you did."

A reluctant sigh whispered past his lips. "I suppose it was a test of sorts." He rubbed his cheek with a long-fingered hand. "If it's any consolation, you passed with the highest marks."

Alexa said nothing. She knew all about such tests. She had been testing men for years—and all of them had failed. "I've got to go in." She started walking, still shaking inside and feeling decidedly unsteady. Damien caught up with her in two long strides.

"You don't have to run away. I promise it won't happen again . . . not unless you want it to."

Alexa turned to face him, caught the play of moonlight on the shadows of his face. "I don't understand any of this. Just what is it you want from me?"

For the longest time he did not answer. "To be honest—I'm not exactly sure."

She knew the feeling. She wasn't sure what she wanted from him.

"When can I see you?" he pressed, his eyes a deep, midnight-blue in the darkness.

Tell him you can't—won't—see him again. Tell him you're not the least bit interested in carrying this mad infatuation any further. "Lady Jane Thornhill will be holding a small soiree this Wednesday eve. If you would like to come—"

"What about your brother?"

"Rayne and his wife have other plans for the evening."

Damien flashed a disarming smile, reached for her hand and slowly raised it to his lips. She could feel the heat of his mouth even through her gloves, and goose bumps feathered up her arm. "You may count on seeing me there."

Alexa turned away from him, her face flushed once more, her heart hammering oddly, and hurriedly walked away. All the way into the house she could feel his bright blue eyes burning into her back.

"You invited him here?" Jane couldn't seem to believe it. "My father will be in a tither." They were sitting on the rose satin counterpane at the foot of Jane's high-tester bed. They had just returned to the duke's home on Grosvenor Square, changed out of their evening gowns, and now wore their long white cotton nightclothes.

"Your father will think someone else invited him.

And his grace is far too much of a gentlemen to ask the earl to leave."

"I suppose you've the right of it there."

"I've got to find out what he's after. I have to know if . . ."

"If what?"

"If he's really as terrible as they say he is. When I look at him, I see . . . I don't know, something. I just don't believe he can really be all that bad."

"Believe it. The man is an unconscionable rake and a confirmed bachelor."

"So was Rayne. So was his best friend, Dominic Edgemont, the Marquess of Gravenwold. Look what wonderful husbands they've turned out to be."

"You're not seriously considering this rogue as a candidate for marriage?"

"I didn't say that, did I?"

"No, but that's certainly the way it sounds to me."

Alexa ran a hand down the heavy rose silk bed hangings. "I know you don't approve, but I can't help it. If he's really as bad as you think he is, surely I shall discover the truth. In the meantime, Lord Falon is the first man who has ever made me feel so much alive."

"Feeling alive is one thing, winding up in his bed is another."

"Jane!"

"Well, it's the truth. You had better be careful, dear girl, and we both know it."

Jane was older than Alexa, and not in the least naive. She had chosen to remain unmarried, much to her father's chagrin, saying she hadn't yet met the right man. But the Season had only just begun. Jane was pretty and pleasantly formed, and with her father's wealth and power, her suitors had always been numerous. Perhaps this Season, Jane would be ready to make her choice.

Alexa leaned over and hugged her much shorter friend. "I'll be careful. I promise."

* * *

It was nearly dawn when Damien returned to the small
suite of rooms he had taken for the Season at the Clarendon Hotel, one of the most fashionable in London.
With its dark wood paneling and thick Persian carpets,
the place had a masculine quality that reminded him of
home and dulled his dislike of the crowded streets, rau-
cous noise, and stench of the city.

A footman held open the etched glass door as he
entered the lobby, dimly lit by gilded chandeliers.
Damien barely noticed, his mind fixed instead on the
evening past. His encounter with the lady in the garden
had left his body strung taut as a bowstring.

For days he had been stalking her, watching her every move, thinking of the prize he would wrest from
her in the end. After the kiss they had shared, the fiery
way she had responded, he needed a woman. Badly.
He'd gone to the Satin Garter, paid handsomely for a
pretty little whore with dark auburn hair, and let her
soothe his passions. He felt rested now, relaxed as he
hadn't been in days, and ready to continue his campaign.

As he climbed the rosewood-paneled stairs, a faint
smile curved his lips. His meeting in the garden had
gone even better than he had planned. Of course he
hadn't meant to kiss her. The last thing he intended
was to scare the woman away.

Damien shoved his key into the heavy brass lock, his
smile turning bitter and harsh. He had known from the
start, Alexa Garrick wouldn't be easy to scare. She was
used to controlling men, used to toying with their affections, used to playing the game.

Until he had kissed her, he hadn't been sure she was
still a virgin, but there was no mistaking that ingenue,
the trembling that had signaled her untried passions.
And the fact she remained untouched made the taking
all the sweeter.

He thought of their next encounter, several days hence, at the Duke of Dandridge's Grosvenor mansion. If all went well, by the end of the night Alexa Garrick would be in his debt. Deeply in his debt.

It was another key he had discovered. Miss Garrick liked the green baize tables. Liked them just a little too much. Usually her brother was there to keep her out of deep play and steer her clear of trouble. With the viscount out of the way and Alexa's mind on the attraction developing between them, there was no telling how much she might lose.

Not that she was that bad a player. If it came down to it, he intended to cheat.

Damien closed the door to his small but elegant suite of rooms. It was stuffy inside, but opening the windows would only let in the oppressive London air. He wished he was home, back at Castle Falon, overlooking the ocean and breathing in the fresh air rolling in off the sea.

He would be, he told himself, perhaps within a fortnight. Alexa Garrick had taken the bait, and soon his well-laid trap could be sprung.

As he crossed the room, he untied his cravat and pulled it off, then began to unbutton his shirt. The little whore had been good, but she hadn't slaked his desire for Alexa Garrick. He meant to take her, to punish her for what she had done. He would do it for Peter.

And now that he had sampled a little of her charms, perhaps a bit for himself.

He didn't bother to deny he intended to enjoy it.

Chapter Two

"HOW DO I LOOK?" ALEXA TURNED IN FRONT OF THE GILT-
FRAMED CHEVAL GLASS MIRROR, HOLDING OUT HER SLEN-
der silk skirt, checking the almost indecently low bust
line of the alabaster high-waisted gown.

It had small puffed sleeves of sheerest tulle, and the
bodice was heavily encrusted with pearls. They trailed
in delicate ropes from beneath her breasts, rustling sen-
suously as she moved and reflecting the soft pale glow
of the lamplight. Pearls were fashioned in her braided
crown of auburn hair, a strand encircled her throat, and
two small pearl ear bobs dangled from her ears.

"You've never looked more lovely," Jane said, and
Alexa smiled.

"Thank you." Thinking of the night ahead and the
handsome dark earl, she took a steadying breath. "I'm
as jumpy as a cat, and he probably won't be here for
hours—if he comes at all."

"The man may be a rogue, but he's hardly a fool. You may be certain he will come." Jane smoothed a disobedient lock of her short, dark curls, looking more than pretty herself. "Most likely he will wait till the end of the evening, hoping he can get you alone."

Alexa nodded. "What about you, Jane? Is there anyone special you'll be looking for this eve? Perhaps Lord Perry will come."

"Lord Perry? The marquess has shown more interest in you than he has in me," Jane said, her cheeks suddenly flushed with color.

"I can't credit that at all. Lord Perry has only been kind to me because of you. He knows we're the best of friends. I believe he's hoping I will aid his suit."

Jane brightened. "Do you think so?" Wearing a pale rose gown heavily embroidered and sparkling with brilliants, her warm brown eyes alight with excitement, Jane looked especially attractive this eve.

"It's entirely possible." Reginald Chambers, Lord Perry, seemed to have caught Jane's interest. Alexa hoped the feeling was returned. "He has certainly been solicitous of late—far more so when you are around."

"Yes, I suppose he has. . . ." She smiled winningly and caught Alexa's arm. "I vow we'll find out soon enough. Come along, Alexa. It's beyond time we made our entrance."

Alexa took a deep steadying breath and the two of them started for the door. Again tonight her stomach swirled with anticipation. It had been a very long while since she had felt that way, and there was no doubt it felt good.

Since Peter's death, she had spent most of her time avoiding people. Blessed with her brother's same love of horses, she rode a good deal, trying fruitlessly to distance herself from her guilt, and as a form of penance immersed herself in her studies, but she'd had no interest in men. And even if she had, those who had called on her at Marden hadn't sparked the least bit of interest.

She thought of Lord Falon and wondered when the earl might make his appearance. She still knew almost nothing about him, yet he intrigued her as no man ever had. Alexa smiled. The tall dark man was definitely an enigma.

One by one Alexa intended to discover the secrets he worked so hard to hide.

The duke's idea of a small soiree turned out to be a three-hundred-person crush, which posed little problem in the huge Georgian mansion on Grosvenor Square. Beneath a blaze of crystal chandeliers, an orchestra played in the Yellow Salon, but Alexa was too nervous to join in the dancing. Instead she walked from one sumptuous room to the next, smiling, working to make conversation, wondering when the earl would appear.

Surprisingly, he had been there for quite some time before she discovered his presence in the India Room, or at least so it seemed from the stack of winnings piled on the green baize table in front of him.

With only a glance at the earl, she approached the short balding man seated across from him. "Good evening, Lord Cavendish. I hope you're enjoying yourself."

"My dear Miss Garrick," the baron said. The earl rose gracefully, the chubby baron clumsily, and the stout little man bowed over her hand. "How good it is to see you."

"It has been a while, hasn't it? As I recall, we played a bit at Lord Sheffield's last month. I hope you're fairing better this eve."

"Not so far, I'm afraid. I'm having a devil of a run of bad luck. But then that has often been the case when I play with the earl." He turned to the tall dark-haired man. "You know Lord Falon, of course."

"I—"

"I'm afraid I've never had the pleasure," the earl put in smoothly, with a graceful bow over her hand.

Cavendish smiled. "She's a tiger at whist. Near put me in the poorhouse."

"Really?" The earl's black brow arched up. "If that is the case, why don't you join us, Miss Garrick? It's only a friendly game."

"I've a better idea," the baron said. "I've lost more than enough this eve, and I'm very nearly starving. Miss Garrick may take my place." He smiled at her warmly, crinkling the plump folds of skin at the corners of his eyes. "German whist, my dear. Two-handed play. You won't be needing me a'tall."

She smiled. "All right." She glanced down at the table, but her mind was not on the cards. It had strayed to the handsome Lord Falon the moment she had seen him sitting in the room.

As Cavendish waddled toward the door, the earl pulled out a chair and seated her across from him, then sat down and picked up the cards. He ruffled through them, the soft hum of the deck concealing the rapid flutter of her heart. As he shuffled and began to deal, his hands were graceful, sure, moving the cards with precision. She remembered their warmth as he had cradled her face for his kiss. The thought made the heat creep into her cheeks and her mouth go dry.

"I heard you liked to play," he said.

"Yes . . . I enjoy gaming very much."

"I thought this might give us a chance to talk."

Her eyes moved over his face, noting the carved planes and valleys, the tiny scar beneath his left ear. "And the baron?"

"An uncollected debt." He smiled. "I told him I wanted to meet you."

Alexa said nothing more. The cards were dealt and she worked to keep her mind on the game. Normally it would have been easy. She loved to gamble. She had played with Rayne and Jo for hours at Marden, and gambled even more since her return to London. She loved the challenge, the blood-pumping thrill of winning. All the ladies of her acquaintance played, usually for little more than pin money, but a few of the women bet more heavily. Alexa had played against them—betting more deeply than she should have—but she had usually won.

Of late she had passed a good many hours that way, or by betting in a lottery or a Little Go—a smaller, not quite legal version not sanctioned by the state. Sometimes she won, oftimes she broke even, occasionally she lost a bit more than she meant to. Rayne had scolded her once or twice, telling her stories of the Duchess of Devonshire, whose unruly passion for cards had ended in the loss of her fortune, but Alexa had continued to play, and Rayne hadn't really seemed to care.

She had promised to be more careful, yet she was hardly a child anymore. She had her own money to spend as she wished; she didn't need her brother's permission.

"Your deal, Miss Garrick." The earl's voice washed over her, drawing her from her thoughts. He looked incredibly handsome in his perfectly tailored dove-gray tailcoat, burgundy waistcoat, and dark gray trousers. The somber colors he usually wore only added to his dark appeal.

Time passed as the two of them played. Alexa eyed the deck and chewed her bottom lip. She had been losing steadily all evening. "Perhaps we should quit for a while. My luck seems to have escaped me."

"Nonsense," the earl said. "Have you forgotten the last few plays? Your luck has already begun to change." Indeed, she *had* won the last few hands. His blue eyes locked on her face, and her heart dipped into her stomach. "Unless, of course . . . you don't feel up to the challenge."

Alexa straightened in her chair. If he thought she was a coward, he was sorely mistaken. "The cards, if you please, my lord. The night is far from over. In fact, I would say we have only just begun."

He smiled at that, and she thought again how handsome he was. Not in the usual sense, perhaps, for Falon was far from pretty. His features were hard, carved, his black brows sleek and male and perfectly formed. He was a man, not a boy, and everything about him said so.

She glanced around the high-ceilinged room, unconsciously comparing him to other men who sat nearby. Several women played loo, while at another green baize table gentlemen and ladies played faro. The earl, she noticed, received more than one covert glance from the women, and more than one hostile glare from the men.

They continued to play, and as the evening wore on, the earl kept her smiling, her face often flushed at the compliments he paid, her hands often oddly unsteady. He'd been more charming than she had ever seen him —and those eyes . . .

Always they were watching, admiring her without words, speaking his desire for her, telling her that her presence at the table was all he had hoped for and more.

The crush of people had long begun to fade, though a few hearty souls still gamed in the India Room, along with her and the earl. Others had gone in to an extravagant late supper served at a long buffet table in the state dining room.

Alexa had not eaten a bite all evening. Instead she sipped a small glass of sherry that had, with the dozens of servants hovering about, begun to seem bottomless. If it weren't for the jangle of her nerves and the dark earl's presence, she would certainly have felt light-headed.

"Your turn, Miss Garrick."

Alexa looked at her hand. She should have quit hours ago—Rayne would be furious when he discovered she had spent this much time in Lord Falon's company, but the cards had once again turned. She was holding a handful of spades, the trump card, and she had the lead.

These were the best cards she had been dealt all evening. If her luck held, she could raise the stakes, win back the money she had lost, and show Lord Falon what a formidable player she could be.

Alexa smiled. "I believe we've been far too conservative, my lord. What say you to doubling the stakes?"

A winged black brow arched up. "Living rather dangerously, aren't you?"

"If the play is too deep, my lord, I certainly—"

He smiled. "Your wish is my command, lovely lady."

And so the stakes were raised and the game continued. Unfortunately, as good as her hand had been, Lord Falon's cards were better, as were his next and his next.

"I—I believe you have completely done me in," she finally admitted sometime later. "I don't think I've ever witnessed a more formidable run of good fortune."

"Luck of the draw, I suppose."

"And excellent playing."

"As did you, Miss Garrick." He smiled as he gracefully came to his feet and moved behind her to pull out her chair. "As for the amount you've lost, I don't expect you carry that sort of currency around on your person. I shall be happy to accept your marker."

"My marker . . . yes . . . I—I'm afraid I've lost track of just how much it is." She glanced down at the tally Lord Falon picked up.

He scanned it and his mouth curved up at the corners. "It appears you owe me just over ninety thousand pounds."

Alexa gasped aloud. "Ninety thousand pounds!" Her heart slammed into her ribs and the pounding grew steadily more fierce. "I—I cannot credit it could be that much!"

"Ninety thousand three hundred thirty nine, to be exact."

"There . . . there must be some mistake, some error in the sums."

"That's what the tally says." He handed her the paper and she looked at the numbers, which seemed almost accusing as the bold black scroll stared back at her.

Alexa read it, then read it again. There was no mistaking that she had wagered and lost a small fortune. She steadied her breathing and fixed her eyes on the earl.

"Is this what you have been after? My money? Is that the reason you've been following me, watching me?"

He glanced around to see if anyone noticed their conversation, saw that most of the others had left or were still engrossed in their play. "It has never been the money, Alexa."

She straightened her shoulders, wondering how she could have been so easily duped, and why it was that she felt so betrayed. "You needn't be concerned that I won't pay you. I'm a very wealthy woman, as you undoubtedly know. Unfortunately, it may take me a little bit of time."

"How much time?" he asked.

"I can pay you in small installments as my allowance comes in, but my brother is the trustee of my estate until I marry or reach the age of twenty-three. There's no way I can pay the full amount I owe you until then."

"Why don't you simply ask your brother for the money?"

"I won't involve Rayne in this. He doesn't owe the debt—I do. I'll see it paid myself."

She thought he would argue. Instead he merely smiled. "I hoped you would say that."

"What—What do you mean?"

"I told you, Alexa, it isn't the money I'm after. It's you, lovely lady. I've wanted you since the moment I laid eyes on you."

Color rushed into her cheeks. "What on earth are you talking about? Surely you aren't suggesting . . . ?"

"Ninety thousand pounds is a great deal of money." Piercing blue eyes locked on her face. "Meet me. Stay with me the night, and your marker will be returned to you."

"You're mad."

"Perhaps I am. Perhaps not. You've become an obsession with me, Alexa. Your brother would hardly allow me to court you. I'm forced to do whatever it takes to make you mine . . . if only for a night."

Her mind spun out of control. *Dear God in heaven.* He meant to seduce her, brazenly, without a dash of honor, and now—if she let him—he had the means. "I shall send my marker round to your lodgings on the morrow."

"You will find me at the Clarendon Hotel."

She nodded stiffly and started to leave, but he caught her arm.

"I'll expect the money by this time next week . . . or your promise to meet me." His fingers caressed her hand, making small sensuous circles on the palm. Heat spiraled low in her belly and tiny goose bumps surfaced across her skin.

"You planned this, didn't you?"

"Yes."

"You desire me that much?"

"That much and more." His eyes bored into her, compelling eyes, beseeching.

Alexa smiled tightly. "My thanks for an interesting evening. Good night, Lord Falon." Lifting her skirts up out of the way, she turned and walked out of the room.

Damien watched her go, suffering an odd mix of emotions. Elation that the next step in his plan had been achieved, uncertainty as to which of the choices she would make, anticipation of what would happen if she chose as he hoped she would. After an evening in her company, his blood ran hot with desire for her. Just the sound of her laughter, rich and warm and slightly throaty, had left him hard and throbbing. One way or another, he meant to have her, to see her ruined, and Peter's needless death avenged.

Whatever happened, she deserved it. All he dealt her and more.

There was just this one small corner of his mind that was having trouble accepting what he hoped was about to happen, the same small part that kept reminding him what an unconscionable bastard he was.

It was this same part, the small, decent part of himself all but forgotten that kept niggling him, kept shaking his resolve and filling him with doubts. It was that tiny shred of conscience that reminded him she was far less sophisticated than he had expected. And far more enchanting. It bothered him that in all the time he had watched her, he had never seen her play the tease, never seen her lead a man on, never shown herself to be the self-centered spoiled young heiress he knew she was.

Damien made his way through the entry, paying little heed to the row upon row of carved marble busts that lined the way or the huge, domed stained-glass window above his head. Instead as he stepped outside the duke's mansion, he inhaled a fresh breath of air. Passing footman in red and gold livery, he descended the broad stone steps, thinking of Alexa Garrick and wondering at the repercussions of the evening they had shared.

There would be gossip about the two of them, yet they had never been left alone, and at one time or another even the staunchest member of the ton had succumbed to the lure of cards. Odds were, Alexa would survive the small indiscretion of his company with only an eyebrow raised here and there and an unpleasant scolding from her brother.

The real question was, what exactly would she do?

Damien continued along the walkway to the street, where a servant summoned his sleek black phaeton. All along the route to his hotel he wondered if his strategy would work. Would Alexa go to the viscount for the money she owed, or try to settle the matter herself?

He was banking on the latter.

Alexa liked playing games. She had proven that in spades again tonight. He smiled at the pun he had made. He had intrigued her, challenged her, and tonight he had bested her, all the while working to build the attraction between them. Would she meet the challenge as he hoped she would?

By the middle of the week, he would know if she still played the game.

Damien saw Alexa two more times before week's end. Once at a house party at Colonel Sir William Thomas's, another night at a soiree given by the fashionable Madam Tremaine. He stayed only briefly, watching his quarry from a distance, never approaching, yet telling her without words how much he desired her. He had received her marker, just as she had promised, but her manner continued to surprise him.

From the letters he had collected during his brief trips home from the Continent, letters his mother and half sister Melissa had written informing him of Peter's suicide and the unrequited love for Alexa Garrick that had driven him to an early grave, he knew exactly what had happened.

The woman had led Peter on, toyed with him, and pretended to return his affections. When Peter had asked for her hand in marriage, she had laughed in his face. In a letter they had found on his desk the day of the shooting, his brother had referred to himself as the "penniless second son." Untitled and far beneath Alexa's level of wealth, young Peter Melford had never been a serious contender for marriage. Alexa had played him for a fool and falsely led him on.

Though Damien rarely saw his mother, Lady Townsend, and they were far from close, he didn't doubt the truth of her letters. Until Peter's death, his half sister had been Alexa's best friend. After the shooting, Melissa had broken off the friendship and Alexa had moved to Marden, one of her brother's vast estates in the country, where she could avoid any scandal that might result from her callous behavior.

Avoid it, that is, until now.

Two months ago Damien had finished his work on the Continent and come back to England. With his return, he had pledged that the woman responsible for Peter's death would receive her just desserts. He had written to his mother and sister, telling them he intended to be in the city for a portion of the Season—which ensured they would stay away—and vowing he would see that the woman paid. The darling of the Social whirl would find herself ruined. If this plan didn't work, he would find a way that would.

Damien crossed the thick Persian carpet to the window in the bedchamber of his suite. Fog hung low over the cobblestone streets, turning the light from the street lamps into a soft, eerie blur. At home he liked the swirling mist that shrouded the cliffs near the shore; here he found it oppressive. For the tenth time he wished he were home.

Not much longer, he told himself. By the middle of the week he would know if his plan would go forward. With a little more of his self-made luck, by the end of next week Peter's memory would be at rest and he could return to the castle. Damien smiled bitterly at the outcome he hoped lay ahead.

"Have you gone completely mad?" Lady Jane Thornhill stared across the carriage seat in horror. They were riding in the duke's splendid black open barouche with the gilded ducal crest, taking the air in Hyde Park along with the rest of the fashionable members of the ton.

"For heaven's sake, keep your voice down. It isn't as bad as all that."

"It's worse than all that." The clip-clop of the four high-stepping, perfectly matched gray horses filled the moment of silence.

"It isn't as though I'm planning to let him seduce me. I've only just agreed to the meeting. I don't for a moment intend to do more than enjoy a glass of sherry with the man and . . ."

"And what?"

She smiled with a tilt of her chin. "Perhaps I might let him kiss me."

"Perhaps you might let him kiss you."

"Would you please stop repeating everything I say? For heaven's sake, Jane, I'm telling you all of this because I'm going to need your help. I didn't expect you to go quite so over the mark."

"Well, you should have expected it. How can you consider doing something so—so—so bloody reckless!"

"Jane!"

"It's obvious Lord Falon intends far more than kissing. You can't be deluding yourself in that. For ninety thousand pounds a man is bound to expect a great deal more."

"That's rather what he said—the man was perfectly honest about his intentions—but I don't think he means to force me. If he intended that, he wouldn't have gone to so much trouble."

"Has it ever occurred to you that he might not have to force you?" Jane reached over and took her hand. "Listen to me, Alexa. You are my very dearest friend, but sometimes you are a bit . . . well, impulsive."

"I haven't been *impulsive* in far too long a time. I can't tell you how good it feels."

"Under any other circumstance, I would encourage you. But this man—and I do mean man—is not going to sit docilely by and let you charm him into doing whatever it is you want."

They rounded a corner of the park and the carriage fell into the shade of an overhanging beech tree. Across the way, sunlight danced on a small lake surrounded by willows where a little boy bent near the edge, sailing a small paper boat.

"I don't believe Lord Falon will do me harm. I believe if I meet him, spend a little time with him, he will return my marker or allow me to pay him later on."

"And what if he doesn't?"

"Then I will know for certain the kind of man he is and these . . . feelings he stirs will not trouble me again."

"It's too dangerous, Alexa."

"Everything in life is dangerous, Jane. I learned that only too well when Peter died. If I hadn't flirted with him so outrageously, if I hadn't led him on—"

"Don't say that. You were younger then. You had no idea Peter would react as he did. If you had, you wouldn't have spent so much time with him."

"No, I wouldn't have. I would have sat demurely at home the way I have for the past two years. I would have let my brother arrange my marriage to some stiff-kneed, boring old aristocrat, the way he would very much like to do now."

"Your brother would never force you to marry some old man."

"All right—some tight-necked, prissy *young* aristocrat!"

Jane smiled, then the smile slipped away. "Your impetuousness has cost you a very good deal already. I thought you had learned your lesson."

Alexa glanced out at the passing greenery, at the sweet briars, buttercups, hyacinths, and crocus that almost always cheered her. "I'll never be the spoiled, selfish, overindulgent young girl I was before. But I'm tired of being afraid to enjoy life, afraid I'll hurt someone else, afraid I'll wind up hurting myself. I've got to do this, Jane. I want to. Please try to understand."

Jane placed a small gloved hand over hers. "If this is what you want, you know I'll help you any way I can. But I won't sit by and let that man take advantage of you."

Alexa leaned forward and hugged her. "I only want the chance to talk to him, to discover a little more about him. I won't be gone more than a couple of hours."

Jane sighed. "All right. But we had better come up with some sort of plan."

Alexa flashed a dazzling white smile. "Thank you, Jane. I can't believe how lucky I am to have you for a friend."

"And I can't believe how queer in the attic I must be to have *you* for a friend." Alexa laughed and so did Jane.

But inside, Jane wasn't laughing.

Chapter Three

WEARING A GOWN OF DEEP SIENNA SHOT WITH GOLD, ALEXA PULLED THE HOOD OF HER MATCHING GOLD-lined cloak up over her head and stepped into the small black caleche that was Jane's own private conveyance. The top was up. The driver, a slender youth with frazzled white-blond hair, Jane assured her was a lad who could be trusted. He would await her outside the Cockleshell Tavern, the small, well-appointed but very discreet inn just outside London the earl had chosen for their meeting.

Alexa referred to it as that—their meeting, rather than the earl's planned night of seduction. There wasn't the foggiest chance she would let it come to that. She could persuade him to play the gentleman, she was sure, and she would have a chance to explore Lord Falon's mysterious nature, to discover what there was about him that so intrigued her.

Alexa leaned back against the tufted red velvet seat of the carriage. Only Jane knew of her mission. Only Jane and the earl. Her brother had allowed her another short visit at the duke's lavish residence in the city. It was obvious she and Jane were enjoying the Season and the time they had been spending together. The duke and her brother agreed: London had been good for both of them.

Just how good, Alexa was about to find out.

The tavern was situated near a small hamlet just off the road to Hampstead Heath. The same road that led to Stoneleigh. Lord Falon had expected her to be coming from there, she supposed, but Rayne would have been far more difficult to fool than the duke and his house full of servants.

As the carriage rolled out of the city, its iron wheels rattling over the cobblestone streets, Alexa listened to the London sounds: apple sellers and rag pickers hawking their wares, beggars pleading for alms, drunken soldiers slurring bawdy tunes. From a second-story window in an alley, someone cursed the ruffians below and heaped refuse upon them in an effort to silence their ribald laughter.

Eventually the sounds grew distant and finally faded away, leaving in their place the stillness of the country. Here the air smelled of fresh-mown grass and sweet evening dew. In the distance she could hear the bawling of a milch cow. Farther down the road, they passed a black and maroon mail coach, its scarlet wheels barreling toward the city.

Then Jane's coachman turned the horses onto a narrow lane, and a few moments later they traveled through the high arched entrance leading into the courtyard of the Cockleshell Tavern.

Alexa's stomach knotted and her palms felt damp. She pulled her cloak more tightly around her as the thin-faced driver jerked open the carriage door. Taking a deep breath for courage, she stepped to the ground and nervously scanned the courtyard. A thatched-roof stable sat off to the rear; a couple of mongrel dogs sniffed for scraps between vacant carriages, but there was no sign of Lord Falon. Her stomach churned uncomfortably and her courage began to fade.

Then he was there, lean and powerful and striding purposely toward her. He was dressed in black, except for his silver brocade waistcoat, stark white shirt, and cravat. His eyes were the bluest she had ever seen, his black hair glistened like jet in the light of the moon. When he reached her, he paused, his eyes taking in her flushed cheeks, heightened breathing, and the daringly low-cut gold and sienna gown.

He smiled and her heart slid into her stomach. "Good evening, lovely lady."

Before she could fashion a proper reply, a hard arm slid around her waist. A long-fingered hand came up to her cheek, he tipped her head back and kissed her. Alexa made a sound in her throat at the warmth that slid through her body, at the pounding of her heart and the rushing in her ears.

He ended the kiss before it had really begun, but kept his arm possessively around her waist. "Let's go inside. We'll be more comfortable in there."

Comfortable was far from how she felt. Unsteady, out of her element, and in way over her head—those were the things she was feeling. Still, she had come this far. With a weak nod of her head, she let him lead her toward the wide oaken door of the tavern.

The inn was a rustic, low-ceilinged establishment with heavy carved beams, a flagstone floor, and a massive stone hearth at the end of the taproom. It was simple in design but furnished exceedingly well, with Sheridan tables and chintz-covered overstuffed sofas and chairs. The small brass whale-oil lamps had been turned down, and combined with the glow of the fire, the inn felt warm and inviting. The succulent aroma of roasting meat drifted in from the kitchen.

They climbed the stairs in silence. She could feel the brush of his superfine coat against her arm and smell the scent of his musky cologne. They reached the landing and headed down the hall, Alexa's heart hammering, her hands shaking, more nervous by the moment, yet more and more intrigued. She wanted to be here, she realized. She wanted to be with *him*.

He inserted a heavy brass key and unlocked the door to a modest suite of rooms. Near the fireplace in the corner, a small round table had been covered with linen and set for two with porcelain and crystal. Steam drifted up from silver-covered platters, a low fire burned in the hearth, and the room smelled slightly of musk. A copy of the *Morning Chronicle* had been neatly folded and set on the arm of the sofa, and through the open door to the left she saw a large four-poster bed. Alexa's cheeks flamed at the sight of it. Her heartbeat increased its uneven tempo and it was all she could do not to run.

When Lord Falon closed the door, the sound in such an intimate setting slammed into her like the muzzle blast of a gun.

"I'm glad you came," he said softly, removing her cloak before she could think to stop him and tossing it over a chair. He waited while she removed her gloves, then took her hand and pressed it against his lips. "I was afraid you might change your mind."

The brush of his mouth against her skin made the heat swirl into her belly. "I changed my mind a thousand times. I'm still not certain what insanity convinced me to go through with this." His gaze was so intense, her stomach churned with warning. She was frightened, yet strangely unwilling to leave.

He smiled, slow and sensual, making her knees feel

weak and the air in the room overly warm. The gravity
of the situation hit her with the impact of a hammer.
She swallowed hard and looked up at the earl, but he
only smiled and released her hand.

"Sherry, isn't it?"

"Yes." A hogshead wouldn't be enough to calm her
nerves, but even a small amount would help. With
long, graceful strides, he crossed to the sideboard and
poured her a glass, which she accepted with unsteady
hands. For himself he poured a brandy.

"To us," he said, raising his snifter in her direction.
"May we both be winners before this night is done."

Alexa couldn't force herself to drink. "To you, my
lord. For being such a worthy opponent." This time it
was the earl who did not drink, and something unreadable darkened his eyes. Alexa took a sip, and the warm
amber liquid slid down her throat and into her stomach. It felt much like the heat of the earl's long-fingered
hand.

"You look beautiful this evening, Alexa. You can't
imagine how I've dreamed of having you all to myself."

She glanced once more at the bed she could see
through the partially open doorway. It was covered
with an apricot counterpane and already turned back at
the corner. Her stomach rolled, and when the earl
stepped toward her, she took a step away.

"I—I'm sorry, my lord. I'm beginning to realize just
how foolish it was for me to come here. I was well-
aware of the danger, and yet . . ." She turned a little
away, but still she could see him. "At any rate, it was
madness, and in truth I didn't come for the reason you
believe."

"No? And exactly what reason is that?"

"I know what it is you're expecting. I know that
when I agreed to this meeting, you believed I meant to
. . . to buy back my marker with the loss of my virtue.

But the truth is, I came here hoping to convince you . . . well, to be a little more reasonable."

A corner of his mouth curved up. "When it comes to you, my love, being reasonable is a difficult thing to do." He moved toward her, but again she backed away.

"What I'm trying to say, Lord Falon, is that I'm not the willing consort you imagined. I'm not some wanton who can barter away her innocence, no matter what the price. I convinced myself that if I came, we could discuss my marker, that I could persuade you to play the gentleman. I hoped that at the very least you would allow me to pay off my debt when I came of age." She smiled at him weakly. "The fact is, my lord, I'm a fraud. I'm just not ready for this sort of—of . . ."

He set his glass away, his light mood suddenly somber. He walked toward her and this time he kept coming. She was trembling by the time he reached her.

"Don't," she whispered, her heartbeat thundering, afraid of what he might do.

"It's all right, Alexa, you don't have to be afraid. I didn't invite you here to force you into my bed." His hand came up to her cheek and he toyed with a strand of hair that curled beside her ear. "I never believed that you were a wanton. I thought that perhaps . . . you were feeling the same sort of attraction I was. I thought that the gambling debt might give us both an excuse to do exactly what we had been wanting all along."

She flushed because she knew it was at least in part the truth. She was there because she wanted to be. Because she wanted to see him, to talk to him, wanted just to be near him.

He smiled in that disconcerting way of his, but beneath the smile there was something inscrutable in his eyes. "It would seem to me," he said softly, "that since we have come this far, we might as well enjoy ourselves. Why don't we have supper? Get to know each other a little? We can discuss the marker, and later you can decide if you wish to stay.''

Alexa chewed her bottom lip. It sounded reasonable enough. The earl wasn't pressing her; he had said that he would not force her. And there was something else. That secret, oddly unfathomable look in his eyes that she had seen before. It appeared when he relaxed his guard—which wasn't all that often—or when he watched her but didn't realize she also watched him. It was a look that compelled her, almost willed her, to remain. A look that spoke of need and longing. Or perhaps it was nothing more than loneliness.

Still, if she stayed, she would be hours late returning to London, and Jane would be frantic with worry. She had promised to be home before midnight, to spend just enough time with Lord Falon to persuade him to give back her marker. She looked at him now, so much taller than she, so dark and incredibly handsome. She wanted to reach out and touch him, to run her fingers through his wavy black hair, to test the smoothness of his skin. She wanted him to kiss her again.

"All right," she heard herself say. Jane was a friend. She would be worried, yes, but once Alexa got back to the city, she could explain that it had taken a little longer than she expected. Jane would understand, and even if she didn't, she would never reveal her best friend's outrageous behavior.

"The cook has made us something special," the earl was saying. "I hope you enjoy it." With a hand at her waist, he guided her across the small salon toward the fireplace and pulled out a carved high-backed chair. As he seated her at the table before the hearth, she felt his warm breath on the back of her neck, and heat uncoiled in her stomach.

"You have no idea how much I've looked forward to this evening." He took the seat across from her, sitting with an easy grace that belied his height and powerful build. His shoulders were broader than she remembered, his skin a little more swarthy. In the lamplight his jet-black hair glistened like the wings of a raven.

"I—I found myself looking forward to it too." That was the truth. Too much so, in fact. Alexa glanced away.

Reaching across the table, Lord Falon refilled her glass of sherry, which had somehow gone dry. "I want you, Alexa. I won't deny it. But for the moment, just the fact that you are here is enough."

Beneath the table Alexa's hands trembled. Secretly, she had yearned to meet a man—a real man—and the earl clearly was one. The question seemed to be whether she was a woman, or still just a little girl.

Standing beside the small black carriage at the rear of the stable, Barney Dillard ran a hand through his unruly mop of kinky white-blond hair. He pulled the watch fob from a pocket in the waistcoat of his gold and scarlet livery, flipped open the lid to the small engraved watch that her ladyship had loaned him, and checked the time.

Midnight! Sweet Mary, the girl had been in there for hours. She should have returned to the carriage by now. They should have been well on their way back to London! He glanced at the horses, who blew and pawed the earth, more anxious even than he was.

What the devil was she doing in there? Sweet Jesu, Lady Jane would fair be in a tither! His mistress had come at the very last minute, holding out the watch, her pretty face lined with worry for her friend. There was something he must do, she said. If his passenger didn't come out of the inn by midnight, he was to unharness one of the carriage horses and ride like thunder to Stoneleigh. He was to find the viscount and tell him his sister might be in danger. Barney was to make all haste in returning with his lordship.

It went unsaid, he was to keep his bleedin' mouth shut about whatever it was that went on.

'Course her ladyship hadn't told him more than that, and it weren't his place to ask. 'Twas his job to do as he was bid, and already he had been lax in seeing it done.

Hurrying now that his mind was made up, Barney unhitched the wheel horse, one of a pair of high-stepping bays, and swung onto its broad sleek back. In minutes he was flying down the road, his scarlet tailcoat sailing out behind him, the sound of hoofbeats strumming against the earth. It wouldn't take long to reach Stoneleigh. On a fast horse the likes of this one, it wouldn't take long for the viscount to return.

Barney wondered what would happen when he did.

Damien refilled Alexa's stemmed crystal glass and listened to her laughter at something he had said. It was rich and throaty, yet more feminine than any he had heard.

As he had promised, they spent the evening in conversation, discussing books they enjoyed, plays they had seen, a little about Napoleon and recent happenings in the war. The subjects were neutral, carefully so. A brief discussion of her family, a few vague answers about his. She was relaxed now, enjoying the thrust and parry, teasing him a little, withdrawing when she began to feel the heat.

It was there, almost palpably. No matter how civilized their words, no matter how mundane the conversation, there wasn't a moment when desire didn't simmer between them.

Not a moment he didn't imagine the time she would spend in his bed.

They finished a light meal of creamed sole and shallots, followed by custard and candied fruits, and she glanced to the clock ticking softly above the mantel.

"I can hardly believe it's already this late." She

smiled, and he recalled the sweetness of those pouty, rose-petal lips. "It's been a wonderful evening, my lord, but I've stayed far longer than I should have."

Wordlessly he stood and pulled back her chair, thinking that though the hours had passed, they were exactly on schedule. He had orchestrated the evening down to the minute. Timing was essential to his plan. So far it had all gone off as he had arranged, but the true test lay ahead.

When she came to her feet, he bent and kissed her shoulder, tasting skin as rich and sweet as cream. "I don't want you to go," he said softly, and in this he spoke the truth.

He turned her into his arms and took her lips in a light, tender kiss she accepted without hesitation. Her mouth was as ripe and sweet as a peach; her breath tasted faintly of sherry. It took a will of iron not to haul her into his arms and kiss her with the fire that raged through his body. Kiss her till she clung to him and begged him for more. He never had the chance, for Alexa pulled away.

"I-It's late and I really must be going."

He captured her mouth again, felt the trembling of her lips beneath his, felt her fingers curling into the lapels of his coat. His hands slid down to her buttocks, cupping the feminine roundness, pressing her the length of him. He could feel her firm flat stomach against his hardened arousal, making him grow harder still. When he parted her lips with his tongue, flames of desire roared through him, as he knew they were burning through her.

Alexa broke away. She was breathing hard, her eyes glazed with passion, backing away from him and looking as though she might bolt and run for the door.

"Don't go." He stopped her beside a small Queen Anne table in front of the sofa. The glow of the candle flickering on top outlined the delicate bones in her face, the arches of her dark copper brows, the leafy greenness of her eyes. All evening his body had been hard and throbbing with desire for her, his blood running thick and heavy. Still, he had waited, determined to bide his time.

Determined to win the game.

"I have to go," she said, but before she could turn to leave, he cupped her chin in his hands, raised her face up to his, and settled his mouth over hers. She made a mewling sound in her throat, then once more tore herself free.

"I—I have to go," she repeated, her breath coming faster, her eyes wide and frightened as she backed toward the door.

"Stay," he said. He leaned forward to kiss her again, but she warily backed away.

"I can't." She reached a slender hand behind her, groping for the handle, desperate to make her escape.

The moment at last had come. She was stronger-willed than he had believed, and though she desired him, she wasn't about to give in. Damien almost smiled. It had been a good long while since a woman had resisted his charms. In a way, he admired her. She had courage and fire well beyond most of the women he had known. Still, his course was set and he meant to see it done.

He stepped closer, pressing her nearer the door. When she finally pulled it open, he gently shoved it closed.

"What—What are you doing?"

He hadn't lied; he didn't intend to force her. He just needed a little more time. He played his hole card, toying with her again, dangling the bait of challenge that had always worked before.

"I presume your brother is in residence at Stoneleigh."

The shift in conversation took her by surprise. "Yes, Rayne is there, but what—"

"You may expect me to call on him first thing tomorrow morning."

For an instant she looked confused. Then the blood drained from her cheeks and she stared at him with a mixture of shock and dawning horror. Her pretty mouth parted but at first no words would come. "You —You can't be serious."

"I'm afraid, lovely lady, I am deadly serious."

"But I—I thought . . . I mean . . . surely, as a gentlemen, what we shared this eve meant something. Surely it more than compensates for my imprudent gaming." She stiffened her spine. "If not, as I've said before, I shall be happy to see the debt repaid just as soon as I come into my fortune."

"It should be clear by now, my love, that I am not now, nor ever will be, a gentleman. As for the ninety thousand pounds, you may be certain for that amount of money I expect a great deal more than just a simple kiss."

Pink flags rose in her cheeks as a wave of anger swept over her, and a look of betrayal so intense it made a hard knot ball in his stomach.

"You're a bastard, Lord Falon."

"That, Miss Garrick, is the one thing I am not. A thousand other socially abhorrent things, but not that particular one."

"Do you really expect me to—to—"

"Yes." But even as he said the word, he questioned, as he had a dozen times since her arrival, the wisdom of what he was doing. She was nothing at all like he had imagined. She was lovely and fresh and enchanting. She was ripe and womanly, yet there was an innocence about her that would charm the most seasoned rake.

For an instant he wished he really was the man she had come to the inn to meet. That he was simply an intriguing stranger charmed by a beautiful woman. That he was so taken with this lovely innocent that he would do anything to have her. Then he thought of his brother, young and eager for life, trusting her, loving her, and being hurt so badly he had put a gun to his head. He thought of Peter lying in a spreading pool of blood, of the pistol still smoking in his hand.

"Perhaps another kiss will do the trick," he taunted. "If you try a little harder, perhaps the next one will persuade me to forget your debt." He reached out and caught her wrist. Hauling her roughly against him, he brought his mouth down hard over hers. She clamped her lips together, twisted in his arms and jerked free, drew back and slapped his face.

She was breathing hard, staring at him as if she had never seen him before and couldn't imagine why on earth she had come to meet him. Something twisted low in his belly even as his mouth curled up in a bitter half smile. With a glance at the clock above the mantel, he stepped away from her, playing another of his final cards, hoping his skill at reading people would prove true again this eve.

"The door is there, Alexa. If your word means so little, why don't you simply walk through it? You can go home to your big brother, beg him to save you from another of your follies. He'll scold you and remind you you're still just a little girl, but what does it matter? Surely it's a small price to pay for saving your precious virtue."

Fury swept her features, which suddenly turned iron-hard. He had won every hand so far—she was determined he would not win this one.

"I came here to get my marker," she said. "What is it you expect me to do?"

There it was, laid out before him in all its blazing glory. The prize he'd been seeking, if only he were smart enough to claim it.

"Why don't you start by letting down your hair? I've had a yearning to see it since the night I first saw you at the opera."

Her soft full lips went thin. Bright green eyes flashed sparks across the room and anger seethed from every pore in her body. With short jerky movements of her hand, hairpins scattered across the floor, and when she tossed her head, thick dark auburn hair tumbled down well past her shoulders. In the light of the candle it hung in waves of red-gold flame, and Damien felt a rush of heat to his loins.

"Take off your clothes. It's time I discovered whether or not you're worth all this trouble."

Alexa's jaw clamped. He wondered if she would really go through with it. His attempt at seduction had failed, but he could still salvage his plan if he could keep her in the room a little longer.

"Do you enjoy humiliating women, Lord Falon? Do you get some kind of perverse pleasure from this?"

"I want you in my bed, Alexa. That is all I care about. You knew that when you came here. You gave me your promise and I accepted it. I'm waiting for that promise to be fulfilled."

Another round of fury darkened her eyes. She was trembling all over, but with rage, not fear. She was furious at his demands, yet unwilling to let him best her again. He had goaded her beyond reason, beyond conscience, just as he had intended. Reaching for the buttons at the back of her gown, she wrenched several loose, tore several more from their loops, but still could not succeed in getting herself undone.

Damien stepped closer, moved her shaking hands away and unfastened the remaining buttons. The gown slid down her body and pooled in a dark golden heap on the floor at her feet. Alexa stepped out of the folds and kicked the dress away. She wore no corset, just a thin white cotton chemise that covered her from the shoulders to well below the knees but did little to disguise the high lush curve of her breast or the tempting dark circles around the peaks.

"Shall I go further, Lord Falon? Or is this enough to satisfy your perverse pleasure?"

"If you intend to please me, you have only just begun . . . unless, of course, you're afraid you'll disappoint me."

She cursed him viciously beneath her breath. With frenzied, violent movements, she stripped the chemise off over her head, tumbling her thick mane of dark copper hair, and except for her small satin slippers, stood splendidly naked before him.

Damien's breath caught in his throat. She was everything he had imagined and more. She was all smooth skin and lush curves, with high round breasts whose rose aureoles ringed softly budded nipples. Her legs were long and supple, her calves delicate and shapely, her feet high-arched and slender.

His eyes moved up to a narrow waist he could nearly span with his hands, to straight slim shoulders and a gracefully arching neck. He was hard and throbbing at the sight of her, his blood heating, desire thick and heavy in his veins. Then his eyes came up to her face, and Damien went rigid, a hard knot balling in his stomach. The breath he'd been holding went out of him in a rush.

Though Alexa faced him boldly, her bottom lip trembled and tears streaked a path down her cheeks. Her lashes were spiked with wetness, and a shiny path of moisture trickled toward her chin.

"I'll never forget the first night I saw you," she said. "You were so handsome . . . like some dark angel come down from the heavens. You were different from the others; bold and mysterious and intriguing, yet there was a gentleness about you. I was drawn to you almost from the start—I don't deny it. I've never felt that way about another man." Damien said nothing. "I wanted to come here this night, more than you will ever know. Even at the risk of my honor, at the chance I might lose everything that I hold dear, I still had to come. In my heart I actually believed that there was something special between us. That if I did end up in your bed, it would be the most beautiful, the most exciting thing that had ever happened." She blinked and more tears rolled down her cheeks. "How pitiful, how naive I must have seemed."

A shudder rippled through him. Every muscle in his body had gone rigid, and his mouth was so dry he could not speak.

She laughed, but it came out bitter and harsh. "I just want you to know, Lord Falon, that if you take me to your bed this eve, you may be certain all I will feel for you is loathing."

Damien's taut control snapped. He had been watching her with a mixture of conflicting emotions. Desire, regret—anger at himself, tempered by the rage he still felt toward her. All those things and something else he could not name. Now he crossed the few paces between them and dragged her hard against his chest.

"Loathing—that is what you feel? Why don't we see?" He kissed her then, a rough, hard, angry kiss that made the blood pump into his loins and the urge to take her nearly overwhelming.

She fought him at first, trying to pull away, pressing her hands against his chest, struggling to break his relentless hold. He could feel her tears on his cheek, and unconsciously he gentled the kiss, no longer wanting to hurt her, seeking only to make her respond, to taste the sweetness he had known before. He knew the moment her anger turned to passion, her uncontained fury to longing.

She swayed against him, her body going soft and pliant, her warm lips trembling, parting beneath his, allowing his tongue inside. He groaned at the heat raging through him, the wanting that clawed its way into his belly. He might have swept her up in his arms and carried her over to the bed if she hadn't made that single pitiful sound. It was soft yet it was fierce, like the cry of an injured bird. It was the heart-wrenching, soul-crushing sound of a young girl's surrender, and Damien found himself completely undone.

It took all his will, every ounce of decency he had left inside, to tear himself free and step away.

For endless moments he just stood there, his eyes locked on her face, his body aching with pent-up desire for her. Ignoring the tension that still rippled through his body, he turned away from her and crossed the room. He picked up the gown she had kicked away and tossed it to where she stood beside the door.

"Get dressed." She clutched it protectively in front of her, her green eyes wide and uncertain, her lips a soft dark rose and swollen from his kisses. "Before I change my mind."

Forcing himself to turn away, he strode across the room to pour himself a brandy. Never had he needed one more.

Chapter Four

WITH A HARD LUMP SWELLING IN HER THROAT, ALEXA
PULLED ON HER CHEMISE WITH TREMBLING FINGERS,
then hurriedly stepped into her gold and sienna gown.
She was trying to fasten the buttons up the back, struggling to no avail as she fought back a fresh round of
tears. The gown made a tearing sound, but she no
longer cared. She felt sick and disillusioned, unsure of
herself, and sad clear to her soul. She refused to look at
Damien, terrified of what she would see if she did, embarrassed by the way she had responded, at a loss as to
why she had lost control.

She missed his approach, since his footsteps were
muffled by the thick Tartan carpet, but at the touch of
his hand she tensed. She steeled herself, prepared once
more to do battle, but it seemed their battle was done.
Instead she felt his hands on her waist, easing her own
aside, doing up the buttons with a gentleness she

hadn't expected and an expertise that said more than words.

When he finished, he stepped away. "I believe this is yours," he said softly, handing her the small slip of paper she recognized as her marker.

She swallowed past the lump as she reached for it with unsteady hands. "Thank you," she said stiffly, taking the paper from his fingers, being careful not to touch him. He had surprised her again. She had been certain he would still expect payment, that the money was all-important, and she would have seen he collected every farthing. Now he had made her wonder about him again.

He stepped away from her, reached for her cloak and enveloped her in its gold satin folds. "Time's running out. We've got to go."

Time had run out for her hours ago. When she should have gone home but hadn't. Even before she had come.

It had all been a lie, a wicked, evil game of some sort. And he had been a master. All through supper he had charmed her, pretending to show an interest in the same things she did, respecting her intelligence, acting as if her opinion really mattered. And more than once there had been that look, that expression of loneliness or longing. She wondered if he pretended that too. Or if it was the single thing in this whole unbelievable evening that had truly been real.

"Ready?"

"Yes." She forced the word past her lips. Damien's hand at her waist guided her toward the stairs. She wanted to shove it away, but she wasn't sure she had the strength to stand on her own. Mostly, she just wanted to be gone from there. She wanted to be returned to her home, safely in hiding at Marden.

No matter what Rayne said, she would make him take her there.

* * *

Damien took a last glance at the clock. One-thirty. They had a little time left, but not much. Lord Beechcroft never arrived with his mistress, an actress named Sophie Lang from the Theatre Royale in Drury Lane, before two. The theatre dismissed at exactly one-thirty, and Beechcroft was as timely as he was randy. Damien's original plan had called for a run-in with the baron on his way out of the tavern somewhere near dawn, after they'd both enjoyed an evening of pleasure in their respective ladies' beds. Now . . . well, at the end of the evening his plans had somehow changed.

He pulled the hood of Alexa's cloak up over her head to cover her fiery dark hair and they started down the stairs. Below them the taproom was sparsely filled with patrons, travelers mostly, while the upstairs rooms were occupied by wealthy young men and their mistresses. *Affaires de coeur* were all the crack, and clandestine meetings were what the tavern was known for, but of course Alexa didn't know that.

They hurried down the stairs, reached the bottom and started across the room to the heavy oaken door at the entrance, when it opened with surprising force and a strong gust of wind.

"Bloody storm's comin' up," said the graying bearded man who walked through the entry with a small cloaked figure on his arm.

Bloody Christ, Lord Beechcroft. He hadn't been early in weeks. Damien knew that for certain. He had paid a small fortune bribing a serving wench to time the man's arrivals and departures.

Beechcroft smiled as they walked past. "Good evening, Alexa, my dear. It is always good to see you . . . though I must admit, I hadn't imagined our paths would cross in . . . such a place as this."

Damien's stomach twisted. He turned to see Alexa

fighting with the hood of her cloak, trying to pull it back into place after the wind had blown it away.

"L-Lord Beechcroft," she said. "I—I was just, that is we were just . . ."

He smiled wolfishly. "No need to worry, my dear. You may be certain that I am the height of discretion."

Damien inwardly groaned. As discreet as the *Morning Post.* It was why he had timed the evening so carefully. Why he had chosen the inn in the first place. Beechcroft and his bloody loose tongue was the key to his plan.

The graying man turned in his direction. He was a baron, a lesser noble who aspired to higher rank and enjoyed any chance to create a hue and cry among the members of the ton. "I'd advise you to take better care, Lord Falon. A lady's reputation is a highly valuable commodity."

Damien forced himself to smile. "This is hardly the scandal it seems. The lady is here merely by chance. She was traveling back to Stoneleigh when a problem arose with her carriage. She stopped here only long enough for her coachman to see it repaired."

It was a lame excuse and all of them knew it. The actress flashed a knowing, painted smile while the baron arched a disbelieving brow. On the morrow, the tale of Alexa Garrick at the Cockleshell Tavern in the company of the notorious Earl Falon would cross the lips of every scandalmonger in London. Alexa would be ruined.

Exactly as he had first planned.

"Let's go," he urged a little too harshly, feeling her tremble, and suddenly filled with remorse. Then again, perhaps this was some sort of justice, fate intervening to punish her for Peter, as he had meant it to happen from the start.

Alexa nodded vaguely. She was reaching the edge, he knew, on the verge of slipping over the brink into hysteria. Any other woman would have broken long ago. In truth, he was amazed at her composure, considering what he'd put her through.

She swayed a little, and he tightened the hold he had on her waist. With a brief farewell to Beechcroft, they made their way out the front door and down the flagstone path toward the stables. They had almost reached the carriage when the distant sound of hoofbeats filled the air. The sound grew louder, the animal pounding toward them at breakneck speed, its sharp hooves churning up mud on the road. They stared in that direction, watching the lone horseman's approach, seeing him ride hell-for-leather through the high arch into the courtyard, his greatcoat flying out behind him.

He drew rein in front of the inn, sliding his huge bay stallion to a halt, dismounting even as the animal reared and pranced. He was a big man, Damien saw, thick-chested and heavily muscled across the shoulders. He started up the path toward the inn, caught sight of them from the corner of his eye and turned in their direction.

"Rayne . . ." Alexa whispered, the word coming out on a soft gasp of air.

Damien steeled himself as long strides carried the big man toward them.

"Alex!" the viscount said, addressing his sister by the nickname Damien had heard him use before. "For Godsake, what the bloody hell is going on?"

Alexa started crying. She didn't mean to. Dear God, it seemed she'd been crying all night, but she couldn't seem to stop herself.

"Oh Rayne . . ." Was that all she could think of to say? She stepped toward him, and he crushed her in his powerful arms.

"Are you all right? Tell me what has happened."

"I'm f-fine. H-How did you find me? How did you know where I was?"

"Lady Jane had instructed her coachmen. She was worried for your safety. He shouldn't be too far behind." He gave her one last hug. "Now tell me what the devil is going on."

"Nothing. Everything. L-Lord Beechcroft is here. He saw me with Lord Falon. Oh God, Rayne, what am I going to do?" She felt his body go rigid even as she'd said the word. *Falon.* Weeks ago, from the first time she had mentioned his name, Rayne had warned her away.

He stepped back from her now and turned his hard brown gaze on the earl. "I take it you have ruined my sister."

A corner of Damien's mouth curved up. He looked ruthless, brutal. But then that was exactly what he was. "It appears that is the case."

Rayne swung a blow that would have sent another man to his knees. Falon stepped away from the punch, but still took the brunt of it. Heavy black hair fell into his eyes as he straightened to meet the challenge, and his lip started bleeding at the corner.

"I'm going to kill you," Rayne said. "I'm going to do it with my bare hands and I'm going to relish every moment."

"No!" Alexa thrust herself between them. She was shaking inside and numb all over. Dear God, would this nightmare never end? "Rayne you can't do that!"

He tore his eyes away from the earl. "For once you are right, little sister. That isn't the sort of thing a young lady should be privy to." He turned back to Falon, who wiped the blood from his mouth with a handkerchief, then stuffed the red-stained cloth into the pocket of his tailcoat. "I shall expect you and your second at dawn tomorrow," Rayne said. "Green Park should do. You've the choice of weapons, of course."

"Dear God," Alexa said.

"As you wish," said the earl. "Pistols will suffice. You may count on my timely arrival."

"Have both of you gone mad?" Alexa turned to her tall determined brother. "Rayne, you can't do this. Lord Falon has already killed three men—the same thing could happen to you."

"Thank you, dear sister, for your vote of confidence."

Ignoring that, her stomach in knots, she turned to face the earl. "Lord Falon, my brother has served in the army. He's a crack shot with a gun. Surely you at least have an instinct for survival. Can't you see that if you go through with this, you may end up dead?"

Damien saw it perfectly. He knew Stoneleigh's reputation and he didn't believe it was exaggerated one little bit. He knew his own capabilities as well. Tomorrow at dawn, one of them would die.

He glanced over at the girl. Her hood had fallen back and her thick auburn hair gleamed like dark molten copper in the moonlight. Even with the tears still damp on her cheeks, she looked lovely. In the eye of his mind he saw her naked, felt the heat in his loins as he had held her pressed against him.

"Please, Rayne," she said, "I'm begging you. I love you. I've already lost Papa and Christopher. I don't want to lose you too."

"Falon is the one who will be dead. You may count on it. And no one deserves it more."

Alexa turned in Damien's direction. "I don't want either of you killed," she said softly, surprising him again, as she had this night a dozen times.

He could still taste her kisses, smell her lilac perfume . . . he could still see the way she had looked at him across that small, candlelit table. He thought of the words she'd said as she faced him so proudly, words that had pierced him to the quick.

He fixed his gaze on her brother. "I know how much

you're looking forward to my demise," he said, "but there *is* another way to settle this."

"Oh, really?" said the viscount. "And just what way is that?"

"You can allow me to do the honorable thing. You can grant me your sister's hand in marriage."

"What!" Alexa gasped.

"You're insane," Stoneleigh said.

Not so insane, he thought. She would finally wind up in his bed, and best of all, he would control her fortune. The castle was in a state of disrepair, and though he was far from poor, he could ill-afford to restore as it should be. Who better to pay for it than Alexa Garrick, the woman who had destroyed his brother? Combined with the pleasures he would wrest from her luscious little body, what sweeter revenge could he have?

"It's quite rational, really. I may not be the greatest catch in England, but I'm still an earl. Marriage to me will silence the scandalmongers and protect Alexa's reputation. Besides, your sister wouldn't be here if she didn't have some feelings for me. Isn't that right, my love?"

She started to rage at him, but he silenced her with a hard look of warning. "I know you're upset, Alexa. All I ask is that you hear me out." He turned to her brother. "I need a moment with your sister in private."

"Not a chance."

"Five minutes." Damien's mouth curved up. "If tomorrow is to be my last day, I don't think that's asking too much."

Stoneleigh still looked uncertain.

"It's all right, Rayne. Lord Falon isn't going to hurt me."

The viscount made a jerky motion with his head, and Damien led Alexa a few feet away. She looked up at him warily.

"What kind of a game are you playing at this time?"

"A deadly game," he said. "The stakes are life and death." He let her take that in. "I'm a very good shot, Alexa. If we go through with this duel, your brother may well end up dead."

She tossed her pretty head in an effort at defiance he couldn't help but admire, considering all she had been through. "Perhaps you're afraid. Perhaps it is you who will end up dead."

"Perhaps . . . The question is, are you willing to take that chance?" She glanced down at her gold satin slippers. The toes were wet, and it bothered him to think that her feet must be cold.

"Rayne has a beautiful wife and baby. I don't want to see him hurt. I don't want *them* to be hurt."

"Then marry me. It's the only other solution."

Her bottom lip trembled and her eyes searched his face. He almost reached for her, caught himself and glanced away.

"Marrying you isn't a solution," she finally said. "You're a rake of the very worst sort. You're a liar—and now that I think of it, probably a cheat. What kind of a life would I have if I married you?"

"I'm not a man to make promises. I can only guarantee that your reputation will be saved and that you will be a countess. That as my wife, I'll protect you with my life, and I'll never mistreat you. I can tell you that if you don't marry me, by tomorrow at dawn your brother may be dead."

"It's my money, isn't it? That's what you've been after from the start."

"I won't deny marrying an heiress is attractive, but the simple truth is I don't wish to die—nor end up killing another man. On top of that, marrying you is the right thing to do. I am, after all, the gentleman who ruined you."

"Gentleman! You're a devil in gentleman's clothes." She eyed him from top to bottom and worried her lush bottom lip. She sighed. "All right. If Rayne is determined to go through with the duel, I'll marry you, but it will have to be a *mariage de covenience.*"

"Not on your life. You'll be my wife in every way, or I'll accept your brother's challenge." He made a gesture of nonchalance. "Who knows, maybe you'll get lucky and I'll be the one who gets killed. Then again—"

"There's a problem you haven't considered."

"Which is?"

"Even if I say yes, my brother won't agree to the marriage."

He smiled. "He will if you convince him we're in love."

"In love!"

"Everyone knows how cockle-headed he is over his own wife. He'll agree if you tell him I'm the man you love."

"I'm not that good an actress."

"Think of the life you'll be saving."

"Only at the price of my own."

Damien winced. It was true, wasn't it? She'd be miserable married to him. He would bed her and ignore her. He cared nothing for her. He was only after her money, and of course her sweet little body. The feelings she stirred, the pangs of conscience he'd thought long dead, meant nothing. He didn't care about her—he couldn't afford to.

"Alex!" The viscount's authoritative bark carried clearly across the courtyard.

She walked toward him like a proud young aristocrat making her way to the guillotine. "Are you bound and determined to go through with this duel?" she asked.

"Of course I am. The man has ruined you. What the bloody hell do you expect me to do?"

"I expect you to think of Jocelyn and little Andrew Augustus."

"I am thinking of them. I would protect their honor just as I am protecting yours."

Men! She would never understand them. Releasing a breath of pent-up air, she rested a hand on his arm. "There's another way to handle this, and we both know it. Lord Falon wants to marry me. He says he's in love with me, and I'm . . . well, I'm in love with him."

"For Godsakes, Alex. The man is a bounder. He hasn't a feather to fly with, to say nothing of the fact he's seduced half the women in London. He's been accused of smuggling, and I've even heard it said he's a spy."

"Lady Jane says he isn't all that poor, and I've heard things nearly as bad about you." Rayne opened his mouth to argue, but she cut him off. "At any rate, none of that matters. What's important is Lord Falon loves me and I love him. Besides, I—I . . . there's always the chance that I'm carrying his heir."

Rayne swore foully. "I had hoped—I thought possibly . . ."

Alexa flushed crimson, and on seeing it, for the second time in a very long time, Damien felt a pang of guilt.

"All right, Alex. You may marry the man, if that is truly your wish. All I want, all I have ever wanted, is to see you settled and happy." Hard brown eyes swiveled in Damien's direction and fixed coldly on his face. "As for you—you may rest assured that I will be checking on my sister's welfare. You will answer to me, should harm come to her in any way."

He nodded. "I never doubted it. As for the marriage . . . three days hence should be enough time to arrange things."

The viscount looked at his sister, who had grown exceedingly pale. "The parish church at Hampstead on Saturday next," Stoneleigh said. "The vicar is an old family friend. He'll see the service performed with as little inconvenience as possible."

Damien walked over to Alexa and reached for her hand. If felt as cold and brittle as a winter leaf. For the first time, he realized the importance of the step he was taking, and exactly what he was taking from her.

"It's all right, Alexa," he said softly. "Everything is going to work out." He brushed his mouth against her hand and ignored the tremor that passed through it. What mattered was Peter and accomplishing what he had set out to do. The chance to set things right had reappeared, and this time he would not be deterred from his purpose.

He forced himself not to think of the haunted look in Alexa's eyes or the trembling in her hand.

Chapter Five

ALEXA'S WEDDING DAY ARRIVED GRAY AND DRAB, MATCH-
ING HER DISMAL MOOD. SHE WAS SOMBER AND WITH-
drawn on her way to the church, sitting in her
brother's elegant black carriage, the Stoneleigh bear
and serpent glittering on the door as they passed
through the mist-enveloping the countryside. In a high-
waisted gown of ice-blue silk, she sat stiffly on the
tufted velvet seat next to Jo, who kept reaching over to
squeeze her hand.

"If you love him, things will work out," Jocelyn said
for at least the hundredth time. Her staunch belief had
come from the overwhelming odds she and Rayne had
surmounted on their difficult sojourn to happiness. In
the years since their marriage, they were desperately in
love, blessed with a beautiful year-old baby boy, and
hoping to increase their family. Surely, Jo believed, if
she and Rayne could make it, Alexandra could find love
with the earl.

Of course Jocelyn didn't really know him. Not like Alexa did. They didn't know how hard and cruel he was, how dangerous, how utterly ruthless. And yet it was that very danger that had intrigued her, drawn her to him like a moth to a devouring flame almost from the moment she had first seen him. It was the dark side of him she had found so exciting. She had wanted to explore it, to somehow get beyond it to the man she sensed inside.

It was that man who called out to her, that elusive man who compelled her—a man who might not even exist.

She had only glimpsed him on occasion, in a secret look or glance. It appeared in his treatment of the people around him, for she had never seen him misuse a servant, or be demanding, or speak ill of others.

It appeared in the touch of his hand when he had buttoned up her dress, when he had guided her so carefully down the stairs. It appeared in the kiss they had shared in the moonlight and for an instant that night in the tavern, when he had forgotten his anger.

It had surfaced as a moment of concern when he had seen Lord Beechcroft and realized their meeting had been discovered.

Or perhaps it was never there at all.

Alexa glanced out the window of the carriage. The road was muddy today, the carriage wheels churning up great globs of heavy black earth. Along the side of the road the grass stood ankle-deep in water, and only the geese that waddled along the lane seemed content.

She gazed up ahead, trying to see past beech and plane trees, searching for the bend in the road that would signal they neared the small, white-steepled church. Her brother waited for them there, and it made her nervous to think of him alone with the earl.

She thought of Rayne and the dark mood he had been in for the past three days. Perhaps it was not too late to call off the wedding. She could tell him the truth —or at least some small part of it. She could admit that she was still a virgin, that she had agreed to the marriage because she didn't want him to get hurt. She could beg him not to challenge Lord Falon, plead with him, implore Jocelyn to plead with him too.

Rayne might listen.

Then again, knowing his outrageous temper, he might not.

She shuddered to think of what lay ahead, and yet she felt resigned to accepting whatever might occur. The path she had chosen seemed almost predestined, and though she might very well destroy herself like the tiny winged moth, she still flew toward the flame.

"We're here, Alexa." Jocelyn's softly spoken words pulled her from her thoughts. "Try not to worry, dear. You wouldn't have gone to him in the first place if you hadn't cared something about him. Trust in your instincts. They can serve a woman well."

The words rang with truth. They gave her heart and a moment of courage. Then she thought of the vicious game the earl had played—the game he was about to win—and her stomach clenched into a hard, tight fist.

Damien stood near the door to the small, ivy-covered chapel at the rear of the old clapboard church. He hadn't been inside a church in years; not since the day they buried his father. He was only nine years old, a lost, lonely little boy trying to be brave, fighting the urge to cling to his mother's skirts. Afterward, he followed the casket back to the castle, to the family plot on the hill overlooking the sea. His father loved the view, he recalled, they both did, and the thought gave him courage.

The wind whipped his hair as he stood by the grave, holding back tears, refusing to let them fall since he was now the man of the family. He tossed a handful of

earth on the casket, then followed his mother back inside the house, wishing he could comfort her, hoping
that she might comfort him.

Instead she left him alone. The following day, she
packed her belongings, said a swift good-bye, and set
off in the carriage for London. She needed to purchase
suitable mourning clothes, she said, needed to be away
from the castle and the memories it held of his father.

It was the first of her endless trips, the first time he
realized how little his mother really cared about him. It
was a turning point in his life, and now, as he stared at
the alter in the small parish church, he sensed that today he had reached another one.

It sobered him to think of taking a wife, no matter
what the reason. There wasn't much place in his life for
a woman, at least not the permanent sort. And what of
the children she might bear? No matter how he worked
to avoid it, chances were there would be offspring
from their union. What kind of father would he be?
Certainly not the dedicated family man his own father
had been. Definitely not the kind of father he had been
blessed with his first nine years.

He glanced around the chapel, at the flickering candles and white-draped altar, at the golden chalice on
the dais beside the open Bible. A few feet away, the
short, balding vicar conversed in quiet tones with the
tall, powerfully built Viscount Stoneleigh, who had
come to him earlier and renewed his previous warning.

"You had better be good to her," he had said, "or
there isn't a square inch of England where you will be
safe."

Damien thought of Alexa and the vows he was about
to make. He shouldn't be there, he knew. He should
call off the wedding, take his chances on the dueling
field, run from Alexa Garrick and this whole unbelievable situation.

Instead the thought of her walking through that door

set his blood to pounding. He smoothed the lapels of his navy-blue tailcoat just to have something to do, then straightened his cravat and the cuffs of his white lawn shirt.

Perhaps she would not come.

The thought made him even more tense, and when she walked through the door, instead of feeling uneasy as he had expected, Damien felt relieved. It bothered him, this odd mix of emotions she stirred, angered him that for a moment he had felt a little like that lost lonely boy. Perhaps that was the reason he steeled himself and smoothed a blandness into his features, replacing his uncertainty with an air of nonchalance.

"Good morning, my love." He smiled as he approached where she nervously stood at the door. "You're looking lovely as usual." That was the truth. Though her cheeks were pale and her ice-blue gown a little too stark, he had never seen her looking more beautiful.

"Thank you," she said stiffly.

"The hour grows late. I thought perhaps you had changed your mind."

She gave him a pained-looking smile. "Why on earth would I want to do that?"

A corner of his mouth curved up. "Why indeed?" He turned to the balding vicar. "Shall we get on with it? We've a long journey ahead if we're to reach the castle in two days' traveling time." A few feet away, the little man's wife stood next to the broad-shouldered viscount and his beautiful wife, but other than that, the chapel was empty.

"The castle?" Alexa repeated from beside him, looking even paler than before. "You don't mean to say we'll be leaving today for the coast?"

"I thought I'd made that clear. I've duties to attend, responsibilities I've ignored far too long. We'll be leaving as soon as the vicar speaks the words."

"B-But I thought we'd be returning to Stoneleigh, at least for a day or two. My trunks are not even packed."

He looked in her leaf-green eyes and saw desperation. Did she hate him all that much? It angered him to think so and stifled any pity he might have felt. "Your sister-in-law can pack a bag and send it on to the inn where we'll be staying."

"But—"

"The wedding night will come, Alexa. You may be certain of it. Whether it happens tonight or the end of the week will make not one shred of difference."

She glanced away, but not before he caught the shimmer of unshed tears. The sight made something pull low in his belly.

"Let's see this thing done," he said gruffly, but when he clasped her hand, he held it gently, then rested it with care upon his arm.

Alexa felt torn. The earl seemed angry and aloof when he should have been self-satisfied and smug. He had won the game, hadn't he? He would soon control her fortune and she would be obliged to share his bed.

She would never understand him. Never be able to discern what it was he felt inside. What was he thinking? she wondered. How would he treat her tonight?

Worry rode like a heavy weight in her chest as he led her to the altar then stood by while the vicar intoned the words that would make them man and wife. Around them the low-ceilinged room seemed to fade into a dull gray blue; the ice-blue gown felt uncomfortably tight and seemed to weigh her down.

From the corner of her eye she saw Rayne's grimly set features, then Jocelyn's teary-eyed effort to smile. Behind the vicar the candles on the altar flickered; one guttered in its bowl of hot wax, sputtered for a moment, then went out.

Digging deeply for the strength left inside her, Alexa

repeated her vows with an unsteady voice, then listened while the earl said his with a surprising amount of clarity. When they were finished, he lifted the short tulle veil that covered her thick auburn hair, drew her into his arms and kissed her.

If she had expected cool reserve, what she got was scorching heat. A drugging, possessive kiss that left her reeling, her cheeks on fire with embarrassment. She wanted to slap the smile off his handsome face, wanted to turn and run from the church. She wanted him to kiss her again.

His expression turned a little bit hard, and she wondered again what thoughts he harbored.

"Our sincerest best wishes, Alexa," Jo said with a warm embrace, dabbing at her tears and smiling brightly, always the optimist.

"Yes . . ." Rayne said, "you know we both wish you well."

Alexa forced a smile. "Thank you." The vicar and his wife gave their congratulations. They signed the necessary documents and in a very short time were ready to leave.

"We'll see you back at the house," Rayne said, sliding a possessive arm around Jo's waist.

Alexa glanced up at the earl. "I—I'm afraid Lord Falon wishes to leave."

"What!" Rayne thundered.

"But you can't possibly," said Jo. "We've planned a celebration. Lady Jane and the duke will be there, and a few of Alexa's closest friends." She turned dark pleading eyes on the earl. "Please, Lord Falon. A woman marries only once."

The earl cleared his throat. Alexa waited to hear his refusal. "I suppose we have to eat somewhere. As long as we leave sometime this afternoon, I see no problem in staying for a while."

Alexa searched his face but it remained inscrutable.

Jocelyn clearly beamed, reading the earl's capitulation as boding well for the future. "Thank you, my lord," she said.

In the end, they stayed far later than Alexa would have guessed. There were gifts to open, a lavish meal served to about twenty guests, and even a brief musicale performed by a London musician on the pianoforte in the West Salon.

Through it all, the earl remained cordial but distant, accepting well-wishers with more grace than she would have imagined, standing at her side and smiling, playing the attentive groom so well she could almost believe he cared something about her. The truth was far different, and both of them knew it.

He had married her to avoid getting shot, or for her money, or both. Whatever the case, when they made ready to leave, a tight lump formed in Alexa's throat.

"Thank you, Rayne, for everything." On the wide stone stairs in front of the house, she rose on tiptoe to kiss his cheek, and he crushed her in a stout bear hug. She leaned over and gave Jo a hug. "I love you both very much."

Rayne glanced away and Jocelyn dabbed at her eyes. "Write as soon as you can," she said.

"Take care of yourself," Rayne said gruffly.

"I will," Alexa promised.

Rayne surprised her by extending a hand to Lord Falon, who surprised her equally by accepting it. "Good luck," her handsome brother said.

"Thank you," the earl responded.

She took her husband's arm and turned to leave, then saw Jane Thornhill making her way through the intimate gathering of friends. As if he had read Alexa's thoughts, the earl stepped away, giving them a moment alone.

"I'm going to miss you," Jane said, embracing her gently. "I just pray one day you can forgive me."

"Forgive you?" Alexa had sent Jane a note, telling her the truth of what had occurred at the inn, and received a letter of friendship and support in return.

"If I had ever imagined . . . if I had believed for a single instant that things would turn out like this—"

"Don't, Jane," Alexa said. "This wasn't your fault. It was my fault, wholly and completely. If I had listened to you in the first place, none of this would have happened."

"Dear God, Alexa, what on earth are you going to do?"

"I'm going to do exactly what I would have done if my brother had chosen the man I was to marry. I'm going to make the best of it. I'm going to be a good wife to the earl and pray that he'll be a decent husband to me."

Jane just nodded. But there were tears in her eyes.

"Ready?" The earl stood behind her. She was tall for a woman, but Lord Falon was a great deal taller. Power and strength radiated from every pore, and as tired as she was, for once she was grateful.

"I'm ready."

Since the weather had turned cold, they were traveling in the Stoneleigh road coach, instead of the earl's lighter carriage. He helped her climb aboard, then handed in her little maid, Sarah.

Rayne had insisted the older girl accompany her, and Alexa was thankful. They were friends of a sort. The plump little blonde had been a companion of Jocelyn's when she had been orphaned and fighting for survival on the London streets. Sarah wasn't a maid in the conventional sense—far from it—but she had learned the skills she needed in order to do her job, and she was even-tempered and cheerful. Within the unfamiliar walls of Castle Falon, Sarah would be a comforting reminder of family and home.

Alexa glanced through the window toward the huge

stone mansion, Stoneleigh, where she had spent her childhood. As friends waved farewell from the massive double doors, the footmen took their places at the rear of the carriage and the coachman climbed up on his seat. The little man picked up the reins, slapped the four sturdy bays on the rump, and the carriage rolled out through the massive iron gates, headed back toward London and on down to the coast south of Folkstone.

They would stop for the night when they reached the White Swan Inn, just outside of Westerham. Tonight the earl would claim his husbandly rights. There was a time she might have looked forward to it with all the anticipation of a blissful young bride. Instead the thought turned her stomach to ice and set up a burning behind her eyes.

Falon would win. Again.

She wondered how much he would take from her before the game was finished.

Damien surveyed his wife from his place beside her in the carriage. She had changed into a dove-gray traveling dress with small black brandenbourgs up the front. Her glorious dark copper hair had been pulled back and hidden beneath a matching gray bonnet. The effect was stark and cool, heightened by the paleness of her cheeks and the glaze of fatigue in her eyes. The strain she had been under showed in the stiff way she sat, the way she clutched her reticule so tightly in her lap.

Damien frowned into the dim yellow rays that signaled the encroaching darkness. They wouldn't reach the inn for several more hours. The horses would be tired from pushing them so hard, and Alexa looked as though she would barely be able to climb the stairs. How could he expect to bed her? Their coupling would hardly be joyous, more a wake than a celebration. He

could only imagine the response he would get, yet he
had promised himself he would take her.

He had waited long enough—Peter had waited long
enough. For a while he had been out of his element,
uneasy with the idea of marriage and more than a little
uncertain. His resolve had weakened; he had weakened. Now she was his, and he meant to have her.
Whether she was tired or not, resigned or not, he
would breach the woman's maidenhead and be done
with it.

At least that was what he told himself, until they finally arrived at the inn a little before midnight. Until he
took his young wife's hand to help her down and she
swayed and nearly toppled into his arms.

He repeated his vow as he led her up the stairs to
their small bedchamber above the taproom, and again
as he opened the door. But instead of joining her inside
as he had planned, he left her at the doorway, placing
her in the care of her little blond maid.

"Your countess will need help in preparing for bed,"
he instructed. "I'll have something sent up for the two
of you to eat. See that she gets whatever else she might
need." It went unsaid that he would be joining her.
That the wedding vows would be consummated before
the night was done.

He meant to. By Christ he meant to.

But as he sipped his brandy in the taproom, he kept
seeing the weariness in his wife's lovely features, her
pale cheeks, and the taut strain marring her beautiful
heart-shaped face. Pity rode hard on his overworked
conscience, and there was something else.

His mind kept recalling the times he had held her,
the fiery kisses they had shared. Long, deep, passionate
kisses, intimate drugging kisses filled with the promise
of desire that blazed between them. It occurred to him
that he wanted more from Alexa than a night of meek
submission while he rutted between her shapely legs.

He wanted to see passion blaze in her eyes. Passion and desire for him. He wanted her to want him.

He lifted his snifter, finished the last of his brandy, and turned to climb the stairs, still unsure of the course he would choose.

"Dear God, Sarah, where is he?" Dressed in a sheer white nightgown Jocelyn had given her as a wedding present, Alexa paced the floor in front of the fire in the small, low-ceilinged bedchamber.

"Perhaps 'is lordship ain't comin', miss."

"He'll come. He's only doing this to make me suffer. He isn't about to miss the chance to share my bed."

" 'E looked mighty bloomin' tired to me. Maybe 'e can't muster the strength to do 'is 'usbandly duty. Or maybe 'e figures 'e'll get more outta a lamb what's rested than one what's plumb done in."

"He'll come, I tell you. He'll come." She made another turn and started back the other way, but Sarah stepped in front of her.

" 'Ere now, luv, why don't ye stop that pacin' and climb up in bed." Sarah reached for the bell pull. "I'll order ye a cuppa 'ot milk and a warmin' pan to take the chill off them sheets. We'll tuck ye away and—"

"No." Alexa shook her head. "You go on, Sarah. There's no reason for you to stay up all night too."

"But—"

"Please, Sarah. In truth, I would rather be alone."

The little blonde nodded, picked up the tray of cold nearly untouched mutton and cheese and headed for the door. Alexa continued pacing, wondering why the earl didn't come, wildly relieved yet strangely upset that he didn't seem to want her. Several hours later, when he still had not arrived, she climbed into the wide feather bed and pulled up the covers, cursing the earl for his treachery. She fell asleep the moment her head hit the pillow, but it seemed only minutes until morning gray lighted the room and Sarah rapped softly on the door.

" 'Is lordship asked me to wake ye," she said as she bustled in. They were only two years apart, but with the differences in the lives they had led, it could have been two lifetimes. " 'E's gone to fetch the coachy. Says we're to meet 'im in the dinin' room for a quick bite to eat. Wants to get an early start on ye journey."

The grogginess she'd been fighting slid away in the blink of an eye. "An early start, is it?" She nearly tore off the sheer white gown in her haste to be rid of it. Marching over to the bureau, she filled the basin with water from a flowered porcelain pitcher and hurriedly washed the sleep from her eyes. Sarah had her traveling dress laid out, a simple dark green bombazine with gold-corded trim and a short matching jacket.

" 'Ere now," the blond girl said when she had finished her morning ablutions, "let me 'elp ye with ye hair."

She had slept with it down, waiting in vain for the earl, now it was matted and tangled. Fortunately, Sarah had it brushed and plaited in no time, and fastened in a coil at the back of her head. As soon as she was dressed, she yanked open the door and headed toward the stairs.

That was where Damien found her, stiff-necked and angry, her cheeks aflame though her face looked even paler than it had the night before.

"Where were you last night?" she demanded, her voice stretched taut as she approached him at the foot of the staircase. "Why didn't you come to my room?"

He arched a wing-shaped brow. "I apologize, my love. Had I known you would be disappointed, nothing could have kept me away. At the time, I thought you'd be far better pleased to see me in hell than walking through your bedchamber door."

"I waited up half the night—as I'm certain you knew

I would. As for the other—you are certainly right there. Devil that you are, Lord Falon, I would as soon see you in hell."

A corner of his mouth twisted up. "Since you're so distraught at my lack of good manners, you may rest assured I won't make the same mistake tonight."

Alexa stiffened. "Whatever game you are playing, my lord, it has just come to an end. Tonight, should you come to my room, you will find the door securely locked."

The muscles in his face went taut. "Should you lock the door against me, madam, you may be certain that I will break it down." He moved closer, cupped her face with his hand, but she jerked it away. "I intend to have you, Alexa. You had better prepare yourself."

"There isn't time enough in this century for me to prepare for that."

Damien felt a stab of anger, followed by a twinge of regret. She had spirit, this woman he had married. No matter how tough things got, there was something inside her that always seemed to carry her through. He almost wished the circumstances of their union had been different.

He sat beside her stiff figure while she finished breaking her fast with a cup of chocolate and several thin wafers, then they made their way out to the carriage.

Inwardly, Damien sighed. He hadn't expected her to be so angry. He had thought she would be grateful that he had left her alone. Now, once again, wrath stood between them. She was hostile and out of sorts, throwing him fiery glances, muttering unladylike words beneath her breath.

Damien almost smiled. Better that than indifference, he decided, his mind darting forward, thinking of the night to come. Perhaps she would grant him some of that fire in his bed.

* * *

Alexa sat rigidly on the carriage seat, pretending to stare straight ahead, all the while watching the play of emotion on her husband's handsome face. Though the muscles across his broad shoulders seemed taut, his features looked rested, while hers looked pale and grim. Outside, the sky was equally grim, a flat-bottomed cover of dense black clouds and a wind that whipped the branches of the overhanging trees.

She pulled her forest-green jacket a little closer, wondering how Sarah could have asked to ride outside with the coachman. Then again, living hand-to-mouth as she had, perhaps she was used to the chill.

"Are you cold?" Falon asked.

"No."

"There's a blanket under the driver's seat. I'll be happy to stop and get it for you."

"I told you I'm not cold."

He said nothing more, and as he stared back out the window, she studied his sculpted profile. With his dark flaring brows and high cheekbones, his glossy black hair and penetrating cobalt eyes, no matter the man he was inside, Damien Falon was incredibly attractive.

Did he find her attractive too? she wondered. Did he mean the words he had said in the garden? If he did, why hadn't he come to her room? More importantly, what would happen if he came to her now? The whir of the carriage wheels filled the silence, but couldn't block the questions echoing in her mind.

She glanced across at him, her patience finally at an end. "Why?" she asked, drawing his attention from the fields they passed along the road. "You've said more than once that it wasn't for the money. If that is not the reason, tell me why it is that you married me."

He stared at her for lengthy, tension-filled moments. Eyes as turbulent as the sea bored into her, making her shift uncomfortably on the seat. "It was never for the

money," he said softly. "That was a bonus I hadn't considered." He looked at her long and hard. "I did it for
my brother."

"Your brother?" she repeated, confused.

"Yes . . ." His mouth twisted up. "I believe you
may recall him. Lord Peter Melford? I gather the two of
you were fairly well-acquainted."

Alexa reeled back in her seat, her mind spinning, certain for a moment that she had misunderstood. "Peter?
Lord Peter was your brother?"

"Yes."

The single word ripped into her like grapeshot from
a cannon. The lanterns inside the carriage seemed to
spin, and her hands gripped the edge of the seat to
steady her. "But you can't be P-Peter's brother. H-His
brother's name was Lee." Dear God, what on earth was
he saying?

"That is correct, madam. Damien Lee Falon. Peter
was my half brother, but we were closer than that."

Tunnels of blackness swirled behind her eyes. "No."
She moved her head from side to side in bitter denial.
"I don't believe you. You're lying again. Y-You have to
be." But now she was uncertain. Peter had rarely spoken of his half brother. He was a black sheep of sorts
and a subject his mother did not approve.

"I assure you, I am exactly who I say."

Dear God, no. The bile rose up in her throat. For the
last two years she had done everything in her power to
forget what had happened to her friend Peter Melford.
She had fought to stop blaming herself, tried to put the
past behind her and her life back in order.

"Peter," she whispered, "dear God, not Peter." Her
stomach lurched painfully and her vision grew dim. For
a moment she thought she might faint. "S-Stop the carriage. I th-think I'm going to be sick."

Lord Falon rapped hard on the back of the driver's
seat and the man tugged violently on the reins. The bile

was close now, her stomach heaving, threatening to erupt and embarrass her before she could get out of the carriage. Even before it rolled to a stop, she threw open the door and staggered toward the small iron stairs.

"Dammit, let me help you. Are you trying to get yourself killed?" The earl blocked her way, jumped to the ground and reached up for her. She felt his hands at her waist as he lifted her down. The moment her shoes touched the earth, she ran for the side of the road. She bent over and retched, bent and retched again. At first she didn't notice the earl's arm at her waist. That he had pulled her dress back out of the way, that she was leaning against him for support.

"It's all right, I've got you," he said, brushing strands of hair from her cheeks. "You'll feel better in a minute." Weakly, she nodded. "Stay here. There's a water bag up with the coachman. I'll get it and be right back." He returned a few seconds later, the canvas bag held in his long-fingered hands, along with a dampened handkerchief bearing the initials DLF.

"Rinse and spit," he instructed. She did it more than once and eventually began to feel better. The earl wiped her face with his wet handkerchief, then gave her some water to drink. "Not too much all at once. Just take it slow and easy."

When she had finished, he led her back to the carriage and helped her climb in. Leaning back against the squabs of tufted black leather, she closed her eyes, feeling drained and empty, and more wretched than she had ever been before.

Damien studied his wife's pale face, the dark feathery crescents beneath her closed eyes, and thought that of the thousand different reactions he had imagined in the last few months, he had never expected this one.

Because he had never believed she cared.

He thought of what had just happened and knew without doubt that he had been wrong. There was no way to affect the pain he had seen in her eyes, and no way to deny it was there. She had suffered from Peter's death, just as he had. Perhaps she had suffered even worse.

The knowledge shook him to the core. And it made him wonder. . . .

"You were in love with him, then?" he said softly. He hadn't meant to ask, didn't want to hear her say it, for the notion was strangely disturbing. Still, it was something he had to know.

Alexa's eyes came slowly open. The pain was still there. It was deeply etched, he saw, an anguish not easily forgotten. It made his own pain resurface, bonding them for a moment as they hadn't been before.

"I loved him," she said, and something twisted inside his chest. "I cared for him deeply, but not in the way you mean. Peter was my friend."

Relief poured through him, surprising in its intensity. Followed by a distinctive sweep of conscience. She was supposed to be self-centered and spoiled, a woman who cared nothing for others, a woman whose own life was all that mattered. A heartless bitch like his mother. But it was obvious Alexa did care.

"You have every reason to hate me," she said softly. "I'm the one responsible for what happened to your brother. I—I was so caught up in Society, so full of self-importance, I didn't have time for him." Her eyes welled with tears and began to etch a path down her cheeks. "I flirted with him outrageously. I didn't know the way he felt . . . not until it was too late. Perhaps if I hadn't been so reckless, so impulsive . . ." She bit her quivering lower lip and wiped at the wetness on her face. A single determined drop rolled steadily toward the small indentation in her chin. "I never meant to hurt him."

Damien dragged in a slow breath of air, but the tightness would not leave his chest. This was not what he intended, not at all. Revenge was supposed to be sweet. Instead he felt nearly as disturbed as she.

"How old are you?" he asked.

"N-Nineteen."

Seventeen two years ago, the summer his brother had been killed. He cursed inwardly. He had been certain she was older. She sniffed and he reached for his handkerchief, only to realize he had used it to wash her face. He picked up her reticule, dug inside, and pulled out a white lace-trimmed hankie. She took it with trembling hands and dabbed it against her eyes.

He wanted to comfort her, but the words wouldn't come. He wanted to say he was sorry, that he hadn't understood, that he had been wrong to force the marriage.

Instead he leaned back against the carriage seat and listened to the soft sounds of her weeping. Even after she had stopped, she didn't look at him. Not until well after dark, when they had reached a small tavern south of Tunbridge Wells called the Boar's Breath Inn. Not the place he'd intended to stay, not as well-appointed nor nearly as hospitable as he would have liked, but it was closer than the Brigantine, his original destination, and he worried he had pushed her too far already.

It was crowded at the inn, a rowdy mix of soldiers making their way toward London from their garrison at Folkstone, travelers, peddlers, and farmers. The taproom rang with course laughter and bawdy jokes, interspersed with the high-pitched female voices of the buxom wenches who served them. Soldiers told stories of war, spoke harshly of Napoleon, and there was talk of a landing on the Continent, rumors Damien had already heard.

Though the inn was nearly full, he managed to secure a suite of rooms, the owner's no doubt, since he'd had to pay twice what the bloody place was worth. He ordered food for the servants, as well as the evening's fare of pigeon pie, cabbage, and apple tarts sent up to their suite, then crossed the entry to where Alexa waited at the bottom of the stairs.

She eyed him warily, as she had all afternoon, then glanced toward the rooms upstairs. "Now I understand why you didn't come to my room last night," she said.

"I didn't join you because you were tired. I thought you would realize that. I thought tonight . . . perhaps you would be feeling better."

She nodded as if she understood the fate that awaited her, deserved it, and placidly meant to accept it. She started to climb the stairs.

"Alexa . . ."

"Yes . . . ?"

"You need to get some sleep. I know all of this has been upsetting. Tomorrow . . . perhaps we can talk things over."

She frowned. "I don't understand. What are you trying to tell me?"

"I'm telling you to get some sleep. That I won't be . . . disturbing you. Not until you're rested."

"But surely—"

"Not until we've talked."

"But I—I thought . . . after today . . . I'm afraid I still don't understand."

His hand came up to her cheek. "Neither do I. Perhaps on the morrow things will be clearer."

Alexa pondered that. She didn't think things would ever be clear again. She was married to the brother of the man she had destroyed. He had done it for revenge. He meant to punish her for her crime—it was as simple as that.

She wanted to hate him for it, to despise him for the deception he had used to get what he wanted, but deep in her heart she felt she deserved whatever justice he meant to extort.

A lifetime of vengeance, she was certain, endless days of penance for the life of his brother, the friend she had so heedlessly betrayed.

And yet, she remained unsure.

Once more Damien Falon had thrown her completely off balance. Ever since they had spoken of Peter in the carriage, he had looked at her differently. The harshness was gone from his features, the brutal determination she had seen there since that awful night at the inn. She had confessed her part in his brother's death—he should have been even more determined to extract some sort of justice.

Instead there had been that soft look in his eyes, a look of caring and concern.

She wondered if she had imagined it.

Chapter Six

"RIPE LIT'LE PIECE O' GOODS, AIN'T SHE?"
THE DRUNKEN PEDDLER EYED HIS FRIEND ACROSS THE
scarred wooden table in the taproom. "Which one?
The blonde with the prime set o' dugs or the redhead?"

"The lit'le blond wagtail. Looks like a tart I once
knew in London. Makes me bleedin' privates 'ard just
to think o' beddin' that one. I'd sure as fire like to get
me 'ands on that lit'le saucebox."

"Then why don't ye?" suggested Darby Osgood. "Ye
seen 'em, same as me. They took the owner's rooms
down at the end o' the hall. Little blonde's nothing but
a servant. Odds are, for tuppence, she be 'appy to give
ye a tumble."

Fergus O'Clanahan chuckled. "I don't think 'is
bloody lordship'd take too kindly to us bustin' into 'is
bleedin' rooms."

"So how's 'e gonna know? The blonde won't be sleepin' with 'im and the missus. She'll be off in one o' them other rooms. Come on, Fergus, 'twas yer idea in the first place. Now me breeches is near to bustin' just to think o' it."

Fergus swayed drunkenly and scratched the whiskers on his chin. "I dunno, Darby. Wouldn't be the first time ye got me arse in a sling with one o' your crack-brained schemes."

"Don't be a puddlehead. Where's ye spirit o' adventure? Besides, 'ow long's it been since ye got yerself a ruddy piece o' tail?"

A surge of heat rushed into Fergus's groin. God's teeth, that was past the truth. His balls had been achin' since he'd seen the rum little blond. They'd be bluer than a too ripe slab o' cheese if he didn't do something to ease 'em soon. He belched loudly and turned to his friend.

"All right, ye bloody old fool. Let's hear what ye've got in mind. But I'm warnin' ye, this had better be good."

"When 'ave I ever let yet down, Fergus, me boy?"

Fergus slurred a vulgar oath, trying not to recall the number of times his feather-headed friend had gotten him into a hogshead o' trouble.

Alexa slept soundly. Too soundly. So deeply in fact she didn't hear the low muffled sound of men's boots on the carpet, the thudding of the pie-crust table against the wall or the low muttered oath the man swore, stumbling forward into the room. She didn't notice the man's raspy whisper or his bulky weight as he pressed his knee on the mattress and climbed up, didn't feel the draught of air across her cheek as he pulled down the covers she was deeply burrowed into.

"God's teeth!" the man spat. "It's the redhead!"

"Jesus! Where's the bleedin' earl? Way 'e was eyein'
her, I figured 'e'd be ridin' 'er 'ard all night."

He muttered a disgruntled curse. "Wherever he is, 'e
sure as bloody 'ell ain't in 'ere."

"The blonde must be sleepin' someplace else. Hurry
up, Darby. We gotta get our arses outta here."

But already it was too late. Alexa's eyes had flown
open and were riveted on the man who straddled her
atop the covers. It wasn't Lord Falon, as she had half
expected. It was the drunken peddler she had seen
downstairs.

A scream tore from her throat the instant before his
hand clamped over her mouth.

"Bloody hell!" the man slurred drunkenly.

"Come on, Darby!"

The peddler seemed uncertain exactly what to do.
Alexa took the moment to bite down hard on his hand.
He yelped in pain and let go. She screamed again just as
the earl stormed into the room.

"Alexa, what the hell . . . ?" He caught her frightened expression the very same instant he saw the two
men, and a look close to madness swept into his eyes.
The devil in a rage would have looked like that, Alexa
thought with a shudder, her gaze fixed on the hard
planes of his face. He swore a savage oath, grabbed the
first man by the shirtfront and lifted him clear off the
floor. The earl swung a blow that sent the man reeling,
crashing into lamps and tables, upending an overstuffed chair and landing him in an unconscious heap
on the carpet.

The other man scrambled unsteadily from the bed
and tried to bolt for the door.

"You're not going anywhere." Falon caught his flap-
ping coattails, hauling him back across the room. "At
least not yet." He jerked the beefy man around and
delivered a crushing blow to the peddler's jaw that sent
him stumbling toward the corner to trip over the body

of his fallen comrade and land in a sprawling heap. The earl hoisted him onto his feet and hit him again, flattening his nose and spurting blood across his shirtfront.

"Me'n' Fergus—we didn't mean ye no harm, gov'nor," the man whined in a mushy, nasal voice. "We come fer the lit'le blonde." Damien hit him again and he went down with a groan. "We didn't mean 'er no harm neither. Just wanted a tumble, is all. We meant to pay 'er for it real good." Crawling to his feet, he held up his hands in supplication. "Please, gov'nor."

Scooting to the edge of the bed, Alexa slid to the ground and raced across the chilly room, her nightgown flying out behind her. She grabbed her husband's arm just as he swung again, stopping the blow and pulling his attention in her direction. He turned on her in a blinding rage, and only checked the punch he meant to throw at the last possible instant.

"For godsake, Alexa, what the hell are you trying to do?"

"I'm trying to stop you from killing this man."

His hand remained balled in a fist. He held it up and it shook with his effort to control it. "I found him in your bed," he said, as if it were a startling revelation.

"They're drunk, Damien. I don't think they realized what they were doing." She kept her hold on his arm, feeling the tension in his muscles, seeing an even more ruthless side of him than she had suspected.

Lord Falon swallowed, still fighting for control. Releasing a long ragged breath, he stepped back and raked a hand through his wavy black hair. "Take your friend and get out of here," he said to the peddler.

"Aye, gov'nor. Anything ye say, gov'nor." The beefy man stumbled, but was finally able to stand. He hauled his friend to his feet and the two men staggered toward the door. The minute they were outside, the earl came toward her, his attention riveted on her face.

"Are you all right?"

"I'm fine."

"How did they get in?"

Alexa wet her lips. He was wearing only a dressing gown, a burgundy silk brocade that brushed softly against her when he moved. The sash was still tied, but the top hung open to his waist. In the light streaming in through the window, she could see his wide dark chest, covered with a swatch of curly black hair. Bands of muscle rippled across a rock-hard stomach. Alexa's mouth went dry.

"Th-They must have climbed in through the window." She was trembling, she realized, whether from what had just happened or the sight of the half-naked earl, she couldn't be sure.

He must have seen it, for he reached toward her, and even though she took a step away, he pulled her into his arms.

"It's over," he said, holding her against him. "No one's going to hurt you. Not while I'm around."

She tried to smile, but her heart still hammered inside her chest. "I'm all right . . . really I am."

He brushed back wisps of her hair. The rest hung down her back in a thick dark auburn braid. "Damn, it seems you're never going to get that sleep you need."

Was that really concern she heard? "I'll be fine by tomorrow." But already he was lifting her up and carrying her over to the bed. He placed her there gently, drawing up the covers and carefully tucking her in.

"Damien?"

He paused, and there was a softness in his eyes that she hadn't seen before. "Do you know how few times you have ever said my name?"

This time her smile came easy. "It's a very nice name." She had said it to herself a dozen times. But that was before all this had happened.

"My mother never liked it. That's why she called me Lee."

"The two of you didn't get along, did you?"

"No."

"Perhaps one day you'll tell me why."

The lines around his mouth grew less harsh. His lips were full and far too close to her own, making her stomach do odd little dances. Dear God, he was handsome.

"Perhaps." He drew the covers beneath her chin. "Get some rest. We'll be leaving fairly early on the morrow." He started to walk away.

"Damien?"

"Yes?"

"Thank you."

She wished she hadn't said it, for he seemed to be reminded of the men he had found in her room. His brows drew together in a scowl. "The next man in your bed had better be me," he said darkly. Reaching the door, he jerked it open, then closed it solidly behind him.

She could hear his footsteps receding down the hall, then heading down the stairs. The peddler and his friend would not return, she was certain of that, as sure as she was that Damien would have done anything in his power to protect her. It was an odd notion, but a comforting one, and holding on to it tightly, her eyes drifted shut and she was able to fall asleep.

Her last thoughts were mixed: an image of Damien Falon ruthlessly dispatching the two drunken men, a memory of his hard-muscled chest, the sound of his voice as he had coldly reminded her he was the man who belonged in her bed.

Yet it was the concern she had seen in his storm-blue eyes that remained in her dreams long after the other images had faded.

Damien paced the floor of the taproom beneath wide bands of sun coming in through the open window. He had let Alexa sleep late and ordered a light meal sent up to her room. With the delays they had suffered, they'd be a full day longer in reaching the coast.

It shouldn't have mattered, yet he found himself eager to return. The castle was the single place on earth he had ever truly belonged. He had never been welcome at Waitley, the mansion near Hampstead Heath where his mother resided since her marriage to Lord Townsend. He was always on guard there, always sparring with the earl, fighting for his mother's meager affections.

And there was certainly nothing of home in his grandmother's chateau outside of Paris. With her husband long dead, Simone de Latour was nothing but a bitter old woman, resentful that her daughter had married an Englishman and determined to extract some sort of justice for the years she had spent living alone.

It wasn't until later, until his return to Falon, that Damien had found some sort of peace. The castle was the only place he was able to let down, to be himself, or at least as much himself as he ever was.

He loved the place, just as his father had. Now he couldn't help wondering what his bride would think when she saw it. He couldn't help feeling resentful that she would compare it to Stoneleigh, or Marden, or any of a dozen of her family's vast estates, and find it lacking.

Yet that, as with most of what had happened to Alexa Garrick Falon since the day he'd first set eyes on her, would be his fault too. He should never have married her. He was hardly her equal financially, and now he'd discovered that his need for revenge had been sorely misplaced. She had been little more than a schoolgirl during her time with Peter, naive in the extreme and merely testing her newly discovered womanhood. That Peter had fallen in love with her he could well understand. There weren't ten men in London who hadn't been captured by her charms.

He should have left her to find a husband among them, left her to one of those dandified aristocrats who sniffed at her skirts and after the first few weeks would have bored her to tears. He wasn't the kind of man who had time for a wife; he didn't have time for permanent relationships. Marriage meant children, duties, responsibilities. With the kind of life he led, he might not be there when he was needed.

He might not live that long.

Still, the deed was done. He was leg-shackled for better or worse, and now that the circumstances had changed, he meant to make the best of it.

Damien looked up from his pacing in time to see Alexa and her little blond maid come into the room. The day had turned sunny and warm, and only a light breeze stirred the flower-scented late spring air. His wife had dressed accordingly, choosing a mint-green muslin day dress sprigged with tiny yellow flowers. Her cheeks were no longer pale, her eyes had returned to their clear leafy green, and when she glanced in his direction, something tightened low in his belly.

"Good morning," he said.

"I'm sorry I kept you waiting."

"I wanted you to get some sleep."

"I do feel better. Thank you, my lord."

"Damien," he corrected, taking her hand. She looked decidedly uneasy, uncertain of what he expected, and after all that had happened, he didn't blame her.

"Damien," she repeated, a flush stealing into her cheeks, but her features still looked wary.

He turned to her little maid, Sarah. "The carriage is waiting out front. Your mistress and I will join you there in a moment."

"Aye, ye lordship." Sarah headed for the door, and

Alexa turned to look up at him, an unspoken question in her eyes.

"I told you today we would talk . . . if you're feeling up to it, that is."

"I feel fine." She gazed off toward the taproom. "What happened to the peddler?"

"He and his friend made a hasty retreat. They really did seem to be harmless. I'm glad you stopped me when you did."

A faint smile tugged at her lips. Damien took her arm and together they walked outside the inn. A small brook babbled along a grassy pathway in the rear, so he turned and led her off in that direction. A meadow fanned out to the left, thick with cat's tail, melic grass, and cocksfoot. Cowslip and marigolds bloomed at the edge of the creek.

"I know these past few days have been hard on you. I'm sorry for the part I've played in that."

She glanced up at him oddly. "Sorry? You went to a great deal of trouble to accomplish your ends, I cannot credit that you would be sorry."

He shoved past the thread of guilt stealing its way into his mind. "I've been thinking about that—about Peter, I mean. Before I met you, I thought I'd worked things out. I held you responsible for Peter's death. I believed you were callous and unfeeling, that you cared nothing at all for my brother, and I meant to see you pay." He cleared his throat. "During the past two days, I've come to realize . . ."

When he didn't continue, she stopped and turned. "Yes, my lord?"

"What I'm trying to say is that I know we went into this marriage for all the wrong reasons. I don't deny I meant to hurt you. The truth is, I set out to ruin you. I planned it for weeks, I followed you and baited you, then in the end . . . well, I tried my best to prevent it. Even then I was beginning to have my doubts."

For a long while she said nothing. When she spoke, there was a disturbing tenor in her voice. "You planned very carefully, my lord."

"Yes, I did, God forgive me. I've always been good at carrying out a plan."

"Strange as it may sound, I cannot fault you for it. Peter is dead because of me. Once I almost lost Rayne. I hated the woman responsible. If he had died, I would have gone to any lengths to see her pay. I know only too well how you must feel about me."

Damien held her uncertain gaze. There were dark turbulent shadows in the depths of her eyes. "It's true in the beginning I felt that way . . . before I met you. But you're nothing at all like I thought you were. You were young and innocent that summer two years ago, merely trying your feminine wings. My brother was equally inexperienced. The combination was explosive —lethal—but I can see now that you never meant to hurt him."

A spark of some hidden emotion leapt in her eyes. The pulse beating softly at the base of her throat picked up speed. "No . . . I never meant to hurt him."

"I'm sorry I forced this marriage, Alexa. I would suggest we have it annulled but the damage to you would be fierce. The fact is, we're married and there is nothing we can do about it."

The spark in her eyes slowly faded. Hot color infused her cheeks. "I resigned myself to that fact some time ago." Alexa turned away, unconsciously squaring her shoulders. He had said something wrong, but he wasn't exactly certain what it was. She started back toward the inn, but he caught her arm.

"I'm handling this badly. With the other women I've known, it didn't matter. With you . . . The truth is, I've never dealt with a wife before; I'm not quite certain how to proceed."

"Just say what it is you are thinking."

He raked a hand through his hair. "I'm thinking that the reason for our marriage is no longer important. What matters is that you're my wife. I thought—hoped —that perhaps, given time, we might be able to make things work between us . . . that is, if you wanted them to."

Alexa's head came up. Her eyes, more uncertain than he had ever seen them, searched every inch of his face. "After all that has happened, my lord, it is hard for me to believe you want a marriage in truth."

"I'm certain that it is. That's why I'm suggesting we take things slowly at first, get to know each other a little. Tomorrow we'll reach the castle. Once we're there, things will settle down. I'll show you around your new home, and we'll have the chance to talk. Perhaps we can gain a new understanding."

Damien reached for her, caught her wrist, and Alexa felt the warmth of his touch flow into her. There was strength in his hands, yet they felt undeniably gentle.

"When the time is right," he said, "I'll come to you as a husband."

Alexa knew a tightening around her heart, a swelling of hope tempered by an edge of fear. She had only just resigned herself to a lifetime of misery with a man who despised her. Now he was offering to forget the past, to build the kind of future she had once dreamed. Did he really mean it? Did she dare to trust him, have faith in him again?

"I want to believe you . . . it's just that . . ."

Damien squeezed her hand, his features suddenly grim. "I know."

She tried to read his expression, saw the tension in the muscles pulled taut across the high bones in his cheeks. What he offered was more than she had expected, and though she risked a great deal in accepting his proposal, it was a chance she had to take.

"I'm willing to try, my lord, if you are."

Damien smiled. It was unlike any smile she had ever seen, like a ray of sun shining down from the heavens, making him look like the handsome dark angel she had once thought him.

"Thank you." Raising her hand, he pressed his lips against her palm, and a melting sensation slid through her body. "My lady."

They said nothing more, just made their way back to the carriage. Some of the strain had eased, yet she sensed a new sort of tension between them. If he meant what he said, the past would at last be forgotten. Damien Falon would come to her, become her husband in truth.

He would hold her as he had in the garden, kiss her as he had at the inn. Her limbs felt weak just to think of it, her stomach tightened, and her mouth suddenly felt cotton-dry. Her gaze swung to his broad, hard-muscled chest, and her nipples peaked beneath the fabric of her dress.

She desired him, she realized, as she had almost from the moment she had met him. And from the smoky, half-veiled look in his incredible blue eyes, he desired her too.

And yet . . .

She couldn't help wondering, was this caring man the real Damien Falon? Or just another facade he had invented to get what he wanted? Was revenge still his goal, or simply a soft, willing woman to warm his bed? Time would tell.

She wondered if he still played the game.

The ride to Falon was uneventful. They went east from Tunbridge Wells to the village of Rye, then north along the coast till they came to the castle. Damien was polite yet reserved, seeing to her needs, solicitous but keeping mostly to himself. For much of the journey, he rode with the coachman atop the carriage, leaving her inside with Sarah. Alexa was grateful. She needed time to sort out her feelings, to prepare herself to accept her husband and the life that lay ahead.

By the time they reached the coast, she began to feel a growing anticipation. Perhaps things would work out after all. Sooner or later she would have been forced to marry. Lord Falon would certainly not have been her brother's choice, but what of her? She couldn't deny the earl was as handsome as he was intriguing, or say that she wasn't attracted. Perhaps marriage to the handsome lord would fulfill her heart's dream.

Or perhaps a lifetime of hell awaited, and Peter would truly be avenged.

Chapter Seven

ALEXA SPOTTED THE CASTLE THRUSTING UP FROM THE WIND-SWEPT, BARREN SHORELINE, ITS GREAT ROUND TURRETS pointing ominously toward a sky leaden with clouds. At first it seemed daunting, like a medieval fortress armed against her—or perhaps an ancient prison.

Then, as they drew nearer, she heard the pounding of the sea and the crying of the gray-winged gulls circling out over the ocean. Frothy waves beat at the shore, and a stiff salt wind whipped in through the open carriage windows. The scene was Gothic and intense, primitive, brutal, and untamed, yet it seemed to call out to her. She found her heart beating madly, her blood pumping with wild anticipation.

The stark land reminded her of its mysterious owner, and just as with him, she felt drawn to its dark, compelling beauty.

And there were other things, she noticed, leaning

forward for a better look at her new home. Lush green
ivy wrapped protectively around the castle turrets and
draped itself over the walls, softening the harshness of
the stone. What had once been a moat had long ago
been filled and now bloomed with brightly colored
flowers. Marigolds winked up from a green bed of cow
parsley, and blue corn cockle and pink snapdragons
waved in the brisk sea breeze.

A few minutes later the carriage turned onto the long
gravel drive, and several barking hounds rushed up to
greet them. Then the coach rolled to a stop. Damien
jumped down from his perch beside the driver and
pulled open the carriage door. Surprised by the somber
look on his face, Alexa said nothing, just let him lift her
down.

"It isn't Stoneleigh or Marden," he said with an odd
note of gruffness in his voice, "but I suppose in time
you'll get used to it." He led her toward the huge oaken
front door, his movements brisk, his touch a little more
formal than she had expected.

Alexa walked past the butler waiting in the entry and
went stock-still. Standing in what had once been the
great hall, surrounded by smoke-darkened beams from
fires a half-dozen centuries past, she stood in awe of
the huge room's timelessness.

"It's incredible," she whispered, entranced by the
heavy iron chandeliers and massive stone hearth. Ancient suits of armor stood sentry near the door, and
silver banners hung from the rafters, bearing the Falon
family crest of a soaring bird.

"This is the oldest part of the castle," Damien said
guardedly. "There are several newer wings, but this has
always served as the entrance, and I am loath to change
it."

"I don't blame you."

"Some of the outer buildings and several of the turrets are in need of repair, but the rest of the house is

adequate. As I said, it isn't Stoneleigh or Marden, but in
time perhaps you will come to accept it as your home."

Was that uncertainty she heard in his voice? He had
been searching her face since the moment she stepped
from the carriage. Could it possibly be that he had worried just as she had that she would not like her knew
home?

She smiled at him softly. "Castle Falon is lovely,
Damien. Unlike anyplace I've ever been. The land
around it is wild and stark, but in its own way, beautiful."

She surveyed the interior of the castle. A warm fire
burned in a hearth so large a man could stand upright
inside it, and the furniture was polished and spotlessly
clean. Across the room, the servants who waited
nearby looked efficient and friendly. In fact they eyed
their lord as if they were truly glad to have him returned.

"It's far more than I had imagined," she added, "and
there is a warmth here I hadn't expected."

She ran a hand gently over a polished oaken table
that looked to be several hundred years old. "You're
correct in one thing. This isn't Stoneleigh or Marden.
They were both quite lovely—exceptionally grand, in
fact, but they never had the feeling of life and home I
sense in here. They were houses to me, nothing more. I
never felt an attachment to either of them, as I believe
I could come to feel here."

Damien flashed one of his most dazzling smiles. The
tension was gone from his face and the light of pleasure
lit his bright blue eyes. It made him look more handsome than ever, more wildly compelling. It occurred to
her she wanted to see that smile again and again.

"I was afraid you would find it dark and depressing.
My mother did. She loathed the place from the moment
she saw it. My father always loved it, and so do I."

Alexa's heart swelled that she had pleased him so. "I'm certain I shall come to love it too."

His smile grew even broader, and as he looked at her, his eyes turned a darker shade of blue. The hunger was there, she saw, the wanting he had lately tried to disguise. It made her own blood heat, made the color rush into her cheeks. She started to say something more about the house, but before she could speak, the butler stepped forward, an uneasy look on his narrow, aging face.

"Excuse me, my lord."

"I apologize, Montague. I've been remiss in not making proper introductions. As I said in my message, at last I have taken a bride." There was warmth in his gaze as it swept over her, lingering a moment on the swell of her breast, making her heart pick up speed. "I'd like you to meet your new mistress. Lady Falon, this is Wesley Montague, our butler."

The thin man bowed formally. "A pleasure, my lady. From myself and the rest of the staff, I bid you welcome to Castle Falon."

"Thank you."

"Most of the servants have been at Falon for years," Damien said. "You'll have time to meet the others once we have settled in."

He glanced back at the butler, who fidgeted uneasily under his close regard. "I'm afraid there's another matter, my lord."

Damien's look once more turned guarded. "What is it?" He stood several inches taller than the thin, graying man, yet the man named Montague appeared not the least in awe of him. It seemed more as if they might be friends.

"You mentioned your mother, my lord. I regret to say she's arrived yesterday at the castle."

"My mother?"

"I'm afraid so, sir, and your sister."

Damien shoved an impatient hand through his wavy jet-black hair. "Sweet Jesus, they haven't been here in years."

"Exactly so, sir."

"Did they tell you why they've come?"

Montague glanced in Alexa's direction and a spot of color rose in his gaunt, pale cheeks.

"They've got wind of your marriage, my lord—almost before 'twas done, it would seem. They say it's the talk of the city."

"I've no doubt of that." Damien sighed. "I suppose they've come to gloat over my brilliant form of revenge."

"Just the opposite, I'm afraid." The color in the butler's face grew brighter. "Perhaps we should discuss the matter in private."

"Out with it, man. The lady is my wife. Sooner or later she'll have to deal with my 'loving family.'"

Montague cleared his throat. "'Twould seem they are highly displeased by your choice of bride, my lord. They feel you've betrayed the memory of your dead brother."

Damien's face went taut, and Alex's legs felt suddenly weak. She knew it had been too easy. She knew it couldn't be over this soon.

"Where are they?"

"Taking tea in the Peregrine Room. I put them there in hopes they wouldn't learn of your arrival until we'd had a moment to speak."

"Thank you, Monty." He turned in Alexa's direction. "I'm sorry this has happened. It never occurred to me my family might come here—not in a thousand years."

"It's all right. I'd have to face them sooner or later."

His smile held regret, yet a trace of the hunger she had seen still remained. "Considering the plans I had in mind, I would have preferred it to have been far later." He reached over and squeezed her hand. "Monty will show you upstairs while I confront the lions in their den."

"Perhaps I should go with you."

"The journey was a long one. I think it better that you rest, then join us for supper. With Rachael in attendance, it's certain to be an interesting affair."

Rachael Melford, Lady Townsend. Damien's mother as well as Melissa's. And of course the late young Lord Peter.

Alexa shuddered. The women made no secret of their loathing. For months after Peter's death, she had written them letters begging their forgiveness for her part in what had happened, but Mr. Tyler, Peter's tutor, had always seen the letters returned. The ladies had refused to read them. He was sorry, he said, but there was nothing he could do.

Now they were here and she was forced at last to confront them. God in heaven, what could she say to them?

What would they say to her?

"Well, if it isn't the blushing bride."

Alexa jerked at the sound, surprised at the sight of her newly acquired mother-in-law and wondering for a moment if the woman had somehow read her thoughts. "Lady Townsend . . ." she whispered, and beside her Damien stiffened. He recovered quickly, forcing a smile to his face.

"Mother. I was just about to join you. I hope you enjoyed your tea."

She was an elegant woman with a trim figure whose once-blond hair was now generously laced with gray. She was still quite lovely, with exquisite skin and fine features. She looked nothing like Damien, except for her bright blue eyes.

"I've enjoyed not a single thing about this wretched place, I assure you. It's as old and musty as it was the day I arrived thirty years ago with your father."

"If you loathe it so much, then why did you come?"

Her mouth flattened into a harsh, tight line. "I came to see for myself if the stories I'd heard were true." She turned unforgiving eyes on Alexa. "Unless the girl travels as your whore, apparently they are."

Alexa flinched at the woman's cruelty, and a muscle jerked in Damien's cheek. Aside from that, his expression remained inscrutable. "I'm surprised you didn't think it was a stroke of brilliance. An heiress worth no small fortune wed to your disreputable black sheep son. I rather thought you'd see it as poetic justice."

"She destroyed your brother. No amount of money is worth the price of making her your wife." She smiled thinly. "Though I find it reassuring to discover your motives. It's comforting to know you haven't changed."

"Nor, it seems, have you, Mother dear."

Lady Townsend's back went rigid. Alexa watched the exchange between mother and son and wondered that a woman could be so cold toward a child of her blood.

Damien's attention swung to Alexa and his harsh tone softened. "Why don't you go on upstairs? You can rest for a while as I suggested."

She nodded and started to leave, but the rustle of fabric coming through the door stilled her movements. She turned to see Melissa Melford walking stiffly into the room.

"If she is to dine, you may be certain that I will not." Dressed in a gown of pale blue silk, she was a shorter, stouter version of her once-blond mother, except that her eyes were a far paler blue.

"Ah, dearest little sister," Damien mocked, making her a sweeping bow. "Gracious as always. So lovely to see you."

"How could you, Lee? Even you couldn't be so cruel."

Alexa laid a hand on her husband's arm and though

his face looked bland, she could feel the tension rippling through him. "It's all right," she soothed. "In a way, I don't blame her."

"Blame is no longer the issue." He turned hard blue eyes on his sister. "I know this is difficult for you, Melly."

"Don't call me that."

For a moment she thought he might smile. "I'm sorry. You're right, it's an ugly name and it no longer suits you. I can see you've quite grown up."

Melissa flushed with what might have been pleasure. Perhaps she felt more for her half brother than the dislike she pretended.

"In the beginning," he continued, "before I understood . . . I felt the same way you do. I know you loved Peter just as I did. But Peter was young and foolish. At the time, so was Alexa. Now Peter is gone and Alexa is my wife. You're going to have to accept that. As long as you're in my house, I ask that you treat her with respect."

"I will treat her with the loathing she deserves," Melissa said. "Peter's dead because of her. For godsake, Lee, how could you have married her?" Tears welled in his sister's pale eyes and began to slip down her cheeks. She stifled a cry, turned away from him and ran down the hall.

"Melissa, wait!" Alexa called after her.

"Let her go," Damien said softly. "It would be best if you went on upstairs. In the meantime, I'll speak to Melissa. Perhaps I can make her understand."

Alexa just nodded. Her throat had closed up and her hands were trembling. Throughout the exchange, Lady Townsend had stood by with a bitter look on her face. At Melissa's outburst, it changed to one of smug satisfaction.

"Your sister will never understand your betrayal," she said coldly. "But I believe I am beginning to." A corner of her mouth curved up in a smile as ruthless as Damien's once had been. "It's obvious you lust after the little slut, just as Peter did. I can see it in your eyes every time you look at her."

Alexa's fingers curled into the palm of her hand until she could feel the sharp bite of her nails.

"My reasons for this marriage are none of your concern," Damien said with a hard look of warning.

"Aren't they? How do you think your brother would feel if he knew you were rutting between the legs of the woman he loved so much it killed him? Surely it's occurred to you. I know how callous you can be, how utterly unfeeling, but I also know you cared very much for your brother. You have betrayed him in this, and I for one will never forgive you." Turning away, Lady Townsend swept regally from the room, leaving her son and Alexa staring after them.

Alexa touched his arm. "I'm sorry, Damien. So sorry. If there was any way I could make things easier, any way I could change what has happened, I would."

Neither Lady Townsend nor Melissa would ever forgive her. Now they would not forgive her husband. Yet what had she expected? That the past could so easily be set away? That she would be welcomed into the family with open arms?

And what of Damien? For all his promises to make their marriage work, his face looked decidedly grim. Lady Townsend's bitter words held a harsh note of truth they couldn't ignore. He did desire her; he had never denied it. Now his handsome face was marred by lines of guilt and pain.

"Go," he said softly, staring at the place where his mother had departed.

Alexa nodded, but the lump rose once more in her throat. Since the morning after they'd talked outside the inn, her hopes for the future had steadily risen. Now, with his mother's cruel words, all her resurrected

dreams seemed to tarnish and fade. The evening ahead
yawned as dark as a cavernous pit. She wondered if the
image foretold the kind of future that awaited.

Damien sat at the head of the table in the dining room,
Alexa to his right, his sister to his left, his mother at the
opposite end.

Above their heads, a huge, hand-wrought, iron chandelier lit the room, each candle set in a holder shaped
like a bird. The long oaken table was massive, yet
carved with exquisite detail. The settings were of gold-
rimmed porcelain, each plate over a hundred years old.

Damien stared into his wineglass, studying the rich
ruby liquid. He lifted it and took a nerve-calming sip.
Fine French wine. A gift from his employer for a job
well done. He wondered how his wife would feel if she
knew.

He glanced in her direction. Alexa looked pale but
lovely in a gown of russet silk the same rich, reddish-
brown shade as her hair. He longed to run his fingers
through it, to see it loose and shimmering, the way it
was that night at the inn.

He fought to ignore an image of her naked, of the
smoothness of her skin and the wine-sweet taste of her
lips. The low-cut gown exposed the tops of her high
lush breasts, making him want to caress them, making
his blood run thick and heavy.

He stared at the pale slim fingers wrapped around
the stem of her wineglass. She had drunk even more
than he had, but touched none of the delicious *grena-
dine de veau,* he so favored, or the delicate *coquilles
de Dieppe* he'd had his chef prepare especially for her.
Her nerves were strung taut, he knew, yet there was
little he could do to soothe her.

He had spoken to his sister and again to his mother.
Melissa had agreed to join them for supper, but refused
to acknowledge the girl she had once called friend. His

mother had restated her opinion that he was the lowli-
est cur for coveting the woman who had destroyed his
brother.

Worst of all, it was the truth.

Until the very moment she had said the words, he'd
been able to deny it. He had rationalized, convinced
himself that he'd married Alexa for revenge but that
once he'd discovered what had actually happened, he
had no choice but to rectify the situation. No choice
but to try and make the marriage work.

Now the truth came home with a vengeance. He had
wanted Alexa almost from the start. He had burned
with desire for her, had sensed her growing desire for
him. He had been drawn to her innocent fire, her frank-
ness and spirit. And he had come to want her for his
wife.

If Peter were alive, what in God's name would he
say? How would he feel if he knew?

It made his stomach twist just to think of it. Made his
chest grow tight and the bile rise up at the back of his
throat. He'd set out to avenge his brother's death, and
instead he had betrayed him. Christ's blood, what
should he do?

"Your introspection is beginning to grow tiresome,
Lee," his mother said, breaking into the silence. "Have
you nothing at all to say? You seemed to have a great
deal to discuss this afternoon."

He arched a brow skyward and forced a blandness
into his tone. "I had hoped we might enjoy the meal
with some measure of civility. Saying nothing at all
seemed the most likely method of accomplishing that
end."

"Really? I thought perhaps your conscience had suddenly awakened."

He smiled sardonically. "Since when have I had one,
Mother dear?"

"Mother's right," Melissa put in, her silver fork

gripped like a weapon. "Your feelings for Peter should have been enough to make you hate Alexa Garrick. Instead you married her and made her your countess."

He gazed at Alexa and saw her pale face. In the beginning he had hoped for such a look of despair, prayed for it, worked carefully to achieve it. Now it twisted his insides and made him want to lash out at the person who would hurt her. He turned a hard look on his sister.

"Whether you wish to believe it or not, Alexa is innocent of any wrongdoing, except perhaps being a naive young girl. You, little sister, are apt to make any number of similar mistakes. I pray that when you do, you are not so cruelly judged as you judge Alexa."

"You dare to defend her!" His mother shoved her chair back from the table, the heavy oak legs scraping loudly against the stone floor. "You were gone on one of your sojourns, off to God-only-knows-where. You didn't see the way she flirted with him, the outrageous way she baited and tried to seduced him. She behaved like a waterfront doxy until your brother fell in love with her. Then, when he proposed, she discarded him as if he were nothing but garbage."

"That's not true!" Alexa came to her feet. "I cared for Peter—Melissa was there—Peter was one of my very best friends. I—I just wasn't in love with him."

"But you *are* in love with his brother."

"No! I—I mean, Damien and I hardly know each other. He . . . that is, we . . ." Her head came up. "Circumstances forced us together. Damien loved his brother very much. He would never have betrayed him." She stared at him from across the table. "He married me for my money. And because he had no choice."

It wasn't the truth. He knew that now as clearly as he knew she would never believe it. He'd wanted her. He still did. Just the way his brother had.

"Leave her alone," he said. "Both of you. If you're finished with your meal, I'd suggest we end this sham of an evening and retire upstairs. It's been a long day for us all."

When he heard no protests, he pulled out his sister's chair, allowing her to join the two women already standing. They walked ahead of him out of the dining room. In the hallway, he pulled Alexa aside and let the other two continue past him.

"I'm sorry this had to happen. Perhaps, in time, they'll see reason."

Alexa just nodded.

"I want to thank you for defending me," he said. "It's been a long time since anyone has."

Her eyes came to rest on his face. "Perhaps that's because you won't let them."

A long moment passed. "Perhaps." He said nothing more as he led her toward the stairs. All he could think of was that she would be sleeping in the room adjoining his. The suite that belonged to the Countess Falon, the woman who was his wife. Alexa belonged to him now, and though his body went hard every time he looked at her, he could not claim her. He had promised to give her time—he meant to keep his word.

And now there was something else standing in their way.

His brother's image loomed large between them, accusing him as it hadn't before. For the first time in years, his mother had been right. How could he sleep with Alexa when Peter had been so in love with her? How could he take what his dead brother could not have? What he had been willing to die for?

It tortured him to think of it, and yet when they reached Alex's door, he found himself leaning toward her, resting his hands at her waist and drawing her against him. He bent his head and kissed her, sliding his tongue along her lips until her soft mouth trembled.

She opened to allow him inside, and a hot rush of passion swelled his loins. It made him want to bury himself inside her, to possess her, and claim her as his wife. Instead he broke away.

"It's time you went in," he said gruffly, his stomach muscles clenched against his effort at control.

Alexa flushed, warm pink creeping into her cheeks. "Good night," she said softly, stepping away from him into the room and closing the door behind her.

He listened as she walked across the floor, heard her speaking to her little maid, Sarah, knew she had begun to undress, and fought a second wave of desire for her. Cursing himself, he turned away and walked to the door next to hers.

That night he tossed and turned atop the covers. In his dreams he could see Peter's youthful face, his pale blue eyes accusing. *She's mine,* they seemed to say.

She should have been. It would have been far better for all of them.

And there was that other to consider. For years death and danger had been his bedmates, not the beautiful flame-haired woman he had not yet truly made his wife. The work he did was all he'd had to live for. It gave him purpose when nothing else could. Now he was married, but the danger still lingered. It could reappear at any moment, would, he was certain, and he would have another job to do.

He should never have married her, he thought for the thousandth time. But his response to the thought was always the same: He wanted her—more than he had ever wanted a woman. He wanted her—and sooner or later, no matter the burden on his conscience, no matter how hard he fought against it, Damien knew he would have her.

He only wondered how he would live with himself once he did.

Chapter Eight

THE NEXT THREE DAYS WERE A JOURNEY INTO HELL FOR ALEXA. CONFRONTED AT EVERY TURN, STARED AT WITH hatred and loathing, she met the women's unspoken challenge with her head held high, but inside she felt as if she might shatter at any time.

Even Damien could not help her, for he was rarely at home.

After that first night, he had stayed off mostly by himself. He left the house at dawn to check the distant fields and see to his small number of tenants, concerned for their welfare, as she wouldn't have expected. At night he worked in his study or ventured out for late night walks on the path atop the cliffs along the beach.

He kept a small boat there, and in the afternoons she had seen its tiny sail in the distance as he fought the whitecapped waves, then finally began to make his way back to the shore.

He was avoiding her, she knew. She wondered what he was thinking and how long he would continue. She wondered, in those few times when she had seen him, at the smoky looks that passed her way, the sensuous heated glances. Yet there was no more touching, no more kisses, not a single moment spent with him alone.

Alexa sighed as she stared out at the frothy sea. His mother's venomous words had done their evil work. Damien felt guilty for the desire he felt for her. The promises he had made her would never be fulfilled. Not as long as his mother and sister remained in the castle.

Perhaps not even after that.

As for herself, since the day she had talked with Damien in the meadow behind the inn, she had once more come to grips with what had happened to Peter and been able to put it behind her. Though she still felt a gnawing sense of guilt and always would, in truth it was much as Damien had said. She had never meant Peter Melford any harm; she had only been young and impulsive, and wildly unthinking. She had suffered from what had happened, and she had changed.

She wasn't the same self-centered woman she had been, and she never would be again. Nor was she withdrawn, as she had been until she had first met the earl. Somehow, some way, she meant to make a life at Castle Falon. A life for herself and the man she had married.

Alexa left her spacious bedchamber and made her way downstairs. There was no time like the present, and besides, it would keep her busy, give her something to do and keep her mind off Melissa and her mother.

"Montague," she said to the thin, graying butler. "I believe it's time I acquainted myself with my new home."

The butler smiled, pleasure creasing the lines of his aging face. "Exactly so, my lady."

"Perhaps the kitchen would be a good place to start."

He nodded. "M'sieur Boutelier is our chef. He can introduce you to the others who work there."

Over the course of the next few days, Montague made her feel at home. She got to know each of the servants, their duties and responsibilities, and what needed doing in the house.

"Mrs. Beckett," she said to the housekeeper, a prissy little woman who seemed to cast lovesick eyes at the butler. "The entire east wing seems to have been left untended. I should like to see that changed."

"His lordship ordered it so," the small woman said a bit defensively. "He had no other choice—there was only so much money. Beg pardon, milady, but the truth is the truth."

"It's quite all right, Mrs. Beckett. I should prefer the truth and I thank you for it. From now on, however, the earl will have sufficient funds to keep that wing open. My family will be visiting on occasion. I should like them to feel comfortable during their stay."

The woman's harsh look faded and a smile swept into her face. "I shall see to it personally, milady."

As each day progressed, she was amazed how easily the servants accepted her. Lady Townsend, it seemed, was hardly a favorite. Anyone the earl's mother disliked was someone to be lauded. It made her task far easier and helped to bolster her spirits.

"I'm going to speak to Damien about making some repairs," she said to Montague late one afternoon, and the stately butler beamed.

"I'm certain his lordship will be more than pleased. The earl has always loved Castle Falon."

"Yes . . ." she said, seeing an image of his darkly handsome face, knowing that soon she would again be in his company. He had bid her join him this eve. They would sup once more with his mother and sister.

It had been all she could do to agree.

"Which o' these will ye be wearin', luv?" Sarah pointed toward a scarlet gown trimmed with gold lace and another gown of cream piped in black.

"Dear God, not the red. They already believe I'm a scarlet woman."

Sarah laughed, her ripe breasts jiggling with the movement. "Scarlet woman—and here ye are, still an untried maid."

Alexa flushed.

"Let 'em think what they will. Ye've nothin' to be ashamed of. Even 'is lordship sees that now."

Alexa smiled softly. "You like him, don't you?"

Sarah lifted the cream silk gown and inspected it for wrinkles. " 'E can be a charmer, 'e can. But I 'ave ta warn ye, luv, a man like that ain't one to give ye 'eart to. At least not for a good long time."

"I know that, Sarah. I haven't forgotten how I got into this mess in the first place. The man is the consummate performer."

" 'E's a man o' many faces, I'll grant ye that. There's times when 'e looks at ye, I can see right well what 'e's a'thinkin'." She grinned, her round face looking even rounder. "He be wantin' ye, there's no doubt o' that. Other times . . . I dunno, luv. 'E could be thinkin' just about anything."

"We hardly married for love," Alexa said. "Damien wanted revenge—and perhaps my money." Unconsciously, she glanced away. "Whatever the reason, the man is my husband. I want this marriage to work. I'll do whatever it takes to make that happen. But I'm not about to fall in love." It was only half a lie, since she was only half in love with him already.

"Good girl!" Sarah said.

Alexa thanked God that Rayne had had the foresight to send the little blond maid along. "What would I do without you, Sarah?"

She chuckled. "That's what Jo used ta say, and she's done all right for 'erself."

Alexa thought about her brother and his wife and felt a rush of longing for her home. If only she could do things over. She would listen to Jane this time. She would tell Rayne about the money she had lost to the earl. She would pay Lord Falon back, tell him to forget his night with her at the inn. If she had, she would be home where she belonged.

Alexa felt the burning edge of tears, but forced them away. It was too late for tears, too late for regrets. Instead she recalled the letter she had gotten from Jocelyn almost as soon as she arrived, and the one she wrote back that same day. She didn't mention her troubles at the castle. Rayne was already worried about her. If he thought things had gone awry, he would descend on them like a wrath from the heavens.

More problems with family was the last thing she needed.

Alexa sighed. Thinking about the past wouldn't change things. She had learned that lesson before. She would have to make the best of whatever lay ahead.

"Come on, luv. Ye'd best be gettin' ready. Ye've a long night ahead, and unless ye in-laws be a'leavin', another long day on the morrow."

Alexa groaned inwardly and let Sarah help her into her gown.

Rayne paced the carpet in front of the marble-mantled fireplace in the viscount's massive bedchamber at Stoneleigh. He reread the message he had received, then crumpled the square of paper into a wide palm and tossed it away.

"I just can't leave, Jo. Not now, not when Alex might need me."

"You have to go, Rayne. You've got to see for yourself how much damage has been done." A storm had ravaged Mahogany Vale, Rayne's coffee plantation in Jamaica. According to the message, several of the workers had been injured, including their friend and overseer, Paulo Baptiste. "You mustn't worry about your sister. She and Lord Falon are doing just fine—she said so in her letter."

"I don't know . . ."

Jo tucked a strand of her long black hair behind an ear and rested a hand on her husband's muscular forearm. "Alexa's all grown up now, Rayne. You've got to accept that."

"What if something happens while I'm away?"

"While *we* are away."

"I told you, you aren't going."

"You want a baby sister for little Anthony, don't you?"

"Yes, but—"

"You won't get one with me here and you there." She rose on tiptoe and kissed his cheek. "Besides, Chita might need me." Chita was Paulo's beautiful Spanish wife and Jocelyn's good friend.

"What about Alex? What if Falon treats her badly?"

"Lord Falon may be a lot of things, but I don't think he would ever mistreat a woman."

"There's no way you can know that for sure."

"I know they're going to have problems. They'll have trouble adjusting to their marriage, just as we did. It's only to be expected."

"I hope to God they don't have to face anything like that."

Jocelyn thought of the time she'd spent in Newgate Prison and suppressed a shudder of revulsion. "I'm sure they won't. Still, whatever lies ahead for them, they've got to learn to depend on each other. They have to work things through on their own.''

Rayne released a long-pent-up breath. He reached for Jo and pulled her against the hard-ridged muscles of his chest.

"I know you're right," he finally said. "It's just that she's so young."

"Little sisters are always young to their big brothers. Let her go, Rayne. Let her make a life of her own."

Rayne smoothed a strand of her long, thick, black hair. "You're right—as always. What would I ever do without you?"

In answer, Jocelyn kissed him. She felt his body respond, and a warm hand cupped her breast. With an inward smile and a rush of heat, she led him toward the huge four-poster bed. Fleetingly she wondered what she should pack for Jamaica.

Damien stopped outside the door of the drawing room simply called Wings. Done in soft pale shades and situated just off the dining room, it was an exceptionally large salon, giving the women a chance to put plenty of distance between them. They took advantage of it, he saw as he walked in, Alexa standing at the far end near the hearth, his mother and sister near the fireplace at the opposite end.

"Good evening, ladies." Determined to set a tone of civility, he strode purposely across the room, intent on bringing them together for one last effort at reconciliation. "Would you care for a drink before supper?"

"Ratafia," said his mother, "should you have it." She turned in his direction and firelight glinted off the silver in her hair. She was still a striking woman, elegant in a way her daughter never would be. He wondered which of her much younger lovers had most recently shared her bed.

"I'm certain Melissa would prefer the same," she finished.

Then again, it was none of his concern. And she was nothing if not discreet. The late Lord Townsend had known nothing of her numerous affairs, nor, Damien suspected, did his still-naive younger sister.

"I'll have sherry," Melissa said, surprising him with a show of spirit, and across the room Alexa confirmed that she would have the same.

His wife wore an austere gown tonight, a high-waisted, silver-gray silk with a moderate neckline, slim skirt, and small puffed sleeves. It appeared as though she had armored herself for battle, yet the gown did nothing to forestall the hot rush of desire he felt for her. Still, she would need that armor for what he had planned.

He poured them each a drink, but refused to deliver it, forcing them to join him at the carved wooden sideboard near the middle of the high-ceilinged room. Whale-oil lamps and mirrored walls softened the lines of the heavy oak furniture.

"Before we go in to supper," he carefully began, "and now that everyone's had time to think things over, I should like to make a last attempt at reaching some kind of understanding." For himself, he didn't give a bloody damn if he ever saw his family again, except for perhaps his sister. He was doing this for Alexa, sensing that the matter of his brother's death and his family's forgiveness still meant a great deal to her.

"If that is what you've called us all here for, you may as well forget it," his mother snapped.

Damien ignored her. "I know it's an unpleasant subject—our dislike of discussing Peter's death appears to be the single thing we all have in common—but just for a moment, I think we should talk about what happened." He turned to his wife, hoping she could read encouragement in his expression. "Alexa, I want you to tell my mother how you felt when you found out that Peter had shot himself."

Her head came up in surprise and a tight sound struggled from between her lips. "My lord, please . . . I—I don't see how something like that can serve."

"Just this once, Alexa. I give you my word you will never have to speak of it again."

Her hand shook and several drops of sherry spilled over the rim of her glass. She set it down on a small round Hepplewhite table.

"Go on, Alexa," he pressed. "I want you to tell us exactly how you felt."

She stared at the tips of his shiny black shoes. For a moment he didn't think she would answer.

"I felt like a murderer." The words were tight, controlled, her voice a little higher than it should have been. There was pain in her eyes, and it bothered him to think that he had been the one to put it there.

"She felt like a murderer," his mother put in, "because that was exactly what she was. That is why she left for Marden—to run away from what she had done."

"That's not true!" Alexa spun to face her. "We had already moved to Marden before Peter was killed. Attempts had been made on my brother's life. We all felt he would be safer there." She turned to Melissa. "You knew that, Melly, surely you couldn't have forgotten."

"I remember," his sister said with forced control. "I remember Peter pining away. He had already asked you to marry him by then, and you had refused him. I remember what he wrote in a letter he penned the night he died. I copied it by hand and sent it to you. Perhaps *you* remember that."

Alexa's face went pale. She remembered the letter— every heartbreaking word.

My Dearest Alexa,

I begin this missive by telling you how much I love you. For the past two years, you've been all I could think of, all I dreamed about. Then I asked you to marry me and you said no. I don't blame you. What would you want with a penniless second son? Still, I was devastated. I thought surely a man could not die of a broken heart, and yet I was that filled with despair.

I thought I had finally found solace, but even that turned to grief. I did things I terribly regret and now my despair is overwhelming. I ask only your forgiveness for what I am about to do. I will love you always.
Peter.

"I—I didn't understand the way he felt," Alexa stammered, fighting the hot sting of tears. "Mr. Tyler said Peter was taken with all of the girls. He knew Peter better than anyone. He—"

"Graham Tyler is a fool," Lady Townsend said. "What would he know of women? He'd rather spend time with his musty old books than in a woman's bed." A harsh smile curved her lips. "I'm happy to say Mr. Tyler is no longer in our employ. As for you, you little whore—"

"That's enough!" Damien's harsh words rent the air. "I don't want to hear another word." He set his brandy glass down a little too hard and the sound cracked loudly across the room. "I'm sorry, Alexa. Obviously, my bringing you all together was a mistake. As a matter of fact, Mother, your staying here is a mistake, one I should have corrected the moment of your arrival."

His mouth curved cynically. "Since none of us wishes to endure several more hours of this torment, I'll have supper sent up to your rooms. After you and Melissa have finished," he said to his mother, "I suggest you pack your things. I'll expect you out of here in the morning."

His mother gasped. "You're throwing us out of your house?"

"Phrase it any way you like. I want you gone."

Lady Townsend seemed to swell with indignation. "I don't know why I should be surprised. You were arrogant and disrespectful when you were a boy. Peter was the only one who ever saw an ounce of good in you. He always defended you, and look how you've repaid him—you spit on his memory by marrying the little slut responsible for his death. You're no good, Lee, and you never will be."

She swung toward the door, the skirt of her plum silk gown swishing softly around her feet. "Come, Melissa. A moment more in your brother's company and I am certain I shall become quite ill."

Melissa hesitated a moment, giving Damien an oddly sympathetic glance, then she followed her mother from the room.

Alexa turned to her husband, but found he had moved off toward the fire. He stood in silence for long, pain-filled moments, one long arm propped on the mantel, his head hanging forward, staring broodingly into the flames.

"Damien?"

He straightened until he was standing, but did not turn to face her. "As I said, I'll have supper sent up to your room."

"But—"

"Good night, Alexa."

Head held high, she turned and left the room.

Alexa saw nothing of Damien for the balance of the night, nor did he make an appearance when his mother and sister left the following morning to return to Waitley. The house was empty, yet two more days

passed with still no word from him. It was not until
supper of the following day came and went that Alexa's
old determination resurfaced.

Perhaps that was the reason she stood at her bedchamber window, staring into the gathering darkness,
searching the distance for the earl's tall figure, wondering if tonight he would walk along the cliffs above the
shore. He'd been gone all day. Montague said he had
traveled into Falon-by-the-Sea, the small, nearby fishing
village named after the castle. On his return, he had
locked himself away in his study.

Alexa had seen him only once, as she had brushed
past him in the hallway on the way to her upstairs'
room. Unconsciously he had reached for her, their
hands had touched, lingered, and for a moment she had
glimpsed the old hunger, the longing for her he now
seemed determined to deny.

He waged a war with himself, she knew. His mother
had fueled the fires of his guilt with each of her bitter
words, and with every passing day he grew more distant. He was retreating from her, going back to the
cold, callous man he had been that night at the inn,
working tirelessly to widen the gap between them.

Tonight she was determined to seek him out, though
he had made it clear she was not welcome. Tonight she
would discover what he was thinking. She would summon her tall dark angel, and if it would somehow mend
the breach, she would welcome him into her bed.

The wind whipped her fur-lined cloak and the air was
heavy with salt and mist as Alexa made her way along
the path that led to the cliffs above the ocean. A thin,
waning moon shone overhead, casting ominous shadows, yet she did not slow. Some distance ahead, near
an outcropping of gray granite boulders, Damien stood
staring out to sea.

He was dressed all in black except for the white of

his shirt, his greatcoat whipping about him, the wind ruffling wildly through his black wavy hair.

She approached him slowly, wondering at his thoughts, uncertain what he would do when he saw her. He must have heard her footsteps on the damp narrow trail, for he started, then turned in her direction.

"Alexa—what are you doing out here?"

Ignoring the harsh tone of his words, she forced herself to smile. "The same thing you're doing, I imagine. Enjoying a stroll in the brisk night air."

"It's dangerous for a woman to be out here alone. Go back inside."

"I'm not alone; I'm with you."

He gave her a long, assessing stare. "I said to go back in."

Instead she pulled the hood of her cloak away from her head and tossed back her hair. She had left it hanging long and unfettered down her back. Now it felt good to feel the wind sifting through the heavy auburn strands. "I'll go inside in a moment. For now, I'm enjoying myself."

Damien's body went rigid. He took an ominous step in her direction, a dark, angry scowl on his face. Reaching out, he gripped her shoulders. "You're baiting me, Alexa. I want to know why."

What could she say to him? That she wanted him to keep his word? That she wanted a marriage in truth? Even she was not brave enough for that.

"I'm keeping you company, that is all. What could possibly be wrong with that?"

He raked a hand through his hair, shoving heavy black locks back from his forehead. In the shadowy moonlight she could see his high cheekbones, his firm, well-formed lips. She wanted to reach out and touch them, to press her own lips against them, to know the heat and yearning his kiss had stirred before. Damien must have read her thoughts, for the pulse began to quicken at his temple.

"You shouldn't be out here," he repeated, but some of the harshness was gone from his voice. Instead it sounded strangely husky.

"I wanted to see you," she said softly. "I wanted you to hold me."

He shook his head in denial, yet even as he made to step away, his arms reached out for her. Alexa went into them eagerly, letting him draw her against him, inhaling his sea-misted, ocean-drenched scent, holding him so close she could feel his ragged heartbeat.

"Alexa . . ." Staring into her eyes, he cupped her face in his palms and tilted her head back. Then he was kissing her, his hard mouth ravishing, his long, lean-muscled body pressing the length of her.

Alexa made a sound low in her throat and slid her arms around his neck. Her breasts crushed into the wall of his chest and she could feel his muscles bunch. Dear God, how she had craved this. She leaned toward him, and his kiss grew even more fierce, his tongue plunging into her mouth, his hands splaying over her back then moving lower, sliding down to cup her buttocks, drawing her into the hardened flesh straining toward her core.

"God, how I want you," he said raggedly, a hand reaching under her cloak, sliding into her bodice to cup a breast. He teased the soft tip into a small taut bud, and the muscles in her legs went weak. He was going too far, moving too fast, frightening her with his intentions, yet she dared not make him stop.

"You shouldn't have come," he said between long, hard kisses, but his hand continued its hot pursuit and her insides turned to fiery liquid.

"I'm your wife," she whispered. "I had to come."

The hand at her breast went still. For minutes he did not move and she wished she could call back the words. Trembling fingers brushed her skin as he eased his hand from inside her bodice. Against the fabric, her breasts felt heavy and achy. Damien's effort at control etched deep lines of pain on his face.

"You should have been Peter's wife, not mine," he said. "For once in her life, my mother was right."

"I never belonged to Peter. I belong to you. Make me your wife, Damien."

He only shook his head. "Go back to the house."

"Please . . . please don't do this."

"I said, go back to the house!"

Lifting her skirts up out of the way, fighting the tears that suddenly sprang to her eyes, Alexa raced back toward the huge stone structure in the distance. She reached the door and pulled it open, raced inside and down the hall, up the stairs and into her bedchamber. She headed straight for the window, leaning against the cool gray stone for support, fighting to catch her breath and ignore the heat still blazing through her body. She stared out toward the cliffs in the distance, searching for her tall dark husband, but she couldn't see him.

She shouldn't have gone to him. He didn't want her —he had made that perfectly clear. She shouldn't have humbled herself that way.

Or else she shouldn't have let him force her to leave.

Alexa sank down in the window seat. Hot tears rolled down her cheeks and her stomach felt leaden, yet she couldn't forget the taste of her husband's lips, the fierce desire that had raced through her when his hand had touched her breasts.

He had felt it too, she knew. It was etched in every line of his handsome face. He had been hard and throbbing with need for her, so much so it had frightened her. Perhaps that was why she had let him drive her away.

Where was he now? she wondered, wiping away the last of her tears. How could he turn her away? But the answer to that, she knew. He was thinking of Peter, warring with his conscience. It had taken her years to accept her own part in her friend's death, but she had finally succeeded.

She wondered if Damien ever would.

"Are ye ready for bed, luv?" Sarah leaned into the room, a concerned look on her face. Alexa nodded, and Sarah silently helped her undress.

"Get some sleep, luv," Sarah said once they were finished and Alexa stood by the bed in her high-necked, long-sleeved, white cotton night rail.

She nodded but made no move to climb in. Sensing her need to be alone, Sarah quietly left her, and Alexa returned to the window. She didn't know how long she sat there. She only knew the hours came and went and the hearth had long grown cold. Damien had never come up to his room; she would have heard his heavy movements. Which meant he was probably downstairs in the study. Alone.

Knowing she shouldn't yet strangely unable to stop herself, Alexa got up from the window seat. Working the circulation into her cold, stiffening limbs, she started determinedly across the room.

Chapter Nine

A LEXA PAUSED AT THE FOOT OF HER BED TO DRAW ON HER HEAVY QUILTED WRAPPER. THERE WERE DRAUGHTS IN THE hall this time of night, and most of the fires had long grown cold.

She slid her feet into soft kid slippers, reached for the oil lamp sitting beside her bed, and made her way downstairs. Just as she had suspected, a sliver of yellow leaked from beneath the study door. Lifting the heavy iron latch, she shoved the door open without knocking and went in.

Damien sprawled on a tufted brown leather sofa in front of a low-burning fire, his long legs stretched out in front of him. His black hair still looked mussed from his bout with the wind, and his unbuttoned shirt hung open to his waist, exposing a wide swath of hard-muscled chest. Alexa wet her suddenly dry lips. She remembered the night she had seen him like that before, the night the peddler had come into the room and Damien had defended her. She recalled the feel of those smooth, hard muscles, and her fingers itched to touch them again.

She walked toward him and he turned at the padding of her footfalls on the thick Oriental carpet. He straightened and sat up on the sofa. "You're supposed to be sleeping."

"We have to talk." She set the lamp on the table in front of him.

"There's nothing to talk about. Go back to your room."

"Not this time, Damien. This time I'm not leaving."

He said nothing for a moment, just stared at her as if he couldn't quite believe her audacity. "Damn you!" With an angry scowl he surged to his feet and strode off toward the fire. He began to pace in front of it, then suddenly stopped and turned. "It's after midnight. What the hell do you want?"

"Tell me what's wrong."

"You know what's wrong."

"Say it," she pressed. "I want to hear you say the words."

"What's wrong is that I want you—is that what you want to hear?"

"If that is the truth."

"The truth? The truth is, I can hardly keep my hands off you." His eyes ran over her, came to settle on the curve of her breast. "It's all I can do to keep from crossing this room and tearing off your clothes. From pulling you down on the floor and thrusting myself inside you."

"Then why don't you?"

For a moment he looked stunned. He shook his head and several dark locks tumbled forward. "We both know why I don't. I don't because of Peter. Because if I do, I don't know how I'll ever forgive myself."

"I thought you didn't have a conscience."

"It may well be limited, but recently I've discovered I still possess such a thing."

She smiled softly. "I'm glad you do. But in this your conscience is sorely misplaced."

"You're telling me it's all right to covet the very thing Peter died for? Sorry, sweeting, even I can't convince myself of that."

"You didn't covet me in the beginning—you didn't even know who I was. You sought me out to punish me for what you believed I did to your brother. You were thinking of him, not yourself."

"That was then. This is now."

"Exactly. You did what you did for Peter. Because you loved him. Peter spoke little to me about you, but when he did, it was easy to see how much he cared. Surely he loved you, just as you did him."

Damien said nothing. His mouth looked grim, his expression intense.

"And he loved me. That's what he said in his letter. Do you really believe Peter wouldn't want us to be happy? If he loved us—and I know he did—causing us pain is the last thing he would want."

Eyes as blue as the tip of a flame searched her face. "Do you really believe that?"

"I believe it with all my heart."

He stood staring for long moments more. There was tension in the dark skin stretched across his forehead. "This has been hard for me," he finally said. "Harder than I ever would have imagined."

Her heart went out to him. "Your brother loved you, Damien. Just as you loved him. He's gone, but you're still here. We both are. We should give him something to be happy for, something to make his needless dying less in vain."

A moment's hesitation, nothing more. He came away from the fire like a panther, his long strides carrying him toward her. Then he was reaching out for her, hauling her against him. His mouth came down hard over hers, taking what she meant to give, giving him solace against the uncertain feelings still roiling inside him. She felt the slick warmth of his tongue, felt a hot surge of pleasure, and opened to him, allowing him entrance. When she did, liquid heat slid through her limbs, and a dizzying wave of desire for him.

"Damien," she whispered, caught up in the warmth of his lips and the feel of his hands on her body. They roamed beneath her wrapper, over her back and down to her buttocks, cupping them, kneading them, stirring the flames that roared through her. He lifted her up on her toes and held her against him, forcing her into his hardness, insisting she feel his raging need.

He was hot and pulsing, bigger than she would have imagined. Dear God, would he really strip her naked and take her right there on the floor?

It frightened her to think of it, and yet she would not stop him. The fragile bond between them could be severed at any time.

He was kissing her neck now, stripping off her heavy quilted wrapper and unbuttoning the front of her nightgown. His mouth moved along her throat to her shoulder, leaving a trail of hot, damp kisses, fanning the fire in her blood into a roaring blaze.

He shoved the nightgown off her shoulders, baring her breasts and leaving her naked to the waist, then he bent his head and took a nipple into his mouth. Alexa moaned as a wave of heat washed over her. Her veins seemed to pulse with liquid fire and her limbs felt strangely boneless. Damien suckled her gently, and her hand slid into the silk of his ink-black hair.

When he nipped her with his teeth, tendrils of flame scorched her flesh and skimmed hotly over her body. Dear God in heaven, she had never felt anything like this. She clung to his neck, her legs so weak she wondered how much longer they would hold her up.

Damien drew back to look at her, and the hunger in his eyes made her tremble. Firelight played over her skin, she saw as she glanced down at her half-naked body, casting it with a golden glow, and her hair tumbled wildly around her shoulders. She looked wanton and wicked, and for a moment she felt afraid. She raised a hand to cover herself, but Damien caught her wrist.

"Don't . . ." he said softly. "In my mind, I've seen you this way a thousand times. I've dreamed of it. I've imagined that night at the inn again and again, but you're even more beautiful than I remembered."

He released her wrist and she let the hand fall free. She shifted, still a little embarrassed, and lifted her gaze to his eyes. They were a deep, smoky blue, more compelling, more fiercely male, than she had ever seen them. The thatch of curly black hair on his chest gleamed like jet in the firelight. She reached toward him, tested the rich, springy texture and heard him groan.

"Alexa . . ." Then he was kissing her again, shoving the gown from her hips, letting it pool in a soft cotton heap at her feet. His hands were everywhere, stroking, touching, caressing, and his mouth—dear God, it was like velvet flame. Her breasts felt heavy, her nipples ached, and the place between her legs throbbed and burned. His hand drifted toward it as if he knew, sifted through the thatch of russet curls, and a finger sank inside her.

She was trembling now, clinging to him, her nipples taut and aching.

"You're so tight," he whispered, a second finger sinking in, sliding easily since she was so wet. He moved them with gentle precision, and unconsciously she arched against his hand. "You want me, don't you, Alexa? You're ready to feel me inside you."

Her throat felt nearly too dry to speak. "Yes . . . I want you." It must be wanting she felt, she had never been so caught up, so totally out of control. She pulled his shirt from the waistband of his breeches, ran her hands over his smooth dark skin and heard his sharp intake of breath.

"We've got to stop now or I'll take you right here."

"Stop? Dear God, you can't mean to stop."

He chuckled deep in his chest, a warm, gently raspy sound unlike any she had heard. "Only till I get you upstairs." He reached for her wrapper, drew it around her and lifted her into his arms. "Our course is set, Alexa. From the moment you walked through that door, there wasn't the slightest chance of turning back, perhaps there never has been."

He strode through the study doors, and she clung to his neck as he climbed the wide stone stairs. "You're mine, Alexa. Once I've claimed you, you'll never belong to anyone else."

She shivered at the intensity she heard in his voice. Under it all, Damien Falon was a ruthless, dangerous man. What would her life be like with him as her husband? She feared what lay ahead, yet her blood still pulsed with desire for him.

They reached Alexa's room, but Damien continued down the hall and into the master suite. The difficult decision had been made. His wife had convinced him, she had come to him of her own free will, and now she would be his. Perhaps he would have come to the same conclusions himself, sooner or later. The past was over. There was nothing he could do to change things. Alexa was right, and the minute she had spoken the words, he had known it for the truth it was.

He swung open the door to his room and walked in.

He would take her here, in the lord's chamber. He wanted to awaken with her in his bed.

Damien crossed the room and set her gently on her feet, letting her slender frame slide the length of his body. His thick shaft tightened at the feel of her feminine curves. His valet had kept the fire going; there was no chill, yet one swept through him. The chill of anticipation, the fever of desire too long contained.

"I need you, Alexa." He had never meant it more. He took her hand and pressed it against the front of his breeches. "Can you feel how much?"

She wet her lips, making them glow like rubies in the lamplight. "I can feel it." She trembled, and he wondered how much was fear, how much was passion.

He turned away from her to strip off his shirt and boots, but left on his breeches. Then he returned to the place in front of her and gently eased the robe off her shoulders.

"Are you frightened?"

In the lamplight her eyes looked unbelievably green and a great deal uncertain. "A little."

"Don't be. I won't do anything to hurt you." Except for that one searing moment. But he couldn't help that, and it was too soon for her to worry.

He cupped her face between his palms, leaned forward and captured her lips. They were sweet as berries, soft as down, and warm as a winter blaze. Sweet Jesus, he wanted her. It was all he could do to control his desire, and at that he crushed her soft breasts against him. He filled his hands with them, molded and caressed her nipples. They tightened into tight little buds, and he bent and drew one into his mouth.

She was shaking all over, her slim hands gripping his shoulders, unconsciously kneading the muscles, making his shaft grow rock hard. "Easy, sweeting. We've the rest of the night for this."

But she only made a soft sound in her throat and

clutched him tighter. He knew what she was feeling, God, he felt near to bursting himself. He took her mouth in a savage kiss, slid his hands down her body and over her hips, then eased her legs apart and slid a finger inside her. She was wet and hot and tight, her slick little passage beckoning more ardently than any lure he had ever known.

He stroked her there and her knees gave way. He lifted her up on the bed and settled her atop the covers, then stripped off his breeches and stretched out naked beside her.

"Damien?" Alexa could barely form the word for the fever that gripped her. She trembled with it, writhed with it, her skin had grown damp and flush, her nipples hard and pouty. It was desire, she knew, yet there was no other man who could have kindled such searing heat.

He's so beautiful, she thought. So sleek and dark and male. He was her husband—and yet she was afraid.

"Damien?" she repeated, forcing the word past her trembling lips.

"Yes, love?" His voice sounded ragged, husky, as if it came from far away.

"I'm frightened. I—I don't understand what is happening to me." Alexa felt his hand at her breast, drawing soft warm circles around her nipples.

She caught the shadow of a smile. "There is always a first time. You have no idea how much it pleases me to know that I am the only man to touch you." Damien kissed the side of her neck, then took her mouth in a ravaging kiss that left her breathless. His tongue dipped softly between her lips, and her skin burned wherever he touched.

She felt consumed by the fire he built inside her, powerless in his grasp, and wildly out of control, as if she raced toward some deep precipice and hovered recklessly near the edge. She stiffened a little and unconsciously drew away, desperate to return to the safety of the world around her.

"Easy, love," he soothed. "I know this is new to you, but I promise I'll take care. Trust me and everything is going to be fine."

"I—I don't know what to do." In that moment she discovered it wasn't him she feared, but herself. Dear God, she had never imagined it would be like this, never realized she would feel such savage emotions.

She trembled violently as he eased her onto her back and came up over her. She could feel his hardened manhood pressing against her leg, huge and hot and throbbing.

"Part your legs for me," he said softly. "That's all you have to do."

She did as he instructed, too caught up to be embarrassed, expecting him to thrust himself inside her, eager, yet dreading the pain. Instead she felt only his fingers, stroking her gently, making her body clench, making her writhe and moan and think only of the wondrous pleasure he was bringing.

"Damien?"

He silenced the word with a kiss. A scorching, searing, blazing kiss that blotted out every other thought until she felt him slowly filling her, felt the stretching of her flesh and the widening, pulsing sensation of his hard length inside her. He hesitated a moment as he reached the final barrier, then plunged his tongue deeply into her mouth and drove himself home.

She jerked upward with pain the instant he broke through, her body arching, tightening around his long, thick maleness, clamping him inside her until his whole body shook with his effort at control.

"Easy, love, the worst is past." A sheen of perspiration covered his forehead. "Are you all right?"

She nodded, though she wasn't really sure.

"Soon you'll know pleasure, not pain."

And she did. Waves of heat that rippled across her skin and welled like great pools of fire deep within her. She clung to his shoulders as his thick shaft moved in and out and his powerful muscles bunched and shifted. His buttocks was moving, flexing, surging, burying him deeper, fanning the scorching heat that distorted her world with white-hot passion. Then the pools of fire were bursting, spilling great droplets of liquid pleasure. She was consumed by the sweetness, the fierce, aching ripples of delight that crested and grew and swept her into a place of mindless joy.

She cried out Damien's name, and he whispered hers as his body stiffened and his wet seed pumped into her. It occurred to her fleetingly that a child might result, and the thought did strange things to her heart. Then she was spiraling down, drifting, drifting, snug in her cocoon of happiness. She curled against him and he cradled her in his strong arms. She closed her eyes, and for a moment she drifted to sleep.

Damien watched his sleeping wife, and desire clutched hotly at his groin. He had only just had her, but it wasn't enough. He wanted to take her again, fill her with his body and brand her as his in the only way he knew how. Instead he brushed damp, burnished hair away from her cheeks and pressed a kiss on her forehead.

She stirred and her eyes fluttered open. They were greener than the earliest spring blossoms, her lashes thick and dark. She blushed prettily when she saw him, and he smiled to think he had been the first to touch her so intimately.

"Is it morning?" she asked, stretching a little, not yet realizing there was nothing between them but smooth, warm skin.

"No. You've slept for only a moment." He smiled. "But I'm glad you're feeling so well-rested." He leaned forward and kissed a soft pink nipple. It tightened into

a bud almost instantly, and her pretty green eyes went
wide.

"What's the matter? This was your idea as I recall."

"Yes, b-but . . ."

He bit the end then tugged on it gently. "But what?"

"But I didn't think we could do it again so soon."

He sighed. "We can't. You're probably sore, and I
don't want to hurt you."

Alexa bit her lush bottom lip. She shifted a little on
the bed, and his shaft ached at the touch of her soft
white skin. "Damn."

She frowned. "What's the matter?"

He took her hand, wrapped her fingers around his
pulsing flesh. "That's what's the matter." If he expected her to release him, he was surprised to feel her
slim fingers running over him, her eyes inspecting the
length and breadth.

"Easy, sweeting. I've only got so much will, and you
test it mightily." Just looking at her lying there naked
took all of his self-control.

"Damien?"

"Yes, love?"

"I don't think I'm sore."

His breath caught in his chest. He let it seep out
slowly. "If we start, I won't be able to stop."

Alexa just grinned. "Neither will I."

Damien laughed. "God, but you are a joy." He came
up on an elbow and kissed her, long and deep. He
suckled her breasts until she quivered, but instead of
entering her, as he had intended, he slid his hands
down to the damp folds of her sex. He wanted to
watch her reach fulfillment, he decided, sliding a finger
inside and hearing her soft mew of pleasure. A second
finger slid in. He stroked her slick flesh, found the tight
little bud of her passion and worked it relentlessly.

She was writhing against the covers, calling his name
and begging him for more. He didn't let up until she'd

reached the summit, her body going rigid, her head
falling back and her eyes sliding closed against wave
after wave of pleasure. The incredible sight was nearly
his undoing. He brought himself under control, but
only for a moment, just long enough to bury himself
inside her. He drove into her hard and deep, feeling the
last of her spasms meshing with the first of his own.

Sweet God, this was heaven. He took her fiercely and
thoroughly, bringing her to climax again. Then he
eased off her and curled her against him. They slept for
a time. At the first gray light of morning, he made love
to her again.

Lying next to her sleeping husband, Alexa had never
felt more fulfilled. At last she was a woman. Damien's
woman. She was the Countess Falon, Damien's wife,
and the knowledge made her heart feel near to bursting.

During the day, he was busy, working with his tenants
or going over the ledgers in his study, yet he always
seemed to find time for her. He showed her the castle,
and seeing it with her husband was as if she'd seen
nothing of the place before.

He knew its history from stories his father had told
him. Portions of the towering stone structure had been
built in the days of the Conqueror, he said with no
small amount of pride.

"It's been in my family since the early fifteenth century. One of my ancestors fought with Henry the Fifth
at the Battle of Agincourt." He led her up an ancient
spiral stairway to a dusty turret that looked out over the
sea. "The castle was his reward for outstanding valor."
Pointing out the machiolation—arrow slits in the floor
used for protection during siege—he smiled at her with
pride and warmth.

"I know little of my family during that time," Alexa
said. "My brother was named after some distant ances-

tor from the twelfth or thirteenth century—a knight named Raynor Augustus—but I don't know anything about him. I wish I had asked my father more before he died."

"My father and I were close," Damien said. "I only wish I could have known him longer."

Alexa knew the feeling. She had been only thirteen when her father died, just a few months after she had lost her older brother, Chris. She still missed both of them terribly. "My father was very gentle, nothing at all like my brothers. I wish you could have met him."

Damien smiled softly. "So do I."

Later that afternoon he shared a part of himself she wouldn't have suspected. In an aviary atop a far wall of the castle, Damien raised magnificent exotic birds.

She walked silently toward the cages, awed by the wild array of colors, shapes, and sizes. "They're beautiful." Wonder edged her voice, her gaze darting from one set of brightly plumed feathers to the next. "I had no idea you would be interested in something like this."

He smiled. "Would you be equally surprised to learn that I like poetry? Or that I enjoy fine paintings?"

"Yes . . ." she said, "I suppose I would." A spiraling warmth slid through her. "But I'm very glad that you do." She studied him a moment more, realizing how complex he was and how much about him there was yet to learn, then she turned back to the birds.

"I recognize those over there"—she pointed toward a large pen with seeds scattered over the gray stone floor—"they're pheasants—from China, as I recall—but I've no idea the names of these others." They walked through the aviary, pausing in front of the cages. Damien spoke to the beautiful birds softly, checking their water and seed, the birds cooing, fluttering up to him as if he were a friend.

"The white one with the topknot of long feathered

plumes is a cockatoo," he said. "The red and green birds are parrots." He pointed toward a short, squat black bird with orange and red colorations and an over-sized, hook-shaped beak. "That's a toucan. It comes from South America, and those little birds are called weavers. They make their home in Africa."

"How long have you been interested in birds?"

"As long as I can remember. It's a legacy of sorts. As far back as anyone can recall, someone in the Falon line has been interested in birds. In the beginning, it was hunting birds: falcons, hawks, other birds of prey. Exotic birds were my father's passion, and before that his mother's. Always there seemed to be someone. Perhaps that's how we got our family crest . . . or the crest gave someone the idea for raising the birds, I don't know which."

"I think it's wonderful."

He turned to face her, the wind blowing softly through his hair. "I think you're wonderful." Bending his head, he kissed her. Alexa felt a rush of heat and a sweep of desire that made her knees feel weak.

They spent several hours in the aviary. There were other birds there, she noticed, chukar and plover raised for food, a whole cage of pigeons.

She stopped before the cage, noting several of the fat gray birds had tiny metal bands around their legs. "Those are carrier pigeons, aren't they?"

His expression subtly shifted. He shrugged. "For a while I found them intriguing. The pigeons are now raised for food."

"Why don't we take them out and—"

"Why don't we go in?" he said. "It's getting late and there are things I need to do before supper."

She eyed him with interest. "All right . . . on one condition."

"Which is?"

"That you tell me about your mother." It was a subject they had both been avoiding, yet she wanted to know why the two were so at odds. She needed to know the truth, as much for Damien as for herself.

"Some other time," he said firmly, and started leading her back toward the house.

Alexa stopped him at the entrance to the garden. It wasn't a tenth the size of the one at Stoneleigh, yet it was beautifully maintained. "Don't you think I have a right to know? I'm your wife now. Your mother and sister are my family too."

He sighed wearily. "The subject of Rachael Falon Melford is hardly my favorite."

Alexa smiled. "I'm very well aware of that, but we'll have to discuss her sometime. What happened between the two of you? Surely she wasn't such a hard-edged woman when you were a boy."

The last touch of warmth slid from his face. "The truth is, she was exactly as she is today." He stared off in the distance, watching the last golden rays of the setting sun. "Though perhaps she hid it better. It didn't seem to matter to my father. For reasons I'll never understand, my father always loved her."

"I don't think we always get to choose the ones we love."

Damien eyed her strangely. "Perhaps not . . . At any rate, he died when I was nine. My mother was twenty-seven. She was self-centered and spoiled, and there wasn't much time in her life for a child."

Alexa thought of her own spoiled youth. As pampered as she had been in those days, she knew her own child would always come first.

"She must have been incredibly beautiful," she said.

He nodded. "She was lovely. Unfortunately, she knew it. She left for London the day of my father's funeral, and from that day forward I rarely saw her. It didn't matter that she was leaving her nine-year-old son home alone, that he had just lost his father and that he might be needing the comfort of his mother."

"Oh, Damien." Alexa laid a hand on his forearm and felt the tension thrumming through him.

"After that, things went downhill. She spent most of her time in the city—and most of my father's money. The castle fell into disrepair. As soon as a suitable period had passed, she married Lord Townsend."

"But surely after that things improved."

He smiled grimly. "Townsend and I were oil and water. I resented the attention he received from my mother, and she resented me for displeasing him. I was shipped off to France when I was thirteen to live with my grandmother."

She started to ask how that had gone, but the look on his face warned her not to. He had said all he intended. Another time perhaps.

"I'm sorry, Damien. I wish there was a way to change things."

"I didn't tell you that because I wanted your pity. I only felt you ought to know." He gripped her arm a little tighter than he should have. "Now it's time we went back in."

He was moody the rest of the evening, but that night he made love to her with the same fierce passion he always did. He seemed different in the morning, as if speaking of the past had somehow helped to heal him. Yet she still wasn't certain of his feelings for her, and there was a secret, enigmatic part of him he always kept hidden away.

The following day they got up early, then went into the tiny fishing village of Falon-by-the-Sea. It was a place of narrow cobbled streets lined with small tiled cottages. The wooden net lofts used by the fishermen dated from the sixteenth century, Damien told her.

"They were built tall and narrow to minimize ground rent," he said as they made their way along the main

street of the village that ran parallel to the ocean. On
the beach below, fishwives sold fresh coddling, plaice,
crab, and lobster.

"Look, Damien!" As they crossed the sand, she
pointed down the beach toward large dark smudges
that appeared to be holes in the upthrusting landscape.
"Aren't those caves leading into the cliffs?"

"Right, ye are, dearie," said an enormous, heavy-
jowled woman, her gray-streaked hair tied back in a
bright red scarf. She stood in front of an open-air booth
selling fish, whose open mouths and opaque eyes
peered up at the woman accusingly. "The coast along
'ere be laced with 'em. Used ta be a smugglers' para-
dise. Some say it still is."

There was certainly a good deal of smuggling going
on. With the war raging, fine French products were a
highly valued commodity, though most of the nobility
used them only in the privacy of their homes.

"Are there caves near Falon?" she asked Damien,
suddenly wondering if that was what had started the
rumors about him.

"Not that I know of." His expression seemed to
change, growing a little bit darker than it had been.
Alexa let the subject drop. The day was far too pleasant
to allow unwarranted notions to ruin her buoyant
mood.

"Which fish looks the freshest?" she asked with a
bright smile instead. "I believe I fancy some for supper."

Damien smiled too. "Supper is already well under
way. André is preparing something special. The fish
will have to wait."

Alexa didn't care. When Damien smiled like that, she
didn't care about anything but making him smile that
way again.

And he was right about supper, she admitted sometime later. M'sieur Boutelier's sumptuous French meals

had gone unnoticed when his mother and sister had been there. Now she relished the rich and delicious fare, and delighted in the fact that Damien ordered the lavish dishes prepared just for her.

They shared *coq au vin,* with *ris de veau aux chanterelles*—a tasty chicken dish served with delicate sweetbreads and wild mushrooms—and a fine bottle of rich red wine. Afterward they walked along the path above the shore. This time when they reached the outcropping of granite, Damien removed his greatcoat and made a bed among the boulders. He kissed her until she was trembling and clutching his shoulders, then he shoved up her skirts, unbuttoned his breeches, and took her without removing his clothes.

It was scandalous—it was wicked—and so incredibly exciting!

"Cold, my love?" he asked, kissing her cheek as she moved into the circle of his arms. "We should probably be going back in."

"Not yet . . . please." She leaned her head against his arm, and he traced a finger along her cheek. "I love to listen to the sound of the sea . . . the way it pounds against the shore. It's almost as if the ocean is alive, as if it has its own heartbeat."

He propped himself up on an elbow. "It is alive . . . at least to me. It's one of the reasons I love it here so much."

Her eyes came to rest on his face. "I love it here too, Damien."

He kissed her softly, teasing the corner of her mouth with his tongue. Then he rose and pulled her gently to her feet. "It's time we went in. There's a nice soft bed upstairs, and I haven't had nearly my fill of you." He drew on his greatcoat, then scooped her up in his arms. "I intend to make mad passionate love to you— until you beg me to quit."

She laughed as he strode toward the yellow lights in

the distance, noticing only vaguely that the fog had drifted in. "You may have a hard night ahead, my lord," she teased as a ripple of heat slid through her.

When they reached their room, they made love swiftly, then once more with slow thoroughness. She was languid and sated by the time she fell asleep.

When she awoke sometime later, Damien was gone.

Chapter Ten

IT WAS DARK STILL, NOT QUITE DAWN. THOUGH THE WINDOW WAS PARTIALLY OPEN, NO TRACE OF MOONLIGHT SHONE IN. Alexa yawned and stretched. Where was Damien? Had he been unable to sleep? She smiled a little at the notion. He had been a demanding lover last eve, and she had been more than willing to meet his needs. They'd been bathed in perspiration and drowsily content when they had finished, and both of them had fallen fast asleep.

Why then had he left her? Beginning to worry when he didn't return, Alexa drew on her quilted silk wrapper and quietly made her way downstairs. There was light beneath the door to his study. She started to lift the iron latch and go in, then realized Damien wasn't alone.

It was rude to eavesdrop, and yet . . . Pressing an ear against the door, she discovered not one, but two unfamiliar male voices speaking in low, hushed tones. With a jolt that set her heart to pounding, she realized the men were speaking French.

Dear Lord in heaven. She moved closer to the door and worked to hear what they were saying. Thank God for Miss Parsons, her crotchety old governess. The woman had hounded her until she had finally mastered the language. For the first time, she was grateful she had learned it. Still, the door was so thick she was having trouble making out the words.

Easing her hand toward the latch, moving slowly, inch by inch, she lifted the length of beaten iron and the door eased slightly open. It wasn't much more than a crack, but it was enough to see Damien in snug black breeches and a white lawn shirt talking to two other men. They were dressed for the damp, chilly weather, with sweaters and mufflers and heavy greatcoats draped over a nearby chair.

Alexa moved a little to the left, giving her a different view of the room. Another man stood in the shadows. He looked windblown and hard, his face weather-beaten and wrinkled. His clothes were those of a peasant, or perhaps a man of the sea. An odd assortment of men, she thought, wondering what had brought them together—and what they could possibly be doing at Falon.

The answer came swift and hard, making her mouth go dry and her insides clench.

Smugglers! They had to be. Dear Lord, the stories were true! Her fingers dug into her palms and her heart thumped with terrifying speed. Sweet God, Damien was involved in smuggling!

Try to stay calm, she told herself, now that you know the truth, you can do something to help him. She shouldn't be so surprised. The clues had been right there under her nose. He was part French, after all, with a taste for French food and wine and expensive cognac. There were the messenger pigeons and the caves along the shore.

She knew he needed money; it was one of the reasons he had married her. He had probably been desperate, gotten involved with the smugglers in order to survive.

Alexa took several calming breaths. There was no reason to panic. He had started smuggling for money—he didn't need that money now. He could end his involvement and no one would be the wiser.

She forced her attention back to the men in the room. They were talking about their mission, asking for Damien's help, saying something about the papers they needed. He had to get them, they said. General Moreau was desperate—he needed the information to plan his next campaign. French lives could be lost without them. Damien must contact his informant, get hold of the documents, and see them placed in French hands. The men would return five days hence—that was how long he had to see it done.

"You may rely on me as always," Damien said in French, and Alexa swallowed the bile that rose in the back of her throat. Closing the door with trembling hands, she leaned against the heavy door, grateful for the solid support. She discovered she still held her breath, and worked to force the air back into her lungs.

Not a smuggler—a spy!

A loathesome English traitor! A man who had sold out his country. A wave of nausea washed over her. It was all she could do to push herself away from the door, walk down the hall and up the wide stone stairs. She was trembling inside and her stomach threatened to erupt.

Dear God, what has he done?

More importantly, what in heaven's name was *she* to do?

Making her way back to the bedchamber, she closed

the door with shaking hands and climbed up into the bed. Damien's bed, the place he had just made love to her. Her stomach rolled once more and hot tears stung her eyes. She wanted to leave the room and never look back, to run and run and never have to face him again. She wanted to pretend that she'd never met him, to forget all the things they had shared . . . the way he had touched her. She wanted to pretend that none of it had ever happened, that she felt nothing for him, that he had not lied to her, tricked and deceived her. That he had not stolen her heart.

Alexa's fingers twisted into the pillow. She wanted to leave, but as the truth came rushing home, she realized she did not dare. She had to stay where Damien had left her. She couldn't let on that she knew, couldn't afford to arouse his suspicions. She didn't dare let him guess that she had just learned his terrible secret.

Oh, dear God, dear God! Tears flooded her eyes and slid in a steady stream down her cheeks. He had lied to her—again. From the time she had met him, he had told her one untruth after another. He had ruined her on purpose, then married her for her money. Still, she had been drawn to him, against all reason, against all logic. She had let him charm her into forgiving him, then allowed him to seduce her.

She flushed to think that in the end it was she who wound up seducing him.

Alexa closed her eyes against the memory of their blissful days together. Everything they'd shared had been a lie. Everything.

She remembered Sarah's words, " 'E's a man o' many faces, 'e is."

He was worse than that. He was a liar and a cheat, a man who would sell his soul to the highest bidder—and obviously had done just that.

Alexa turned her head into the pillow, trying to muffle the sound of her tears but unable to stop herself from crying. She had to gain control, she knew. It was a matter of life and death for the people of her country.

That thought sobered her. If French lives could be lost without the information Damien was to bring, English lives could be lost if he succeeded. Her brother Christopher had been killed by the guns of a French navy warship, his packet sunk by mistake off a rainy Dartmouth coast. Rayne had spent a year in a filthy French prison.

She hated the war, hated Napoleon and his Grande Armée, hated the loss of life and senseless destruction. She hated the French, and she wasn't about to let her husband assist them in killing more innocent young British men.

She wiped her eyes on the lace-trimmed pillowcase. She couldn't let him succeed. No matter the cost, it was up to her to stop him. But how could she do it?

Alexa bit her lip. Rayne would know what to do; he had been a colonel in the army. But her brother had left the country. When she'd received his missive telling her he and Jocelyn would be leaving for Jamaica, returning to Mahogany Vale, it hadn't seemed important. Thoughts of Damien had filled her mind and heart, as his loving filled the newly awakened needs of her body.

Damien. The man who was her husband. The man who was a traitor to everything she held dear. He had tricked her again, lied and deceived her. He had taken her innocence and drawn her into his web as artfully as a deadly spider.

He was a master of the game; she had known that from the start.

She stared up at the heavy blue velvet canopy. His performance had been superb, she thought, recalling bitterly the hours they'd spent together, fighting the fresh bite of tears. Each day her feelings for him had grown. Even now her heart ached for him, for the future she had begun to believe they would share. Tears clogged her throat, and her chest felt leaden.

Damien Falon, husband, lover—spy. His roles were as varied as his collection of beautiful birds. He was an actor par excellence. Now, in order to defeat him, it would take a consummate performance of her own.

Alexa steeled herself. He had played her for a fool from the moment he had met her. He had bested her, wrenched out her heart and trampled it beneath his feet. He had won every hand so far—but the game wasn't over.

She pushed herself up from the bed on unsteady legs and made her way over to the window. Though it was dark outside, the fog had lifted. She caught a hint of movement along the cliffs above the sea. The men were returning to the beach, to the boats that must have carried them ashore. Damien's tall, imposing figure was among them.

Alexa closed her eyes against a stab of pain and the image of her husband with the Frenchmen. No matter what it took, no matter how painful it was, this was one game she couldn't afford to lose.

Damien pulled his greatcoat closer around him. A biting wind had blown in with the tide, and now that same harsh breeze would carry Lafon and his men back to France.

He hadn't expected to see them, had secretly been hoping this day would not come, that the war would end and his life could go on as it had been since his marriage. But in his heart he knew, sooner or later, they would need him again.

His life would return to the way it was before, his idyll with Alexa would be over.

He sighed as he made his way back to the house. Monty would be waiting, concerned for his welfare as always, a loyal and trusted companion, no matter what course his life took. Yet it wasn't his old friend who dwelled in his thoughts, it was Alexa. He would be forced to lie to her again. He hated to do it, and yet he had no choice.

Perhaps it was better this way. The lies put distance between them, and he needed that distance now. Besides, he wasn't sure he liked these strange new feelings she stirred. Tenderness and caring had rarely been a part of his life, nor had conscience or compassion. She appealed to his more gentle nature, dredging up old yearnings, making him ache for things that could not be.

Lafon and his men had put those thoughts to rest. He had a job to do, and conscience wasn't a part of it. Tenderness and caring would only get him killed.

He spoke to Monty in the hall, thanking him for his discretion, for rousing him and seeing to the men. When he headed back upstairs, he found Alexa curled up in his bed, but he didn't join her. Instead he added fuel to the dying fire, took a bellows to the embers till they erupted into flame, then sat down in an overstuffed chair to soak up the warmth. He would watch Alexa sleeping, enjoy these few moments before he had to leave her.

He wondered if she missed him as she slept alone in his big bed.

"I've got to go into the city." Damien took a sip of his thick black coffee, the fine china clattering as he set the cup down in its saucer. "I'll be back just as soon as I can." They were seated in a small salon near the rear of the house, where they could watch the sea.

Alexa smiled, steeling herself, hiding her anger yet using it to blot the pain. "You're taking me with you, of course." The game had begun hours ago, when she had lain in her husband's wide bed, pretending to sleep while he had watched her, her mind churning with what she had learned and exactly what she must do. "You know how much I love the city."

He only shook his head. "Sorry, sweeting, not this time." He glanced out the window as if his mind were already far away. Sea gulls circled beneath flat gray clouds, and a stiff wind beat at the low-lying shrubs atop the cliffs. "I'll be busy most of the time, and even if that weren't so, the scandal hasn't yet died down. I don't want you suffering a bunch of wagging tongues."

"What about you? You're bound to be a target, just as I am. Perhaps even more so."

"I'm used to it. Besides, I haven't got a choice."

"What is it you have to do?"

"Speak to my estate man. I was gone for quite some time." Italy, he had told her. To settle some business for his mother. Now she doubted that it was the truth. "Things still aren't completely back in order."

Alexa sighed. "I suppose you're right," she conceded, with what she hoped was the right amount of reluctance. "It's probably best I stay here, but I'm going to miss you awfully."

He leaned over and kissed her. "I'm going to miss you too."

Anger and pain lanced through her, and hurt and a feeling of betrayal so vast she fought not to cry. Miss me? she thought, wondering how far the lie went, sick to think how shallow his feelings for her must be, fighting the notion his nights might be spent in another woman's bed. He would miss her? Highly unlikely. Yet even after all she had discovered, she couldn't help wishing it were the truth.

"When are you leaving?" She hoped he wouldn't notice the pulse beating heavily at her temple. It matched the pounding in her head she had suffered since dawn.

"This morning. I'm already packed to go. Monty is seeing to the carriage."

Alexa just nodded. Her throat felt tight and tears

burned the back of her eyes. Dear Lord this was hard—
a thousand times harder than she had imagined. Still,
when all was in readiness, she let him walk her to the
door.

"Take care of yourself." She forced a tremulous
smile.

"You too," he said, his voice a little husky.

Standing in the entry, she tilted her head back and
waited for him to kiss her. Instead of the perfunctory
good-bye she half expected, he gave her a searing,
blood-heating kiss that left her breathless and sad and
overcome with longing.

"I'll be thinking of you every night as I fall asleep,"
he said, and she braced herself against a fresh rush of
pain.

"Good-bye, Damien," she said softly, holding her
tears at bay, wishing with all her heart that things
could be different.

But wishing wouldn't change things. And as she
watched the carriage roll away, she knew nothing
could change what she had to do. With a brief nod at
Monty, Alexa returned upstairs to pack a small tapestry
satchel and make ready for her journey.

Rayne was no longer in England. She couldn't ask for
his help, but she believed she knew what he would do.
During his years in the cavalry, his best friend had been
a man named Jeremy Strickland. Colonel Strickland was
General Strickland now. He had stayed in touch with
Rayne, and the last she'd heard, he was stationed at
army headquarters in London.

It was eighty miles into the city, better than a two-
day ride for Damien in his carriage. She would take the
mail coach. Since it stopped to change horses every ten
miles, she could make the same trip in less than
twenty-four hours. She could see the general, enlist his
aid, and be back at Castle Falon before Damien's scheduled return.

"What on earth are ye doin', luv?" Sarah stood in the open doorway, a stack of fresh linens folded neatly in her hands.

"A m-message just arrived," Alexa lied, repeating the tale she had come up with. She stuffed garters and stockings into her bag beside a navy-blue day dress with a matching pelisse. "Lady Jane has taken sick. I've got to go to London."

"Well, why didn't ye tell me? I'll 'ave me bags packed in a jiffy."

Alexa started to call her back, then thought better of it. It was a long way to London. She would be far less conspicuous traveling with her maid. She would think of some explanation for Sarah once they reached their destination. In the meantime, it would cause fewer problems with Monty.

"We'll be taking the post chaise, Sarah," she called after her. "It's the fastest way to travel, and Lady Jane may need us."

Exhaustion. There was no other word for what she was feeling, and even the several hours sleep Alexa had gotten at the fashionable Grillon's Hotel on Albemarle where she had taken a suite of rooms hadn't helped.

Dressed in a dove-gray day dress trimmed with bands of plum satin, she had left Sarah there, and for a scant few vails, the desk clerk had arranged for a carriage. She had chosen Grillon's since Damien often stayed at the Clarendon, and though the ambience was more serviceable than elegant, the establishment was considered highly respectable.

She leaned back against the carriage seat, her body battered and bruised from her tenuous ride over the rutted roads, her mind still sluggish from her grueling, madcap flight into the city. Yet as tired as she was, the sights of London captured her as always. Though she had loved the barren freshness of the ocean, the simple fishing village of Falon-by-the-Sea, and the people in the castle, the teeming, pulsing city somehow made her feel alive. It gave her courage when she needed it so badly, hope when she felt so utterly hopeless, and strength when she was certain she hadn't a drop of it left.

The surging crowds of people, the merchants of the Strand, the coffeehouses, print shops, and bookstalls, the wickedness round Covent Gardens. She loved the cobbled streets, the boys who hawked the penny post, the chimney sweeps and ragpickers, the sights and sounds and even the odious smells.

It lifted her spirits just to see them, and it strengthened her resolve. These were her people, and she loved them. England was her country and she meant to stand by it.

She would do what she had come for.

Forcing its way through the traffic, past phaetons and broughams and tiny one-horse gigs, the carriage bowled through the crowded streets of the West End, finally reaching its destination, the Horse Guards building in Whitehall Palace.

Pulling the hood of her cloak up over her head, Alexa stepped down from the carriage and hurried toward the finely proportioned structure beneath the clock tower. Guards in scarlet tunics glittering with shiny brass buttons stood out front, the white plumes on their helmets rustling in the early morning breeze.

She moved past them and went in, her insides quaking with the enormity of what she was about to do.

Dear Lord, help me get through this. She refused to think of Damien. After all he had done, she owed him nothing. Yet his handsome dark image hovered like a specter in the corners of her mind. If there had been the slightest doubt, the smallest chance that she was wrong, she wouldn't be there. If there had been any other way she could have stopped him. . . .

Alexa knew that there was not.

Taking a deep breath for courage, she crossed the gray marble floor, making her way toward a uniformed soldier behind the wide front desk.

"E-Excuse me." The young man looked up. "I wonder if you might be able to help me." He had hazel eyes and an easy smile. She thought him no more than three and twenty.

"What can I do for you, miss?"

"I've come to see General Strickland. My name is Alexa Garrick." She felt nothing at all like Lady Falon. And Jeremy Strickland wouldn't recognize her by that name.

"I'm sorry," said the soldier, "but General Strickland is out of the city."

"When . . . when will he be back?"

"I'm afraid, miss, I don't rightly know."

"It is extremely urgent I see him. Can you tell me where he has gone?"

"I am not at liberty to say."

"But I've come all this way! The general is a friend of my brother's . . . Colonel Garrick? I'm certain if he knew I was here—"

"I can't tell you where he is, miss, but I can say that the general is out of the country."

"Out of the country!" She was making a disturbance, but was too tired to care. A woman across the room glanced her way, and the officer to whom the woman spoke placed his lorgnette in his eye and gave her a lengthy stare. "I'm sorry. I—I just thought . . ." She started to turn away, but someone stepped in front of her.

"Perhaps I might be of assistance, Miss . . . Garrick, did you say?"

"Yes . . . that is what I said, but—"

"Colonel Douglas Bewicke, Seventh Light Dragoons, at your service."

She only shook her head. "I'm sorry, but I don't think you can help me."

"It is obvious that you are upset. Why don't we go into my office where we can speak in private?" He gave her a reassuring smile. He was a slight man, shorter than most, with light brown hair and brown eyes. His complexion was a little bit ruddy.

"I don't—I don't know . . . Dragoons, did you say?"

He smiled. "I too am acquainted with your brother. How is Colonel Garrick these days?"

"I'm sorry to say he is also out of the country."

A light brown eyebrow went up. "In that case, I insist you let me help you. I'm certain your brother would be highly upset if we let you leave here unaided."

Douglas Bewicke led the woman into his office and settled her in a tufted red leather chair, one of two across from his desk. She was a beauty, he saw, with finely formed features and a slender yet womanly figure. It didn't surprise him. Good looks—like arrogance and money—ran in the Garrick family. Douglas crossed to the sideboard and poured her a snifter of brandy.

"Here"—he handed her the glass—"drink this. Perhaps you will start to feel better." She took a fairly healthy swallow. Her hands were shaking, he noticed as he moved behind his desk and sat down in a high-backed leather chair. A tremor of excitement slid through him. What did the girl want with Strickland? Why was she so upset? The Garricks were wealthy beyond belief. Her brother had always been a little too high and mighty, and knowing such a wealthy family's secrets was always a source of power.

"All right?" he asked, and she nodded. "Good. Now, why don't you tell me what this is all about?" For a moment she said nothing. She looked uncertain, and he thought she might try to leave. Then her bottom lip trembled and tears filled her pretty green eyes.

"I—I'm sorry." She dug into her reticule, pulled out a white lace-trimmed handkerchief and dabbed at the wetness spilling down her cheeks. "I still can't believe this is really happening."

"It's all right, Miss Garrick. Just take your time. There's no need for you to hurry."

She took a steadying breath, her expression tight and drawn. "To begin with, my name is no longer Garrick —it's Falon. Alexa Falon. Damien Falon is my husband."

"The earl?" He leaned toward her across his oak desk.

"Yes."

Interesting. He'd despised the blackhearted rake since their days together at Oxford. Falon had been the better student. He was almost too good-looking, more athletic, and far more successful with the ladies. But it was the day the young earl had caught him cheating that had put them at odds forever.

Douglas's hand beneath the table unconsciously tightened. Though Falon had never mentioned the incident, from that day forward, his disdain had been apparent. It was there in every glance, every curl of his well-formed lips, every smoothly uttered word. One day, Douglas had vowed, he would wipe that condescending expression off the handsome earl's face.

He smiled at the countess. "And this . . . problem you are facing, it has to do with the earl?"

She came to her feet in front of his desk, her slim hands still clutching the handkerchief. "I'd very much like to trust you, Colonel. If I am to do that, I must have your word, as an officer and a gentleman, that my husband will be treated fairly."

"That goes without saying, Lady Falon. I give you my

personal guarantee. Now . . . what exactly is it that
your husband has done?''

"M-My husband—is a spy.''

The breath escaped from his lungs, making a hissing
sound as it did so. Falon a spy? He'd heard rumors, of
course, but no one believed them. In fact, as he recalled, one of the higher-ups had personally checked
on the matter and dismissed it.

"Surely there's some mistake. Why, the late earl,
Lord Falon's father, was highly patriotic.''

"Perhaps that is so. Unfortunately, he died when
Damien was young. Damien is part French on his
mother's side. He lived with his grandmother for a time
in France. Apparently, that . . . that is where his loyalties remain.''

He rounded the desk until he stood before her,
watching the play of emotion across her face. Kneeling
at her side, he took her hands, which were icy cold and
trembling.

"You've done the right thing, Lady Falon, I assure
you.'' The right thing for my career, he thought, with a
gleeful inner smile. Catching a traitor would make him
a hero. It was just the boost he needed. That the man
was Damien Falon made the accomplishment even
sweeter.

"I've a feeling there's a good deal more to this than
you have told me.'' He gently squeezed her hands, then
sat down in the chair beside her. "Why don't we begin
at the beginning?''

Chapter Eleven

ALEXA LEANED BACK AGAINST THE HARD LEATHER SEAT OF THE MAIL COACH, WHICH ROCKED AND JOLTED AT A breakneck pace along the rough road home. Across from her, Sarah eyed her with a worried expression. They had just left Rye, headed north along the coast to Castle Falon. Their journey from London was almost ended.

"Are ye certain yer all right, luv?" Sarah asked around the shoulders of a stout, ale-bellied merchant. "Ye be lookin' as pale as a lily. Are ye sure ye ain't comin' down with what it was ailed Lady Jane?"

"I'm fine, Sarah. I'm just tired is all." She had told Sarah that Jane's illness had, for the most part, turned out to be a false hue and cry, that by the time they had reached the city, Jane was already up and about and nearly over her illness completely.

"Lady Jane is fit as a fiddle, and yer feelin' poorly. I

was afeared ye shouldn't 'ave gone off so 'alf-cocked. Yer 'usband will 'ave a conniption when 'e finds out what ye've put yerself through.''

Her husband. Dear God, what had she done? She had told Colonel Bewicke the truth, gone through with her plans as she had set out to. The pain had nearly been unbearable—the pain and the unexpected guilt.

You had no choice, she told herself for at least the hundredth time. But it didn't ease the pain. *He was only using you. He doesn't care a fig for you; he only married you for your money, and perhaps to assuage the lust he felt for your body.* Still, the guilt would not leave her.

She thought about her husband's return and the documents he was certain to have in his possession. Colonel Bewicke would be waiting with his troops when the Frenchmen arrived to steal England's secrets. The men would be captured.

Damien would wind up in prison.

Or worse. A traitor might be hanged, mightn't he? She had known that in some far corner of her mind, but refused to accept that it might actually occur. She'd had to end his spying, and yet . . .

The ache rose up, solid and fierce and nearly overwhelming. Why had all of this happened? What had she done to deserve a man like him?

Why had she fallen in love with him?

The knowledge that she had, nearly doubled her over with pain. She had tried to deny it, fought it with every heartbeat, feared it, and yet could not stop it from happening. Dear God, how could she love a man like that? She had asked herself the question nearly a dozen times, but no answer came. The knowledge simply gnawed at her, refusing to let her rest.

When she finally arrived back at Falon, weary and heartsick and desolate clear to her bones, Alexa went straight to her bedchamber. Sarah clucked over her with bowls of broth and warming pans for her feet, Monty worried for her health, and the cook made remedies and potions. In truth, the sickness she felt was of her own making. It gave a dull gray pallor to her skin, left her in tears, and ate at her very soul.

The minutes ticked by, the hours stretched and grew and seemed interminable. Still, she knew he would be there. His meeting with the French was set for tonight. A man like Damien would not fail to come.

Alexa stiffened, hearing noises below in the entry, footsteps and muffled words, orders being shouted, and knew that the earl had returned.

"Where is she?" There was no mistaking that voice, silk edged with steel. It drifted up from the stairwell as dusk grayed the windows. Damien had come to complete his mission.

"Upstairs, my lord," the butler said. "Her little maid, Sarah, took her some broth. Perhaps by now she's feeling better."

He took the stairs two at a time and her heart tripped over itself. She had known this would be hard, but she hadn't expected the terrible burning ache she felt inside.

"Alexa?" He stepped in through the door that connected their rooms. "Are you all right? Monty says you've been ill." He was wearing buckskin breeches and a white lawn shirt, his long legs encased in knee-high riding boots. His tousled hair glistened blue-black in the lamplight. "How are you feeling?"

"I'm fine," she said with a glance away, "or I will be in a day or two. I'm sure it's nothing to worry about. Perhaps a touch of what Jane had." By now he was certain to have heard the story of her trip to the city.

He took her hand, leaned over and brushed her forehead with a kiss. "Monty told me about your little expedition. It isn't safe for a woman alone on these roads." He smiled at her with such affection it made her heart turn over. "I ought to put you over my knee."

Tears formed in her eyes but she willed them away. "I missed you." She meant it. Dear God, she wished it wasn't the truth. She had missed him every moment, missed him even as she had spoken the words that betrayed his secret, even knowing what would happen this very eve. She should hate him, should see him as the traitor he was, but when she looked at his beautiful face, she saw only the impossibly handsome man who had stolen her heart.

"I missed you too," he said, his voice a little husky. "I've thought of nothing but making passionate love to you for the past four days." He brushed her lips with a kiss. "I guess it will have to wait."

Had he really been thinking about her? Had he been faithful to her after all? She supposed she would never know the truth.

"I'll be better by tomorrow—I promise." But she knew she would never be better again. "Perhaps we can take the carriage down to the village, or picnic by the shore." She closed her eyes, unable to look into those of piercing blue a moment more. If she didn't know the truth, she would believe he really had missed her, that he really and truly cared.

"You've got from now until morning. If you aren't back on your feet, I'm sending for the doctor."

She merely nodded. By tomorrow it wouldn't matter. By tomorrow the life they had shared would be over and done.

"Get some rest, love. I've got plans for you in bed, but they've nothing to do with your being sick." He smiled at her, then kissed her again with tenderness and compassion, yet his hunger for her showed in his expression.

It made her chest go tight and a fierce ache wrap around her heart. It made her want to weep, to pound

her fists and cry out in despair. It made her want to rail
at the unfairness of it all. She watched him leave, then
heard him moving around in his bedchamber. He was
speaking to Monty, then the old man left him alone.

Alexa shivered, suddenly feeling a chill. How long before the men would come? Or would Damien leave the
house and meet them on the beach? Whatever occurred, she intended to be there. She had come this far;
no matter the outcome, she meant to see it through.

With unsteady hands she dressed in a serviceable
dark brown woolen dress and plaited her hair into a
single long braid that hung down her back. Wrapping a
blanket around her shoulders to keep out the chill, she
seated herself in front of the window. Outside, a heavy
mist had crept in, obscuring the sliver of a moon.
Waves beat at the shoreline, matching the heavy dull
throbbing of her heart.

She wondered where Bewicke and his men were.
Had he brought them from nearby Folkstone as he had
told her he would? A number of soldiers were gar-
risoned there, she knew, manning a row of Martello
towers built for coastal defenses against the French.

The house slipped by; the ormolu clock ticked op-
pressively loud in the silence. Hearing a noise, Alexa's
senses went on alert. Damien was moving around
again, his long strides unmistakable, then she heard the
sound of a closing door as he stepped out into the hallway. Gathering her courage and fighting down the
panic that threatened to envelop her, Alexa picked up
her heavy woolen cloak and swung it around her, then
pulled the hood up over her head. She waited a moment, then quietly followed her husband downstairs.

At the back door she paused, watching his tall silhou-
ette move toward the cliffs, her heart hammering hard
inside her chest. She edged out of the house, but stood
quietly in the shadows until he began his descent to
the beach. Hurrying now, her breath coming in short,

uneven gasps, she raced along the narrow path to the shore. At the top of the cliffs she paused again, her gaze searching madly for the Frenchmen—and Bewicke and his soldiers.

Two small boats bobbed in the surf, their masts lowered into the hull, out of sight. Six men stood near the water line and three were crossing the sand. Damien walked in their direction. Beneath his arm he carried a square leather satchel, which she guessed must hold the documents the men had come for.

With her breath frozen somewhere inside her chest, Alexa crouched behind a nest of boulders. On the sand below, around a curve in the shoreline and an outcropping of rock that blocked them from view, Bewicke and his men moved stealthily forward. Uniformed in scarlet, each of the soldiers carried a musket armed with fixed bayonet. Bewicke unsheathed his saber and it glinted with menace in the tiny sliver of moon.

Alexa glanced back toward Damien and her heart rose into her throat. Images of her husband holding her, kissing her, whispering soft words of passion, rushed into her mind, moments he'd been caring and gentle. She thought of the night he had burst into her room at the inn, how wildly protective he had been, how worried for her safety. She thought of him defending her against his own mother, of how he had suffered to think that in marrying her he was betraying his brother. She thought of his beautiful birds, of walks they had taken on the beach, of the little things he had done to please her.

With a rush of clarity she realized that no matter what he had done, she couldn't stand the thought of his being in prison, or facing a scandalous trial, or perhaps being hurt or wounded in the coming confrontation.

She couldn't in her wildest imaginings accept the thought of him winding up dead.

Dear God in heaven, what have I done?

Alexa started running. If she could get to him before the British rounded the corner, she could warn him of the danger. He and the Frenchmen could escape. If they could make it back to the boats, they could get away—in France he would be safe.

She raced along the cliffs, the harsh wind stinging her cheeks. She would have to wrest the documents away—God in heaven, she had to protect her country's secrets—but if she succeeded, England would be safe and Damien could escape.

She scrambled down the steep sandy trail, slipping and sliding, rocks and pebbles cutting into her hands, scraping her knees and tearing her dress. By the time she reached the bottom, her shoes were filled with dirt and sharp little stones dug into her feet. She kicked her slippers away and kept running. The deep sand pulled at her muscles, and something cut into the bottom of her foot. Alexa stifled a groan of pain and raced on.

So far the men hadn't seen her, and she dared not cry out. Her legs were burning and so were her lungs. Her heart pumped fiercely, yet she drove herself forward. A few more yards—Damien whirled toward her just as she reached him. She jerked the satchel from his unsuspecting hands.

"It's a trap," she said, gripping the leather to her chest as she backed away, her breath coming hard and fast and making it difficult to speak. "Th-The soldiers are right behind me—you've got to run!"

Even in the dim light of the moon she could see his face go pale. "Sweet Christ, Alexa—what have you done?" He started moving toward her, but she only backed away.

Her legs were shaking and hot tears trickled down her cheeks. "There isn't time. You've got to go—before it's too late."

He saw them then, rounding the point, crouching

low and running across the sand in his direction. The first shot rang out, cutting through the air with the buzz of death just inches above their heads.

"Run back toward the cliffs." Placing himself between her and the soldiers, he gripped her arm and dragged her in that direction. "You've got to get up where it's safe." More shots ripped through the air, a volley of them that scattered the Frenchmen and filled the night with the acrid scent of gunpowder. Bewicke shouted the order for another round, and Damien shoved her into the sand, shielding her with his long, hard body.

"You mustn't do this," she gasped, unable to believe what he was doing, her mind nearly numb with fear for him. "You've got to get away!" Why hadn't he tried to escape? Dear God, he was risking his life for her, ignoring his own safety and any chance he might have to avoid being captured. "Damien, please!"

More shots sliced the air, and while the men reloaded, Damien dragged her to her feet. He pulled her toward the path leading up to the cliffs, determined to see her safe.

"Damien!" she cried, but already it was too late. Six of Bewicke's soldiers set upon him, dragging him down into the sand.

At the same time, Alexa felt a hand clamp over her mouth and a thick arm wrap around her waist. "No!" she screamed as one of the Frenchmen, a big burly dark-haired man, began dragging her back toward the sea. "Let me go!" She tried to struggle, fought to break free, but his hold was relentless. He swore at her foully but kept moving steadily backward, then he was wading into the ocean, lifting her aboard one of the sailboats, shoving her down roughly and following her in.

"Damien!" she cried out, staring back toward the shore, but he was surrounded by soldiers, taking blow after blow from their fists and their feet. The French-

men fired their pistols and several British soldiers went
down, their bodies sprawling lifeless in the sand.

"Faites vite!" someone ordered. Hurry Up! And the
men who manned the oars began to stroke rapidly
away.

She tried to tear free of the burly man's grasp, but he
easily stilled her movements, pressing her down between the runnels even as he fired his pistol at another
group of soldiers rushing toward them from the beach.
Around them men worked feverishly to hoist the sails,
and in minutes they had left the shore behind, the
small boats fighting the waves then breaking through
the surf to the opposite side, the white canvas burgeoning, the stiff wind catching then filling it, carrying
them even farther out to sea. The sound of pistol shots
still cut the air, but now they were sporadic, muffled
and indistinct.

Alexa stared at the water and knew her last chance
of escape was slipping past the hull in a great dark,
freezing wake. She crouched, then surged to her feet,
determined to toss herself over, wondering how long
she could swim with the heavy weight of her clothing
dragging her beneath the sea.

"Ah, non, anglaise," said the beefy man, gripping
her shoulders until she winced, and stopping her head-
long flight. "It would be my pleasure to let you
drown," he continued in French, "but the colonel has
need of you."

"Have a care with the lady," said a tall, imposing
figure from behind them. Silver touched his dark brown
hair and there was a gauntness to his features. "She is
the wife of our good friend. He might not wish to see
her harmed."

"The little whore betrayed us!"

"You cannot know that for certain." The colonel
reached toward her, slid the satchel from her trembling
fingers. Until that moment Alexa hadn't realized she

still carried it. "Perhaps she is an ally, *n'est ce pas?* You can see that she brings us what we have come such a long way to get."

Alexa gasped at the thought that she had unwittingly helped them. "Whoreson Frenchman! I am no ally of yours!"

The colonel chuckled softly. "We know who you are, Madame Falon. We also know that your family is a powerful one. Perhaps the English will want you back badly enough to give us what we want in return."

A surge of hope shot through her, along with a thread of trepidation. "What is it you would seek?"

"Why, your husband, of course. The major is a man of many talents."

"My—My husband is a major?" The bile rolled in her stomach.

"An officer in the Grenadiers de Cheval, Napoleon's elite Guard Cavalry. Only an honorary rank, of course, but one that is well-deserved. Though his value here has ended, there are other places for a man of his skills." He pinned her with a long hard glare. "In the meantime, madame, you should be grateful your usefulness has not yet ended."

Damien groaned and raised a hand to his battered face. His knuckles were cut and throbbing, his lips puffed and swollen, his body black and blue all over. With his ribs cracked, it even hurt to breathe. He winced as he sat up on the dirty straw pallet in the corner of his cell in a thick-walled, musty old building at the rear of the garrison at Folkstone. Reeling with the effort, he fought a wave of nausea.

Bloody Christ, was there an inch of his body that didn't hurt? If there was, he had yet to discover where it was.

On the other hand, he was probably lucky to be alive

at all, most likely wouldn't be if it hadn't been for Alexa.

He thought of her now, and a wave of fury washed over him. She was his wife, by Christ, yet she had betrayed him. He was battered and beaten and languishing in a dingy, rat-infested cell because of her. His jaw tightened as he thought of the lengths she had gone to oppose him. Bloody hell, she had married him for better or worse. She owed him her loyalty, if not her trust.

Then he thought of her racing toward him on the beach, saw once more the tears streaking hotly down her cheeks. Perhaps in the end she had honored her vows when she risked her life to save him.

Some of the anger slipped away, and in its place he felt a grudging admiration. It had taken incredible courage for her to speak out against him. He was her husband, after all, and women rarely defied the men they married. And there was her family to consider. The scandal would be devastating. But Alexa was a woman of conviction. She had done what she felt she had to, and in some remote corner of his mind he was proud of her.

Damien sighed into the darkness, trying to ignore the secret part of him that wished she had cared for him enough to overlook whatever it was he might have done, that he had come to mean more to her than politics, or even the bloody destruction of war. He remembered the tenderness they had shared, the passion, the feelings of closeness.

He remembered the nights she had slept in his arms, and wondered if she remembered them too. Perhaps she did. Perhaps that was the reason that she had tried to help him—at no small risk to herself, heedless of the shots that nearly cut her slender frame in two.

Damien shuddered to think of it, and the movement sent a fresh round of pain slicing through him. The beating on the beach was bad enough, then, once they'd reached Folkstone, Bewicke had questioned him for hours. The man was determined to wring out the answers to his questions—by any means at hand—whether or not it was the truth.

"Who were the men you were meeting on the beach?" Bewicke has asked for what seemed the hundredth time. "What is the name of your informant?"

"I told you before, I'm not saying anything—not until I speak to General Fieldhurst."

"You'll speak to me, you bloody bastard, and you'll tell me what it is I want to know!"

"What about my wife?" he pressed, getting another solid blow to the stomach for his trouble. The square-jawed sergeant that Bewicke employed seemed to revel in his assignment.

"Your lovely wife is a patriot and an extremely courageous young woman. Her only mistake was in trying to help you get away. If your comrades in arms do not harm her, we will find a way to see she is returned."

She wasn't in danger. Damien was certain of that. The last time he had seen her, she had been in the boat with Lafon. Politically, the man might be a snake, but he was a colonel in the Grande Armée and he was a gentleman. He would never hurt a woman, especially one who was married to a man they still needed. The certainty that Alexa was safe—at least for the moment—was the only thing that made this whole ordeal the least bit bearable.

"Listen to me, Douglas—"

"You dare to speak to me as if we are friends? We haven't been that for years . . . if ever we really were." He nodded to the sergeant, who swung a blow that rocked his head back and sent a knife-sharp pain through his temples.

"S-Sorry . . . *Colonel* Bewicke." Damien spit out a

mouthful of blood. "But I'm still not talking until I see Fieldhurst."

"Why? What is so important you cannot simply say it to me?"

"Fieldhurst is a man of honor. I have to be sure that no matter what happens, my wife will be returned safely home."

"The general has more urgent matters to attend. Your only hope is to confess what you have done. Give me the name of your informant and tell me what was in those papers, and I will see your wife gets home."

Damien shook his head, and the sergeant hit him again. When his breath returned, he smiled crookedly, his upper lip split and swollen, taunting Bewicke when he should have been doing everything in his power to appease him. "I told you I'm not talking. In the meantime, I suggest you get my wife back. When her brother finds out what has happened, you can bet there'll be bloody hell to pay."

Bewicke went white with fury. He motioned to the thick-muscled, square-jawed sergeant, and more pain exploded in Damien's head. He thought of Alexa, imagined her beautiful face, and prayed she was safe. A vision of her tear-filled eyes was the last thing he saw as the sergeant's great fists battered his agonized flesh again and again.

"The blackguard's right, you know." That from Lieutenant Richard Osborne, the lean-boned, sharp-tongued man who was Bewicke's aide and closest ally in the regiment. They stood before the fireplace in the adjutant's quarters at Folkstone, a neat little white-walled room, only sparsely furnished, Bewicke pacing, trying to decide what to do.

"As soon as word gets back to London the girl has been taken," Osborne said, "they'll be on our bloody backs like a taste of the cat."

Cat-o'-nine-tails. It cut into flesh and muscle, and unmanned the stoutest of men. Thinking of former Colonel Garrick and his outrageous temper, Bewicke knew that Osborne wasn't that far off the mark.

"Damn and blast, I hate to give the whoreson back." Bewicke moved to a sideboard and poured them both a brandy. He handed Osborne a drink, took a sip of his own, then noticed a piece of lint on the front of his scarlet tunic. He picked it off and flicked it away.

The lieutenant took a sip of his brandy. "I can't see that you have much choice."

Bewicke knew his aide was right, still, he wasn't quite resigned. "Has our courier yet returned?"

"He's been gone for some time. I expect him back at any time."

"With luck they'll accept our terms, as well as the hour and place we've suggested for the meeting."

"Why shouldn't they? It's very near Falon. They're more than familiar with that particular stretch of coast."

"Why indeed?" Bewicke agreed. He took a sip of his drink, swirling the amber liquid against the sides of his glass. Suddenly he smiled, a feeling of excitement beginning to stir through him, dulling his irritation. "Except that perhaps they've yet to discover the caves below the cliffs that lie just round the point."

"Caves?"

"Exactly so. What say you, Richard? Perhaps we'll have the girl—and the traitor."

Osborne looked uncertain, but Bewicke smiled. He looked at himself in the mirror and could almost see the glittering gold on his uniform that would signal his promotion. He felt in that moment as if the deed were already done.

Alexa reached the top of the stairs and took a steadying breath, preparing herself for the uncertain day ahead.

In the rooms below, the smell of fresh-baked bread drifted up from the kitchen, along with sounds of the cook scolding her young son in a colorful flurry of French.

Alexa's hand closed around the banister as she descended the stairs of the farmhouse. Built of white stone, thick-walled and tile-roofed, it was small but comfortable, well-furnished and immaculately clean.

"I see that you are ready. Good. I hope your stay has not been entirely unpleasant."

She fixed her gaze on the man at the bottom of the stairs and forced herself to smile. "You've been a surprisingly congenial host, M'sieur Gaudin, considering the circumstances. I suppose I must thank you—you and Colonel Lafon." Since her arrival last week in Boulogne, the boats having landed on the beach just south of the small fishing village, she had been staying at the home of a man named André Gaudin. Of course, *staying* wasn't exactly the word.

The word was imprisoned.

"A beautiful woman is always a welcome guest, *miette,* regardless of her political opinions." He was an older man, barrel-chested, with a shock of thick white hair. He was a fatherly sort, a kindly man who had ignored her bursts of temper, her demands that she be released, and her sullen, heartsick moods.

"Welcome or not," she said, "I am grateful for the comforts you've provided."

"And the company? Perhaps it was not so very unpleasant either."

Her smile came in earnest. It was hard to stay mad at a man like Gaudin, a man who had sympathized with her plight, though his loyalties were unquestionably French. His calmness was somehow reassuring, his gentleness a welcome relief from the brutality she had expected. From the start he had assured her that she would not be mistreated, that sooner or later she would be returned to England and her husband brought back to France.

"You will miss 'im?" the Frenchman once asked when he had found her staring out the window of her room. In the distant hills above Boulogne, she could see an ancient castle with its crumbling outer walls.

"My husband is a traitor. I should be happy to see him in prison, but . . ."

"But . . . ?"

"But yes . . . I will miss him. I know I shouldn't, but I will."

"Perhaps when the war is over, you will join him in France."

"No, m'sieur, that is not possible." She wouldn't come back, even if Damien wanted her to, which after what she had done, he most assuredly would not.

The Frenchman sighed, his thick white brows making an odd sort of ripple in his forehead. " 'Tis a sad thing, war, *n'est ce pas?*"

"*Oui,* m'sieur . . . a very sad thing indeed."

She had said so then, and she thought so now as she stood in the entry. She was wearing the same brown woolen dress she had worn the night of her capture on the beach, though it had been cleaned and pressed, as had her heavy woolen cloak.

M'sieur Gaudin reached for her hand and gave it a gentle squeeze. "Perhaps one day we will meet again."

She smiled. "I believe I would like that."

"May *le bon Dieu* keep you safe."

"*Merci,* m'sieur. If all Frenchmen were as kind as you, there would be no need for war."

He seemed pleased by her words, smiling as he reached for the door. When he opened it, Colonel Lafon stood on the porch, sunlight sparkling against the brass buttons on his uniform coat. He wore the dark blue and white of the Grenadiers de Cheval—just as

her husband would. Threads of silver at the colonel's
temples stood in contrast to his thick, dark brown hair.

"The boats await, madame. I hope you are ready."

"I assure you, Colonel, I am more than ready."

Chapter Twelve

D AMIEN STRETCHED HIS STIFF MUSCLES, THOUGH IT WAS NO
 EASY TASK WITH HIS HANDS BOUND IN FRONT OF HIM. HIS
shirt hung in tatters, his breeches were covered with
dirt and filth, and his hair hung in heavy black ropes
across his forehead.

Still, he marched along the beach in front of Bewicke
and his soldiers, more than eager to reach their destination and make the trade that would see his wife safely
home. Though he felt certain of her care, he knew first-
hand how impulsive she could be. Hadn't he used her
impetuous nature to his ill gain on more than one occasion?

Though he had prayed that she would behave herself
and nothing untoward would happen, he'd worried
about her every moment he spent in his dismal cell.
And cursed her, and then cursed himself for ever getting her involved in this.

Damien scanned the inky horizon, searching for her now, or at least for the boats that would carry her ashore. A bank of fog lay just off the shoreline. Already tentacles of mist crept in to shroud their movements. It was nearly ten o'clock, the time they had set for the rendezvous. Lafon was meticulous. Barring any unseen difficulties, he would arrive right on time.

Bewicke said something to one of his men, then turned his attention to Damien. "You're a lucky man, Falon. My questions remain unanswered, and now you return home to France."

"You seem to forget, Colonel, that Castle Falon is my home."

"Ah, yes, so it is. Then am I to believe you will miss it once you are gone?"

"You may rest assured I will miss it."

"And your wife, Falon? Will you also miss her?"

Something squeezed inside his chest. "I'll miss her," he said gruffly.

Bewicke flashed a smile of satisfaction. "Never fear, your lordship, I will see to your lady wife's welfare. Perhaps I can find a way to console her for the grievous loss of her husband. Perhaps the countess will enjoy the solace of my bed."

Damien lunged for him, but the guards beside him gripped his shoulders and jerked him back.

"You had better take care, Lord Falon, lest you receive another lesson in manners before your friends arrive."

Damien said nothing. Already he could see the dark outline of two small sails in the distance, just inside the fog bank. Several minutes from now the boats would reach the shore.

They did so with swift efficiency, their bows sliding up on the sand, Lafon and his men climbing over the sides, their boots sloshing noisily in the surf. When the colonel reached up to help Alexa alight, Damien breathed a sigh of relief.

She was home and she was safe. For now, it was all that mattered.

The men were still some distance away. Bewicke shoved him in that direction, and he stumbled forward, fighting to stay on his feet. A gust of wind tugged off the hood of Alexa's cloak, and he caught his first real glimpse of her. Her cheeks looked pale, her dark copper hair clung damply to her throat and shoulders, but her beautiful face was no less arresting than it had been the first time he had seen her. It made his insides clench and his mouth go dry. It made him want to hold her, to make love to her for hours on end. It made him wonder what he would do without her.

"Time to go home, your lordship." Bewicke shoved him again, and Damien continued walking, his boots crunching softly in the sand. Her eyes searched him out, and he wondered at her thoughts. He wondered if she would ever forgive him.

Alexa watched her husband coming toward her, her gaze locked on his face. One of his eyes was blackened and nearly puffed closed, and a line of dried blood trailed from his lips. His shirt gaped open, and even in the pale light of the moon Alexa could see the bruises on his ribs.

Dear God, Damien, what have they done to you?

But he seemed to be moving with his usual graceful stealth. She noted a bit of stiffness, but it was obvious no bones had been broken. He looked beaten and bruised, yet hardly defeated. He held his head high, his back straight, his broad shoulders squared. Part of her yearned to run to him, to throw herself into his arms, while another, saner part denounced him as a traitor and swore that she no longer cared.

They faced each other across a narrow stretch of

sand, Bewicke and his soldiers on one side, she and
Lafon and his small group of men on the other.

"I am sorry, madame," the French colonel said, "but
there will be no chance for a farewell to your husband."

Alexa straightened her spine, drawing on her courage, ignoring her feelings of loss. "It doesn't matter.
There is nothing I have to say."

"I am sorry, madame."

At Colonel Lafon's urging, Alexa started forward, and
so did Damien. His eyes held hers, yet, as always, he
carefully masked his emotions. She had taken only two
uncertain steps when the blast of a musket split the air.
Alexa whirled toward the sound and so did her husband. Men began shouting in both English and French,
waving their arms, and then she heard the sound of
running feet.

"It is a trap!" Lafon shouted, and Alexa's heart
dropped into her stomach.

Before she could think what to do, one of the
Frenchmen grabbed her and twisted an arm behind her
back. He turned and started shoving her toward the
surf.

"No! I'm not going with you!" She tried to pull free,
but already they had reached the boats and he was
dragging her into the sea. He lifted her up over the
gunwale and tossed her into the hull, drenching her
skirt in the brackish, stagnant water. Alexa surged
toward the bow, shouting for someone to help her,
searching frantically for Damien even as the boat was
pushed into the sea.

She saw him fighting two of Bewicke's men, down-
ing one with a blow of his still-bound fists, kicking out
at the other then sprinting on toward the water. A pistol shot rang out. She realized Lafon was in the other
boat and his shot had brought down the second British
soldier. Her heart beat madly as Damien fought two

more men and continued running forward, determined to reach the boats and his last chance for escape.

She found herself praying he would make it, felt her heart aching for him so fiercely a flood of tears washed her cheeks. Her hopes began to fade as her own small craft plowed into the waves and farther out to sea. Then she saw him thrashing through the surf toward the boat that held Lafon and the rest of the men.

Dear God, please help him! Insanely, she wondered if God were an Englishman—if he closed blind eyes to the perils of the French.

She never knew whether her husband made it, for a volley of musket fire cracked through the air and a burning pain tore into her chest. She cried out at the feel of it, her flesh erupting in blood, the world spinning sideways as a wave of dizziness assaulted her.

"Mon Dieu," one of the men in the boat said, "the little *anglaise* has been hit."

"Serves the little whore right," said the beefy Frenchman she had heard called Rouget.

"Damien . . ." she whispered, wishing she knew what had happened, the sharp pain growing, her fingers pressing into the ragged wound just inches above her heart. She tried to search out the second boat, but they had already entered the fog bank. She thought she heard the dip and glide of their oars but she couldn't be sure.

"We must stop the bleeding," the first man said. "Press something over the wound."

"Why should I? Major Falon is safe—the woman is of no use to us now. After what she has done, if we let her die, 'e will probably be grateful."

The first man seemed to ponder the other man's words. "I have no love for the English myself. I do not believe the major will want a wife who has betrayed him." His smile looked wolfish and cold. "But there is a

better place for a beautiful woman than the bottom of
an angry sea."

"I do not see what you mean," Rouget said.

"It is simple. If she lives until we reach Paris, we will
take 'er to Madame Dumaine at Le Monde du Plaisir.
She can join Madame's *fille de joie*. We will be well-paid
for such a prize—in money, and perhaps ways even
more pleasant."

"What if the major finds out?"

" 'E will not be long in France—they will set him to
spying someplace else. And 'e is not the type for Le
Monde."

Rouget nodded. "I heard he keeps a mistress."

"More than one, so they say."

"What if she dies?" Rouget asked, stuffing a dirty rag
against her shoulder.

"If she dies . . ." The first man merely shrugged his
shoulders. The men's coarse laughter was the last thing
Alexa heard as she sank deeper into the fiery pain and
her mind slid into darkness.

Damien paced the beach south of Boulogne. Though
the sun had come up, thick, flat-bottomed clouds darkened the horizon, and the wind blew bitter and cold.

"Nom de Dieu—where are they?" he said in French,
speaking more to himself than the man who stood beside him.

Victor Lafon followed his gaze, the hollows in his
gaunt cheeks even more pronounced this morning.
"Two of the men were killed in the fighting on the
beach. That left only Rouget and Monnard to crew the
boat. The seas have been rough. The boat has obviously
been swept off course. If that is the case and the men
are forced to land somewhere else, their orders are to
make their way as quickly as possible back to Paris."

"If that happens, it's going to take them some time."

The colonel nodded. *"Mais oui,* that is so. If their

boat has not been sighted within the next two hours, I suggest we make ready to leave."

Two hours. It seemed more like two days. Was Alexa all right? This time Lafon wasn't there to protect her. Damien didn't know the two Frenchmen she had wound up with, only that they were enlisted men chosen because of their seamen's skills. There was no way to judge how an Englishwoman would fair at their hands. He could only pray that her status as his wife would offer her some protection.

As he had for the thousandth time, he damned Douglas Bewicke to hell.

The hours passed, but the sky grew no clearer, and there was no sign of the boat.

"I think we had better go." Lafon approached where he had walked to the edge of the sea. "The trip to Paris will take several days. You will wish to be there when the men arrive, *n'est ce pas?*"

Damien only nodded. He was worried about Alexa, but he didn't want Lafon to know just how much. In the game of intrigue, it was unwise to betray one's emotions. His care for Alexa was his Achilles' heel. It was the kind of knowledge they might one day use against him. It was a mistake he couldn't afford to make.

"How are you feeling?" the colonel asked as they made their way toward the carriage waiting in the distance.

"Like I've been set upon by the mob at the Bastille."

"You will feel better once we have arrived back in Paris and your pretty little wife is returned to your bed —although on that score, I do not think I envy you."

Damien smiled thinly, falling into the role of the hard-edged, conscienceless man they expected. The tough, unfeeling man he had been.

"Her loyalties to England are strong. It is a fault I should have dealt with sooner. Perhaps if I had, none of this would have occurred." He glanced at the shrewd man standing at his side. "The fact is, the girl is my wife. Her loyalty belongs to me—a lesson she will learn soon enough. As for her return to my bed—that is another of her duties I mean to see she soon fulfills."

With some amazement, Damien realized just how much he meant the latter.

"Colonel Lafon is here, m'sieur." The small dark maître d' stood in the open doorway. Damien sat behind his desk in the study of his town house—*hôtel*, the French called it—in the Rue St. Philippe, Faubourg St. Honoré. They had reached Paris two days ago.

Two days. And still no word of Alexa.

Now Lafon was here, and Damien's heart set up an uneven rhythm inside his chest. *"Merci,* Pierre," he said to the butler. "See him in."

The little man nodded, his slicked-back, pomaded hair unmoving, and hurriedly left the room. A few minutes later he opened the heavy oak door and Lafon walked in. One look at the tight lines and bitter expression on the colonel's gaunt face and Damien came up from his chair, his hands biting into the wooden armrests.

"What's happened? Have you found her?"

"You had better sit down, *mon ami.*"

Damien did not move. "Tell me."

His blue and white uniform spotless, Lafon walked forward until he stood in front of the desk. They faced each other across the polished rosewood surface. "Your wife took a musket ball in the chest as her boat escaped the beach. The wound was a mortal one. I am afraid she did not survive the voyage."

Damien said nothing. Just slowly sank down in his chair. "There must be some mistake."

"I am sorry, Major Falon."

"You . . . you're certain of this? There can be no mistake?"

"Corporal Rouget was with her when she died. He says she did not suffer."

"Where . . . where is her body?" He tried to remain in control, fought desperately to hide his turbulent emotions.

"I am afraid that is part of the tragedy. The boat capsized in the waves as it was approaching the shore. Madame Falon's body was lost at sea."

Damien's eyes slid closed. Sweet Christ, it couldn't be true. He felt sick inside, his chest so tight he could barely breathe. "Bewicke. I'll see that bastard dead, I swear it."

"We should have known better than to trust an Englishman."

Damien could do no more than nod. "I appreciate your bringing the news." He swallowed past the lump in his throat. It took all of his will to pull himself under control. When he did, he looked up at Lafon and slowly shook his head. "I wished my wife no ill." He tried to sound matter-of-fact. "In truth, I had grown rather fond of her."

"Your wife was a beautiful young woman. You have my deepest sympathies."

Damien shoved back his chair and rounded the desk. He prayed Lafon wouldn't notice that his legs were shaking. "Thank you, Colonel." He sighed. "Our marriage was hardly a long one. Money was involved, of course—but I had yet to grow tired of her sweet little body. Ah, but these things happen."

"So they do," Lafon said, moving toward the door.

"Ironic, isn't it? Were I still in England, I would be a very wealthy man. Fate can be a ruthless enemy, *n'est ce pas?*"

"*Oui*, Major Falon. Fate has always been more fickle than the vainest of women."

Damien waited for the colonel to leave, closed the door behind him and leaned against it. His head was pounding, his stomach felt leaden, and there was a roaring in his ears that blocked out all other sound. God's blood, he couldn't believe it. Yet these uncertain feelings he had harbored all week had warned him that something was wrong.

Woodenly, he moved to the ornately carved sideboard near the fireplace in the corner. With trembling hands he lifted the stopper from a crystal decanter and poured a liberal dose of cognac into a snifter. He took a long nerve-dulling sip and then another.

In minutes he had finished the glass, refilled it, and finished that too. He meant to get good and drunk. He knew it was futile, yet he prayed it would help ease the pain. Alexa was dead because of him—there was no way to deny it. Dead and gone and missing from his life forever. The pain seemed to grow, to swell with every heartbeat, to gouge and tear and twist. The fiery ache expanded, filling every muscle and joint, sliding through his veins like white-hot oil.

For years he had cared about nothing. For a while he and Peter had been close, then his brother had died and he was once more alone.

For a brief, sweet moment in time he had cared for Alexa, known feelings for her he hadn't believed himself capable of. Now, however unwillingly, she had abandoned him too.

Damien picked up the bottle of cognac and returned to the chair behind his desk. He slumped into the deep leather seat, his head hanging forward, the glass once more empty.

There had been pain when he lost Peter, but it was nothing compared to this. This was a soul-crushing, mind-numbing ache that the liquor he consumed did not begin to dull. He felt as if his chest had been ripped open and his heart torn out. As if he had died and now burned in the fires of hell.

He refilled his drink and downed the contents, his fingers painfully gripping the empty glass. He reached for the bottle and, on the small silver medallion hanging from the neck, caught a glimpse of his reflection.

For the first time he noticed that his face was wet with tears.

Celeste Dumaine stood in silence at the foot of the old iron bed, its white-painted brass chipped and peeling. Beneath the worn pink satin counterpane, the young girl lay sleeping. She was a slight woman, not unlike herself—twenty years ago. Now Celeste's once-taut body had turned fleshy. Her breasts were no longer firm, her skin no longer supple. Her long chestnut hair had begun to thin, to fade and lose its luster. Ah, but she had been a beauty once—not unlike the girl.

Celeste moved toward her around the side of the bed. Her breathing was still too shallow, her pulse a fluttery thread at the side of her neck. Celeste reached a hand in that direction, tracing a finger down the alabaster column of her throat, gauging the texture of her skin. In the glow of the lamp, the large ruby ring Celeste always wore on her third blunt finger glittered like a drop of blood against the girl's pale cheek.

She trailed a light touch across it. Never had she seen smoother skin, the color of priceless ivory. Never had she seen finer features. Or hair such a vibrant shade of auburn, the dark red hue of polished rosewood. Celeste had brushed it, then fanned it out on the pillow, the long shimmering curls like flaming silk beneath her hands.

She leaned forward to smooth the heavy strands, and the shimmering mass seemed to sear into her fingers. Under Celeste's black lace robe her nipples grew hard, the stiff peaks pulsing, growing tender beneath the abrasive fabric. The blood in her veins seemed to thicken, to pump a little slower, and the vee at the base of her legs began to dampen and burn.

She bent over the bed and eased back the covers. Below the bandage that covered the young woman's wound, her full breasts rose and fell softly. Each of them was perfectly formed, full yet firm, and pointing erotically upward. Celeste's hand shook as she cupped one. A fever still raged, making the skin hot, making the girl toss and turn.

Reluctantly, Celeste pulled up the covers. It had been years since she had been afflicted with such yearning. Whether the object of her desire was man or a woman did not matter. It was the beauty of the subject, the exquisiteness of form. It was an elegance, an exuding of grace, an essence of purity that made her blood pulse heavily and a dampness settle between her legs.

What a splendid creature, she thought, tasting a hunger long forgotten, her anticipation growing, swelling just as her breasts did. And she belongs to me.

Celeste vowed the woman would live. She would see to it personally. Once she was healed, she would break her in carefully, use her to the best advantage without destroying her spirit. Money was all-important, of course, but with the proper care, there was more to be gained than just added coins for her purse. Far more.

She had plans of her own for the beautiful young girl.

Damien roused himself a little at the insistent knock on his bedchamber door but didn't get up from the chair.

The knob turned, the door opened, and his *valet de chambre*, a tall, stately man with sandy brown hair, walked in. Claude-Louis Arnaux was just two years older than Damien, a married man with a young son, whose wife served as his housekeeper.

"General Moreau is here to see you. He is downstairs now, waiting for you in the study."

Moreau. Christ. He sure as hell couldn't let the general see him like this. "Tell him I've been ill. Tell him I apologize, but I'm not yet dressed to receive callers. Tell him I'll see him in his office, later this afternoon."

Claude seemed relieved. Damien knew his friend had been worried about him. "As you wish. I will have a bath sent up and see to fresh clothes."

Damien nodded, grateful as always for his friend's unwavering loyalty. He dragged himself up from the overstuffed chair he had pulled in front of the now dead fire. He hadn't come out of the room in days. His hair was dirty, his face unshaven, his clothes a wrinkled mass of stains and creases. He kicked aside an empty bottle of cognac. A broken glass crunched beneath the heel of his boot.

"Nom de Dieu," he muttered, followed by an indrawn hiss of breath as he passed by the cheval glass mirror. God, he looked like hell.

He felt like it too.

He smelled of stale brandy, his head pounded, and his tongue felt leathery and dry. He wished he could crawl back into the bottle he'd been living in for the past four days, but the liquor hadn't really helped, and he couldn't hide from himself forever.

Alexa was dead—he would never forgive himself for that, and inside, his grieving would continue. Outside, his absence would soon be noticed and the depth of his feelings made note of—he couldn't afford that.

Claude-Louis walked back in. He was one of the *ci-devants,* a former member of the aristocracy, one of the *emigrés* now returned home. If the Revolution had not occurred, if Louis still remained king, Claude would be a count. Instead he was a servant . . . or at least so it seemed.

"I am glad to see you've come back to the living," Claude said.

He only wished he had. "I was a fool. No woman is worth that much grief." Behind him, servants walked in carrying a steaming *cuveau* of hot water. Claude-Louis waited till the servants had left and closed the door behind them.

"There is no need for pretense with me. We have known each other far too long for such folly, *n'est ce pas?*"

Damien sighed. "That is so, *mon ami.* I did not mean to play games." He raked a hand through his wavy black hair. "Sometimes I'm no longer sure where the games leave off and the real world begins."

"It is all right, my friend. I believe that is so for us all."

Damien stripped off his clothes and sank into the steaming copper tub, welcoming its cleansing warmth. He rested his head against the rim and his eyes drifted closed. For a moment he saw Alexa smiling at something he had said. She was admiring his beautiful birds, her eyes filled with happiness and admiration. He saw her speaking to his mother, her eyes flashing, standing up for him when she should have been fighting for herself.

Then he saw her running toward him on the beach. There was fear in her eyes, regret, and terrible sorrow. A world of emotion shown in a face filled with worry—for him. The sight was so heart-wrenching, it jerked him fully awake. He groped for the white muslin towel with a trembling hand and Claude-Louis held it out for him.

"You are weak. You have not eaten in some time. Even now Chef Masson prepares a tray. You will feel better with something in your belly."

Damien said nothing. The thought of food made his stomach turn over. Still, he would force himself to eat.

He had a job to do, and though it hadn't gone as he had planned, he would find a way to salvage the situation. Work would help ease the pain, for it was work that gave him purpose. He would cling to that purpose now as he never had before.

Cling to it, though he knew without doubt that no matter how successful he was, the price he had paid was more than a man should have to bear.

"So, *ma belle,* how are you feeling?"

Alexa studied the garishly dressed woman seated in the faded chintz chair across from her. "Nearly as good as new, thanks to you, Madame Dumaine." They were sharing a cup of mocha, sipping from fine porcelain cups, incongruous in the shabby, tastelessly decorated room.

"Another few days and you will be ready to face the world, I think. You will set them on their ears."

Alexa's face went pale. "Madame, I know how generous you have been, I—I know I owe you my life, but I beg of you to release me."

"We have been over this a dozen times, my pet. I have paid a small fortune for you. I have spent hours at your bedside. I have fed you and nursed you and protected you. It is a debt that must be repaid."

"I told you, I'm a very wealthy woman. If you will see me safely returned to England—"

"England, bah! You will remain right here!"

"But surely—"

"The past is finished, my dove. The sooner you accept that, the happier you will be. You are mine now. You will do exactly as I say." Her expression was implacable, the lines of her mouth thin and grim. She was a hard woman—she'd had to be. Whatever softness she had known had been burned out by the past she had led. And yet . . .

Her voice grew soft, almost cajoling. "Trust me, *ma*

belle. Your life here will not be so hard. There will be men, yes—a good many of them. But you are intelligent. In time you will learn how to please them. It is not such a bad life, really."

Alexa shivered to think of it, her blood running suddenly cold. "Please, madame, is there nothing I can say to convince you?" She had tried—dear God, she had spent hours pleading and crying, begging the woman to see reason. She had tried to escape, only to discover the windows had been barred from the outside and a huge bearded blackamoor posted outside her door.

"Hush, my pretty. The time for talking is past. Resign yourself, and perhaps the day will come when your debt has been repaid. When that times comes"—she smiled—"your body will belong only to me."

Alexa said nothing, but a tremor of dread slid down her spine. She watched in silence as the thick-waisted older woman crossed to the door and went outside. She could hear the blackamoor speaking to her in soft suggestive tones, then the sound of their mutual laughter.

A chill stole over her. What would happen to her now? she wondered. When would the first man come? What would he look like? How would his hands feel on her body?

How would she bear it?

She thought of Damien and her mind cried out with longing. She wondered where he was—wondered if he still lived—and a bleak despair crept over her soul.

She thought of Bewicke and her heart filled with loathing. It was Bewicke and his treachery that had brought her to this. A man she had trusted, a man she had foolishly believed would help her.

But he had not helped her. He would not help her now.

In truth, she had no one.

She could not even help herself.

Chapter Thirteen

DAMIEN DESCENDED THE STAIRS OF HIS *PETIT HÔTEL* IN THE RUE ST. PHILIPPE.

Built before the Terror by Aristos frightened of losing their heads to the guillotine, it was a heavy stone structure of high windows and wrought-iron balconies, elegant, yet it seemed more a fortress than a home. With its thick walls, escape tunnels, and secret passages, the house had provided worried nobles a quick means of escape, or a place to hide should the need arise. It also made it easy to watch the occupants within, which, in all likelihood, was why the marshals had provided the house for his use whenever he was in France.

Damien crossed the hall toward the door. Pierre Lindet, his maître d', stood in the entry, holding his hat and gloves, his long black, satin-lined cloak, and a sleek ebony gold-headed cane.

He was dressed for the opera, joining Lafon and

Moreau; the architect, Cellerier; Mayor Frochot; and the Duchess d'Abrantes, wife of the governor of Paris. Afterward they were expected at a party at the Hotel de Ville.

In the past he might have enjoyed himself. Before his marriage . . . before he had known Alexa. Now he dreaded every moment.

"Your cape, m'sieur." Pierre held it out. Damien took it and swirled it around his shoulders. He affixed the jeweled clasp, then tugged on his gloves and reached for his cane.

"I presume my carriage waits out front."

"Oui, m'sieur."

"Where is Claude-Louis?"

"I have not seen him, m'sieur. He went out some time ago and has not yet returned."

Damien nodded absently.

"Will there be anything else, m'sieur?"

"That will be all, Pierre. Tell Claude-Louis he needn't wait up."

The quiet little man slipped silently away, and Damien started once more for the door. The sound of a small voice and the shuffle of running feet stayed his movements and drew his attention down the hall. He turned to see little Jean-Paul Arnaux running toward him, his short legs pumping though his stride was uneven as he dragged his twisted leg.

"M'sieur! M'sieur!"

Damien lifted the boy into the air. *"Bonsoir, mon petit,* when did you get home?" The dark-haired, dark-eyed child had been away in the country, visiting one of his dozens of cousins.

"I have just returned this day, m'sieur. Then Maman took me with her to the market. I was hoping to see you before it was time for bed." Jean-Paul was only seven, yet he had always seemed older. Perhaps it was the accident he had suffered three years ago that had forced him to grow up too soon.

Damien hugged him hard, his chest suddenly taut at the thought of the child he and Alexa might have shared. "I am glad to see you. It's been far too quiet around here without you."

His mother approached down the hall, smiling softly. "I will take him, m'sieur." Claude's wife, Marie Claire, reached out and took the boy, holding him solidly against the plump mounds of her breasts. "I hope he was not too much bother."

"Jean-Paul is never a bother," Damien said, and watching them together made the words come out a little bit gruff.

"Bonsoir, m'sieur." The little boy waved over his mother's shoulder.

"Bonne nuit, mon petit," Damien called after him. The child was another of his weaknesses. He had tried to remain aloof, but the boy would not let him. His own attachment had grown, and though their encounters were seldom and usually brief, the boy staunchly remained in his affections, and apparently Jean-Paul felt the same.

Damien sighed at the notion, wondering how long it would be before circumstances changed and their friendship forced to end.

Wishing the prospect didn't seem so grim and recalling a time when he wouldn't have cared, he adjusted the collar of his cloak and started for the door. Before he could pull it open, Claude-Louis sailed in, yanking off his tall beaver hat, his sandy brown hair falling over his forehead as he reached out to grip Damien's shoulders.

"Thank *le bon Dieu* you are still here."

"What is it? What's wrong?"

Claude-Louis glanced around, then pointed toward the study. Damien followed close behind him.

"There is not time to prepare you for this, so I will just come out and say it. Your wife is not dead."

Damien jerked as if he'd been shot. A numbness slid into his chest and for a moment he forgot to breathe. "Tell me I heard you correctly." Surely he hadn't, but God, how he wanted it to be true.

"Madame Falon is alive. She is being held right here in Paris."

"If you are wrong," Damien said softly, "I swear I shall never forgive you."

"I am not wrong—at least I do not think so. There is only one way to be certain, of course."

"Where is she?" His heart was racing, thrumming, beating so fast his hands had begun to shake.

"That is why we must hurry. She is being kept at Le Monde du Plaisir, a brothel down by the Seine."

Damien's mouth went dry. "How can you be sure it's Alexa? What have you heard?"

"The first rumor surfaced three days ago. From a sailor down at the docks who had been with a girl from Le Monde. He said there was a woman, an *anglaise,* a girl more beautiful than Aphrodite. He said she was new to Le Monde, that she had been sold into *les femmes* by two of Napoleon's soldiers."

"That hardly proves it's Alexa."

"That is what I also thought and why I did not tell you. Instead I spoke to some friends, called in a few favors. I discovered that the girl had been injured, that Celeste Dumaine had personally nursed her back to health. They say she's being held against her will. They also say that on the first evening in August—tonight— there is to be an auction. The woman will be sold to the highest bidder."

The breath hissed softly from Damien's lungs. *"Nom de Dieu."* He glanced toward the door then back to his friend. "We still can't be certain she is the one." But the doubts no longer mattered; he knew that he would be there. A regiment of French soldiers couldn't have kept him away.

"The place is well-guarded. If it is your wife, you will need some sort of papers—or Colonel Lafon and at least a half-dozen men."

Damien shook his head. "The auction may have started already. We haven't got that kind of time."

"What will you do?"

Wordlessly, he turned and crossed the study. From a drawer in his desk he pulled out a pistol, checked the load, then stuffed it into the pocket of his cloak. Moving aside the painting behind his desk, he worked the combination of his safe and pulled out a heavy sack of coins.

A corner of his mouth twisted into a ruthless half smile. "If it is my wife, the price will be a steep one. I don't intend to be outbid."

Claude-Louis clapped his friend on the back. "I will get my pistol and join you in the carriage."

Damien nodded and the two men started for the door.

Dear God in heaven, how am I going to get through this? Alexa glanced down at the vulgar white lace corset she wore over a short, nearly transparent chemise that barely covered her bottom. Her breasts were pushed up, exposing the top half of her nipples, which had been lightly rouged pink. She cringed to remember the way Madame had touched her there, applying the color with trembling hands, licking her thick lips as she did so.

Alexa had put on the garments herself, knowing she would be forcibly dressed if she refused. Madame had laced up the corset while Alexa drew on sheer white stockings and the white satin garters with their tiny pink roses. Madame had brushed her hair but left it loose and flowing down her back, then the woman had tied a pink satin ribbon around her throat.

Alexa had not cried. Not this time. Not tonight.

She had cried every day until this one. She had begged and pleaded and taken several beatings with a willow switch. Madame had warned her the beatings would get worse, that the blackamoor would surely take his belt to her if she continued to disobey. She said that the man would enjoy it, and Alexa believed her. She had seen his lascivious smiles, seen the lewd way he fondled the women. There was no end to the man's demented cravings—no escape from this madhouse that was meant to be her home.

And no mercy from its inhabitants, who all believed she should simply accept her fate.

Perhaps she had, she thought, as she stood at the top of the stairs looking down at the crowd below her, at the drunken officers of Napoleon's army, the foul-mouthed merchants, and gouty, overindulged members of the "new nobility."

Perhaps she had, for she felt nothing but numbness and resignation. Nothing in the space that had once been her soul.

Madame stood beside her, bent and kissed her cheek, then gave her hand a gentle squeeze.

"Do not fear, *ma belle.* I will pick a man worthy of your charms for your first night here. He will have to pay the price, of course, but I will make certain he initiates you properly into the world of demimonde."

Alexa bit her lip. In the salon at the bottom of the stairs, the men crowded closer, leering up at them, pointing and making bawdy jests. They mingled with a dozen half-dressed women, speaking to them crudely and squeezing their naked breasts.

"I—I cannot do this," Alexa said, a surge of spirit returning, a last brief flash of the woman she had left behind. "Please, madame, I beg you to let me go."

Celeste slapped her face. "You will do it. You will do exactly as I say. You will lie beneath whatever man I tell you to and you will let him have his way."

Alexa made a whimpering sound in her throat. Her cheek stung and her knees had begun to shake.

Celeste Dumaine merely smiled. "That is better, my dove. Now you will follow me down the stairs."

Alexa did as she was told, stopping midway while Madame Dumaine continued on to the bottom. On the landing above, a brawny Frenchman who worked at Le Monde grinned and barred that path of escape. The huge bearded blackamoor stood at the bottom, and there were more men posted near the doors.

Alexa swallowed the tears that collected in her throat. She wouldn't cry, she wouldn't! She would survive this night and those to come. She would find a way to escape. She would make her way back to England. She would forget the things that had happened to her body—and she would once again be safe.

From the shadows beneath the overhanging hallway above him, Damien watched the stairs. A tense muscle bunched in his jaw, and unconsciously his hand balled into a fist. He forced himself to relax it.

He still wore his long black, satin-lined cloak, the collar turned up, helping to shield him from view. He had spoken to Celeste Dumaine upon his arrival, told her of his interest in the Englishwoman, and even tried to buy her. Celeste had merely laughed.

"You may buy her favors, m'sieur, but only for the night. La Belle Anglaise belongs to me. I will choose her suitors—men with coin enough in their purse, and hands that will be gentle on her tender young body. She is worth more to me than a fortune in gold."

He still wasn't sure the woman was Alexa, but to press the issue would have been folly. Instead he merely shrugged. "A night of pleasure is enough for a man . . . if the woman is as worthy as you say."

"She is worthy—you will see. The question is, are you?" Celeste had laughed again, a husky rasp that sounded strangely lewd, and he had moved into the shadows.

He steeled himself as he waited for the auction to begin, certain it wouldn't be Alexa, praying it would be —and that if it were, she hadn't been hurt.

Then she stood at the top of the stairs, her unbound hair a fiery cascade around her shoulders, and the last of his doubts slid away. His heart beat savagely and a wave of emotion washed over him, making his legs feel suddenly weak.

Alexa. The word formed in his mind but not on his lips. Silently he thanked God for her safety, thanked Him again for bringing him here. Relief and gratitude welled up inside him, so powerful he fought to keep his hands from shaking.

He watched her from his place deep in the shadows, burying his need for her, forcing his thoughts to focus on the task ahead. She was dressed appropriately for the evening, he saw with a new surge of anger, her body exposed in the most erotic manner, covered just enough to tantalize, not nearly enough to protect her from the savage, leering throng of men.

She looked wan and pale and distraught. She looked numb and desolate and more beautiful than he had ever seen her. He wanted to draw his pistol and put a lead ball into each of their lecherous faces. He wanted to climb the stairs, sweep her into his arms, and carry her away from this terrible place.

He wanted to hold her and kiss her and tell her how much he had missed her.

Instead he bided his time, centering his mind on his purpose, waiting with casual nonchalance as he lounged among the shadows. He kept himself carefully hidden so that she could not see him and somehow give him away. There would be no room for error, no second chance. The Seine would pose a cold grave for him—and for her? He dared not imagine the consequences.

The bidding finally started, and the room erupted in chaos. Ten francs, twenty, a hundred. A fat merchant tried to climb the stairs, determined to inspect the prize more thoroughly, but the huge black man at the bottom sent him sprawling against the door. The bidding continued. Damien raised the head of his cane, and Madame Dumaine smiled with pleasure. She approved of him, he saw, as long as he came up with the money. He doubled the last bid, hoping to end it, but the price kept on rising.

He doubled the tally again, and the room fell silent. Alexa started toward the shadows, her face even paler than before. Another short flurry of bids, a subtle lift of his cane, and the auction was ended. A cheer went up from the men, and a terrible scream tore loose from Alexa's throat.

She stumbled blindly down the stairs, fighting and clawing her way toward the door, but the huge bearded blackamoor and two other men caught her up and lifted her high above the crowd. She was crying now, moaning so pitifully it was all Damien could do to keep from tearing his way through the mob to reach her.

It was imperative he did not, though beneath his cloak waves of tension rippled through his body. Forcing a smile to his face, he handed the coins to Madame Dumaine. "I like a woman with spirit. I believe your price is just."

"You have purchased a treasure—as you will see when we join her upstairs."

Damien merely nodded. He was fearful for Alexa, anxious to see her, and more eager still to be shed of

this godawful place. He let the woman guide him up
the stairs.

Alexa struggled, twisting and trying to jerk free of the
men's determined hold. She opened her mouth to cry
out, but a rag was forced between her teeth. It was tied
around her head, and as they pressed her down on the
mattress, her wrists were bound to the iron frame of
the bed. Her ankles were also bound, her legs pulled
roughly apart, each one secured to a corner, leaving
her open and exposed, embarrassed and vulnerable to
the man who would take her. She thought of him now,
or the shadow of him that was all she had seen in the
corner.

What did he look like? she wondered, shivering as
she recalled his long, swirling cloak with its high standing collar.

The devil himself, she thought bitterly, and I am the
devil's prize.

Misery assailed her, and regret, and haunting despair.
She would lose control of her body this night, but her
soul would remain locked away. No matter what happened, no matter what evil they did to her, she would
not lose that part of herself that belonged only to her.

The part she'd once given to her husband.

She thought of him now, and a well of sorrow rose
inside her. Perhaps if she kept her eyes tightly closed
she could pretend he was the man who loomed above
her. She could see the longing in his features, the
yearning that had drawn her to him from the moment
she had first met him. Perhaps, if she pretended, she
could feel the joy of his taking, the incredible depth of
emotion that loving him once had brought her.

A sound in the hall, and her eyes flew to the door.
The man would be here any moment.

Alexa shuddered. How could she deceive herself? No
man's touch would be like her husband's. No man

could move her as he had. No man could make her blood boil and her heart pound. Dear God, where was he now?

The door flew open and Celeste Dumaine walked in. The tall man in the black cloak turned before she could see him, unfastening the jeweled clasp beneath his white cravat, swirling the cloak off and draping it over a nearby chair.

"I look forward to a pleasant evening," he said. *"Merci beaucoup,* madame."

"Ah, *non,* m'sieur, you do not understand. Our business is not yet ended. I will stay for a while. I would be certain *ma belle* is handled gently."

A thick black brow arched up and Alexa's breath caught in her throat.

"Surely you do not mean to watch," the man said, and the familiar cadence of his soft French words made the room begin to spin.

Damien! Dear God in heaven! Surely she was dreaming, surely the man could not be her husband.

Across from him, Celeste merely smiled. "What do you care if I stay? You will have far more pressing matters on your mind."

"But that is absurd. Surely, I have paid enough money. If you need more—"

Celeste's broad back went rigid. "If that is the way you feel, m'sieur, you may take your coins and leave. I told you before, La Belle is under my protection. If you do not wish me to stay—at least for a time—then I will find a man who does."

Damien eyed her a moment, then the blackamoor who stood just a few feet away. He shrugged with nonchalance. "I suppose it does not matter. Perhaps it will heighten the pleasure, *n'est ce pas?"*

A brow arched up and she smiled. "Perhaps." She seemed satisfied with that, settling herself in a chair near the foot of the bed while the blackamoor took up a place outside the door. "I suppose we will just have to see."

Damien inwardly cursed. Perhaps he could silence her before she could sound the alarm, perhaps not. He dared not try it unless there was no other way. His senses still on alert, he turned his attention to Alexa, drinking in the sight of her, aching for her, yet burying that ache in a steely resolve to see her safe. His eyes searched her face, conveying a silent message, hoping she could see the tenderness he felt for her, his joy that she still lived.

When he had seen her bound and gagged, he was angry, yet some of his tension had eased. Whatever she was thinking, she would not give him away, and soon he would be able to release her.

He knelt beside the bed, his gaze locked with hers, reading the uncertainty, the pain, the hope mixed with fear.

He leaned over her, gently cupped her face between his hands. "It's all right, *chérie*. You must trust me."

She nodded and her eyes slid closed. Several tears leaked from beneath her thick dark lashes. When he leaned over and kissed them away, some of the tension eased from her body. He untied the gag and slid it from between her lips. She wet them and he noticed that they trembled.

"Do not be afraid," he said, loud enough for Celeste to hear. "I will not hurt you." He bent forward and kissed her, running his tongue across her lips, testing the gentle curves, remembering the taste of them, fighting the need that swept over him. He sank his tongue inside, slid it out and into the soft damp corners. He kissed her again and she kissed him back, molding her mouth to his, her tongue stroking softly, saying what she dared not say in words.

His hands moved down her shoulders, his lips moved along her throat, trailing hot damp kisses. "Trust me," he repeated, thinking of the woman across from them, knowing what she expected, cupping a breast and squeezing it gently, making the small rouged nipples grow hard and distended.

Alexa made a soft mew in her throat, then she glanced at Celeste and a flood of pink rose into her cheeks.

"Would you like Madame to leave?" he asked, and she nodded.

"Soon, my dove," Celeste promised. "Soon you may have him all to yourself."

Damien silently cursed her. Lowering his mouth, he began to suckle at his wife's lovely breasts, laving the rouge off with his tongue, trying to ignore the erotic, slightly bittersweet taste of it. Though he willed it not to, his shaft grew hard against his leg, held down uncomfortably in his tight black satin breeches. He shifted and it rose up hard against his belly.

He reached for the silk rope binding Alexa's wrist, pulled it loose and freed her hand. He kissed her breast, tugging the rigid peak softly. She moaned and her fingers slid into his hair. When her back arched upward, he opened his mouth to take more of her, the taste of her soft smooth skin making him forget where he was and that the Frenchwoman watched them. He reached for the second rope and pulled the knot. Alexa's arms came around his neck. He took her mouth, kissing her long and deep, his tongue sinking in, the taste of her like honey.

"Mon Dieu, but you are sweet," he whispered, fighting a fresh wave of desire for her, angry at himself for his lack of control, madder still at the woman who had put them in this position.

Alexa started to speak, but he silenced her with his lips, a deep, thorough, wet-tongued kiss that left them both shaken and only dimly aware of their surroundings. God, he wanted her. She was alive and she was his and he had never needed her so badly.

His hands strayed down her stomach, past the flat plane below her navel, his fingers sliding into the thatch of red curls at the junction of her legs. For a moment she responded, moaning softly, pressing herself against his hand. When she sucked in a breath and tugged at the ropes around her ankles, he paused, suddenly aware of what he was about to do. There were tears in his eyes as she looked at him, and he cursed himself for a fool.

Damien turned his piercing blue gaze on Celeste. "Do you leave us now, madame, or do you make the lady suffer for your perversities?"

Celeste came up from her chair. She was angry, and he prepared himself to silence her, hoping he could do it before she could cry out. Then Celeste saw the tears on Alexa's cheeks.

"You are right, m'sieur," she said with a sigh. "The fault is mine. The girl has no experience in such matters. There is plenty of time, *n'est ce pas?* Perhaps one day in the future . . ."

Damien smiled. "You are a woman of wisdom, Madame Dumaine. You may rest assured that your lovely Belle Anglaise is in good hands with me."

Celeste returned the smile and started for the door. "Enjoy yourself, my pet," she said. Crossing the room, she stepped into the hall and closed the door behind her.

Damien turned back to Alexa. With swift, sure movements he pulled the cords from around her ankles, freeing her legs, and eased her into his arms. "Alexa . . . sweet God, I thought you were dead."

"Damien . . ." She clutched him tightly, crying against his shoulder, holding him as if she were afraid to let him go.

"It's all right, *ma chére,* no one's going to hurt you

now." He held her for a moment more, kissing her cheek and smoothing back her hair, then left her to retrieve his cloak. He returned to the bed and swirled it around her, encompassing her protectively in its folds.

"How—How will we get out of here? Madame has barred the windows."

He strode across the room in that direction and drew back the heavy fringed curtains. The narrow-paned windows had been locked from the outside, a wooden board nailed across them so they would not open. The boards now dangled loose on one side, and a worried Claude-Louis stood on the tiny wrought-iron balcony.

"We must hurry," Claude said, "they could spot the carriage at any moment."

Damien nodded, grateful his friend had been clever enough to discover which room they were in. He returned to the bed, slid an arm beneath Alexa's knees, lifted her up and carried her over to the window. Handing her into Claude-Louis's arms, he climbed over the balcony and jumped down to the street.

"Whenever you're ready," he said, and before Alexa could discern what he intended, she was sailing through the air, her heart in her throat, landing solidly in her husband's powerful arms.

"All right?" he asked with a tender smile, and she nodded, burying her head against his shoulder and tightly clutching his neck.

Then he was climbing into the carriage, settling her securely on his lap and holding her snugly against him. The man he called Claude climbed up on the driver's seat, took the reins and urged the horses at a fast trot down the dark, narrow alley.

With infinite care Damien smoothed her hair away from her cheeks. "You weren't . . . they haven't . . . hurt you, have they?" She shook her head. "Thank God." He cradled her face in his hands and then he kissed her.

It was a searing, burning kiss that stirred all the fires he had unleased in the shabby room upstairs. Then, she had been embarrassed by her responses. This time no one was watching. She kissed him back, opening her mouth to him, sucking his tongue inside, teasing it, feeling the smooth slick muscles that reminded her of another smooth muscle she longed to feel inside her.

"Damien, I've missed you so."

His kiss was soft and deep. "If I'd had the slightest idea . . . if there had been the least chance that you were alive . . ." He kissed her eyes, her nose, her lips, then opened the cloak and lowered his mouth to her breasts. The heat was incredible, a simmering inferno that burned out of control.

He suckled and tasted, ringing her nipple with his tongue, tugging on it, making the fire burn brighter. Beneath the cloak she felt his hands on her buttocks, cupping them, squeezing them gently, making the ache return to the place between her legs.

"Damien," she whispered, unbuttoning his shirt, desperately needing to touch him. She ran her hands over the hard-ridged muscles of his chest, making them flex and tighten, her finger circling a flat copper nipple, lacing through his curly black chest hair. Then he was easing her back on the seat, pressing her into the black tufted leather. She could feel the red satin lining of his cloak, smooth and cool against her skin, unlike the fever raging inside her.

He kissed her deeply, fiercely, then he was parting her legs, settling himself between them, unbuttoning his breeches and letting his shaft spring free. She reached toward it with trembling fingers, eager to touch him, to feel the weight of him inside her, out of her mind with wanting and need and something else she refused to name.

"Easy, *ma chére,*" he said, sliding the tip of hardness inside her. But it wasn't easy she wanted, and it wasn't easy she got. Damien surged forward, filling her to the hilt, every inch of him hard and pulsing, throbbing with fiery heat. He held himself still for a moment, as if he savored the tightness, then he pulled out and savagely thrust back in. Out and then in, out and then in, pounding, pounding, riding her like a madman, taking his pleasure yet giving it too, his fierce need matching her own.

"Damien!" she cried out as he drove into her hard and deep, the fire in her blood blazing hotter, her heart hammering, her loins damp and aching, gripping him as she neared the edge of release. Beneath her the carriage rumbled, rocking and swaying over the paving stones, the horses' hooves pounding, just as he was pounding into her.

In seconds she was soaring, rising through the flames like a phoenix, sailing out over the edge. She was blinded by circles of sweetness, alight with joy and a pleasure so intense she was certain she would die of it.

He whispered her name as he joined her, his narrow hips pumping, his seed spilling into her. She was damp and sticky and warm with his fluid, but she didn't care. He had come for her, saved her from a fate worse than death. Tomorrow she would think of this night and all that had happened. Tomorrow she would battle her conscience, her loyalties, prepare herself for this new twist of fate.

Tomorrow . . . she thought as she snuggled against his wide, hard shoulder, unafraid for the first time in weeks, grateful to God for sending him to save her. Exhaustion swept over her. Still clutching him tightly against her, Alexa closed her eyes and drifted into an exhausted sleep.

Damien carried his sleeping wife up the stairs to his bedchamber. Gently, he rested her on the canopied bed, unlaced and stripped off her corset and stockings.

When he touched her shoulder, a smudge of powder came off in his hand, and he realized it had been used to disguise the scar left from her wound. He checked it carefully, saw that it was well-healed, and pressed his lips against it.

With tender care he pulled up the covers and tucked them around her. For the first time he noticed the circles beneath her eyes, the waxy hue of her skin. She was exhausted, he saw, weary from the strain and her fear of the unknown, tired to her bones from the battle she had been waging.

He let her sleep, though what he wanted most was to join her in the bed, to fill her again as he had in the carriage, to claim her and make her his. Instead he left her and went downstairs to join Claude-Louis in his study. He sent a messenger to the Opéra, carrying his apologies to the group he was to have joined, then poured himself a cognac and sat down in a chair across from his friend.

"She sleeps?" Claude asked.

Damien nodded. "There will never be words enough to thank you."

"Thanks are not needed among men who are friends."

It was true, so he said nothing more, just finished his drink and returned upstairs.

Still, he did not join his wife in bed. He knew if he did, he would wake her. She needed her rest and he meant to see that she got it. Instead he sat down at her bedside to watch her gentle breathing, more grateful to have her returned than for any gift he had ever received.

Chapter Fourteen

ALEXA STIRRED, DISCOVERED SHE WAS NAKED, AND HER EYES SNAPPED OPEN. *DEAR GOD, WHERE AM I?* THE ROOM SHE was in wasn't faded and shabby; it was sumptuous in the extreme. She lay in a gold and green silk-draped canopied bed, atop a deep feather mattress. Heavy silk brocade draperies in the same gold-green hues hung at the tall-paned windows, and the polished wooden floor was warmed by a thick Persian carpet.

Alexa sat up in bed, the covers clutched tight beneath her chin, her memory slowly returning. Bewicke and the English, the musket shot and the awful pain in her chest, the terrifying days at Le Monde, Celeste Dumaine and the auction, Damien . . .

Her heart fluttered and so did her stomach. Alexa carefully surveyed the room, hoping, yet somehow fearful, that she would encounter her husband. Damien was not there, but his musky male scent still lingered.

She remembered the way he had swept into her room, looking like the devil reincarnate. She recalled the fierceness of his gaze, the way his blue eyes touched her, willing her some of his strength. She saw tenderness there, mingled with relief and savage determination.

With a rush of embarrassment she remembered the way he had kissed her, caressed her half-naked body in front of Madame Dumaine. As wicked as it was, she responded to him as she always did, her body on fire for him, craving him as a sun-parched flower thirsted for rain.

She thought of the carriage ride, of the horses' hooves pounding against the paving stones just as he had pounded into her. Her cheeks grew hotter to think of it, to remember her wanton behavior—to remember the way she had given herself to him with no thought of the past.

No thought of his ruthlessness, of the vicious games he had played, the lies he had told.

Without the slightest concern that her husband was a traitor.

Alexa's stomach clenched. She owed him her life, yet it was because of his disloyalty that she had come to such an end in the first place. It was his fault—but last night she had not cared.

A light knock sounded at the door. When Alexa granted entry, a dark-haired woman, short, buxom, and pretty, stepped into the room. Surely not one of Damien's mistresses, she thought with sudden panic, recalling for the first time the soldiers in the boat and their cruelly taunting words. A hot surge of jealousy rolled over her.

"*Bonjour,* madame," the woman said. "I am Marie Claire, housekeeper here, and wife to Claude-Louis, your husband's *valet de chambre.*"

Alexa felt such a wave of relief it made her a little bit

dizzy. "Good morning." She flushed a slight shade of pink, feeling foolish for her anger, and resentful that her husband's infidelities could upset her so much.

"Since we did not know you were coming, there is as yet no lady's maid to attend you. I thought perhaps you could make do with me until your husband can make suitable arrangements."

"*D'accord.* Thank you, Marie Claire." Alexa climbed out of bed and allowed the dark-haired woman to attend her, ordering a bath up to the room, helping her wash and dry her hair then put on a borrowed muslin day dress. The gown was quite stylish, high-waisted and trimmed with embroidered roses. It was a little too short, the bosom a little too tight, but it was the finest thing she had worn in weeks. When they had finished her toilette, she felt better.

"Your husband will be pleased," said Marie Claire with a pleasant smile, surveying her clothes and her upswept auburn hair. They turned in unison at the sound of the door bursting open. Marie Claire frowned, but Alexa merely smiled at the small, dark-haired child who stumbled wide-eyed into the room.

"Jean-Paul, *mon Dieu,* what are you doing? You know better than to enter a lady's room without knocking."

"I am sorry, Maman. I did not know a lady was here."

"It's all right," Alexa said to him gently. "I only arrived late last eve. There is no way you could have known."

"Who are you?" he asked, taking an uncertain step backward toward the door. For the first time she noticed his foot dragged unnaturally and the shoe he wore tilted at an unusual angle. His mother's gaze followed hers and the Frenchwoman's posture shifted protectively toward her son.

"Do not be rude, Jean-Paul," she said. "The lady need not answer to you."

Alexa kept her gaze fixed on the boy. "It's all right. We would have met sooner or later. I am . . . M'sieur Falon's wife," she admitted almost reluctantly.

The little boy surprised her with a smile. *"C'est bon!* Then it is certain that we shall be friends."

Her heart twisted oddly inside her chest. "I would like that. I would like that very much."

"Since you are here with M'sieur Damien," he said, "does that also mean that you like birds?"

She smiled. "Yes, I do."

"Then I shall show you mine. His name is Charlemagne. The most beautiful bird in the world."

"I would love to see him."

"But not today," his mother put in, no longer looking defensive. "Run along now, *mon chou.* Madame Falon has better things to do than to waste her time talking to you." But there was no censure in her voice, and a well of affection glinted in the depths of her pretty dark eyes.

"He's a darling little boy," Alexa said as the child limped off at a fast pace down the hall. She couldn't help wondering what had happened to his leg or feeling sad that such a tragedy should have befallen a child.

"Your husband has always been kind to him. He dotes on the child more than he should."

Damien did that? Doted? She could hardly believe it. Still, he must have been the one who brought the child the bird.

"Where is he?" She worked to sound matter-of-fact, but as images rose sharply of the night they had shared, she wasn't feeling matter-of-fact at all.

"If you're looking for me," came the answer from the door, "then I am happy to say that you have found me." A smile lit his darkly handsome features, and his bright blue eyes ran over her with warm appreciation.

He looked fit and well-rested, and far too attractive. Alexa felt drawn to him as she always did, but this time she was determined to ignore the attraction.

"Thank you, Marie Claire," Damien said. "That will be all for now. I can see to my wife's care for the balance of the morning."

"If there is anything you wish, madame, you need only let me know."

"Merci, Marie Claire," Alexa said.

"How are you feeling?" Damien strode toward her, his dove-gray tailcoat spotless, his breeches indecently snug over his lean hips and muscular thighs. He was still speaking French, as he had since the moment she had seen him. It was a reminder of all that had occurred, and unconsciously, Alexa drew away.

"I—I'm fine," she answered in that same soft language, the words second nature to her now. "Thank you for last night . . . I—I mean thank you for coming. I don't know what I should have done if—if . . ."

He closed the distance between them and took her into his arms. "Don't think about it. You're safe now. Your time at Le Monde is no more than a terrible dream."

A trace of bitterness edged the smile that curved her lips. If only she could forget the past, live as though she had been reborn last night. "Perhaps that is so. But we are still in France, England is still at war, and you—you are still a traitor."

Something flashed in his eyes—pain? regret?—then it was gone. "Perhaps that is your way of seeing it. It all depends on one's point of view."

Alexa pulled away from him. "How can you do it, Damien? You're an Englishman, for Godsake. You're a member of the aristocracy."

"I'm also a Frenchman. Or have you forgotten?"

"Apparently I have . . . or at least I seem to have done so last night."

"Ah, yes . . . last night." His eyes swept over her as if he could see through her clothes, and a blush rose into her cheeks.

"I'm not saying that I am not grateful."

"What exactly are you saying?"

"I know very well I owe you my life, however . . ."

A black slashing brow arched up. "However?"

"I wouldn't have been in that situation in the first place if it hadn't been for you. You and your spying— your treachery and deceit. It's beyond everything that I believe in. It isn't something I can live with."

"Last night you certainly had no trouble—"

"What happened last night should never have occurred. I don't intend to let it happen again."

The muscles across his high cheekbones went taut. He forcibly relaxed them. "I know that you are upset. You've been through a lot—more than most women could have endured. You're living in a strange country, with a man you no longer trust. I can't fault you for being confused."

"Then surely you won't mind finding me another room."

His piercing blue eyes bored into her. The gentleness was gone from his features, leaving his face a mask of stone. "Oh, but I do mind. I'll give you some time to get used to the way things are, but the fact is, you're my wife, Alexa. As long as you remain in France, you will sleep in my room—in my bed. You agreed to do that when we were married. I expect you to keep that agreement now."

"I didn't know you were a traitor when I married you."

A cynical smile curved his lips. "Remember, sweeting, a traitor to one country is a patriot to another."

Alexa said nothing, just clamped her lips and stared at him grimly. If only she could believe he *was* a patriot. Perhaps she could understand . . . in time she might even forgive him.

She looked at him now, trying to read his face, wanting desperately to believe his motives were somehow more noble than simply personal gain. In her heart she knew they were not.

His features harsh and grim, Damien turned away from her and stalked out of the room. For a long while after he had gone, Alexa stared at the place where he had been.

Damien stepped from his carriage onto the paving stones near the entrance to Ecole Militaire in the Faubourg St. Germaine. He had a meeting with General Moreau, one of the great horse generals of the Grande Armée and aide-de-camp to Napoleon.

He was wearing his uniform today, the blue and white tunic and tight white breeches of the Grenadiers de Cheval, the gold braid on his jacket glittering in the warm August sun. He didn't dress this way often, only on formal occasions and meetings like this one, and today the clothes felt oddly uncomfortable. He hadn't thought much about them, not until he had passed Alexa in the hallway and her face had turned ashen at the sight.

She had brushed past him without a word, ignoring him as she had all week, moving woodenly off toward the garden. He had watched her from the window, seen her sitting among the hyacinths and daffodils, staring blankly off in the distance. He knew what she was thinking, knew she would never forgive him for his lies and his deceptions, for spying against her beloved country.

If only he could tell her the truth.

He couldn't, of course. Danger surrounded him like a pool of stagnant water. The tiniest ripple could suck them both under, and into a watery grave.

Damien passed along the colonnaded hallway of the huge stone building, thinking about Alexa and the tension that existed between them. The house was like a battleground, every word guarded, every movement gauged, every strength tested against every weakness. His actions were limited by the part he played. He was being watched, he knew, and so was she. He didn't dare involve her in this. He had to protect her, no matter the cost."

Every day she stayed in France, she was in danger.

He entered a small domed vestibule with a heavily molded ceiling, crossed the black and white tiled floor, and opened the twelve-foot doors leading into the general's suite of rooms. A young lieutenant in the antechamber stood up as he entered, then ushered him inside the general's massive office. Damien came to attention in front of the stout thick-chested man sitting behind the huge gilded Louis XVI desk.

General Moreau returned the salute and they both sat down. "Good news, eh, Major? Your lovely wife returns to you from the dead."

"Very nearly, General. She is now home and safe, I am happy to say."

"You may rest assured the men responsible have been dealt with severely."

"Thank you, sir." They spoke briefly about the English menace, Moreau recounting events in Spain and Portugal that influenced the Peninsular Campaign, including the not-so-long-ago victory of General Wellesley, recently appointed Viscount Wellington, at the battle of Talavera in May.

"His success was only a small one," Damien reminded him. "The man was lucky to escape so unscathed."

Moreau grunted because it was the truth. "Wellington himself said, 'If Boney had been there, we should have been beaten.' "

"I do not doubt it," Damien agreed. But Wellington had been lucky. Napoleon had put his faith in his brother Joseph and returned to Paris to settle problems there.

They spoke about rumors Moreau had heard that the English might be returning. "Our sources believe they will land once more on the Continent."

"When?" Damien leaned forward, bracing a hand on his knee.

"Any day now."

"Where is the landing expected?"

Moreau chuckled. "If you were still in England, Major, you might be able to tell us, *n'est ce pas?*"

He sighed. "An unfortunate ending to an invaluable operation."

"Do not despair, Major Falon. There is always a place for a capable man like you."

Damien saw the opening he had been seeking, the reason he had requested this meeting. "I am certain there will be. Which is why I am here."

"And that reason is . . . ?"

"I would like to ask that my wife be returned to her homeland."

A busy dark brow went up. Moreau scratched his curly brown side whiskers. "But your wife has only just arrived—she has seen nothing of our beautiful city. And you are only newly married—you said yourself you had yet to grow tired of her."

"That is true, General, but—"

"They say she is more beautiful than a goddess."

He forced down a swell of emotion, careful to keep his voice bland instead. "My wife is a very lovely woman."

"Is that not reason enough to keep her here?"

"What about my assignment?" he argued. "She knows no one in Paris. Once I am gone, there will be no one to take care of her."

"That time may yet be some distance away. When it comes, we will see that she gets home." He smiled. "In the meantime, I believe I would very much like to meet her. Perhaps you would care join me this week's end at my château. It is not so very far away, only a few miles out in the country at St.-Germain-en-Laye. Others will be joining us, of course. My wife has planned quite a lavish affair. It would be the perfect opportunity for you to introduce your Belle Anglaise."

Damien inwardly tensed. Word had slipped out of what had happened at Le Monde, of the auction, of the beautiful woman who was Major Falon's wife and the way he had saved her. The affair had piqued the general's interest. His invitation was in truth a command.

"We would be delighted, General Moreau."

"C'est bon!" The stout man rose from behind his desk, and Damien stood up too.

"In the meantime, I presume you will be attending tomorrow night's ball in support of the Emperor's Austrian campaign."

Another thinly veiled command. "Of course." He would have to find Alexa something to wear, but that was a problem already on his agenda.

"Unfortunately, I must see to more pressing matters." He sighed. "Ah, to be young and unfettered again. It would surely be heaven, *n'est ce pas?*"

"Absolument."

The general dismissed him with a reminder of his upcoming visit to the country, and Damien gave him a smart salute.

"Have a good evening, General." Turning away from him, he made his way out the door.

Standing just down the hall, Victor Lafon watched him leave. He studied Moreau's closed door, a little uneasy at the meeting that had just occurred. He wondered what had gone on inside the room, and why, as Major Falon's direct superior, he hadn't been invited to attend. Whatever the nature of the meeting, he didn't like it. It wasn't wise for a man like the major to garner too much favor.

He turned to his aide, a young lieutenant named Colbert, with keen gray eyes and a solid dose of ambition. "I want him watched more closely," the colonel said. "Tell Pierre he had better be keeping his eyes open."

The lieutenant just smiled. "Pierre Lindet is a loyal servant to the Emperor. Besides, our little maître d' hotel has five hungry mouths to feed—he needs every franc he can get. With certainty, you may count on Pierre."

Spying on a man left a bitter taste in the colonel's mouth. Then again, perhaps in Falon's case it was only poetic justice. He shrugged it off as another unpleasantry of war and went into the general's office.

Alexa spent the morning with little Jean-Paul and his beautiful bird. Charlemagne was a snow-white cockatiel who was kept in a cage in the carriage house. The pet was obviously the child's pride and joy, and Damien had done a fine job of showing the boy how to care for it.

She wondered again what had happened to the boy's twisted leg, but hadn't yet had the chance to find out.

Instead she said good-bye, leaving him in the care of his father, and made her way back to the house. Damien returned sometime later, calling her name as he entered the small salon where she sat reading, his voice rich and smooth as the finest of wines. She ignored the shiver of warmth that slid into her stomach.

She turned to watch him walk in, admiring his tall lean frame and the impeccable fit of his clothes, though it galled her to do so. He had spoken to her little since the morning they had argued, and had slept by himself in the room next to hers.

She wondered what he wanted with her now.

"Ah, there you are." He was no longer wearing his uniform, but a dark plum tailcoat, gray pique waistcoat, and light gray breeches. He looked less forbidding, more casually controlled, and she relaxed a little in his presence. He bent over her hand as if nothing untoward had passed between them and softly brushed his lips against her fingers.

"You look as lovely as ever." Still holding her hand, he returned to his full height above her. "But I believe it is time you had something of your own to wear."

Alexa stiffened and pulled her hand away. "I presumed I wouldn't be staying that long."

"I had presumed that as well. Unfortunately, General Moreau has other ideas."

"You mean I'm not going home?"

He shrugged indifferently. "The general is determined to meet you, and now that I think of it, I see no reason for you to leave so soon."

"No reason? But I am an Englishwoman—and there is a war going on."

"You are also my wife," he said with a soft hint of warning. "It is your duty to remain with your husband for as long as it should please him."

"But—"

"Be a good girl, Alexa, run upstairs and get your wrap. We've several functions to attend, and I would see you properly clothed."

Be a good girl, Alexa? Who the devil did he think he was? But she went to fetch a shawl, for she needed time to think. He wasn't sending her home, at least not yet. She could try to return on her own, but after her experience at Le Monde, she wasn't too fond of the notion. It might be smarter to stay in Paris until she was assured of safe passage back to England.

It would happen, she believed, sooner or later. Rayne would be returning from Jamaica, and the British would begin making demands. Though a war raged between them, there were diplomatic channels for such matters. A woman of her wealth and position would not be considered merely a casualty of war.

And Damien had been respectful of her wishes and continued to leave her alone. Surely she could keep him at bay a little longer. Perhaps he would tire of her constant refusal to share his bed and convince the general to return her.

Her mind still whirling, Alexa collected her borrowed cashmere shawl and joined her husband at the bottom of the stairs.

"Ready?" he asked.

"I suppose so."

"Good." With an inborn grace she had always found attractive and now fought to ignore, he took her arm and led her out to the carriage. He was smiling, his expression relaxed, yet it didn't seem completely sincere.

What role was he playing today? she wondered, wishing that she could understand him. What were his motives—and why did she still care?

Yet a part of her did care. She wanted to deny it, but every time she tried, she remembered him as he was that terrible night at Le Monde. His concern for her had been stamped on his handsome face, and no amount of acting could disguise it.

Alexa sighed at her turbulent thoughts and the uncertain future ahead. Resolving to forget her troubles for a while, she turned to look out the window and focus her mind on her surroundings. For the first time that day, she smiled. Paris was a city just as vibrant and alive as London, its crowded streets surging with humanity, the colorful sights, sounds, and pungent odors quickly capturing her interest. They passed a street sweeper scrubbing the paving stones, a broom merchant, a knife grinder, a furniture maker with an up-ended chair over his head.

They traveled by a small café, its patrons sitting out
front, pigeons at their feet picking at scraps that had
fallen from the tables.

"Where are we headed?" she asked absently, not
really caring, her eyes still fixed on the small wrought-
iron balconies and high arching windows, the sights
and sounds of the crowded Parisian streets.

"There is a seamstress in the Rue des Petits Champs.
She will see us well taken care of."

They traveled the Rue St. Honoré, past the Elysée
Palace to the Rue Richelieu and onto the Rue des Petits
Champs. Next to a sidewalk puppet show in front of a
small shop with tiny paned windows, the carriage
rolled to a halt. A bas relief sign out in front read SEMP-
STRESS in raised bold red letters.

Damien ushered her inside, and a wrinkled, frail little
woman scurried toward him from a curtained back
room. The shop had high molded ceilings, tables piled
high with bolts of cloth, and the air was tinged with
the slightly acrid odor of fabric dye. Several women
chatted at the counter, one of them admiring a pair of
pink satin slippers.

"M'sieur Falon, how good it is to see you." The frail
little woman stopped before Damien's tall figure,
dwarfed by his height and the width of his shoulders.

"As it is you, Madame Aubrey."

"And who is it you have brought me this time?"
Rheumy old eyes scanned Alexa from top to bottom. "I
believe you have outdone yourself, m'sieur." She
smiled, exposing teeth worn low in front by so many
years of use. "You have always chosen women of great
beauty, but this one—"

"This one is my wife," Damien broke in, with no
small hint of warning. It went unsaid that talk of his
mistresses should end, but the damage had already
been done.

"Your reputation proceeds you," Alexa said to him

bitterly as the small woman left them and returned to the rear of the shop for her fabrics. "I suppose I shouldn't be surprised. You were a rake in London— why shouldn't you be one here?"

"Alexa—"

"At least you dress your women well—with the blood money your spying brings."

"My *patriotic* efforts are none of your concern," Damien said shortly. "As to the other, content yourself with the knowledge that you are the only woman with whom I seek to share my bed." He glanced up and caught the little woman watching him. "A condition that will not change—as long as you continue to please me."

"Please you! I will do everything in my power *not* to please you!"

An amused smile curved his lips. His next words came out softly. "The fact remains, *ma chére,* that you do." Bending over, he brushed her mouth with a kiss.

Alexa just stared. Already her heart thumped uncomfortably. Sweet God, how could he do that with just a few soft words? But there had been that look in his eyes when he'd said them. It was as if for an instant he had let her see inside him, behind the facade of whatever role he played.

"Come," he said gently. "Madame Aubrey will grow impatient."

Alexa let him lead her into a small salon where several women helped to remove her clothes. Dressed in only her thin chemise, she stepped up on a low round pedestal and Damien sat down on a brocaded sofa.

"Such a figure . . ." Madame Aubrey said, clucking like a pleased mother hen as she surveyed her. She gripped the chemise from behind and drew it snugly against Alexa's curves, studying her from several different angles. "Our best endeavors will not be wasted on this one." The frail woman smiled at Damien while her helpers began to drape Alexa in lengths of expensive cloth.

Diaphanous muslins, silks and satins, tulle, gauze, taffeta, and Mechlin lace were all carried into the room. A tunic dress of emerald silk over an undergarment of gold was chosen for the upcoming ball they would attend. A delicate ivory taffeta combined with an amethyst gauze trimmed with pearls created another stunning gown; and a length of royal-blue satin enhanced by an underskirt embroidered with silver thread completed the list.

Damien insisted she choose a number of different bonnets and a half-dozen pair of short and long gloves in a variety of colors. There were cloaks, redingotes, and spencers, a tiny pagoda parasol, a tippet of swansdown, and even a lovely jeweled comb.

A few simpler gowns were chosen, and each time she undressed, Damien watched her. His expression remained inscrutable, but hunger blazed in the fierce blue eyes that moved over her nearly nude body. It was a look of such burning need, it stirred an odd, hollow flutter in the pit of her stomach. It made her own hunger build, made her breasts grown achy and a dampness gather between her legs. It made her recall the imprint of his hands on her body, the heat of his mouth on her flesh.

She was shaking by the time they had finished, Damien's hot gaze nearly devouring. He came to his feet with graceful, pantherlike stealth, his sleek muscles moving beneath his coat and breeches. The heat of his eyes seemed to stroke her wherever they touched, and images of his powerful build and firm, well-formed lips set off a tingling in her limbs.

He must have read her thoughts, for his touch was different this time, no longer casually reserved but determinedly possessive. The minute they left the shop and entered the carriage, he dragged her into his arms.

"Sweet Christ, do you know how much I want you?"
He kissed her then, taking her lips in a slick, hot kiss
that made her insides burn and sent all her convictions
flying out the window.

For a moment she allowed herself the pleasure, sliding her arms around his neck, kissing him back, touching her tongue to his, pressing herself against him. Her
nipples grew stiff against the fabric of her dress, and
Damien's solid arousal throbbed hotly beneath her
hips.

Need sliced through her, more powerful than she
could have imagined. But with it came a heavy dose of
conscience.

Dear God, I can't let this happen!

Trembling with the effort, she pressed her palms
against his chest and pulled away. "I—I can't," she
whispered. "I can't do this."

"You want me. Surely you can't mean to deny it."

"I want the man I thought I married."

Damien swore foully, his eyes boring into her, chal-
lenging her without words. With a heavy sigh he set
her away from him and raked a hand through his wavy
black hair. Still, he said nothing, and neither did Alexa.
She was stunned by the depth of her emotions. How
could she still care for him so much? How could she
respond to him, knowing the things he had done, the
lies he had told? How could she still want him?

She had to stay away from him, that much was clear.

The only question was, how in God's name would
she do it?

Chapter Fifteen

T HE GOLD AND EMERALD GOWN WAS READY BY THE NIGHT
OF THE EMPEROR'S BALL. IT WAS TO BE A GRAND AFFAIR,
though Napoleon himself would not attend, ensconced
as he was at the palace of Schönbrunn outside Vienna.

Four thousand people from all classes of Parisian society had been invited, with an emphasis on the mili-
tary, commerce, and banking. The square and quays
leading up to the Hotel de Ville were brightly lit with
lanterns, and the magnificent interior had been richly
decorated in the Emperor's gold and green.

For the first time it occurred to Alexa that Damien
had chosen those same colors for her.

"You did it on purpose, didn't you?" she said
through clenched teeth as they made their way through
the crowd.

Damien only smiled. "I did it because it matches the
green of your eyes . . . and because I knew it would

please them. Moreau might not be here, but there are a number of other important people who will be."

"I should have refused to wear it."

A black flaring brow arched up. "You might have found it a bit unnerving to arrive in just your chemise."

She glared at him but said nothing more. He was the epitome of the handsome French soldier this eve, in his tight white breeches and tall black hussar boots. Gleaming gold buttons marched up the front of his scarlet-trimmed, white and navy tunic, and his broad shoulders glittered with epaulettes and braid.

As the orchestra played in the background, he led her through the richly garbed assembly, past walls dominated by Imperial eagles and decorated with the Emperor's dark green colors dotted with tiny gold bees. At the foot of the huge marble staircase in the grand salon, he paused.

"There are some people I would like you to meet." He said a few words of hello to the group who stood gathered there, then began to make introductions.

"Enchanté," a gentleman named Brumaire addressed her.

"Bonsoir, m'sieur," she replied somewhat stiffly. It was an odd assortment: a man named Fouchet who was Minister of Police; a colonel of dragoons; a captain of hussars; the architect, Cellerier; a commander of the carabinier brigade; an actress of the Comédie Francaise; and an abbot of the clergy who had no abbey. He wore ecclesiastical dress but did not belong to a church— taking his degree instead "in Society."

The actress, an attractive blonde with oversized breasts, eyed Damien far too boldly. Alexa found her hold on his arm growing tighter, a line of tension forming around her lips.

"You must not worry, *miette,"* came a once-familiar voice beside her ear, "Gabriella is no longer his *cher amie.* I believe your husband's eyes are only for you."

"M'sieur Gaudin!"

"It is good to see you, Madame Falon." He bent over her hand then squeezed it with some affection.

Damien smiled at him warmly. "Good evening, André. I had hoped I might see you here."

"Oh? Why is that?"

"To thank you, of course, for caring for my wife in my absence."

"It was my pleasure, though I am sad to see that she is still here."

"Frankly, my friend, so am I. But if General Moreau wishes it, who am I to disagree?"

André frowned, his thick white brows coming together. "Alas, that is so." He turned back to Alexa. "In the meantime, one can only make the best of things, *n'est ce pas?*"

"I am trying, m'sieur."

M'sieur Gaudin introduced them both to the group of people he had come in with. Colonel Lafon was among them, the Duchess d'Abrantes, and a handsome blond man by the name of Julian St. Owen, whom everyone called Jules. He was just in from the country, someone said, a keen-eyed man in his early thirties, with a pleasant manner and obvious intelligence. When he bowed over her hand, holding it a little longer than he should have, Damien broke the contact by asking her to dance.

"Are you certain you wouldn't rather be dancing with the actress?" Alexa couldn't help asking.

"They're playing a waltz. There is no one here I would rather dance it with than you."

His serious tone surprised her, but not the heated look in his eyes. It had been there all evening, since he had first walked into the drawing room and seen her in the low-cut gold and emerald gown. The expression on his face made her heart speed up and her palms grow damp. It made her yearn for those few brief moments of the waltz when he would hold her in arms, though in truth she knew she should refuse him.

Instead she let him guide her onto the dance floor, turn her to face him, and gently take her hand. Around them couples swayed in rhythm to the music, dipped and twirled in the candlelight beneath the crystal chandeliers. The music swelled until it filled the massive mirrored ballroom.

"Do you realize this is the first waltz we have ever danced?" he said, his eyes moving over her face. They came to rest on her lips, and her legs felt suddenly shaky.

"I know." Yet it did not seem so. Every muscle in their bodies moved in perfect rhythm, every turn, every step, every sway of their hips. His leg brushed intimately between hers and unconsciously he tightened his hold.

"You're the loveliest woman here," he said, and his hot gaze told her he meant it.

"Merci, m'sieur," But there was a catch in her voice.

"I want you. I have since the moment I saw you in that dress."

Alexa glanced away. "Wanting isn't everything. Sometimes we can't have exactly what we want."

"Sometimes we can."

She turned her gaze to his. "You want me and yet I am your enemy."

"You are my wife. That is all that matters. Can you not put our differences aside—at least while you are here?"

Alexa stiffened in his arms. "How can you ask me that? Do you believe I should accept what you have done? Pretend that I approve? That I should welcome you into my bed then return home to England and simply go on with my life as if you had never existed?"

"Perhaps there is an alternative," he said softly.

"And exactly what is that?"

"That you entrust yourself into my care and believe that somehow I will make things work out for us both."

Alexa swallowed past the ache that suddenly rose in her throat. She wanted to—dear God, she had never wanted anything more. But in truth she did not dare. Damien had lied to her a dozen times, deceived her in more ways than she cared to remember. It would be madness of the wildest sort, and yet . . ."

"I wish I could. You will never know how much I wish it, but . . ."

"But?"

"But the fact is I cannot."

Damien's hold grew tighter, indecently so, pressing his long hard body the length of her, making her aware of his growing arousal in his immodestly tight white breeches.

"Dammit, you're my wife!" he bit out beneath his breath. She tried to pull away but he held her fast. "Sorry, sweeting, but you aren't leaving." His grip remained tight on her waist. "That would surely prove embarrassing for both of us." And yet he eased his hold, letting her draw away from him, giving them time to regain control.

When the dance had ended, he returned her to the place beside André Gaudin. "If I might impose upon our friendship, André, I would like to leave Alexa for a moment in your care. I need a word with Colonel Lafon."

"Of course," André said.

"If the two of you will excuse me . . . ?" He bowed curtly and walked away.

"He is a difficult man to figure, *n'est ce pas?*" Gaudin said.

"Practically impossible."

"And yet you have feelings for him."

"Yes."

"Why is that?"

She tore her gaze from her husband's tall retreating figure. "Perhaps I see something in him." She sighed. "Then again . . . perhaps it isn't really there."

Whatever he might have replied went unsaid as Jules St. Owen returned.

"Madame Falon." The blond man smiled, and she noticed his eyes were a light sky-blue. With his aquiline nose and the cleft in his chin, she realized once more how handsome he was. "With your husband occupied elsewhere, perhaps you will grace me with a dance."

Why not? she thought. Damien might not like it, but she didn't really care. "It would be my pleasure, m'sieur."

Again a waltz was playing. So much the better, she thought, hoping her husband would see them. Perhaps he would be angry. If he treated her badly, it would help put some distance between them.

At the edge of the dance floor St. Owen put a hand at her waist and led her into the steps of the dance. He was shorter than Damien, but well-built and attractively male, and nearly as proficient a dancer. Still, she felt a little more reserved in his company, and St. Owen must have sensed it for he leaned a little bit closer.

"Relax, Lady Falon," he whispered in her ear, and to her amazement, the words were spoken in English. "I have come to help you get home."

"Who—Who are you?" she asked, drawing away to look at him.

"Speak French," he warned, for she had slipped into her native tongue. He eased her back into the dance and continued as if nothing had happened. "I am a friend. For now that is all that is important."

"Who sent you? Why should I trust you?"

"General Wilcox sent word. He is Colonel Bewicke's superior."

"Bewicke is the last man I would trust."

"It is Wilcox I am here for."

"Then you are a spy?"

"No. I am a loyal Frenchman."

"Then why are you—"

"This isn't the time. I'll tell you more when next we meet. Just be assured there are those here who will help you."

They finished the dance, and Jules St. Owen returned her to André Gaudin. She felt shaken and ill at ease, unable to grasp what had just occurred. When she turned once more to St. Owen, he had melded into the crowd. She watched his blond head disappear through the doorway.

"Did you enjoy your dance with Jules?" André asked, and she wondered if he knew what had transpired between them.

"He seems like a nice enough man."

"Jules is a wealthy export merchant—a captain retired from the sea. I have not seen him in a while. In the past he has often been at odds with the policies of the Emperor. Apparently, he has put such notions to rest."

So André had no knowledge of what St. Owen had planned. But then neither did she.

"You have caught the eye of at least a dozen other young men here. If it is your wish to continue to dance—"

"In truth, I should prefer being home." She had too much on her mind, too much she needed to consider. And now with this latest turn of events . . .

"Perhaps your husband will agree."

She saw him striding toward her, his darkly elegant features setting him apparent from the rest of the men in the room. Several pairs of female eyes fastened on his narrow hips and long, muscular legs as he moved, and Alexa felt an unwelcome twinge of jealousy.

"I've a meeting with Lafon early tomorrow," Damien

said when he reached her side. "Would you mind very much if we went home early?"

"As a matter of fact, I should be greatly relieved."

He eyed her a moment. "Then I'll see to your cloak and summon the carriage."

They left just a few moments later, shouldering their way through the crowd then waiting out front while the carriage was brought round. Though Damien said little along the route home and they entered the house in silence, his eyes followed every move she made. His desire for her had not lessened. It was there in the way he touched her, in the smoky blue of his gaze. She knew what he was thinking, that he was her husband, that he had rights to her body she could not deny him.

Yet he said nothing as she climbed the stairs, nothing as she walked away from him down the hall and into her bedchamber. With a wave of relief she closed the door and leaned against it, then turned to see Marie Claire.

"I will help you undress," the dark-haired woman said, and Alexa nodded. Though her mind remained on the man she had left in the hallway, she stripped off her clothes with quiet efficiency and pulled the pins from her hair. Marie Claire handed her a long white night rail, but a voice from the door stopped her before she could draw it on.

"You may go, Marie Claire," Damien said softly.

Alexa clutched the nightgown protectively in front of her, waiting in silence as the woman left the room. If only she could ask her to remain, but she knew all too clearly where the Frenchwoman's loyalties lay.

"What—What do you want?" The words cut into the silence left when Marie Claire closed the door.

Damien's stormy eyes raked her. "You know very well what I want." He came away from the door, his black silk dressing gown exposing his long sinewy legs as he moved. A few feet in front of her he pulled the

sash, and the robe fell open. When he stopped, it slid
from his shoulders and she saw that he was naked.

*Sweet God in heaven. Was there ever a more beauti-
ful man put on this earth?* Her vision seemed filled
with his long lean limbs and a torso banded with muscle.

"I'm your husband, Alexa," he said softly as he approached, but she only turned away.

"Don't. Please don't." She took a step toward the big
four-poster bed, her back and hips exposed to him, her
hands catching one of the bedposts to steady her. She
felt his hard body pressed full-length behind her. He
bent and kissed the side of her neck.

"I need you, Alexa." Warm kisses trailed over her
shoulders, his groin cradled her buttocks and the long
muscles of his thighs pressed into the backs of her legs.

"I can't," she whispered, but already fire raced
through her body. His hands splayed over her stomach,
her ribs, then came up to cup each of her breasts.

"You can," he said, his thumb and forefinger working her nipple, making it peak and distend. The flat
plane of his stomach went taut against her buttocks,
then he bent his head and the warmth of his tongue
ran over the ridges of her spine. A hand slid up the
inside of her thigh and into the dampness between her
legs. He stroked her there, making her tremble, making
the blood roar in her ears. Her mouth felt dry, her
limbs weak and disjointed. Her stomach fluttered and
her body went hot with anticipation.

"Part your legs, *ma chére.*" His finger slid inside her
as she mindlessly obeyed, her hands biting into the tall
wooden bedpost, her head falling back, her hair hanging down below her hips.

His shaft rode high and hard against his belly; she felt
it against her hips, and fiery need tore through her. Her
blood was pumping, surging, flowing like molten lava
and setting her aflame. Then he was parting the petals

of her sex, guiding himself inside, driving into her with one long powerful thrust.

"I need you," he whispered, and there was something in the way he said it that made her believe it was the truth.

He turned her a little and took her mouth in a savage kiss, his hands on her breasts, kneading them, molding them, making them grow heavy with desire for him. Then his grip settled firmly at her hips and he held her immobile as he drove himself inside her, the powerful thrust and drag of his shaft urging her to the edge of her control.

"Say it," he whispered, "tell me you want me."

She tried to fight it, bit down on her trembling lips and tightened her hold on the bedpost. Damien withdrew nearly full-length, then filled her hotly again.

"Say it," he commanded. He held her hips and ruthlessly thrust himself inside her.

"I want you, Damien. I want you so badly it hurts."

"Sweet Christ," he groaned. He was taking her hard and fast now, his lean hips pumping, his hands hot, his mouth devouring.

"Damien!" she cried out as she reached her release, then she was swept away, rocked by one powerful explosion of heat followed by another and another.

She didn't notice when he spilled his seed, that her knees had given way beneath her, that it was he who held her up. She was shaking all over with the power of her emotions, and suddenly she was afraid. Then she felt his gentle kisses on her face, felt his arms wrapped protectively around her, heard the reassuring whisper of his words.

"It's all right, *chérie*. There's no need for you to be frightened."

But there was every reason to be afraid. Alexa knew it, yet the knowledge hit home with the force of a blow. She straightened and pulled away, turning to face

him as if she faced her greatest foe. "You shouldn't
have come here."

"Alexa—"

"Don't. Don't say anything more." At the agonized
look on her face, he picked up her high-necked, long
white night gown and silently held it out to her. She
took it with trembling hands and quickly pulled it on,
all the while backing away.

"I want you to go," she said, her voice a little too
high and strangely uneven.

Damien shook his head. "I don't want to leave you.
Not like this."

"Please, Damien—" But his expression was determined as his long strides moved him toward her.
Sweeping her into his arms, he carried her over to the
wide feather bed.

"I'll just stay here for a while." Drawing back the
covers, he settled her carefully on one side and adjusted her pillow, then stretched his tall frame out on
the other. "Just until you fall asleep."

It seemed an odd thing for him to do, and yet she felt
comforted by it. Damien joined her under the blanket,
drew her close against him and cradled her in the circle
of his arms. Surely he would try to make love to her
again, she thought, keeping her body rigid and her
guard up. Instead he stroked his long dark fingers
through her hair, leaned over and kissed her temple.

Finally she began to relax. Her emotions still in turmoil, eventually she fell asleep.

Damien awoke to the sound of the clock ticking loudly.
For a moment he strained to get his bearings. Where
was the ice-blue canopy that should have been above
him? Then he remembered he slept in his own bed this
eve . . . beside the woman who was his wife. His
body tightened to recall the way they'd made love, the
heat and the fury, the incredible way she had re-

sponded. He reached for her, wanting her again, needing her . . . only to find she had gone.

He sat upright in bed. Alexa wasn't in the room and
no sounds came from the room next door. The fire had
burned low, casting the walls with ominous shadows,
and small scurrying noises betrayed a mouse in the
walls. He climbed from the bed and pulled on his black
silk dressing gown, opened the door and stepped into
the hallway. Perhaps she was hungry and had gone
down to the pantry to find something to eat.

He assured himself that was so, smiling to think what
had caused such a craving for food, yet already his
unease had begun to build. She'd been more than a
little disturbed by what had happened between them.
Was she upset enough to have done something foolish?
What if she ran away? What if she tried to return to
England on her own?

His insides twisted even as he formed the thought.
He shouldn't have gone to her, shouldn't have taken
her, he knew, yet he'd wanted her as he had never
wanted a woman, and he had sensed that she'd wanted
him too.

He had known her conscience would rebel. At the
time, it did not matter. Her conscience be damned,
he'd thought then.

Now . . .

His worry grew as he descended the stairs and made
his way to the rear of the house, for no light came from
the kitchen. He should have left her alone, he silently
repeated, knowing it was the truth, but his need for her
had been strong, and deep inside he'd been angry.

Or perhaps it was only disappointment. Regret that
what she felt for him wasn't enough for her to set aside
her loyalties and accept him as he was.

Disappointment that she could not trust him.

Who was he kidding? He had no right to that trust—
he had done everything in his power to destroy it. Not

on purpose, at least not after they were married, but it had happened just the same. He had known it might, yet prayed he could avoid it. Now he wished for that trust with a need that ate at his soul.

Intensifying his search, Damien changed direction and walked purposefully back toward the main salon. At the door to his study he paused. Yellow light leaked from beneath the heavy wood, and the soft sound of weeping seeped out from within.

He wasn't sure whether to be relieved or upset. He knew without doubt it was Alexa. That it was she who wept, and that he was the cause. Taking a steadying breath, he opened the door and quietly stepped in. Alexa didn't hear his approach, curled up on the sofa as she was, her slender feet tucked up beneath her nightgown. She sat slumped over the end of the couch, her head resting in the cradle of her arms, her long auburn hair a dark crimson fall shielding most of her tear-streaked face.

Damien sat down beside her and gently eased her into his arms. "Don't cry, *ma chére,* there is no need for tears."

She didn't pull away, as he more than half expected, but accepted his embrace and continued to cry against his shoulder. "Please, Damien," she said, "please let me go home."

He drew back to look at her. Tilting her chin with his finger, he pressed a soft kiss on her lips. "If there was any way it could be done, *chérie,* you may be certain that I would arrange it." That was the truth and then some. She would be safe in England as she never would be here. "Unfortunately, General Moreau wants you to stay."

"I'm English. I don't belong here."

"You're my wife. You belong with me."

"If—If things were different, then maybe I would agree. Unfortunately, they aren't." She shifted, raised

tear-glazed eyes to his face. "You know the way I feel
. . . you know I cannot accept things as they are. You
know, and yet when I am with you, you make me forget what I believe in. You force me to . . . to . . ."

"To what, Alexa? Give in to your needs? Accept that
at least in some ways you still have feelings for me?"

"Yes!" she admitted, and it tore him apart to see her
anguished expression.

"You must hate me very much," he said softly.

She made a small sound in her throat. "I hate what
you stand for."

Damien stared over the top of her dark auburn head,
at the walls that surrounded them, the walls in a house
full of enemies, the walls that might have ears. He
wanted to ask how she felt about the man he was inside, but when had she ever had the chance to really
know him? Sometimes he didn't even know himself.

"You feel something for me; you've admitted that
much already. How would you feel if I were a loyal
Englishman? If I had never betrayed my country?"

Her eyes searched his face. There was pain in them
and uncertainty, a well of turbulent emotions. "If that
were the case . . . perhaps, one day . . . I would
love you."

His whole body tightened, the words slicing through
him, making him feel things, want things, he knew he
could not have. Bloody Christ, he knew better than to
say it. He knew that it was too dangerous, that in utter-
ing the words, he was putting both of their lives at risk,
and yet . . .

"I'm a spy, Alexa. I have been since my fifteenth
year. But it isn't France I spy for—it's England."

A strangled cry tore from her throat. Her green eyes
looked huge as she pulled away to look at him. "I don't
believe you. You—You're making this up. It's just another of your tricks."

"It isn't a trick."

"Bewicke would have known. Someone would have known." She leaned forward, her fingers biting into his shoulders. "Dear God, you can't expect me to believe this."

"Almost no one knows. It's dangerous for you to know. We're both being watched. It's insane for me to tell you, but when I see you like this . . ." He wiped away a tear that clung to her thick dark lashes.

"Do you know how much I want to believe you? Can you possibly imagine?"

"I know you have every reason not to, but—"

"Say it's the truth, Damien. Say this isn't just another of your lies."

"It's the truth, Alexa."

"Swear it. Swear it's the truth upon your father's grave."

He glanced at the walls. It was late—he prayed the servants were sleeping. "I swear it."

She reached out to him then, and he crushed her against him. He could feel her trembling, feel the dampness of her tears against his cheek. She clung to his neck and her long, silky hair seemed tinged with fire across his shoulder.

He held her like that as the clock ticked long minutes past, stroking her back, running his hands through her hair, happy just to hold her. Finally she pulled away.

"If what you say is the truth," she said with a look of despair, "then it is I who have betrayed you. Dear God, you've lost your home. You were beaten and thrown into gaol. You are here and in danger. You—"

"Hush," he soothed. "I didn't tell you this to upset you. I did it because I . . ." He glanced off in the distance, uncertain of what he had been about to say. "Because I can't stand to see you hurting."

"Damien . . ."

"I shouldn't have told you, but I did. Now it's your turn to swear." She stared at him blankly. "You must

swear that from this moment on, you'll say nothing
more about this. You'll act as if these words were never
spoken. I'll see you returned just as soon as I can, but
in the meantime we've got to be careful. If anyone dis-
covers the truth, neither of us will leave this country
alive."

Worry lines formed across her forehead. "Can't you
tell me a little bit more? Explain how—"

"No. I've said too much already. I want your promise, Alexa. Swear this subject is closed."

Uncertainty clouded her eyes, and endless unanswered questions. "I—I swear it."

He hoped he could believe her. He could almost see
her mind working, ideas forming, being discarded,
some of them making their way to the surface.

"Damien?"

"Yes, love?"

"Since now we are both on the same side, perhaps
there is a way I can help."

"For God's sakes, Alexa, your involvement in this is
the last thing I want."

She reached toward him, cupped his cheek in her
hand, and the warmth in her eyes made his chest grow
tight. "All right. I'll do whatever it is that you say."

He smiled at her softly. "There's just one last thing."

"Yes?"

"It's important our roles remain the same. Gradually,
we can adjust them, but we can't afford to make anyone suspicious."

"I can be a very good actress when I want to."

"I'm counting on it." He bent forward and kissed
her, a slow, lingering kiss that made his blood pound
hotly and desire burn once more through his veins. "In
the meantime, why don't we go back upstairs?"

Alexa nodded, and he took her hand, anticipating the
balance of the night they would share. He smiled, but
already he was regretting his actions. It wasn't like him

to take such chances, especially with a life besides his own. Damn, but the lady had a way of getting to him.

He hoped to hell it wouldn't wind up getting them killed.

Chapter Sixteen

TWO DAYS PASSED. THE KNOWLEDGE OF DAMIEN'S SECRET BUOYED ALEXA'S SPIRITS AND FILLED HER WITH HOPE. HER instincts had been right about him from the start. Damien was a hard man, but he had very good cause. In truth, there was more to her husband than even she had suspected.

Sitting in front of her mirror, brushing her long auburn hair, Alexa smiled. Damien was a patriot, not a traitor. A spy for England—not France. She wanted to shout her joy to the world, to thank God for the unbearable weight that had been lifted from her shoulders. She wanted to lie in bed with her husband for hours on end, to learn every inch of his sleekly muscular body. She wanted to rejoice with him, to show him how much she cared.

Instead she kept her expressions carefully bland, her feelings tightly controlled. Only in bed did she allow

her emotions free rein. Those heated moments were
alive with passion and wonder, times when the world
outside ceased to exist and for a few brief minutes both
of them were free of the dangers around them. On several occasions after they had made love, she started to
tell him about the man named Jules St. Owen she had
met at the Hotel de Ville, but each time the promise
she'd made held her back.

She had vowed not to broach the subject of his spying again, and she meant to keep her word.

And in truth, something deep inside kept her silent.
A tiny voice of caution that warned her to beware.

Perhaps it was in part a reaction to the role her husband continued to play, for most of the time and always
in the presence of others, Damien remained coolly reserved. He treated her much as he would one of his
mistresses—a fact that galled her, though she now believed she understood. She consoled herself with the
hope that they would soon be returning to England, to
home and safety and the life they had shared before all
of this had occurred.

She kept the thought fixed firmly in her mind that
night as they traveled to the Opéra. They were seeing
Cherubini's *Les Deux Journées,* along with Colonel
Lafon, M'sieur Celleries, and a captain of the hussars
named Francois Quinault.

Unfortunately, it turned out that Quinault was ac-
companied by the big-breasted actress, Gabriella Beaumont, Damien's former *cher amie.* All evening, the
voluptuous blonde rudely ignored her escort and flirted
outrageously with Damien, fluttering her hand-painted
fan and laughing as she whispered in his ear.

Sitting in the blue velvet armchairs in Lafon's private
box, Alexa told herself it did not matter. Damien wasn't
flirting back, and though he accepted the woman's
overtures as if it were his due, he laced his fingers pos-

sessively with her own as if he willed her to understand.

I do, she inwardly repeated. He is playing a role and I must play one too.

In the light reflected from the metal-backed lamps, Alexa suddenly smiled. If he could act his part, she could act hers too. Damien might not like it, but there were limits to what she was willing to endure. Pulling her fingers from his dark-fingered hand, she rose from her seat and turned to the small buxom blonde who sat at his side, next to Captain Quinault.

"Madame Beaumont," she said, eyeing the impertinent blonde from head to foot. "I realize you and Major Falon are extremely well-acquainted, but in case the fact has escaped you, he is now married to me. In the name of good taste, I ask that you please remove your hand from his leg."

The woman gasped and surged to her feet, her tiara tilting sideways atop her lavish coiffure. "How dare you!"

"I dare because it is my privilege to do so. Perhaps in this country a wife allows such a thing. Perhaps it goes unnoticed. In my country—"

"That's enough, Alexa," Damien cut in shortly, rising to his full height between them, but there was a trace of humor in his eyes and perhaps a hint of approval. "You will insult Madame Beaumont no further." He turned to Gabriella and bowed formally over her hand. *"Excusez,* madame. My wife is not usually given to such bursts of ill manners." He spoke once more to Alexa. "The performance is nearly at an end. Perhaps it is time we went home."

Alexa eyed the blonde with cool disdain. "Nothing would please me more." Ignoring the woman's gloating expression, she lifted her chin and strode regally from the room.

Damien said nothing as he led her outside the theatre

onto the Rue Richelieu, but in the shadows around the corner, he pulled her away from the crowd and up against the wall into the darkness. Alexa held her breath, awaiting his rebuke, but instead saw a corner of his mouth curve up and amusement sparkle in his eyes.

"Jealous, were you?"

She arched a dark auburn brow. "Perhaps. Then again, perhaps I was only acting."

"Were you?"

"That depends on why you encouraged the woman to behave as she did."

"Because it's what Lafon and the others would expect of me."

"And as an Englishwoman—and your wife—they would expect nothing less of me than to put such a scene to an end."

He laughed, a sound she hadn't heard in far too long. "I suppose that is true."

"Then you're not angry?"

In answer, he leaned forward and kissed her, his mouth claiming hers in a thorough taking that shimmered through her limbs and made her knees feel weak.

"No, *ma chére,* I'm not angry." In truth, he seemed glad that she cared enough about him to have done what she did. "Let's go home." The gruffness in his voice said exactly what his plans were, but the words stirred a different thought inside her.

She raised her eyes to his face. "I want to go home, Damien. I want that more than anything else in this world." But it wasn't a return to the house in the Faubourg St. Honoré that she meant, and her husband knew it. "When can we go back where we belong?"

A long finger stroked down her cheek. "I'll get you home just as soon as I safely can."

"What about you?"

"I can't return until I have something of importance

to give them. When this is over, my usefulness will be ended. I want to bring back something the British can use."

"But surely—"

"No more, Alexa. You gave me your word."

She said nothing else, just let him guide her round in front and help her into their carriage. As he settled his long frame back against the seat, Alexa leaned forward and kissed him. In seconds he was kissing her back, pulling her onto his lap and sliding his hands inside the bodice of her gown. He didn't stop until they'd reached the house, and then only for a moment.

They held hands on their way up the stairs, and once they reached their bedchamber, hurriedly dispensed with each other's clothes. They made love until three in the morning, then finally fell asleep.

Later that afternoon, Damien suggested a ride through the city, which suited Alexa perfectly, since the sky had cleared to an azure shade of blue and a breeze kept the temperature from being overly warm. Fewer carriages clogged the streets, more people, it seemed, deciding to enjoy the day and stroll among the gardens.

"Incredible, isn't it?" Damien said with obvious affection as he stared outside the carriage window. "Unlike anywhere else in the world."

She eyed him with some speculation. "I'm surprised that you like it. You never seemed to care for life in the city."

"Paris is different."

"Yes . . . I suppose it is. It must be difficult having your loyalties so divided."

His expression shifted just a little. "Loving so beautiful a city has nothing to do with my loyalties. Nor is that a subject that we should be discussing." He softened his words with a kiss. "Please, *ma chére,* this is difficult enough as it is."

Alexa merely nodded. There was so much she wanted to ask, so much she needed to know. Instead she kept silent, determined to keep her word.

The day passed in warm companionship. They strolled the Tivoli Gardens and luncheoned at the Café Godet in the Boulevard du Temple, a crowded place filled with soldiers in colorful cockaded hats and ladies eating ices and oranges. They walked the streets of the Palais Royale in the shade of low-branched plane trees, and near the corner of the block discovered a small traveling sideshow.

"May we go in?" Alexa asked excitedly, enthralled by the antics of a huge brown bear and a bare-chested gravel swallower performing for a small crowd out in front.

"If you like." Damien smiled with such warmth it took her breath away. "Though I have to admit there is something else I would rather be doing." He bent and kissed the side of her neck as he led her into the tent.

That night they made love, leisurely this time, since the day had been a long one. She felt sated and content that next day, and more hopeful about the future than she had been in weeks.

Marie Claire helped her dress and make her way downstairs, but Damien had already gone. There were a few things he needed for the general's house party they would be attending at week's end, he had told Pierre. As Alexa thought on it now, there were several things she needed as well. When she discovered that Damien had not taken the carriage, she vowed to make a quick trip to the small shop she had seen near the Rue des Petits Champs for a fan to match her blue and silver gown and an extra pairs of slippers.

"Do you wish for me to go with you?" asked Marie Claire.

"*Ah, non,*" Alexa replied, looking forward to a little time alone. "I will only be gone for an hour."

"At least let Claude-Louis drive you. Your husband will be angry if you go out alone."

Alexa easily agreed. She liked the sandy-haired man who was her husband's valet—she liked the entire Arnaux family. And being unfamiliar with the city, it would be comforting to have him along.

Her hour-long endeavor turned into three. The carriage was laden with boxes when she returned home, departing the conveyance out front, next to a coach she had never seen. It was a sleek black caleche, heavily trimmed in gold. Four matched blacks stood in harness, which, with the war going on and the shortage of horses, could only mean the rig belonged to a man of some importance.

She went into the house with no small amount of trepidation, wondering who their guest might be and hoping it boded good instead of ill.

Outside the main salon she paused. She could hear men's voices, but she wasn't about to go in. Still, she was suddenly determined to discover what went on. Two doors led into the room, one from the foyer, the second from a small informal drawing room off toward the rear of the house. Alexa made her way there.

The doors were closed but, to her relief, not snugly. It was easy to see through the crack, easier still to make out Colonel Lafon's tall lean profile, as well as that of a stout, dark-haired man with bushy brows and thick, curling side whiskers. Both of the men were in uniform, the shorter man wearing enough gold braid to light the room without candles.

"It is always good to see you, *mon general,*" Damien was saying, "but I'm beginning to think this isn't a social call."

"Hardly," Lafon put in, his bearing nearly as rigid as the general's. He held a glass of cognac, as did the other two men, but hadn't yet taken a drink.

"No, my dear Major, I am very much afraid it is not."

Tension rippled through the general's thick body. "Unfortunately, it is about a conversation you had in this house several nights past."

"Oh?" Damien arched a slashing black brow. "And just what conversation was that?"

"The one where you informed your lovely wife that you were a spy for the British."

Dear God in heaven. Alexa's nails dug into the palms of her hands. Damien's fears had not been unfounded. Sweet Lord, what would they do?

Terrified, she watched him through the door, his hesitation so slight she knew she had imagined it. A rich burst of laughter bubbled up from his throat.

"Clever, wasn't it?" Moving to the sideboard, he refilled the glass of cognac he cradled in a long-fingered hand, his grip not the least bit unsteady. "She was surly and ill-tempered before. Now she welcomes me into her bed. She's even jealous of my mistresses—Gabriella in particular. Isn't that right, Lafon?" He turned away from the colonel and looked the general square in the eye. "I said what the woman wished to hear. I didn't think I'd be expected to report my marital machinations to a general of the Grande Armée."

"You're telling us it was an act?" Lafon said, clearly incredulous, but no more stunned than Alexa.

Damien merely shrugged. "I thought it was a stroke of brilliance, myself, but as I said, I didn't expect my ruse to be reported to the Grande Armée."

The general eyed him a moment, carefully stroking his side whiskers. "We have known each other through very many years, *n'est ce pas?*"

"Very many years, *mon general*—and very many women."

A smile touched the general's lips. It turned into a grin, and then he burst out laughing. His barrel chest shook and his eyes crinkled up at the corners. "I should have known." More deep laughter, enough to

rattle the medals across his thick chest. "You never
cease to amaze me, *mon ami.*"

Alexa stood at the door in stunned silence. It's only
his way of protecting us, she thought wildly. Dear God,
it couldn't be the truth. Still, her chest ached and her
throat felt so tight she could not speak. She heard Lafon
join in the laughter, saw him shaking his head and
Damien chuckling softly. It was all too real. Too terribly, unbearably real.

She remembered the way he had manipulated her
from the beginning, his ruthless attempt at seduction,
then forcing her into an unwanted marriage. She
thought of the lies he had told, the lengths to which he
had gone for revenge, the threats he made against her
brother. She recalled the night he met with the French.
He had lied about that too, and later when he'd gone
into the city.

If he had been an English spy, why hadn't he told
her about it then? She remembered Jules St. Owen.
Surely General Wilcox would know the truth. Surely
someone would!

Dear God, she wanted so much to believe him.
Surely Damien would tell her about the men, she
thought with desperation, explain his words and prove
where his loyalties lay. Perhaps she should simply confront him, tell him what she had heard and ask him to
explain.

And he would, she was sure. Logically and sensibly,
and the fact remained it would not be the truth.

Alexa's stomach knotted; for a moment she thought
she might be sick. *You're a fool, Alexa,* a voice said
inside her. *You defend this man again and again. You
believe his lies when every particle of common sense
screams that it can't be the truth.*

*You believe he is the man you fell in love with,
when no such man exists.*

Fighting back tears, Alexa left the drawing room and

headed for her room upstairs. She felt battered and
bruised, used and abused and deceived. Dear God, she
was tired of being duped.

It was her fault, she knew, for wanting to believe in
him so badly. For seeing something inside him that
wasn't really there. Closing the door behind her, she
moved woodenly to the window and sat down in a
high-backed chair. Through a glaze of tears she stared
out into the garden, but it was only a colorful blur.

She had cried too much since her marriage, since the
night at the inn when her heart had first clashed with
Damien Falon. He had bested her time and again, and
yet she had not learned her lesson. She had been abducted, manhandled, shot, and sold into bondage, and
still she had not learned. She loved this man who was
her husband, and yet she had never really trusted him.
Was he using her again, or was he telling her the truth?

Alexa heard the front door close and jumped up from
the window seat. Dashing the tears from her eyes, she
checked her image in the mirror, turned and hurried
from the room toward the servants' stairs in the rear.

You've got to stay calm, she told herself, you've got
to at least pretend. Forcing herself to smile, she descended the stairs and hurried down the hall to the
door that led to the carriage house in the rear. She
opened the door and slammed it behind her, pretending she had only just come in.

"I'm home," she called out, approaching her husband in the entry, working to appear as if nothing were
wrong, praying he couldn't detect a trace of her tears.
Praying with all her heart and soul that he would tell
her about the men and convince her once more that
she was wrong. "Did you miss me?"

"Of course I missed you. I always miss you." He gave
her a smile as well, but she noticed a trace of tension
around his lips.

Alexa glanced toward the entry. "I thought I heard someone at the door. Did we have visitors?"

"Colonel Lafon and General Moreau stopped by."

"Wh-What did they want?" Hope rose. Her pulse leaped hard inside her chest.

He simply shrugged his shoulders. "Nothing much. The general wanted to be certain we'd be joining him in the country."

"I see." But her heart wrenched painfully and her stomach nearly rebelled. Tears burned behind her eyes. She quickly blinked them away and continued to smile. "I'd like to change, if you don't mind. My feet are beginning to hurt, and it's time I got out of these clothes."

"Perhaps I should help you." His eyes swept the length of her, then settled on the swell of her breast.

Alexa smiled but shook her head. "I've a bit of the headache, I'm afraid. I think I'll lie down for a while."

"If that is the case, then it's best that you do. Later, if you're up to it, Colonel Lafon has invited us to join his group at the theatre."

It took all of her will, but she nodded. "That sounds lovely. I'm sure I'll be fine by then." Damien kissed her cheek and she left him, forcing her unsteady legs to climb the stairs. As she reached the safety of her room, tears flooded her eyes and a wave of despair swept over her.

Lies. More and more of them, one of them heaped upon another.

What did you expect? came the voice in her head. *Even you can't be that big a fool.* Deceptions, deceit, a constant assortment of games. Dear God, she hated him for it!

Misery washed over her, weighing her down like a water-soaked skirt, sucking her under, leaving her drained and confused. Leaving *him* once more the victor, the man who would surface undefeated. Perhaps she should simply give in, let him win the game completely.

Perhaps she should simply succumb to despair, curl up in a tiny ball of misery and let matters run their course.

Alexa clamped her jaw, her mind crying out in denial, her resolve turning hard as something rebelled inside her. Her English blood perhaps, or simply her pride and her strong sense of will. She hurt deep down. Despair soaked into her very bones, disappointment and loss as harsh an enemy as she had ever known. Yet there was anger there, too.

Damn you. Damn you to bloody hell for the bastard you are! she thought, and in that moment, if she had owned a knife, she might have plunged it into his heart.

Stay calm, the little voice warned, *it is you who have everything to lose. It is you has suffered at this man's hands, you who will continue to suffer unless you do something about it.*

The voice was right, she knew. There had to be a way to redeem things, a means to save herself . . . a way to even the score.

Her mind began working, sorting through her thoughts, piecing them together then discarding them one idea after another and forming new ones again.

Alexa whirled toward the window, her heart leaping hard inside her chest. She needed an answer to her problem. Sweet God in heaven—suddenly she knew what it was.

Her fingers pressed against the window, her thoughts beginning to focus, the solution becoming crystal clear. Damien was a spy—a very successful one, it seemed. If his story had been true, his purpose in France would have been to gather information. He mingled with Napoleon's top advisers, with his generals and most trusted staff. He was invited into their homes, into their confidence, treated as a good and loyal friend.

He had access to a great deal of knowledge. Perhaps, if she were careful, she could gain access to it too. Alexa's heart pumped as her thoughts whirled and the last of her tears dried on her cheeks. Her blood was thrumming with new resolve, determination stirring, anger and resignation slipping away.

If Damien could do it, so could she. All she had to do was learn to control her emotions. He had played so many games, she finally lost count, and he'd won every hand. Her emotions had caused her defeat, the feelings he aroused in her, the need she believed she saw in his eyes whenever he looked at her. If she could learn to control those emotions, she could win.

Alexa moved from her place inside the door and began to pace the carpet. At week's end they would be attending the general's house party. Surely she could glean some useful information, something she could take back home.

Until then she would find a means to avoid him. An argument, perhaps, something that would anger him enough to stay away. For a moment she considered telling him what she had heard. Damien would be angry, furious that his deception would no longer work. He might stay away from her—then again, he might not. He'd have no reason to maintain his caring facade; he might simply take what he wanted. Worst than that, he would once more be on guard.

No, the truth here would not serve her. She needed a ruse, something that would keep him away from her bed and focus his attentions elsewhere from what she had planned.

Alexa took a long, courage-building breath. She would do whatever she had to and hope she would find some way to help her country. She would ignore the terrible pain, the throbbing ache of despair, ignore

the rending of her soul, so deep it nearly tore her in
two. She would shoulder her loss, steel every thread of
her being, and pretend not feel the heartache.

She would pray for God's help to lighten the load,
and pray that she heard from Jules St. Owen. Jules
would see her back to England. She would be safe at
last, and there would finally be an end to this terrible
nightmare.

Alexa thanked the Almighty and her own common
sense that she hadn't succumbed to her urge and given
the poor man away.

Chapter Seventeen

D AMIEN STEPPED OUT OF THE CARRIAGE IN FRONT OF GEN-
ERAL MOREAU'S CHÂTEAU IN ST.-GERMAINE-EN-LAYE, JUST
northwest of Paris.

Designed for le Duc de Torcy, the château stood four
stories high with two long colonnaded pavilions, one at
each end, and rows of high arching windows, each
with a small wrought-iron balcony. Dozens of tall brick
chimneys rose up through the steep slate roof, and
wide lawns beckoned guests toward the high carved
front doors.

"It's beautiful," Alexa said as Damien slid his hands
around her waist to help her down. "I wonder what
nobleman lost his head so that General Moreau might
own it."

"Alexa—" he warned, and a tight smile settled on
her lips.

"Sorry. We're guests here, aren't we? I'd almost for-

gotten." The smile remained in place, just as it had for
the past three days. His wife had been cool and reserved since the night they had gone to the theatre
with Lafon, her manner the result of a heated argument
involving Gabriella. Since that time, Alexa had been
pleading the headache, ignoring his advances, and gen-
erally keeping him an arm's length away.

At first he had humored her, allowing that she had
good cause. Gabriella had behaved outrageously,
openly approaching him in the lobby of the Theatre
Francaise as he stood next to Lafon and kissing him full
on the lips.

Unfortunately, Alexa had seen them. She had been
furious, and he could hardly blame her. He tried to explain, but she refused to listen, simply ignoring him
instead for the balance of the evening. At home they
had argued again, Alexa demanding that he put the
woman in her place, then leaving him alone and sleeping since then in the room next to his.

Her resentment of the woman was hardly a surprise,
yet he had begun to suspect the problem went deeper.
He sensed a tension between them that hadn't been
there before, an underlying desire to avoid him. He began to suspect that it wasn't just Gabriella, but Alexa's
feelings for him—or lack of them—that were keeping
her away.

Or perhaps it was the sea-captain-turned-wealthy-
merchant, Jules St. Owen, Alexa had met the night of
the ball at the Hotel de Ville. Damien had seen her
dancing with the man that evening, but at the time
he'd thought little about it. Then she had seen St.
Owen again at the Theatre Francaise, the damnable
man taking the seat right beside her.

Unconsciously, Damien's hold on Alexa's waist grew
tighter as he guided her up the wide stone stairs leading into the château. The blond man was handsome

enough to turn any woman's head, and it was obvious St. Owen had more than a passing interest in Alexa.

Damien watched the sway of her slender hips as she moved past footmen in the general's gold and crimson livery, the afternoon sun dancing like fire in her dark auburn hair. She was beautiful and incredibly desirable. Before they had married, half the men in London had thrown themselves at her feet, his brother Peter among them.

Perhaps she missed the attention. He had yet to know a woman whose interest could be captured for long. Perhaps she had already grown tired of him. Perhaps, like his mother, like the woman his sister Melissa had described and he had first believed Alexa to be, she fed on the attentions of other men. Perhaps she needed them to convince herself of her beauty and her charm.

Damien worked a muscle in his jaw. He would give her a little time, try to discover the truth, but whatever the reason for her rejection, she was his wife and she would remain so. For the first time, he understood his father's obsession with his mother. He had been willing to keep her, no matter the cost. It was a disturbing thought, one that made his insides feel cold and uncertain.

Yet far worse than that was the gut-twisting, mind-numbing rage he felt that his wife might seek the company of another man.

Her plan was working, and yet it was not easy. Damien was sullen and brooding, studying her with turbulent eyes, angry that they had argued and not quite sure of the cause. He was polite, of course, and in the presence of their host and hostess, he was charming. In their elegant suite of rooms, ivory and gilt with lavish Baroche, painted ceilings, he paced the carpet with angry strides, demanding she tell him the truth of what was wrong.

"I've told you what is wrong. You and that—that woman! I'm beginning to believe you are still carrying on with her. I wouldn't be at all surprised if you had invited her here!"

It wasn't too difficult a performance, since she merely had to remember the way she felt when she saw the woman kissing him. That, combined with the latest round of lies he'd told, was enough to enliven her temper and bolster her charade.

Damien raked a hand through his hair. "I've told you before, Gabriella is no longer my mistress. Why is that so difficult for you to believe?"

"You can ask me that after the way she behaved at the theatre?"

"I thought you understood. I thought—"

"Well, I don't understand, and I no longer wish to discuss it."

"Fine!" But he seemed even more confused as he stormed out of the room and slammed the door.

Alexa sank down on the bed. He'd seemed so troubled, as if her feelings really mattered. As if . . . Dammit, no! She would not play the fool for him again. Her course was set; she meant to do what she had to.

Several hours later she heard him in the room adjoining hers and knew he was dressing for the evening. She had been ready for some time, choosing the high-waisted, royal-blue satin gown with its silver underskirt, her hair swept into a heavy braided crown atop her head. A lady's maid had been summoned to help her. Now she merely stood waiting for her husband's knock at the door.

She heard it not long after, though he made no pretense of manners and simply strode in without permission. Dressed formally in a black swallow-tailed coat with a rolled velvet collar, he wore a silver waistcoat and tight-fitting black satin breeches. The white lace cravat at his throat enhanced the darkness of his skin, and his eyes had never appeared more blue, or, as he gave her a lengthy perusal, more undeniably hungry.

"You look beautiful." His hair looked nearly blue-black in the lamplight, his expression so sensual it made the heat creep into her cheeks.

Alexa steeled herself from the melting sensation that swept into her stomach. "I'm glad that you approve," she answered somewhat tartly. Dear God, why did he have to stare at her like that, with eyes that devoured her, with a look of longing and need and some other emotion she could not name.

"I had hoped that by now you would have come to your senses." His deep voice rang with disappointment. "Apparently you have not."

Alexa said nothing. It was hard to think of the proper reply when her heart was pumping so fiercely.

He reached out a long dark finger and ran it along her cheek. "If I really believed you were jealous, I might be flattered. I might even see it as a sign that your feelings for me have grown. Unfortunately, I do not believe that jealousy is what this is about . . . is it, Alexa?" His gaze searched her face, determined to seek out the truth. She was equally determined to hide it.

"I—I have no idea what you're talking about, but I do know we're beyond being fashionably late. It's the height of bad taste to keep our host and hostess waiting any longer."

Anger crept into the hard planes of his face. Tight lines marred his features, and his eyes seemed to glow from within. For a moment he said nothing, then stiffly he held out his arm and Alexa accepted it. She walked beside him down the wide marble staircase, trying to ignore the fury rippling through him, the tension she could feel in every muscle. How much longer could she avoid him and still carry on with her plan? A day or two perhaps. Damien wasn't a man to be thwarted for long. If she didn't leave France soon, he would demand a

return to her bed. Alexa's stomach clenched at the
thought, but with desire, not revulsion. Dear God, just
the notion of them making love made her insides swirl
and her stomach flutter with excitement. Images of
smooth dark skin and sleek male muscle danced along
the edges of her mind.

Beneath her hand, the sinews in his arm flexed as he
moved, and she imagined the feel of his long hard torso
above her. In her mind he was parting her legs, sliding
his hardness inside her.

A strangled sound slipped from her throat and he
glanced at her oddly. Her knees felt weak and she
started to tremble.

"What's the matter, *chérie?* You're not afraid of the
general, are you?"

"No, no, of course not." *It's not the general I fear,
it's you. And myself.*

"Then it's time we got on with the evening."

Alexa simply nodded, and Damien led her into the
Grand Salon. It was huge and imposing, with gilded
walls and golden candelabra, with mirrors and high
molded ceilings. The inlaid parquet floor had been
cleared, except for an array of gold brocade sofas and
high-backed chairs along the sides and rear, and a huge
marble-manteled fireplace stood at both ends.

"So, Major, at last you and your lovely wife have decided to join us."

"We would have been here sooner," Damien said
with a reckless smile, "but alas—with a lady such as
this in my quarters, it is easy to let time slip away."

Moreau chuckled deep in his chest, and she recognized him immediately as the man in her husband's
study. "I quite understand, *mon ami.* I was told that
your wife was a goddess—and indeed, in no way was I
misled." The general bowed over her hand, his dark
eyes taking in every curve then moving to her face
with blatant appreciation.

Alexa couldn't help wondering how many battles he had fought. A number, she would wager, for the man had the look of a well-seasoned soldier. How many times had he fought with the British—how many young Englishmen had he killed?

"How are you enjoying our country?" he asked. "I know your introduction to Paris was hardly as we would have liked, but those things happen, *n'est ce pas?*"

So he knew about her time at Le Monde. Had his spies informed him, or had her husband told him the story simply to amuse him?

"It's quite a lovely city," she replied with careful nonchalance. "There are, of course, parts I should prefer not to visit again." It hurt to think Damien might have told him the tale. She found herself searching for the answer in his face. "Like any big city, Paris has its share of undesirables."

She felt her husband's hand slide possessively around her waist. "From now on my wife will see only the good side of our beloved city." There was an undercurrent of tension in his words, and she realized he was silently warning Moreau not to pursue the subject. She sensed his protectiveness, and in that moment she knew he'd said nothing to the general or anyone else. A wave of gratitude slid through her and an almost unbearable yearning for him to hold her.

"I am certain, Major Falon, that your wife will grow to love our country just as you do." Moreau turned back to Alexa. "And now, Madame Falon, may I present my lovely wife, Lucile." A graying woman cut short her conversation with a woman dressed in black and smiled in her husband's direction. She was small and stately, with a slightly Roman nose and expressive slate-gray eyes.

"*Bonsoir,* Madame Falon," the woman said. "It is a pleasure to meet you."

"The pleasure is mine, Madame Moreau." They made conversation for a time, the general still taking Alexa's measure, then eventually they were excused from the powerful man's presence.

"I almost wish he weren't so impressed with you," Damien said as they walked away. "Perhaps he would send you back home."

Alexa made no comment. Was he eager to return her to safety, or did he simply wish to be free to return to his mistresses? Half of her longed to be gone while, oddly enough, the other half wished to remain.

For the first time since she had escaped Le Monde, she thought of her home near Hampstead Heath and felt a wash of homesickness. Had Rayne received word of her abduction? If he hadn't, he very soon would, but they couldn't have yet returned to England. She was certain that would happen, just as soon as they learned what had occurred.

Once it did, if St. Owen failed her and she was still here, Rayne would press the government to arrange for her release or to make a trade of some sort. She would get home one way or another. Damien would be gone from her life, though the heartache would remain. Perhaps she would have discovered something of value to take with her, some piece of useful information. Something to make the hurting less in vain.

As they made their way beneath the gilded candelabra, listening to the strains of the orchestra, Damien continued his introductions, meeting and greeting the fifty odd people who were also guests at the château. Alexa listened carefully, working to remember each name as they chatted politely. The men often talked of the war, discussing an article that appeared in the *Moniteur* or the *Courrier Francaise,* frequently adding small but possibly significant details.

They spoke of the Emperor's Austrian campaign, and she learned that at Wagram, the price of French victory had been extremely costly. It was hardly the triumph she had read in the papers. In truth, the Grande Armée had paid a goodly amount in blood.

They spoke of English troop movements, and her interest piqued even more. Just three days earlier, she learned, the British had disembarked at Walcheren. Though the news had not yet reached the papers, it had stirred quite a fervor in the government, and was apparently the reason M'sieur Fouchet, Minister of Police and acting Minister of the Interior, had not been able to attend the gathering.

Alexa kept them talking whenever she could, guiding the conversation yet careful to remain nonchalant. If Damien had truly been working for the English, she could easily see how valuable he would have been.

She turned to see him glaring down at her. "I'm glad that you are enjoying yourself," he said with some annoyance, since little of the conversation had been directed at him.

"Now that I've accepted my . . . visit here in France, I thought I might as well make the best of it."

"I would agree wholeheartedly—if you also accepted your duties to me."

"My duties to you? What about your duties to me?"

"Alexa—" but she only turned away, smiling sweetly, and continued to converse with the guests she'd just met.

They were surprisingly friendly, she discovered, perhaps because she was there at the general's insistence and somewhat under his protection. Perhaps simply because she spoke such fluent French.

Whatever the cause, it made her task all the easier. She had already learned a great deal about Paris itself; most surprising, the keen personal interest Napoleon had taken in the city's development, everything from paving the streets to sewer systems and waterworks, hospitals, schools, fountains and gardens.

The aqueduct in the Rue St. Denise had been built at his insistence, as well as an orphanage called La Pitie. There were temples and monuments, of course, but most were dedicated to the men who had sacrificed their lives in the war and not to Napoleon himself.

On that subject, in these surroundings at least, she heard only praise for him. Several of the women spoke in whispers of Josephine and the emperor's marital discord. There was talk of a possible divorce, a rumor she had heard before, though she hadn't believed Napoleon would actually go through with it. Now she wasn't so sure.

"Do you really think he would divorce her?" she asked.

Damien frowned. "Almost certainly he will."

"Marriage must mean very little in this country," she said, feeling an unwelcome pang.

"The emperor wants an heir. Desperately. He is willing to go to any lengths to achieve that end. Even giving up the woman he loves."

Surprise touched her features. "You believe he loves her?"

"Yes. I believe in the end their relationship will continue, whether there is a marriage between them or not."

Alexa watched him closely. She couldn't decide if Napoleon was a worse scoundrel than she had imagined, or only far more human.

Alexa continued through the crowd, Damien walking beside her. The hand he rested at her waist felt oddly possessive, then his long slim fingers went tense. Near the corner of the room, just a few feet away, Jules St. Owen stood with a drink in his hand.

The handsome blond man moved toward them. "Good evening, Major."

"St. Owen. You remember my wife, Alexa, of course."

"A man would have to suffer a fever of the brain to forget so lovely a creature." He bowed formally over her hand, and Alexa felt her face go warm at the look of pleasure she saw in his sky-blue eyes.

"I'm certain he would," Damien said dryly. His own eyes had turned a piercing shade of cobalt, a shimmering, stormy color that held a note of warning—and some other turbulent emotion he worked to hide.

They spoke for a time, then St. Owen excused himself and bowed once more over her hand. Beneath her fingers she felt him press a note into her glove, and her fingers curled tightly around it.

"Adieu, madame." He smiled at her, and she forced a smile in return.

"Bonsoir, M'sieur St. Owen. It is always good to see you." As discreetly as possible, she stuffed the note into her reticule, then later read it quickly while Damien went to fetch her a glass of punch.

La bibliothèque, it simply read. The library. Alexa started to tremble. She didn't know where the room was, but she could find out. If only she could somehow slip away.

"Your punch, my love," Damien said, his cool gaze sliding over her, looking to decipher her thoughts.

What was *he* thinking, she wondered, and how could she possibly steal away? But her prayer was shortly answered when one of the servants arrived, carrying a small silver salver. A note for Damien rested in the middle. He picked it up and scanned the contents.

"I'm afraid I'm being summoned by our host. I shall leave you in the company of M'sieur Cretet's wife, Jacqueline." She had met the minister's wife earlier in the evening, and they had conversed with ease. "I'm sure I won't be long." When Alexa merely nodded, Damien leaned over and kissed her cheek. "I'll be back just as soon as I can," he said softly, and then he was gone.

Alexa watched his tall frame passing through the

crowd and something stirred inside her. Dear God, the
man could affect her with only the slightest glance. He
was impossible to figure, impossible to trust, and
yet . . .

What was it about him that always left her in turmoil? She would never understand her feelings for him
—never!

With Damien gone from the salon, she excused herself from Madame Cretet and made her way toward the
ladies' dressing room upstairs. Long before she got
there, she rid herself of the note and discovered the
location of the library from one of the servants.

Jules St. Owen was waiting when she walked in.

"Close the door," he instructed softly, and she made
all haste to do so.

Crossing the magnificent book-lined chamber, she
nervously approached where he stood between the
narrow rows stacked floor-to-ceiling with leather-bound
volumes. Above their heads majestically carved gilded
ceilings arched above frosted-glass chandeliers, and a
number of rosewood desks, each with a small glass-
shaded lamp, formed a line down the center of the
room.

"I have come as you wished, M'sieur St. Owen, but
this time you must tell me why it is you've decided to
help me. It is the only way we can go on."

"First I would know if returning to your home is
what you want."

"If you are asking do I wish to leave my husband
. . . the answer is . . . yes." Even as she said the
words, something twisted inside her. "Too much has
passed between us." *Too much misery and not
enough love.* "And there is a war going on."

He made a slight inclination of his head, his golden
hair gleaming in the lamplight. Reaching inside his
coat, he pulled a small wax-sealed enveloped from the
breast pocket. St. Owen handed her the letter, and she

recognized the seal as belonging to the British Army. She hurriedly broke it open and began to read. Quickly scanning the words, she glanced up when she was through.

"As I told you before," the blond man said, "I am not a spy. I am merely a loyal Frenchman doing what he believes is right for his country."

" 'Right.' I've begun to wonder what in God's name right really is."

"There are times I feel much the same, but a man is often forced to take a stand."

She handed him back the letter, an introduction of St. Owen from General Wilcox and an urgent plea that she place herself in the man's capable hands. "Exactly what is your stand, M'sieur St. Owen?"

"To be frank, Madame Falon, my beliefs—and those of a number of others—are no longer the same as those of our beloved Emperor. Though I dare not speak out in public, there are other things I *can* do, and helping you is one of them."

"I'm afraid I still don't understand."

"It is quite simple, really. There are men in your government, men like General Wilcox, who have known for some time that I am dedicated to ending the war. They have asked me to help you, and in doing them this favor, my ties with them are strengthened. Perhaps in time, with our continued mutual efforts, our countries' disagreements may come to an end. If that should occur, we can stop this carnage the Emperor calls the glory of war."

"So you would have peace?"

"Yes."

"At what price?"

"Not at the price of French honor, if that is what you are implying. But I believe it can be done."

Alexa studied him with speculation. He appeared to be forthright and loyal, a determined man who was exactly what the general's letter had said. A man she believed she could trust. "How? How can you help me?"

"I was a ship's captain for quite a number of years. I can arrange things, see you returned in much the same manner you arrived. During the dark of the moon two weeks hence, a small boat will be sailing from Le Havre. You will have to leave the city several days before then, of course, make your way from Paris to Rouen, then go north. I will see you safely as far as the coast. The boat will set sail from there, and the following day you will be home."

Home. The word made her heart squeeze up inside her. Dear God, how she wanted to go home! Gratitude swelled for this man who would risk his life to help her. Her thoughts veered for a moment to another man who had once done the same. The tall, dark, enigmatic man who was her husband. The stranger she still loved no matter how hard she tried not to. She imagined never seeing him again, never touching him, and her heart felt leaden with despair.

Don't be a fool, the voice said. *You have no choice and you know it.* "You say you came because of the men in my government. Has General Wilcox or any of those men ever mentioned my husband?"

"In what regard?" he asked, his light eyes probing.

"Is it possible . . . is there any chance at all that he is not an English traitor? That perhaps he is working for his homeland?"

St. Owen's manner softened. *"Je suis de sol, chérie.* I am sorry to say this, but I am very much afraid that your husband is a man whose loyalties run only so deep. In a way, that is what has made him so valuable. It is also the reason that he is watched so closely."

"Your government pays him well, I gather. Perhaps the English have offered him an even greater sum."

"I do not think so. From what I have learned, he has been working for us for some time."

"But you can't be sure."

"I can only say what I believe—what General Wilcox has told me—your husband has been spying for France."

A hard knot tightened in her throat. Perhaps if he had done it for more than just the money, if he had been a loyal Frenchman working for his cause, she might have been able to forgive him. She looked at St. Owen and started to say something else, but a sound at the door interrupted them.

"You will hear from me again," Jules said softly even as he turned to walk away. He was halfway down the narrow aisle when she heard her husband's deep voice cutting harshly into the silence.

"She is here, is she not?"

"Mais oui, I chanced upon her, yes. We spoke only briefly."

"I ought to call you out."

"I would decline, Major Falon, for as you can see, there is no cause for your concern." Alexa stepped from the shadows. "Do not insult your lovely wife with groundless accusations."

She was grateful now for her well-groomed appearance—every hair in place, her cheeks pale except for the light dusting of rouge she had applied up in their suite, her lips as untouched as they were when her husband had left her.

"I was tired," she said. "I merely wandered in, seeking respite from the crush. M'sieur St. Owen came in search of something to read." Even she was surprised when he held up a small red leather volume.

"Les Dangereuses," St. Owen said. "I assure you, my friend, this is all the seduction I had in mind."

Damien bowed formally. "My apologies—to you both."

He waited for St. Owen to leave, then walked to the door and set the lock into place behind him. The noise of the brass key turning grated harshly in the silence of the room. Alexa wet her lips as he moved toward her, his pantherlike strides carrying him with an ominous grace that spoke of some deadly intent.

"It is evident the man did not touch you. The question remains—did you want him to?"

Alexa shook her head. "No," she said with some conviction. "I didn't want him to."

"Perhaps you did." Icy control dripped from each word, and she realized just how angry he was. "Perhaps you were craving a man's touch—needing it the way you once did mine."

"Damien, please—"

"Perhaps *this* is what you wanted—" He cupped her face between his palms, his thumbs beneath her chin, forcing her head back. Then he bent and took her mouth in a savage kiss. It was reckless. Brutal. Punishing. Yet underlying the fierceness there was something far more urgent. He took her with his tongue, claiming her in a roughly intimate fashion that spoke of possession, but his hands trembled against her cheeks, and she was utterly undone by the longing in his eyes and the desire that rippled through his powerful body.

"Damien . . ." Need seemed to swell between them, and an incredible yearning that throbbed like a wound in her heart. She found her hands in his hair, her nipples hard and pressing into his chest. She wanted to tear the buttons from his shirt, to pull it open and run her fingers across his hard-muscled chest. She wanted to feel him naked above her, pressing her into the carpet at their feet.

Damien must have read her thoughts, for he was forcing her backward, up against the wall of books until her bottom pressed into the leather-bound volumes. Gripping the hem of her skirts, he slid the blue and silver fabric up her thighs, then lifted her thin chemise.

Another ravaging kiss, his mouth molded hotly over hers, his tongue claiming, mating, relentless.

"Part your legs," he commanded.

"Damien, dear God . . ."

"Do it, Alexa. You know it's what you want."

Her limbs were trembling, barely able to hold her up. She eased her legs apart, opening to him, and he knelt between them, propping his arms on the walls at her sides, her skirts gathered up in his fists. Damien kissed the flat spot below her navel, ringed it, bent and kissed the inside of her thighs, laving a damp trail of fire along her flesh.

Heat rippled through her, a fiery wave that torched her blood and weakened her limbs, made her nipples pucker and tighten. His mouth teased the petals of her sex, tasting her, ravishing her in a way she couldn't have imagined. He parted the soft folds with his tongue and pressed a hot kiss on the small bud hidden between them.

She moaned when his tongue sank inside her, trembled at the heat of his mouth on so intimate a part of her body. She could feel the warmth of his breath, and talons of heat seared through her.

"Damien . . ." she whispered, barely able to force out the word, her body shaking and on fire for him. "Sweet God . . ." Unconsciously, a hand slid into his hair while her fingers dug into his shoulder.

Her skin seemed to burn with heat, white-hot tendrils licking upward from the core of her, flames leaping, making her spin out of control. He suckled the tight bud gently, then again plunged inside her with his tongue.

Alexa cried out as her body went rigid then spiraled into climax. Great shudders ran through her, spasms of pleasure, splinters of heat that blotted her surroundings, had her writhing against him, then left her boneless and numb.

When she opened her eyes, Damien was unbuttoning his breeches.

"Tell me you want me."

There was no hesitation. "I want you." He took her savagely, there against the wall, filling her with his long, hard length, driving into her again and again. He captured her mouth and kissed her, a deep thorough kiss that rekindled her need and drove her again toward the chasm of pleasure. She pressed her hands against his chest and felt a rippling in the wide bands of muscle, felt his incredible strength.

She spun out of control a second time, the pleasure bursting free, soaring through her, the incredible scorching heat. She felt caught up, lifted like a flower by unseen winds then scattered like petals upon the sand. Damien followed her to climax, his powerful body tensing, muscles flexing and tightening, shuddering again and again as he filled her with his seed. He bowed his head and rested it a moment on her shoulder, let go of her skirts, and slowly they slipped downward, along her trembling legs.

"Do you really believe St. Owen can make you feel that way?" he finally said, easing himself from inside her. He adjusted his clothes and her own, then buttoned up his breeches, his gaze never leaving her face. "I don't think he can."

Dear sweet God, she had never seen him look that way, his beautiful blue eyes so turbulent, so filled with unhappiness and longing. They spoke of incredible need and great depths of passion. How could that be, in a man with such iron control?

Silently he turned and walked away, his back perfectly rigid, his shoulders squared, though she noticed a hint of defeat in his long-limbed, smoothly graceful strides.

She meant to let him go. There was nothing to be said, and even if there were, what good would it do?

She meant to let him go, and yet . . .

"Damien!" He paused at the door, but he did not turn. "Jules St. Owen means nothing to me. There has never been any other man for me but you." Her voice broke on this last, and Damien went stock-still.

He reached for the door with hands that were suddenly unsteady. Turning the key then gripping the handle, he pulled it slowly open and stepped out into the hall. The door closed softly behind him.

Alexa stood there trembling. Her heart felt ravaged. Her stomach was tied in knots and her mind so numb she could barely think. Still, she did not regret her words. Whatever the outcome, she had told him the truth.

Since the very first moment she had seen him, tall and bronzed and standing alone in the garden, there had never been another man for her. She knew there never would be.

And there were enough lies between them.

It was Damien's choice whether or not to believe her. She knew only too well what it felt like to live day-to-day with the pain of uncertainty and distrust.

Chapter Eighteen

STANDING IN AN ALCOVE NEAR THE WINDOW, DAMIEN WATCHED THE DOOR TO THE LIBRARY UNTIL ALEXA OPENED it and fled down the hall. He relaxed a little as he watched her climb the stairs, making her way to their plush suite of rooms, safe from wagging tongues and prying eyes.

He felt odd inside, strangely unnerved by what had occurred. He rarely lost control, but with Alexa it had happened more than once. He'd been out of control tonight—way out—the moment he discovered her missing. And then when he'd found her . . .

Jules St. Owen was lucky to be alive.

Damien sighed as he stepped out onto the terrace. She wasn't involved with St. Owen—at least the man wasn't her lover. He'd known that the moment he kissed her, was sure of it by the time they finished making love.

And in truth, she had never given him cause to believe that she would be unfaithful. What had happened was his fault, not hers.

Bloody Christ. Thinking of the damnable way he had handled things between them, he slammed his fist against the rough stone wall. He should have trusted her, yet for him trust didn't come easy. His father had trusted his mother, but she had abused it. Damien had trusted her, and she abandoned him. He had wanted to trust his grandmother, after he had been sent to her in France.

But Rachael and Simone were a pair. Like mother like daughter, he had often thought. She treated him more like a servant than a grandson, taking the birch rod to him whenever he did something wrong, never satisfied with any of the tasks he completed. Damn, but he'd grown to despise her. If it hadn't been for Fieldhurst, he might have refused to return.

Damien drew out a slim cigar, clamped it between his teeth, leaned toward one of the torches lighting the path to the garden and dragged in a deep puff of air. Fieldhurst had been his salvation, he thought, exhaling a thin plume into the clear night sky. He recalled their first meeting, on his fifteenth birthday on a similar night at Waitley, his stepfather's country estate near Hampstead Heath.

Fieldhurst had been an acquaintance of Lord Townsend's. The major was a stalwart, serious man as steeped in British tradition as a strong cup of tea. With his uncompromising loyalty and unyielding determination, he reminded Damien of his father, and he liked the man almost from the start.

Surprisingly, Fieldhurst seemed to like him. They went hunting together the following day, each of them bagging a nice fat grouse. The major, as Anthony Fieldhurst ranked at that time, had given him the idea of providing information, nothing complicated at first, just keeping his eyes open while he was in France, then reporting anything of interest that he might have heard.

That was in 1794. The year he had watched Robespierre and St. Just march up the steps to the guillotine. Danton and Desmoulins lost their heads—there were dozens in all—and his grandmother had insisted they attend a goodly number of the bloody executions. The first time he had seen one, he had run from the crowd and retched into the shrubbery. His grandmother had laughed and called him a coward. He had steeled himself after that, but the sight continued to disgust him, and he had never forgotten.

It was a driving force in the commitment he made to Fieldhurst the year he turned twenty-one. That was the year Napoleon advanced into Syria, the year the Little Corsican defeated the Turks at Abukir.

All the while, Damien had been pretending his loyalty to France, building his growing number of contacts in Paris—not so difficult a task, considering Simone's second husband had risen quite high in the government.

That was also the year he made the deal with General Moreau.

The deal to sell British secrets to the French.

Except that the secrets he sold them came directly from England's Minister of Defense, and were strictly used to mislead them. Fieldhurst, by then a colonel; William Pitt, the Younger; and King George himself, were the only ones who knew. Pitt was now dead and the king rarely lucid. General Fieldhurst was his only contact now.

Damien propped his back against the wall of the terrace and stared out into the garden. He could almost imagine Alexa standing at the opposite end, her dark copper hair reflected in the glow of the lanterns, her beautiful green eyes flashing as she watched him walking toward her.

He shouldn't have married her. The thought had occurred a thousand times. Yet he wouldn't have missed a single moment of the days they had spent together, and if it weren't for the danger he'd unwillingly placed her in, he knew he would never let her go.

Damien didn't come back to their rooms, and part of Alexa was glad. The other part tossed and turned and wondered where he might have gone.

And just who might be with him.

She wasn't naive enough to have missed the heated glances that passed his way from some of the women. But surely after they had made love—the intimate way he had taken her—he wouldn't have need of another woman. Alexa's face grew warm at the memory, and yet she couldn't be sure.

In the morning, she paced her bedchamber then stopped in front of the high-paned, silk-draped window to scan the meadows beyond the château. She wouldn't see her husband at least until nightfall. Most of the men had gone hunting, Damien among them. Perhaps it was just as well. It would give her a chance to gain control of her emotions, to put things back in perspective and decide what she should do.

And she would have a chance to explore the château and spend a little more time with the guests. Who knew what secrets they might reveal?

The day passed far more quickly than she had imagined, the women friendly if somewhat reserved, the general's wife giving her the acceptance she needed. Except for Damien and the uncertainty that lingered between them, the afternoon passed pleasantly, and in the hour before sunset she discovered something intriguing.

In the west wing, the family wing, she located the

general's study. The door was open, but she didn't dare enter, not with so many people around. Still, she could see his massive rosewood desk, its leather top scattered with official-looking papers. Better yet was the desk itself, for she had seen one like it before—in Rayne's study at Stoneleigh. Her father had shown her its secret compartment when she was a little girl. There were only a handful like it, he had said, constructed by Farrier, one of the greatest furniture makers in France.

Yes, she remembered it well, and this one looked exactly the same. Rayne kept his most important papers in the secret compartment.

What would a general keep in there?

It was certainly worth a look, she decided as she readied herself for supper and the lavish entertainment scheduled for the evening. Damien had finally returned and was even now dressing in his room. He hadn't said much, had seemed to be surprisingly subdued. Perhaps he was regretful of what had occurred, but with a husband who rarely spoke his thoughts, she figured she would never know for sure.

She heard him enter even before she saw him, turned to find him standing in the doorway in a perfectly tailored pearl-gray tailcoat. His immodestly snug black breeches reminded her of his manly attributes, and a ripple of heat slid into her stomach.

"Ready?" he asked, surveying her with a look of approval. "You look lovely . . . but then you always do."

She walked forward and accepted his arm. "Thank you."

"About last night," he said, surprising her, "I'm . . . sorry for what happened. I'm sorry for a lot of things. I shouldn't have lost control."

She lifted her eyes to his face, searching the hard planes and valleys, her heart thudding softly. "Why did you?"

For a moment he said nothing. "I was jealous." He

tried to appear nonchalant, but a flush rose up his throat, darkening the skin above his cravat. She had never seen him look quite that way. "St. Owen is a handsome man, and he's obviously taken with you."

She tried to avoid feeling pleased that he should care. "I meant what I said—Jules St. Owen means nothing."

"What about me?" Deep blue eyes searched her face. "What do I mean to you, Alexa?"

She nervously moistened her lips. Everything, and nothing at all. For nothing was all the feeling for him that she could allow herself. Yet even to think it would have been a lie. "You—You're my husband."

He nodded and his face closed up once more, but not before she glimpsed his disappointment. "It's time we joined the others," he said.

"Yes." Dear God, what did the man expect of her? Whatever it was, she couldn't afford to give it to him.

They made it through supper, both of them smiling, making conversation, almost maddeningly civil. How could he say so much with his eyes and so little in words? How could his gaze say one thing while his deeds said something else entirely?

Alexa had an overwhelming urge to leap up from the table and run from the room. She wished she could snap her fingers and arrive back in England, clap her hands and return to the time before she had met him, a time before Peter's death, before the months of guilt and self-loathing, a time when she had been innocent and carefree, nothing but a foolish, dreamy-eyed young girl.

You're just tired, she told herself. You've been mired in intrigue for so long you don't know which way to turn. But she did know what she had to do.

And several hours later the perfect opportunity arose. Damien was ensconced with the general and a small group of men, while she conversed with several of the women. Eventually she was able to slip away.

Lifting her gold silk skirts up out of the way, she circled the drawing room and headed for the west wing. There was no one around, just a well-meaning servant here and there, and no one at all in the corridor outside the general's study.

Careful to stay in the shadows, her heart beating madly, she eased open the door and peeked in. Again seeing no one, she quickly went inside and closed the door.

It was dark in the high-ceilinged room. She tripped on the fringe at the edge of the carpet and nearly went sprawling, caught herself and continued on unsteady legs to the wall at the opposite end. Her pulse was pounding; a buzzing of fear filled her temples. Dear God, if they found her in here . . .

With trembling hands she opened the heavy damask curtains behind the desk enough to let in a crack of moonlight, carefully set aside ink stands and sand shakers, and began a careful search of the paperwork lying on the dark green leather insert. She found nothing of interest, mostly supply requisitions and a stack of daily orders. She fumbled beneath the desk, searching for the tiny wooden lever that released the door to the hidden compartment.

It wasn't where she thought it would be. She checked several inches to the left and again to the right, all the while listening for a sound at the door, her heart hammering plaintively against her ribs. Frustrated, just when she thought to give up, her fingers found a crack in the smooth wooden surface.

Alexa smiled in triumph. The desk was even more finely crafted than her brother's, the lever so perfectly concealed it was nearly impossible to find. She tugged on it gently, heard the release of the small brass catch, eased her hand away and pulled open the drawer in the middle. She felt along the seam at the rear and pressed on it firmly. The compartment silently slid open.

Alexa probed inside. The walls were smooth, the compartment mostly empty. Then her fingers brushed a rolled-up tube of paper. It felt like a scroll of some sort, but longer and several layers thick. She hurriedly removed it and rested it on the top of the desk.

Untying the tiny gold ribbon around it, she unrolled the papers and realized they were plans of some sort. As she hurriedly scanned the document, her heartbeat kicked up even more.

Sweet God in heaven. Frantically, she began to turn the pages, then a sound marked the opening study door.

"Damien—" She tensed as he closed it softly behind him, her hands beginning to tremble at the long, purposeful strides carrying him to her across the room. In the moonlight slanting toward him, she could see his harsh features, and fury darkened every one.

"You little fool," he ground out. Rounding the desk, he grabbed the plans from the table. Behind him the door flew open once more, lamplight flooding in with the sound of heavy boots. Damien's hand came down hard across her cheek and Alexa hit the floor with a whimper.

"What the hell do you think you're doing?" he demanded, towering above her, his body fraught with tension, his hands balled tightly into fists. He turned at the general's approach and handed the stout man the long roll of papers.

"I'm sorry, General Moreau. I hardly know what to say. A servant told me she was in here. When I walked in, I found her rifling through your desk." Damien sighed and shook his head. "We both know my wife is a patriot. Unfortunately, her loyalties belong to those who oppose us."

The general took the plans from his hands as Alexa climbed unsteadily to her feet.

"Mais oui, so it would seem," he said tightly. Only

the muscle ticking in his cheek put the lie to his careful control. He stroked his curly brown side whiskers. "And it would also seem we have underestimated her once again."

He turned a hard look on Alexa, who lifted her chin, but inside she was shaking. Her cheek stung, her eyes burned with unshed tears, and worst of all, her heart ached unbearably.

"You are brave, my bold little Belle Anglaise," the general said, "but more than a little foolhardy. What should I do with you, I wonder?"

Sweet God, what would *he do?* Damien's face was set in taut, unreadable lines. Anger was all she could decipher. He said nothing in her defense, and she wondered if he worried about his own fate as well.

"Tell me, *mon ami,*" the general said to him, "does your pretty little wife still please you?"

A sleek black brow arched up. He eyed her and a corner of his mouth curved into a lecherous smile. "Take a look at her, *mon general.* Have you ever seen a riper temptation? I'll grant you she can be impertinent. Headstrong and willful—a handful for the strongest man." His hand lightly skimmed across her breast. "But she is a fiery little piece in bed. It could take a man months to get his fill."

The general chuckled without mirth. There was an edge to his voice, and his eyes held a subtle command. "It would hardly heighten French moral should we appear threatened by one small Englishwoman. For the time being, your wife's . . . indiscretion will remain between the two of us. However, I would suggest in the future you keep her more firmly in hand."

"You may rely on it, sir." Damien gripped her arm and dragged her close against him. "Beginning tonight," he said harshly. "With your permission, General Moreau, I would like to return to Paris." He smiled sardonically. "I have several lessons in mind for the lady's misconduct. The next time you see her, I promise you she will be the height of the well-behaved young woman."

Alexa shivered at his words. Moreau just nodded. "See that she is."

Victor Lafon watched Damien Falon drag the woman from the room. The major's face was set in stone.

His wife looked as proud and defiant as she had that foggy morning Victor had dragged her from his tiny sailboat on the beach near Boulogne. He remembered it only too well, for as much as he despised her betrayal, he admired her for the courage it had taken to do it.

He wondered what she had done now.

He knocked on the door to the general's study, and the man's raspy voice commanded him to come in.

"Colonel Lafon," the general said, cigar smoke drifting up from where he sat behind his desk. "Come in."

"I saw Major Falon leave your study. He seemed to be rather at odds with his wife."

Moreau stared at him glumly. "His little Belle Anglaise may prove more than our major can handle. We discovered her in here, breaking into my desk."

"*Nom de Dieu,*" Victor said.

"Exactly so, *mon ami.* That one bears watching, *n'est ce pas?*"

"I am sorry to say—they both do."

Moreau just nodded. "And you have seen to this, yes?"

"Almost since the moment the major's wife arrived."

"Good." Moreau sighed. He studied his cigar, watching the thick plume swirl toward the ceiling. "It is a sad thing, war . . . but the saddest of all is not knowing who one's enemies are."

Victor glanced toward the door. "That is true, General Moreau. If the major turns out to be one of them, it is only a matter of time until we find out. The woman will give him away, or his concern for her, or both. Should that unfortunate happenstance occur, I assure you, our people will know."

"You are a good man, Victor. Let us hope Major Falon's loyalties run half as deep as your own."

Partly relieved and equally frightened, Alexa let her husband drag her up to their lavish suite of rooms. He said not a word as he ordered the maid to pack their clothes, nothing as he led her firmly down the stairs and out in front to their waiting carriage.

Once they left the château, his anger seemed to slowly slip away. As the journey wore on, his tension gradually eased and his posture became less stiff. He tilted his head back against the leather seat of the carriage, but his expression remained lost in the shadows.

As for Alexa, she felt worse by the moment. The documents she had found had been beyond just important. They were imperative. Crucial. But she had failed to get them.

Her mission had not succeeded, yet somehow that *other* seemed far worse. In all her life, no one had ever raised a hand to her. Perhaps they should have, her father or Rayne, or perhaps when she was younger, her mother or her older brother, Chris. She had often been impetuous. She was stubborn to a fault and too often spoiled. But they had simply indulged her. They had loved her far too much to hurt her.

Unlike the man who was her husband.

Even now her cheek stung from the blow he had delivered, and thinking of the rage that had darkened his handsome face, Alexa's stomach knotted at what might yet occur. She closed her eyes against a vision of him towering above her, talking about her as if she were nothing but another of his strumpets. Tears welled up, and though she closed her eyes in an effort to keep them from falling, they seeped from beneath her lashes, forming hot damp trails toward the small cleft in her chin.

When she looked once more at her husband, she saw him leaning forward, his stormy gaze fastened on the gathering drops of moisture and the darkening bruise on her cheek. A trembling hand reached out to tilt her chin up. He surveyed her face beneath the light shining in from a passing street lamp.

"I'm . . . sorry." His voice sounded oddly uneven. "Christ, I didn't mean to hurt you. I tried to ease the blow, but I had to make it look real . . . somehow I had to convince them." His fingers felt so unbelievably gentle, turning her cheek first one way then the other, his scowl growing blacker as he realized the damage he had done. "If there'd been any other way—anything else I could think of to do . . ." She felt his fingers shaking wherever they touched.

Damien's gaze probed her own. "I've never hit a woman before. For that woman to be you, I—" He broke off on this last, but there was no mistaking the anguish in his features. "For the first time in my life, I couldn't seem to think. I knew they were right behind me—bloody Christ, I've never been so frightened in my life."

Alexa blinked up at him, trying to make her mind work, trying to reason, telling herself she couldn't be hearing him correctly. "Frightened? For me or for you?" Dear God, it made her heart hurt just to look at him, made fresh tears gather and slide down her cheeks.

"For both of us! For godsakes, Alexa—they shoot spies in this country. Flog them in public and then shoot them! Bloody hell, what were you thinking? How could you take such a risk?"

"Are—Are you trying to tell me what happened back there was an act? That you were merely pretending?"

"Of course it was an act. I had to think of something.

I had to convince them of my loyalty in no uncertain terms.''

"How—How did they know where I was?"

"One of the servants saw you going into the general's study. He went looking for Moreau. Fortunately, he found me first.'' He frowned at the tears on her face, her look of hurt and betrayal. "Surely you didn't think that I . . . you can't possibly believe . . ." The pain in his features grew more intense. "Tell me you don't believe I truly meant to hurt you.''

She only shook her head. "You don't have to pretend anymore. I know everything. I heard you talking to Moreau that day in your study. I know that everything you said about being loyal to the British was a lie you made up to keep me docile . . . and to get me b-back in your b-bed.''

Silence descended on the carriage. "Bloody Christ.''

Alexa bit her lip to keep it from trembling.

"I was trying to protect you,'' Damien said gruffly. "I was trying to protect us both.''

"That's why you lied to me about those men? That's why you didn't just tell me the reason they were there?''

"I didn't want you to worry.''

"You're lying again. That's all you've done since the day I met you.''

"I'm not lying, dammit! I'm trying to keep us alive!''

"Stop it!'' Alexa covered her ears, rage and pain welling up, washing over her in great unchecked waves. "I can't stand this anymore. I just can't stand it!''

She found herself wrapped in his arms, his body shaking nearly as hard as her own. "I've got to get you home,'' he said softly. "I've got to find a way . . .''

"Tell me the truth,'' Alexa pleaded, feeling torn in two. "Admit just this once that you've been lying all along. That you're working for the French, that what happened in the general's study is the way things really are."

He only tightened his hold. "I had to convince them. I didn't mean to hurt you. I was trying to protect you. I love you, dammit, I—"

Damien went stock-still. Alexa stared up at him in stunned disbelief.

"What—What did you say?" She had never seen such turmoil in his features, so much bitter regret, such unbelievable longing.

His voice came out on a soft breath of air. "I said I love you. I didn't mean to say it, but it's the truth. That's what you asked for, isn't it?"

Alexa's eyes slid closed and the last of her strength seemed to drain from her body. Damien's strong arms were the only thing holding her up.

"I didn't mean to hurt you," he repeated, drawing her even closer. "I just couldn't think what else to do."

She wanted to believe him. God help her, she wanted him to love her more than anything on this earth. She started to cry against his shoulder, unable to stop the flood of tears. His hands splayed over her back, soothing her gently, then he pulled the pins from her hair and sifted his long dark fingers through it.

"Don't cry, *chérie.* Please don't cry." A corner of his mouth tilted up. "I promise you I am not worth it."

It took all her force of will to bring herself under control. When she did, he tipped her head back and gently kissed her lips. "I'm telling you the truth. I have been all along. I should have told you about the men, but I didn't want you to worry. I know the kind of man I am. I know how hard this must be for you." The merest brush of his finger touched her cheek. "If only you could see inside my heart."

Alexa closed her eyes. More tears welled and slid down her cheeks. She only shook her head. "I don't—" She swallowed past the ache in her throat. "I don't

know, Damien. I don't know what to believe anymore.
I've never been so confused."

"What can I do to convince you?"

She accepted the handkerchief he held out to her,
dried her eyes and blew her nose. Did he mean what
he had said? Could he possibly be in love with her?
Dear God, how she wished it were the truth.

"You'd have to tell me everything. You'd have to explain it all in detail—exactly as it happened—from the
very beginning."

Damien glanced out the window. They were passing
near the Seine, a quiet section with very few people
around. He was grateful Claude-Louis had handpicked
his driver. He rapped on the wall and ordered the man
to stop, then stepped down to the paving stones and
lifted Alexa down. He held her a moment, felt wisps of
her dark auburn hair against his cheek and the steady,
reassuring beat of her heart.

The bruise on her cheek damned him for the bastard
he was, and his insides twisted up inside him. Christ,
he had never brought her anything but grief.

With an arm around her waist, he guided her away
from the carriage to a path along the river. Through a
light covering of clouds the moon appeared like a new
silver coin, its rays a glistening trail across the water.

"I don't know where to begin," he finally said, stopping near a small wooden bench and turning her to
face him. "I've been doing this for a very long time,
Alexa. Almost as long as I can remember. And I'm good
at it—very good. So good, in fact, that the roles I play
are almost a part of me." He told her about his grandmother and how much he had disliked her, how Major
Fieldhurst, one of Lord Townsend's acquaintances, had
become his friend, and together they had come up
with the notion of his gathering information.

Damien shook his head, the memories rushing to the
surface. "Anthony was cagey—and bold as brass.

'They'll see you as nothing but a boy,' he said. 'You won't pose even the slightest threat. But you're not a boy, are you, Damien?' 'No,' I said, 'I haven't been that for a very long time.' " Something flickered in her eyes. He prayed it wasn't pity.

"So whenever you were in France, you spied for him?"

"Yes. I gave them very little at first, just an interesting tidbit or two, but my contacts continued to grow, and by the time I was a man, I knew a number of people well-placed in the government. They were used to my presence, convinced of my loyalty. That's why they listened to the offer I made them the summer I turned twenty-one."

"What offer was that?"

"To sell them British secrets. It appealed to the French sense of justice that I—a member of the English aristocracy, an earl, no less—was willing to provide them information—for a price, of course. But that was exactly what Fieldhurst and I had planned."

He carefully explained how all of it worked, how the information he gave them was actually *mis*-information, designed to lead them astray. He was careful to leave nothing out, only too aware of the risk he was taking.

"What was in the documents you were carrying the night Bewicke came for you on the beach?" Alexa asked, but she found it hard to concentrate. Her mind kept straying to the moment he had said that he loved her.

"Incorrect British troop movements. Oh, there was enough of the truth in the papers so the French would believe them, but most of it was designed to lead them in the opposite direction."

"Who told General Moreau what you said to me that night in the study? Who could have been spying on us?"

"Any one of the servants, excepting Claude-Louis

and Marie Claire. The house is a maze of hidden rooms and secret passages. That's the reason I tried to be so careful.''

She watched him for several long moments. "Why?" she finally asked. "Why do you do it?"

He shrugged his broad shoulders, uneasy with so personal a question. "A number of reasons, I guess. For the money. The excitement. Perhaps just because I can." In the beginning he had done it for his father. Because it was the one thing he could do that would have made his father proud. As he grew older, he did it because it made him feel good about himself, good that he was doing his part to help end the war. But those things were too intimate to share, even with Alexa.

"Is there anything else you want to know?"

"Why didn't Fieldhurst get you out of gaol?"

"Because that whoreson Bewicke wouldn't let me speak to him. When this is over, I swear I'll have that bastard's head."

Alexa turned to him and wondered if the guilt she felt reflected in her eyes. "That last night at the castle . . . I never meant for you to be hurt. I only wanted to stop you from handing over the papers. I was terrified at what might be in them. I wasn't thinking clearly. I was angry and hurt and confused. *And desperately in love.* When I saw you down on the beach . . . when I realized that you might be killed—" She broke off and fresh tears slid down her cheeks.

He leaned over and kissed her forehead. "You did what you thought was right. In a way, I was proud of you."

"Oh, Damien." She went into his arms and he held her, her mind spinning with everything he had said. It all made sense of a sort, but then she'd never thought that a man with his skills wouldn't be totally convincing.

"Do you believe me now?" His cheek was pressed to

hers and she could feel the dark stubble of his day's growth of beard.

"I believe you." She wanted to—desperately. And why shouldn't she? At this point he had no more reason to lie.

His hold tightened fiercely. "I'll get you home safely. I promise you that. But you've got to promise me you won't ever do anything so foolish again."

She mulled that over, then drew back to look him in the face. "I saw what was in those papers, Damien. We have to go back and get them."

"Sweet Jesus!"

"Do you know what those were? Plans for building ships propelled by steam—a whole French fleet of them. Can you imagine what that means? Do you know how important those are?"

Only the most important documents he had stumbled upon in his fifteen years of service. "I know."

"In London last year I saw a steam-propelled carriage. It was running on a track in a huge wooden pavilion."

"I remember. Catch-Me-Who-Can, it was called. A man named Trevithick built it. I read about it in the *Chronicle.*"

"It could work for ships too, Damien. We have to go back and get those papers."

"We don't have to do anything. You're staying out of this. You're going home."

"Not without those papers." Her jaw tilted stubbornly and green fire flashed in her eyes.

"Bloody hell, Alexa. I won't let you get involved in this."

"How can we get back in?" she asked, ignoring him.

"We don't have to get back in."

"Why not?"

He released a weary breath. "Because by now the general has undoubtedly moved them and . . ."

"And what? Go on, Damien. For once, please, just tell me the truth."

"And because there might be an easier way to get hold of them."

"Which is?"

He stared out over the river. A small boat drifted past, its wake stirring a ripple of moonlight. "I can get them from the man who drew them."

"How do you know who that is?"

"There was a maker's mark in the corner."

"Yes, I remember it. A tiny circle with two little triangles that look like miniature sails."

"I know whose mark it is."

Excitement flushed her features. "Whose?"

Damn, he didn't want her involved in this. "A man named Sallier. He's famous for his shipbuilding designs. Odds are good he'll have kept a set of the plans."

"I'll bet they'll tell us when the ships are scheduled to be completed. Do you think they'll mention where the boats are being built? Give us the location of the shipyards?"

"There's a very good chance they will."

"Then we've got to get them. We have to be able to stop those boats from being launched. If enough of them are built, Napoleon can cross the channel any time he wants. He won't need to wait for the wind. He can use the fog for cover, land his forces anywhere he wishes—and we won't be able to stop him."

He looked at her hard. "I know."

There were people on the path ahead. Damien turned and started guiding Alexa back toward the carriage. Neither of them spoke along the way. As the horses came into view, she stopped on the path and turned to face him.

"Did you mean what you said?" she asked softly, her eyes fixed on his face. "Before . . . when we were in the carriage?"

"I meant it. It isn't easy for a man like me to say. I love you, Alexa. I think I have for a very long time."

She wanted to tell him that she loved him too, but she kept seeing him as he was in the general's study, cold and cruel and utterly ruthless. Her cheek still stung where he had slapped her. Her eyes still burned from the tears she had wept, and the words seemed to lodge in her throat. Damien leaned forward and kissed her, a tender, gentle kiss that left her aching inside, her heart throbbing painfully, her stomach churning with turbulent emotions.

They walked in silence until they reached the carriage and Damien helped her climb in.

"I'll be glad when we get home," she said, her feelings still raw and uncertain.

"Yes . . ." he agreed with a troubled expression.

She still couldn't tell what he was thinking. She just prayed that England was the home he had in mind.

Chapter Nineteen

*I*F ONLY YOU COULD SEE INSIDE MY HEART. THE WORDS
HAUNTED HER, TUGGED AT HER LIKE THE TORMENT SHE HAD
seen on his face. Damien didn't come to her room that
night, and Alexa was glad. Too much had happened.
Her mind was a dizzying swirl of emotions, fears, and
uncertainties.

Damien must have sensed it, for he let her sleep far
later than she should have, and when she finally
dressed and went downstairs, she discovered he had
gone.

"He is out in the carriage house," Claude-Louis told
her. "Your husband is helping my son feed his bird."

Damien's elegant, sandy-haired valet stood at a window overlooking the garden. Damien had told her that
before the revolution, the Arnaux family had been in
the aristocracy. Claude-Louis's inborn grace and intelligence spoke of his noble blood.

"My husband and your son—they're very close, aren't they?"

"That surprises you?"

"A little."

"Your husband is a hard man, but only on the surface. It is something even he does not seem to understand."

"He didn't have much of a childhood. Perhaps that is the cause. People always seem to expect him to be something more than he is."

"Or perhaps he is more than he believes he is."

She mulled that over as she left the room and made her way toward the rear of the house. There were endless facets to the man who was her husband. It was part of the reason she found him so intriguing, part of the reason she had always been so attracted to him.

It was also the reason she was afraid to give him her heart completely, to put all of her trust in him.

Alexa walked through the French doors leading out to the garden, then down the path to the carriage house in the rear. It was cool inside. It smelled of aging wood, paint, and axle grease. In the loft above her head, pigeons roosted in one corner, sailing out with a noisy flutter, then returning to their nests to fluff their feathers and coo.

Alexa walked toward the sound of voices drifting in from a small room at the rear. When she made her way in that direction, little Jean-Paul came running toward her.

"*Bonjour,* Madame Falon," the little boy said, a bright smile lighting his face. "We hoped that you would come."

"Did you?" She glanced from the short, dark-haired child to her tall, handsome husband.

"Yes," Damien said, "we were hoping you might join us." His eyes were a dark, enigmatic blue, searching eyes, probing her thoughts.

"I used to wonder if you liked children," she said softly. "It is easy to see that you do."

"I don't like children—at least not all of them. Jean-Paul is . . . special."

Alexa smiled. She didn't like all children either. Not really. But she liked Jean-Paul, and she would love to have a child of her own. Especially Damien's child. "Yes, he is very special." Lowering herself to his small stature, she smiled. "Damien is lucky to have you for a friend."

"Ah, non, madame. It is I who am lucky to have him. If it were not for M'sieur Damien, I would not be here."

She glanced up at her husband, but he merely shrugged his wide shoulders. "We met the day of the accident. If I had been quicker, perhaps Jean-Paul would not have been injured at all."

She swung her attention to the boy, her heart beginning to throb uncomfortably. She had wondered what had happened to the child, but it had never occurred to her that Damien might have somehow been involved. "Is that right, Jean-Paul? Damien was there when you got hurt?"

He nodded. "It was a day when the soldiers marched through—so many you could not count them. They looked grand in their bright-colored uniforms, with all of their medals and shiny brass buttons. There were horses and wagons—lines so long you could not see the end. My mother and I, we were watching when a cannon passed by. Something scared one of the horses. I remember my mother screaming. I remember M'sieur Damien's face as he ran toward me. . . . The rest I do not know . . . only that my leg hurt and I was crying."

"Jean-Paul was struck by a wagon?" she asked Damien, her chest going tight at the image.

Damien shook his head. "A cannonade pulled by

horses. Someone fired off a pistol and the animals
bolted. When they rounded the corner, the wagon
tipped over, dumping the cannon off its bed, along
with several iron balls. I was able to save Jean Paul from
the cannon itself, but one of the cannonballs crushed
his foot."

"Oh, Jean-Paul, that must have been terrible for
you."

He shrugged in a gesture that reminded her of her
husband. "For a while it hurt. Now, I mostly do not
remember."

"That's how I met Claude-Louis," Damien put in.
"He was grateful that I had helped his son. In time we
became close friends. Eventually, he and Marie Claire
came to work for me."

"M'sieur Damien saved my life," the boy said sol-
emnly.

"Then we have something in common." Alexa
smiled at him softly. "For once he saved my life too."

Damien gazed at her, tenderness in his expression. "I
am also the one who put you at risk. Now, why don't
we give Charlemagne a handful of seeds, then go down
to the park for an ice? I'll bet Madame Falon would like
that nearly as much as Jean-Paul."

There was warmth in his gaze and it sparked something deep down inside her. "*Oui,* m'sieur," she said.
"I would like that very much."

There was only one loose end. Jules St. Owen. Whatever happened between her and Damien, Alexa was
willing to chance. But she owed a certain amount of
loyalty to Jules. She wasn't about to do anything that
might put him in danger.

So when little Jean-Paul came running to her room
carrying a small piece of paper, crumpled and sweaty
from its ride in his tiny fist, she read it with a certain
amount of urgency.

"Where did you get this?" she asked.

"From a blond man out in front of the house. He said that I should not give it to anyone but you."

She smiled, but her heart increased its rhythm. "You did exactly right. Thank you, Jean-Paul." She smoothed back an unruly lock of the little boy's thick dark hair. "Run along now and play—and thank your mother for sending up the tea."

She had been feeling a little out of sorts. Too much on her mind, she knew. Too much at stake and still so many unanswered questions. "Tell her it was just what I needed."

Jean-Paul nodded and hurried off down the corridor, dragging his misshapen leg. Her eyes trailed after him for a moment, the sight tugging gently at her heart. Still, he was a strong child, intelligent and quick-witted. She believed whatever occurred in his life, Jean-Paul would be all right.

She sat down and reread the message. *Your husband has a meeting with General Moreau tomorrow at two o'clock to discuss his next assignment.* So St. Owen had his own informants in the government. Dear God, what kind of a world did they live in? *Meet me at the Café de Valois in the Palais Royale at two-thirty.*

As usual, Damien had told her nothing about such a meeting. He expected her to trust him, but when would he learn to trust her?

The afternoon of the following day, he dressed to leave the house, just as Jules had said. Standing in the grand salon, she saw him heading for the door dressed in his brass-buttoned uniform.

"I see you're going out," she said lightly, but it bothered her that he still refused to confide in her.

"I've a meeting with General Moreau."

"Why didn't you tell me?"

"Because it isn't important." His expression subtly shifted and he gave her a hard look of warning. "And even if it were, it is none of your concern." It dawned on her that someone might be watching. She had unwittingly forced a return to his hard-edged role.

"Walk me out to the carriage," he demanded, "there is a matter I would discuss." He picked up his plumed bicorn hat, tucked it under an arm and jerked open the heavy wooden door.

"As you wish," she said somewhat meekly.

Outside the house he stopped and turned. "I'm sorry I had to do that. They'll be watching us more closely than ever."

"I know. I shouldn't have pressed you."

"I'm not exactly sure what the general wants. I'll tell you when I get back home."

"Be careful."

He gave her a brief, hard kiss. "I won't be gone long."

Long enough for her to reach the Café de Valois, she hoped, but Jules seemed entirely competent. He would have this plan well thought through. Standing on the wide front porch, she watched her husband leave, feeling an unwelcome tug at the handsome sight he made in his perfectly tailored grenadier's uniform, then hurried inside to fetch her reticule and a parasol as protection from the sun.

Checking to be certain that no one saw her leave, and seeing nothing out of the ordinary, she hailed a cabriolet at the corner and made her way to the small café in one of the arcades of the Palais Royale.

Jules was waiting when she arrived.

"It's good to see you." Dressed in an expensive dark brown tailcoat, he guided her out to one of the pavilions in the garden and ordered each of them a cup of coffee. It arrived with a pitcher of hot steamed milk. "I've been worried about you."

"Worried?" Alexa leaned forward in her chair. "Has something happened? Is something—"

He shook his head and lifted a fine hand toward the bruise on her cheek. "There were rumors, speculation as to why you and your husband left the château in such a hurry. There was gossip that he beat you."

She sighed. "It's a long story, Jules. And not at all what people think."

"Then you are all right?"

How much should she tell him? "I'm fine. I came to tell you I won't be leaving Paris with you after all."

"Nom de Dieu, why not?"

"My husband is taking care of things. He is going to see that I get home."

"Alexa—"

"It's the truth. I would explain, if I believed that you would understand. I'm afraid I would be putting him in danger."

Jules's hand covered hers where it rested on the table. "Listen to me. You and I are friends. I would never do anything to hurt you—not you, or your husband."

She studied his attractive face. Wisps of golden blond hair touched his smooth, refined forehead, and his light eyes were shadowed with concern.

"I wish it were that simple, but the fact remains— you are French, I am English. I cannot be certain our goals are one and the same."

"My goal is to end this war. To bring peace to my country. To stop the killing and save good men's lives."

Alexa chewed her lip. Dare she risk it? She had trusted Jules before, and he had not failed her. He was working with General Wilcox, and Damien might need help. They both might need it. "My husband is a patriot. An English patriot."

Jules leaned back in his chair. "So he has once again convinced you."

"He explained things. Answered my questions. It all made perfect sense."

"Your husband is an expert at making things make sense."

"I believe him."

"Why?"

"Because he has no good reason to lie—and because he loves me. He told me so the night we left the château, and of all the things he might say or do, I don't think he would make up something like that."

"Neither do I," Jules said, surprising her.

"You don't?"

He shook his head. "I saw him in the library, remember? The man was blindly jealous. He obviously has feelings for you—deep ones. Which is exactly the reason he *would* lie about who he is."

She hadn't thought of that. It was an insane notion. Surely Jules was wrong.

"There is a general named Fieldhurst who can verify his story. I've read about him in the newspapers. Surely your people can reach him, confirm once and for all that Damien is telling the truth."

"In time perhaps, yes."

"I've found something, Jules, something important. My husband is going to see the information gets back to England."

He leaned forward, his face growing suddenly taut. "Will it help to end the war?"

"I can't say for certain. But I *can* tell you, if we don't get the information to the British, Napoleon is sure to invade England. Do you know how many thousands of lives that will cost? There will be carnage on both sides —untold useless deaths—and for what? So the Little Corporal can be emperor of the world?"

"Surely you are wrong, Alexa. His last chance for invasion died at Trafalgar." The great sea battle that had ended in British victory and left the French Navy broken and almost entirely destroyed.

"Unfortunately, I am not wrong."

"Then what if you are wrong about *him*?"

"I—I'm not wrong about him either. Fieldhurst will tell you. Get your sources to find out the truth."

"How much time do we have? How long before this information becomes worthless?"

Alexa swallowed hard. Every day was crucial. And there was always the chance someone might discover the attempt they were about to make and stop them. "I —I'm not sure."

"The boat will be leaving Le Havre in a little over a week. We've got to leave Paris no later than the twenty-third in order to make it. If your husband is telling the truth and the two of you are safely away, it will not matter. But if something goes wrong and you need my help . . . or if you have the information and you want to be sure it gets to England, I will be ready. Just get word to my friend at the Hotel Marboeuf. His name is Bernard, and you can trust him to help you. Bernard will know how to get in touch with me, and he will keep you safely hidden until I can come for you."

Jules squeezed her hand. "Do you understand, Alexa?"

"Yes," she said weakly, for all her old doubts had just crept back in, and though she was determined to ignore them, her limbs felt suddenly unsteady. "Thank you, Jules. No matter what happens, I'll always be in your debt."

He brought her hand to his lips and kissed the palm. "Falon will never know what a lucky man he is."

"I cannot believe it!" Rayne Garrick, Fourth Viscount Stoneleigh, paced in front of the sofa in the drawing room of his comfortable plantation house in Jamaica. "I knew something like this would happen. I should have shot that bastard when I had the chance!"

"Calm down, Rayne. It might not be as bad as it sounds." Jocelyn eased the letter from her husband's

clenched fingers and silently reread the contents. The
letter had arrived in Kingston with the latest ship from
England, then been delivered to Mahogany Vale along
with the weekly supplies. It was written by one Colonel Douglas Bewicke and posted on the third day of
July, two days after Alexa had been abducted. "From
what it says here, your sister is in France, but so is her
husband."

"Her husband? Surely you aren't referring to that
whoreson French traitor I allowed her to marry?"
Rayne's dark brown eyes snapped with fury. Lines of
tension and worry hardened his features.

"Perhaps there is some mistake. You said you knew
this man Bewicke. You said he was nothing but a snivel-
ing little coward—I believe those were your words. Perhaps he is wrong about the earl. Alexa believed in Lord
Falon enough to marry him—"

"Alexa is the one who turned him in. The only sane
thing she has done since she met him."

"I don't believe we should condemn the man just
yet. He told her that he loved her that morning outside
the inn. Even if he is a French spy, if he loves her, he
will see that she is kept safe."

"And if he cares for her not one wit? If he ruthlessly
seduced her and married her for her money? Where
will my sister be then?"

"W-We mustn't think that. We must hold good
thoughts until we get back home, and that is still quite
some weeks away."

"If that bastard has hurt her, if he has harmed a single hair on her head, I shall track him to the ends of the
earth. I won't rest a day until I see him dead."

Jocelyn placed her hand on her husband's muscular
forearm. Tension rippled through every sinew and
cord.

"It's going to be all right, Rayne. Alexa will be safe in
France until we can arrive back home. Once we are

there, you can speak to your friend General Strickland,
arrange for a trade of some sort. You will find some
way to see her returned—I know you will.''

Rayne sifted his fingers through his wife's long black
hair. In the sunlight streaming in through their bedchamber window, it shined like onyx and felt like silk
against his hand.

''Always the optimist, aren't you, my dearest little
love? What in the name of God would I ever do without you?''

''Your sister is going to be all right.''

Rayne smiled and then nodded, but he was far less
certain. Alexa had always been impetuous. For a while
after young Lord Peter's death, she had been quiet and
withdrawn, but it wasn't really her nature. She hated
the French for the death of their brother Chris, and for
the tortures Rayne suffered during the year he'd spent
in one of their prisons.

Now that she was forced to live among them, could
Alexa keep her temper under control and her wits
about her? Could she survive whatever cruelties she
might be forced to endure?

Where was she now? he worried. And where was
that bastard she married?

Rayne cursed himself for allowing them to wed, and
that whoreson Falon to the depths of a fiery hell.

If only he hadn't kept putting her off.

''What are we waiting for?'' Alexa kept asking. ''Why
can't we simply break into the shipbuilder's office, get
the plans, and leave?''

''Because it's too dangerous. We've got to pick just
the right time.'' He paced the bricks of the terrace, his
black boots echoing into the garden, his expression
dark and unreadable, as it had been since that night by
the Seine.

''And if we wait long enough, it isn't going to matter.

We have no idea how many of those ships have already been built. For all we know, they might be ready to launch any day now.''

"I told you—we have to wait. Every detail has to be perfect, our escape route securely in place. There won't be room for mistakes.''

"But—''

"That's the end of it, Alexa. And dammit, please don't bring it up again—we don't know who the hell might be listening.''

She knew that much was true. She knew as well that what she had said was also the truth. And as far as she could tell, Damien was no closer to arranging a safe passage home than he had been in the beginning. Even if he was, she had no way of knowing because her husband wouldn't discuss it.

Which was part of the reason she had never mentioned St. Owen. Jules was her ace in the hole in this deadly game. When the doubts crept in, as they steadfastly continued to do, he was her link to sanity. If all else failed, she could always go to Jules.

Alexa bit her lip. What would Jules do if he knew about the plans she had seen in the general's desk? Would he be able to help her get them? He was as opposed to bloodshed as she was. He was working with Bewicke and Wilcox, trying to get her back home —and Jules had a boat leaving France at the end of next week.

Standing now in front of her bedchamber window, Alexa wondered if she should have told her husband about St. Owen's offer, about the boat that could get them back to England. Once he knew the truth, they could simply steal the plans and leave on the boat together.

Then again, what if, by some small chance of fate, Jules was right—Bewicke and Wilcox were right—and she was wrong?

Damien would never let the documents leave France.

The notion gnawed at her, keeping her up late at night, making her wonder. . . .

And there was Damien himself. He had left her alone since the night they had fled the château, had kept himself carefully apart from her. She didn't know what he was thinking, didn't know whether he regretted his hastily spoken words.

Didn't know for certain whether he had truly meant them.

I love you might come easier for a man like Damien than she had guessed. After all, he was an actor, a chameleon, a man of a thousand faces.

The fact was, she could risk all—trust Damien with the fate of her country, her very life—or she could find the shipbuilder, break in and get the plans. She could give them to Jules, who could get them to General Wilcox. She could be certain beyond most doubt they would safely reach her homeland.

Jules could help her . . . if she continued to trust him.

Dear God, it always seemed to come down to that. She loved Damien, but the bitter truth was she still didn't trust him. Jules was French, but he was working with the English, and he'd been honest and forthright from the start.

Whatever she decided, the first step was to secure the plans. Alexa resolved to see it done.

"Bonjour, Jean-Paul." Damien strode into the entry. "Have you seen Madame Falon?"

"Oui, m'sieur. Madame went for a walk. She said that she would return very soon."

A muscle tightened in his jaw. He didn't like her going out alone. Dammit, he had told her that more than once. They had to be doubly careful now; the slightest mistake could be fatal. Still, he worried constantly that something might go wrong.

His glance strayed from Jean-Paul to the window looking out onto the street, where a group of children kicked a small leather ball across the paving stones. There was no sign of Alexa, but when he looked back at the boy, he saw her walking toward them.

"Good morning," she called out, a soft smile lighting her face.

"I wondered where you were. You shouldn't have gone out alone." He had kept himself away from her since that night beside the Seine, now his chest went tight just at the sight of her.

"I know, but it was such a lovely day." Her cheeks looked flushed from her time out of doors, her hair mussed by the wind. "What have the two of you been up to while I was gone?"

Jean-Paul glanced at the children playing outside the window. "I was watching my friends. I was wishing that I could play ball with them."

"Then why don't you?" Alexa asked. "Surely your mother would not mind."

He only shook his head. "They will not let me. They say I cannot play with such a twisted leg."

Damien sighed. "Children can be cruel, Jean-Paul. They don't realize how awful their words can make someone feel."

"I do not care what they say. I only wish I could kick the ball as they do."

Alexa knelt beside him. "Perhaps you can." She studied the angle of his twisted leg. "What do you think, Damien? Jean-Paul is strong and agile. I think perhaps there is a way he might learn to kick."

She was wearing green today, a soft embroidered muslin that set off the color of her eyes. There was warmth in her expression, but also a guardedness. It

made his insides clench and regret to well up inside
him.

Why had he told her he loved her? It was a stupid
thing to say, considering their uncertain future, and
even if it was the truth, it had only made her more
wary. He'd stayed away from her bed since then, and
she had seemed grateful. He wished he knew what she
was thinking.

He fixed his gaze on the little boy's oddly angled leg.
She was right, he saw. If the child could learn to swing
it just so, he could kick with the side of his foot. It
might actually give him better leverage than he could
get with the toe of his shoe.

"Yes, I believe you could do it, Jean-Paul, if there was
someone who could teach you."

"You could teach me!" The little boy's big brown
eyes lit up. "I know you could. And I am a very fast
learner."

Alexa laughed and Damien's chest squeezed at the
feminine sound. How long had it been since he'd heard
her laugh that way? Too long. Far too damned long. She
was young and innocent. She deserved to laugh more
often. She didn't belong caught up in war.

"Damien?" Alexa's voice brought him back from his
thoughts.

He forced himself to smile. "What do you say, Jean-
Paul? You'll have to change clothes first, or your mother
will have my head."

"*Oui*, m'sieur—I will do whatever you say. I will
hurry. You must wait for me right here." The child
dashed off toward the stairs, leaving the two of them
alone.

When Alexa looked up at him, he saw the same uncertain feelings he had seen in her eyes before. The
green depths looked troubled and wary, but there was
tenderness there too, and something else he could not
name.

"You've made him terribly happy," she said softly.

What about you, Alexa? Will I ever make you happy? But he didn't say it. He was afraid of hearing the truth.

"He's a good boy," he said instead, his voice a little gruff. He looked at her and his blood began to quicken with desire for her. Since the night they had fled the château, every time he saw her, he wanted to tear off her clothes and bury himself inside her. But he felt guilty for the last time, guilty and oddly afraid.

Forcing his eyes from the soft swell of her breast, he glanced back out the window. "I suppose I had better change too. I have a feeling this task could be harder than it appears—at least for someone who hasn't played ball in years."

His wife only smiled, so he turned and walked away.

Alexa watched him go, feeling her heart tug painfully. She wondered at the turbulent emotions that had shifted across his face, the softness in his eyes whenever he had looked her way.

An ache rose up at the wall that continued to stand between them. For a time at Castle Falon she had crumbled the wall a little and begun to pierce the armor he wore so solidly around him. Then the French had come and she had gone to Bewicke. She had lost him then, and she really couldn't blame him.

Still, he had come for her at Le Monde, and she realized her feelings hadn't changed.

The hunger remained strong for them both, but a sea of doubt also remained. That night by the Seine, he had told her that he loved her, convinced her firmly that he had spoken the truth. But since that time, once again his guard was up, and she had no way to know what he was thinking.

Perhaps she should try once more to breach the wall, take the risk and give him her heart completely. But she had done so once and the pain had been unbearable. She wasn't sure she could survive that kind of grief again.

She thought of Jean-Paul, at the warm look on Damien's face whenever he and the child were together, and wondered why it was the only person he ever seemed at ease with was the tiny dark-haired boy.

Perhaps because the boy expected nothing of him. Perhaps because he accepted Damien just the way he was.

It was a disturbing thought as she made her way upstairs. The child loved Damien for himself, no matter what he had done, no matter what he believed in. The little boy trusted him, and won Damien's trust in return.

If only she were brave enough to do the same.

Alexa knew that she was not.

She had made her decision. She would put her trust in Jules St. Owen. She didn't love Jules. When it came to St. Owen, she could remain objective. With Damien her thoughts were constantly in turmoil, incessantly confused, nothing but a vicious tangle of emotions.

When it came to her husband, she couldn't trust her own judgment.

Good judgment was imperative now. There was too much at risk—too many British lives at stake.

Alexa crossed the floor of her bedchamber, feeling suddenly weary. She had just come back from the Hotel Marboeuf, where she had spoken to the man named Bernard and left a message for Jules. If he were willing, they could break into the shipbuilder's office and search for the plans. If they found them, Jules could see them safely on to England.

As for herself, that was another matter entirely.

Deep inside, she had known all along that she would not be going with him.

Chapter Twenty

J ULES ST. OWEN SAT AT A SMALL CORNER TABLE IN THE CAFÉ
DE VALOIS, SIPPING A STRONG CUP OF COFFEE. IF HE LEANED
forward in his chair, he could see the door leading in
from the street. He stiffened then came to his feet
when he caught sight of the slender cloaked figure
who had just come into the café.

Making his way purposefully toward her, he took her
arm and led her back to the table. "I was beginning to
worry." Removing her wrap, he draped it over the
back of her chair.

"I took the long way getting here." She let him seat
her, a slender hand shoving wisps of dark auburn hair
back under her bonnet. "I wanted to be sure I wasn't
being followed."

"*Très bien.* I am thankful for your good judgment."
He ordered her a cup of thick black coffee, and the
waiter brought it, along with some steaming milk.

"Is everything ready?" She was gowned in a light blue figured-muslin day dress, simple and modest, her breasts a tantalizing curve beneath the fabric, her eyes bright and searching. She looked lovely as always, but he couldn't help noticing the paleness of her skin.

"All the preparations are in place for our departure, as well as for the theft of the documents. That, I intend to see to personally . . . as soon as you tell me where they are."

"I told you before, Jules, I'm not telling you until that night. I intend to go with you, and that is the only way I can ensure you will take me."

He swore a muttered oath beneath his breath. "I am sorry, *chérie*, it is far too dangerous. I hoped by now you would have come to your senses."

"Just being here is dangerous. I have to go along, Jules. I won't have it any other way."

"And just how are we supposed to get you out of the house?"

"I'm leaving that up to you. I know you'll think of something." She was beautiful and determined. He realized he could not thwart her.

"All right. It seems that you have left me no choice." She smiled at the victory she had won, and Jules felt a tightening in his chest. He sighed. "I will see that your husband is called away, then you can leave unnoticed and meet me a few blocks from the house."

"When?"

"Thursday night. We only have until Friday to leave if we mean to reach Le Havre in time to catch the boat."

She chewed her soft bottom lip, and he forced down a swell of desire for her. He had never lacked for women. Most of the ones he wanted were more than willing to share his bed. Not this one. Alexa felt only friendship for him. He wondered if her husband appreciated her strength and determination anywhere nearly as much as he did.

"About the boat . . ." she said softly, glancing nervously down at the table. "I haven't changed my mind, Jules, I'm still not going with you."

"But I thought—"

"I know what you thought. For a time even I wasn't sure. But the truth is, I have to stay."

"You can't. Not once the plans have been stolen. They're bound to be suspicious. *Mon Dieu,* you saw the papers in the general's desk."

"I have to stay with my husband." Her eyes came up to his face and he caught the shimmer of tears. "I love him, Jules. I love him and I'm not going to leave him." She blinked hard several times and forced the wetness away. "Besides, if we're careful, they might not discover the documents are missing for weeks. By then, Damien and I will be safely back home."

"You obviously still have your doubts or you wouldn't even be here. What will happen to you if you're wrong?"

"Until we hear from Fieldhurst, there's no way to be completely certain of anything. I'm not willing to risk the lives of the people of my country because I'm in love with him, but I believe he cares for me. I believe he will protect me. My husband will see I get home . . . even if he can't come with me."

Jules started to argue, but the stubborn look on her face told him not to. *Mon Dieu,* but the woman had courage. And in her own way, loyalty to the man she loved. Still, he could hardly let her remain. He would bide his time, get hold of the papers—if indeed they were there, then worry about convincing her to leave.

He reached for her hand across the table, felt her soft warm skin, and gave her fingers a reassuring squeeze.

"All right, we will do this as you wish. I will leave a message at the Hotel Marboeuf with the final instructions. Thursday night we will get the plans."

"Thank you, Jules."

He brought her fingers to his lips. *"Avec plaisir, chérie.* Now let us pray that nothing goes wrong.''

Damien stood inside the room at the rear of the carriage house, the only place he felt safe from being overheard. Claude-Louis stood beside him. Jean-Paul's big white bird flapped its wings and cawed, accepting the treat Damien shoved through the bars of the cage.

''Then everything is set,'' he said, glancing past the cage to his friend.

''It is all arranged as you requested. On the evening of Monday next, the two of you will dress formally, then leave the house as if you were going to the Opéra. I will meet you at the corner with a carriage and clothing for the journey from the city. Your wife will go with me, and you will go after the plans.''

Damien nodded.

''There will be a man waiting outside M'sieur Sallier's shipbuilding office. His name is Charles Trepagnier. He is a good man and one you can trust. He will be there to help you.''

''Hopefully I won't need him, but it's good to know there'll be someone else there.''

''Once you have the plans, you will meet us north of the city and be on your way out of town.''

''And the boat?''

''Will be waiting four days hence, south of Boulogne. Make it safely that far, and you will soon be home.''

Damien clasped his friend's shoulder. ''Thank you, *mon ami,* you have always been a faithful friend.''

''You have not said what you will do should the plans not be there.''

''If they're not there, we'll leave without them. At least we know what Napoleon is up to, and I can't risk keeping Alexa here any longer. Things have already gotten too far out of hand.''

"I am glad to hear it. I had begun to worry for your safety."

"Just take care of yourself and that wife and boy of yours."

"You may rely on it. And Damien—as I have been a friend to you, you have also been a very good friend to me."

"I won't forget you—none of you—especially Jean-Paul. Tell him that for me, will you? Tell him if he should ever wish to come to England . . ."

"I will tell him."

Once more Damien nodded. There was nothing else to be said. Tonight he would tell Alexa. After supper they would take the carriage and go for a walk by the Seine, where they could speak in private. She was bound to rest easier, knowing things were in order and that they would soon be leaving.

He would rest easier.

The danger of discovery grew stronger every day. Alexa's presence had triggered it, as had his feelings for her, though he had done his best to disguise them. Going after the documents would heighten the risk, but too much was at stake for him not to chance it. If anything happened to him, if he did not make it to the rendezvous point, Claude-Louis would see Alexa to safety. He would get her to the boat and be certain that she reached her home.

He could count on Claude-Louie.

He just prayed that all would go well and he would be leaving on the boat along with her.

On Thursday night Alexa ordered a special meal prepared, an added touch to set the scene of a comfortable evening at home. And in truth, she wanted these few hours with her husband.

She leaned over and lit a taper, wanting everything to be perfect, strangely needing to breach the wall, if only for one night. They wouldn't have much time. She trusted that Jules's plan would work as he had explained in his note, that a messenger would arrive around nine o'clock with an urgent summons for her husband.

A number of officers of the grenadiers were being briefed on upcoming troop movements. It was a simple matter, Jules said, to have the major's name included on the roster of those men ordered to attend.

And it would give him the perfect alibi, should something go wrong at the shipbuilder's office, or the theft be discovered before she and Damien had time to leave the city.

She felt better knowing that whatever occurred this eve, she was not putting him in danger.

She straightened a crisp white linen napkin beside his plate, the table exquisite with china and crystal and bouquets of lovely fresh flowers. The chef was serving *côte de veau belle des bois,* veal chops with creamed wild mushrooms, though Alexa was too nervous to eat.

She turned when she heard his approach, her pulse picking up just to see him walking toward her so incredibly tall and handsome.

"Mon Dieu . . ." he said on a slow breath of air, his dark gaze running the length of her. The rough-smooth cadence of his voice made her heart throb painfully. "How could I have forgotten in such a short time just how lovely you are."

Alexa felt the warmth seeping into her cheeks. "I hoped that you would like it." She had chosen a sapphire silk gown with a gossamer underskirt. It was daringly low, revealing the rounded swell of her breasts, and split up the side to display a tantalizing portion of her leg.

"C'est extraordinaire. But far better still, I like what is in it."

The rose in her cheeks grew more pronounced. She

had chosen the gown on purpose. She wanted to see
him look at her the way he used to, with desire burning hotly in his eyes, his face dark and seething with
hunger for her. Whatever happened this night, she
wanted to see that look one more time.

She saw that it was there even now, scorching in its
intensity, firing her blood and making her heart beat
wildly. Blue eyes blazing, the skin across his high
cheekbones taut and his hard mouth curving sensu-
ously, he narrowed the distance between them, long
muscles bunching in his thighs as he moved. He
reached her side and slid an arm around her waist,
catching her hard against him, his mouth coming down
over hers.

The kiss he gave her sizzled with fiery heat, firm lips
slanting over soft; plundering, relentless, determinedly
possessive.

"I've missed you," he said, his voice thick and husky.
"I shouldn't have waited. I should have come to you,
made love to you, made you want me the way I want
you."

"Damien . . ." Another searing kiss, this one so
thorough her knees nearly buckled beneath her. She
was clinging to his shoulders, accepting the thrust of
his tongue, melting as his hands found her breasts. She
could feel the bands of muscle across his chest, feel the
hot rigid thickness of his shaft as he pressed himself
against her.

"I want you," he said. "I need you, Alexa."

She made a soft sound in her throat. For a moment
she thought he might take her right there, lift her skirts
and drive himself inside her as he had done that night
in the library. Heat roared through her at the thought,
but instead he broke away.

A seductive smile curved his lips. "Perhaps your
lovely supper should wait."

"I-It would hardly be fair," she said breathlessly,

though the protest was a weak one. "Chef Masson has worked on this meal all day."

"We could make it up to him. I'm sure we can think of a way."

She wanted to say yes. Dear God, she wanted him so badly. It occurred to her suddenly that she should have done this sooner, that he had been waiting for her, letting her set the pace. He had told her he loved her, and she'd said nothing in return. She had left him feeling uncertain, left him vulnerable and unsure.

He smiled at her before she could speak. "Of course, waiting has its benefits too. I've discovered that certain . . . appetites are enhanced by a generous amount of patience." He nibbled the side of her neck. "It would give me time to think of a new way to seduce you." A wicked black brow arched up. "Or perhaps we'll pretend we are once more in the library."

Color infused her cheeks. She had seen him seductive before, but never quite so playful. It was relief, she saw, the knowledge that she still desired him. Dear God, how could he have doubted it? It made her heart twist painfully, made her want to ignore the plans she had made and let him carry her back upstairs, make love to her for hours on end.

"Surely a slight delay would be no problem," she whispered, rising on tiptoe to kiss him, sliding her arms once more around his neck.

He gave her a devilish smile and eased himself away. "Now that I think on it, I believe your plan is better. We'll take it slow and easy. All through dinner I want you to imagine exactly what I'm going to do."

A shiver of desire rippled across her skin. Time was limited. She wanted to forget the meal, make love instead, but the moment had passed and it was too late now to change things.

Damien seated her in a high-backed chair, then sat down himself, smiling with eyes full of tenderness. The hunger remained, but it was tempered with some other emotion she could not read. She found herself praying it was love. That he had told her the truth the night they had walked beside the Seine.

"Thank you," he said, leaning toward her, reaching out to clasp her hand.

"For what?"

"Coming back to me."

Her heart clenched. Had she really gone away from him? But she knew in truth that she had. Just as he had gone away from her.

Perhaps they had both been afraid.

He lifted his wineglass, his gaze still resting on her face. "To us," he said.

"To us," she repeated, her heart swelling with love for him, and a rising tide of hope for the future. Yet the night had only begun. Danger lay ahead, and she was no longer sure she had made the right decision. Was it too late to call off her meeting with Jules? Was there a way to reach him?

She was growing more anxious by the moment. She reached for her wineglass, took a nerve-calming sip— then a hard knock sounded at the door. Frantically, she glanced at the tall grandfather clock against the wall. It was only seven-thirty.

"*Pardon,* M'sieur Falon." Pierre Lindet, the short, dark-haired butler stood at the dining room door. "There is a messenger here from General Moreau. Your presence is required in the general's private quarters."

Damien stiffened. He was worried, she saw, and suddenly she was worried too.

"Gen-General Moreau wishes to see you?" Surely the man had been sent by Jules. Just a small change in the way they had worked things out. Surely there was nothing to be afraid of.

"I'm certain it's only routine. Information he needs

or an opinion on something involving British movements."

"Yes . . . I am certain it is." Still, she was frightened.

Jules had said nothing about Moreau. It would merely be a briefing, officers only, he said. He had never mentioned Moreau. She came up out of her chair and moved with Damien into the entry. "How long do you think you'll be gone?"

"It's hard to say. Probably not too long." But he didn't look all that certain. He turned his attention to the thin-faced corporal who had brought him the message. "It will take a moment for me to change into my uniform."

"There is no need, Major Falon," the soldier said. "The general sends his apologies for requesting a meeting so late."

Damien relaxed a little and turned to take his cloak from Pierre. He swirled it around his broad shoulders. Flashing her a dazzling white smile, he bent his head and kissed her, a searing, blazing, fiercely possessive kiss that left them both trembling.

He was gone before she realized his smile had been far too bright. It was the sort of mistake he seldom made, and it only made her worry all the more.

Still, there wasn't time to ponder fears that might be groundless. For the present, she had to assume that things were progressing as planned, that Jules would be waiting and all would go well.

Determined to keep appearances normal, she ordered the rest of her dinner sent up to her room, but didn't bother pretending to eat it. Marie Claire helped her undress and pull on a night rail, then she paced the floor until the hour reached half past ten.

Dressing quickly in a simple dark brown bombazine dress, she cloaked herself in black, opened the door and scanned the hall for servants. Seeing no one about, she made her way quietly down the back stairs and out the door leading to the carriage house. Checking to be sure she wasn't followed, careful to stay in the shadows, she walked the two blocks down the Avenue Gabriel to the rendezvous point that she had set with Jules.

She sighed with relief when she saw him striding toward her. His face looked taut, but not unduly strained.

"They came for him?" he asked. "You had no trouble slipping away?"

"I had no trouble, but the messenger came early. He said he had come from General Moreau."

"Moreau?"

"Th-That's what he said. Is something wrong, Jules? Is Damien in some sort of trouble?"

"Not that I know of. No other messenger arrived?"

"No."

"Perhaps there was a last minute change of some sort. My people are good. As long as the task was accomplished, they wouldn't care how it was done."

She relaxed a little at his words. Moreau had always been demanding. This wasn't all that unusual a request, and if Jules's people got wind of it, they would consider it as good a diversion as any.

"Since we can no longer be certain how long he may be detained, we had better get on with it."

"Yes." She hadn't thought of that. She prayed Moreau would keep Damien occupied until she could get back home.

"I think it's time you told me where we are going," Jules said as he helped her up in the carriage.

"The office of a shipbuilder named Sallier. It's quite some distance away, on the Rue St. Etienne near the Quai de la Mer. Do you know it?" She had discreetly asked around about the shop and finally gotten the location from the driver of a cabriolet.

"I know the street. It shouldn't be too hard to find the office."

He picked up the reins to the single bay horse that pulled his small black phaeton. It was an unobtrusive conveyance, obviously chosen so as not to be noticed as it moved through the busy Paris streets.

It took a while to reach the Rue St. Etienne and pull into the narrow dark alley at the rear. Jules left her sitting in the carriage while he made his initial inspection, then came back and helped her down from the seat.

"There is a window above a small door leading down to the basement. I have already pried it open. I presume you are bound and determined to go with me."

She smiled. "But of course. How would you know what to look for if I didn't go along?"

He made a sound of exasperation, but didn't bother trying to talk her out of it. He led her to the back door, then went round the building and climbed through the open basement window. A few minutes later the door swung open and he motioned her in.

"There are only two rooms," he said. "A workroom where the designs are made, and one that is M'sieur Sallier's office."

"Where shall we start?"

"The workroom. If the plans are here, it will be because they are working drawings. Most likely they will be kept with others of their kind. To a man who works on such plans every day, it might not even occur to him that he has something worth stealing."

"Perhaps that is what Damien was thinking."

"I'm certain it is."

Lighting a small whale-oil lamp, but careful to keep the wick burning low, they began to pull open the heavy oak cabinets that held shipbuilding designs. Each drawer contained a several-inch-deep stack, and it took long minutes to check each set of plans to discover if they were the ones showing the steam-propelled ships.

They finally finished the first chest.

Nothing.

"You go through that one," Jules said, understanding now what to look for. "I will do this one."

Alexa nodded. Every moment more they spent in the shop increased their chance of discovery. She crouched in front of the set of drawers, pulled the first one open and began to sift through the stack of designs. Nothing.

The second drawer yielded nothing. Neither did the third.

"Find anything?" Jules called softly.

"Not yet." But she wasn't about to give up. She finished the last drawer, stretched the muscles that had begun to ache in her back and neck, and turned to survey the room.

Jules was searching what appeared to be the last place in the room that plans could be kept. Alexa moved toward Sallier's office. There was nothing on his desk, and the drawers in the desk weren't large enough to store a set of plans.

Making certain nothing appeared out of place, she surveyed the walls of the office, looking for more of the storage chests. Nothing. Beginning to feel the stirrings of defeat, she started to leave, but as she reached for the door, she noticed a stout wooden bureau sitting behind it.

"Find something?" Jules asked from the doorway.

She surveyed the bureau with a last thread of hope. "If they aren't in here, I don't know where else we can look."

"We had better hurry," he said, kneeling beside her.

Alexa nodded and pulled open the drawer to see a stack of plans, just like those in the drawers in the workroom. She lifted each set and scanned the first page. Near the bottom of the pile she paused, her heart beginning to beat erratically.

"I've found them," she said softly, almost reverently. "They're here, Jules, just like Damien said. I only hope they mention where the ships are being built."

"We can study them once we get out of here. Take a last look around. Make sure that nothing appears to have been disturbed."

She did as he asked, praying she had replaced everything properly on top of Sallier's desk, and hurried to the door at the rear of the shop. Jules locked it behind her, then went down to the basement and left by the window he had pried open to get in. He wedged it back into place and joined her in the carriage.

"We did it," Alexa said as Jules coaxed the horse into a trot and the carriage pulled away.

"Naturellement, chérie, surely you had no doubt."

She laughed along with him, relief and triumph making them both a little giddy, but already she was scanning the documents, looking for the crucial information.

"It's all here, Jules. Where each ship is being built and the proposed completion date. Sweet God, they'll be ready to move in six weeks."

"Time enough for the English to act—once they get word."

Alex looked up at him, a portion of his handsome face lit by the light slanting down from the moon. "You'll see it done, Jules, just like you said? You'll make certain these papers get to England?"

A fine hand cradled her cheek. "I will not fail you, *chérie.* As much as I do this for my country, I also do it for you."

She smiled at him fondly. "Thank you, Jules."

"Come with me, Alexa. Let me help you leave France and return safely home."

She only shook her head. "Damien will get me home."

"*Nom de Dieu,* it isn't safe for you to wait."

"I have to."

For a long, tense moment he did not speak. Then a soft oath tumbled from his lips. "Is there nothing I can say?"

"You know there is not."

"If Falon is lying . . . if he hurts you in any way—I swear I will kill him myself."

Tears stung her eyes, but she forced them away. "You're a good friend, Jules. I will never forget you."

"Nor I you, *chérie.*"

He left her on the street several blocks from her home, then waited as she made her way off through the darkness. It didn't take long to reach the carriage house. She crossed the courtyard then used the key to the servants' entrance at the rear of the house. Quietly climbing the stairs, she proceeded down the hall toward her bedchamber. All the while, she prayed that Damien had not returned home. God only knew what he would do should he find her gone, and any steps he might take could sound the alarm.

She closed the door behind her and leaned against it, then crossed to the room that was his. Nothing was out of place. Since none of the servants had been roused, she felt safe in assuming he had not yet returned. With a sigh of relief, she glanced at the clock.

Two-thirty.

It had taken far longer than she had expected. She was bone-tired and her stomach growled with hunger. She wished she had eaten, yet the cold veal and limp vegetables left on the tray still sitting beside the hearth only made her stomach churn.

Alexa moved toward the mirror above her bureau and silently began to strip off her clothes. Dressed once

more in her simple cotton night rail, she listened for
her husband's return.

She would not tell him what she had done—at least
not yet. It was unfair to put Jules at risk. She was exhausted from her foray this night, yet she strained
toward every sound, hoping to hear his heavy footfalls,
secretly hoping he would come to her, join her in her
bed. She needed his comfort this eve. She needed to
feel his strong arms around her. She wanted to tell him
she loved him. She wanted to hear him say the words
to her.

Instead she lay awake, listening to the eerie creaking
timbers in the house, to the sound of insects outside
her window and the wind rustling softly through the
trees. She was still awake when the gray light of dawn
crept into the room.

And her husband had not yet returned.

Chapter Twenty-One

D AMIEN RAKED A WEARY HAND THROUGH HIS HAIR AND SAT UP STRAIGHTER IN HIS UNCOMFORTABLE SEAT. ACROSS from him, around a long rectangular rosewood table, General Moreau, Victor Lafon, Grand Chamberlain Montesquiou, acting Interior Minister Fouchet, and several of the Emperor's marshals surveyed a large detailed map of Holland.

The British had landed at Flushing.

The men had been up all night discussing the situation, and it was now late into the day. The conversation had ranged from incredulity, to anger, to concern for what the English might do next.

Still, there wasn't a great deal of worry, except in Fouchet's quarter, and Damien suspected that was merely a front to bolster the man's political ambitions. Two weeks earlier, after the English landing at Walcheren, he had ordered the *levée en masse* of the National Guard, and mobilized the National Guard of Paris.

The Emperor had been livid. From his headquarters in Schönbrunn he had denounced Fouchet as an alarmist and accused the man of plotting against him. As Damien watched the minister now, it appeared the man was up to his same old tricks.

Damien glanced once more at the map, at the shaded-in areas of British occupation, and felt the same uneasiness he had experienced before. Although he couldn't be certain, he was more than a little bit wary of the tack the English had taken. The area in Holland where the men were camped was swampy and known to be rife with fever.

Wellington was still in Spain. Damien was far less certain of the man who led British forces to the north, and far less confident that the landing had been a wise one.

He prayed that he was wrong.

"Don't you agree, Major Falon?" The general's voice jerked him from his thoughts.

"I'm sorry, General. My mind must have strayed. Could you repeat—"

"Excuse me, General Moreau . . ." Sergeant Piquerel walked into the high-ceilinged, well-appointed room. He was a big brawny man with dark red hair; a brutal, battle-hardened soldier whose posture today looked unusually tense. "I am sorry to interrupt, but Lieutenant Colbert has an urgent message for you. He requests a moment in private with you and Colonel Lafon."

The general shoved back his chair, the legs scraping harshly on the polished wood floor. "You will have to excuse me, Major. It appears our conversation will have to wait."

"Of course, General Moreau."

Damien watched the stout man cross the room followed by Victor Lafon, and suddenly felt a little uneasy. Colbert was Victor's aide. He was ambitious and keen-minded, a man who intended a quick rise through the ranks. What information had he uncovered? How would it affect the British . . . or was it something else?

He waited in silence, while the occupants of the room buzzed in speculative conversation around him. A few moments later the sergeant jerked open the door.

There was some commotion in the hallway. Damien heard the sound of tramping boots, then six uniformed guards of the general's staff swarmed into the room, sending the men at the table all surging to their feet. Moreau walked in behind them, followed by Lafon and Lieutenant Colbert. They proceeded across the staff room—making their way straight toward him.

"Major Falon," said Colonel Lafon. "It is my most unpleasant duty to place you under arrest."

A hard knot clenched in his belly. "On what charges?"

"Treason."

The hand he held at his side balled into a fist. He forced himself to relax it. "I assure you, Colonel Lafon, there has been some mistake."

"That, Major Falon, remains to be seen," said General Moreau, stepping into the circle of men. "Sergeant Piquerel—you may do your duty. Take him away."

The uniformed guards surrounded him. There was no place to run, no way to escape. And there was Alexa to consider. Damien let them lead him away. As their movements echoed along the empty hall, his mind swirled with questions: What had happened to alert them? Where were they taking him? What would happen to Alexa?

A number of answers came to mind, actions were considered and discarded, possibilities weighed, along with potential solutions.

Overriding it all was his fear for Alexa. What would happen to her with him in prison . . . or perhaps even dead? Was it possible they intended to arrest her

as well? There was no way to know, no way to help her
unless he kept his head. He couldn't let his worry for
her distract him.

As they marched him out the door and into the
courtyard, Damien felt the sun's warmth on his back,
then they were wrenching his arms behind him, knot-
ting a rope around his wrists, and shoving him up in
the back of a wagon.

He had no idea where they might take him. No idea
how he might escape. He thought of Alexa and could
almost see her pretty green eyes growing dark with
worry as they had last night when the messenger arrived. He could almost see her soft bottom lip begin to
tremble.

Damn! If only he could get word to Claude-Louis,
the man could see her safe.

He cursed himself. If only he had left sooner, she
wouldn't be in danger.

If only . . .

Whatever happened, he would play the game
through to the finish, but the hard truth was, it just
might be too late.

Alexa paced the floor of her bedchamber. Damien
didn't return all that day, and it was now well into the
evening. Where was he? Why hadn't he come home?

She worried endlessly, imagining all sorts of terrible
possibilities, then chided herself for her groundless
fears and convinced herself the theft of the plans had
nothing to do with her husband's tardy return.

It was during one of those more optimistic moments
that she went downstairs in search of something to oc-
cupy her turbulent thoughts. A book perhaps, something to distract her. She pulled a volume of Rousseau's
Confessions from a shelf in Damien's study and had
started back upstairs when she spotted Marie Claire in

the entry, staring out through the windows that faced
the street.

She approached the woman in silence, wondering
what it was she watched so intently. The dark-haired
woman was smiling, Alexa saw, and her eyes held a
slight mist of tears.

"What is it, Marie Claire?"

For a moment the woman did not answer. Then she
simply shook her head and pointed out the window.
Alexa searched the brick path leading to the street, and
in front of the house her gaze came to rest on little
Jean-Paul. He was surrounded by a circle of children,
his round cheeks flushed with excitement. His white
linen shirt was streaked with dirt, his breeches slightly
rumpled, but he didn't seem to mind, and neither did
his mother.

"He is doing it," said Marie Claire with gentle pride,
seeing him kick the leather ball with the side of his
foot, making it sail farther down the street than any of
the other boys. "You said that he could do it, and
M'sieur Falon taught him how it could be done."

"Yes . . ." Noticing the children were almost in awe
of him, Alexa felt a soft tug at her heart. "I believe your
son could do almost anything, if he wanted to badly
enough."

The tiny Frenchwoman turned big dark eyes on
Alexa. "I will never forget the gift of your friendship
that you and your husband have given to my son."

Alexa's own eyes stung with tears. "If my husband
were here, he'd be very proud of Jean-Paul."

Marie Claire just smiled. "He will be a wonderful father—you will see. Even he does not know, but I do. I
know what I speak is the truth."

Alexa bit her trembling lip. She wanted Damien's
child, more than she ever would have believed. Unconsciously her hand came to rest on her flat stomach. It
was possible even now she might carry his babe. She

found herself praying it was so, that he would want a child as much as she did.

She prayed that he had been telling the truth and that they would return to England, but as she thought about Jean-Paul and the child's unwavering love for her husband, it was becoming more and more clear that it didn't matter which side he was on.

It didn't matter what he had done or what he believed in. It only mattered that she loved him, and she prayed that he loved her.

If only he would return, she would tell him.

If only she knew for sure that he was safe.

She squeezed Marie Claire's hand, her worry once more making its way to the surface. She turned away from the woman and her son and went back to her room upstairs.

All the way there she prayed for Damien's safe return.

Victor Lafon stood outside the door leading down to a small dark chamber below the office of the Prefect of Police. Lieutenant Colbert stood beside him. Sergeant Piquerel was downstairs with the prisoner.

"Should we confront him with the theft of the plans?" Colbert asked, his keen eyes shrewdly assessing.

Victor shook his head. "Not yet. We will give him some rope, see whether or not he hangs himself." Victor had been assigned the task of uncovering the truth of the theft that had occurred at the shipbuilder's office and recovering the crucial information—before it fell into the enemy's hands.

"He could not have accomplished the theft himself," Colbert said. "He never left the general's office."

"Falon did not take the plans, but he was one of the few men aware of their existence. I know without doubt he is behind the deed, and in time we will discover his accomplice."

"What about the woman?"

"I have already sent men to bring her in."

"Surely she couldn't have done it."

"Highly unlikely. She has courage enough to try, but Pierre did not see her go out last night, and even if she did, it would be a difficult task for a woman to accomplish alone."

"What about St. Owen? We know she's been spending time with him."

"Jules has always had a way with the ladies. We have no reason to suspect him of anything other than a lovers' tryst. Still, in the past he has had his differences with some of the Emperor's policies. It cannot hurt to question him."

Colbert nodded.

"The woman may well be the key," Victor said. "The major obviously has feelings for her. Perhaps we will be able to bargain with him, promise her safe passage home if he will return the documents."

"From what I know of Falon, I would think he'd be more willing to bargain for his own safe passage than for that of his wife."

"Perhaps you are right. At any rate, we will soon find out. One way or another, we will recover those plans. We will also find out whom the major meant to sell them to."

"But I thought—"

"What? You assumed he would sell them to the British? Our informants have never uncovered any real loyalty there. It is my belief Major Falon meant to sell them to the highest bidder. There are at least half a dozen countries who would pay a small fortune for such valuable information."

"*Dieu de Ciel*, I never thought of that."

"Perhaps that is why General Moreau assigned the

task to me. I have known the major far longer than anyone else. If anyone can uncover the truth, I am the one to do it.''

Colbert smiled. "With Sergeant Piquerel's help.''

Victor glanced toward the heavy wooden door, thought of where it led, and inwardly shuddered. He released a weary breath and shook his head.

"Nasty business, torture. I had hoped it would not be necessary, but in truth, with the major, I never believed it would come to anything else.''

Colbert followed his gaze, hearing the thud of fists against flesh even through the heavy wooden door. "Personally, I never liked the man. But I know you felt at least a grudging respect for him. I am sorry for the way things have turned out.''

"Nothing is surprising in war, *n'est ce pas?*''

"*D'accord,* Colonel Lafon. Unfortunate as that may be, that is so.''

Victor pulled open the door and glanced down the stairs. The passage was dark, hiding the walls in the distance. He forced his mind not to think of what lay in the shadows, and fixed his gaze instead on the small circle of light at the bottom of the stairs.

A whale-oil lamp sat atop a scarred wooden desk, and torches flickered eerily from small brass holders stuck into the sides of the tunnel. Sergeant Piquerel stood with his thick legs splayed and his beefy hands balled into fists. The major slumped against the ropes binding him to his chair, an eye puffed closed, a corner of his lip cut and swollen.

Victor steeled himself. "Let me know when they bring in the woman," he said to Colbert as he started down the stairs. Hearing the ominous words, Falon roused himself, straightened his battered body and fixed him with a piercing blue-eyed stare.

* * *

Alexa came away from the window, exhaustion making her weary, yet the tension she felt would not leave her body. It was dark outside, no moon, no stars—and still no word from her husband. The wind blew branches against her window, and the scratching of the leaves against the panes set her nerves on edge even more.

She left the room to go downstairs—anything to distract her—but halfway down the hall a pounding at the door grabbed her attention. It was an urgent sound, harsh and determined. It made her mouth go dry and her chest grow tight as she hurried down the stairs.

Pierre scuttled past, muttering softly, heading for the entry, intent on quieting the intruder. Alexa followed him nervously onto the black and white marble floor, her heart thudding uncomfortably inside her breast.

"Bonsoir, m'sieur," the butler said, "there is something that you wish?"

Alexa sucked in a breath. "Jules, what on earth—" She broke off at the worried expression on his face.

"I am afraid I must speak to you. It is a matter of utmost importance." Ignoring the tiny dark-haired butler, he strode into the room, gripped her wrist and urged her down the hall.

"For godsakes, Jules, what is it?" The moment they reached the study and closed the door, she whirled to face him.

"Something has happened. I want you to go upstairs and get your cloak—and put on a sturdy pair of shoes. We have to get you out of here."

"Wh-Why? What has happened?"

Jules's already dark expression turned even more grim. "They have arrested your husband for the theft of the plans. They were discovered missing from Sallier's office only this afternoon."

"But they know he couldn't have done it—he was with them!"

"They believe he arranged it. Now the soldiers are on their way here. They are coming after you."

"Dear God in heaven."

"You must stay calm. Get your cloak and shoes as I have said. Do it quickly, Alexa. We do not have much time."

She nodded, turned and hurried back upstairs. Battling down her terror, she quickly packed a small traveling bag, put on a pair of brown leather shoes, and grabbed her black hooded cloak. In the entry, Jules took her arm, and together they left the house. He handed her up in his small black phaeton, then climbed up on the seat beside her.

"Where . . . where are we going?"

"The Hotel Marboeuf. Bernard will be waiting with a wagon. He can take you north out of the city. You still have time to catch the boat to Le Havre."

Alexa's mind refused to absorb what he was saying. All she could think of was that Damien was under arrest. "The Hotel Marboeuf?" she repeated dully.

He nodded. "Bernard will take you north."

"What . . . what about Damien?"

Jules squeezed her hand. "I am sorry, *chérie,* there is nothing we can do."

Alexa stiffened in the seat, her mind slowly turning, at last beginning to function. "What do you mean there is nothing we can do? Damien is innocent. We have to get him out of there."

Jules only shook his head.

"Where is he?"

For a long moment he did not answer. "In the catacombs. There is a chamber beneath the office of the Prefect of Police. Eventually he will be placed in La Force Prison."

"The catacombs . . . Dear God, how could they do such a thing?" Tears welled in her eyes as macabre images surfaced in her head. She had heard about the catacombs. They were great limestone quarries that had lain under the city since Roman times. During the Terror, they were used as burial chambers for the thousands of prisoners who had climbed the steps to the guillotine. That Damien should be held prisoner in one of the grisly chambers, that he should be surrounded by aging bones and rotting corpses, was almost more than she could bear.

"I have to get him out of there," she said softly, wiping the tears from her cheeks. "I'm not leaving him in there."

"You must listen to me, *chérie*—"

"No! You must listen to me! It was my idea to steal those plans. I will not let him take the blame for it."

"If we had not taken them, he would have stolen them himself."

"Yes, I believe he would have. Which proves he has been telling the truth all along."

"That is not what General Moreau thinks."

"Wh-What do you mean?"

"The general believes that your husband meant to sell the plans to the highest bidder. Napoleon's army is a threat to a number of countries. Any one of them would pay very dearly for such valuable information."

"I—I don't care why he would have taken them. I don't care where he would have sold them. None of it matters anymore—none of it! I love him, Jules and I'm going to help him. There is nothing you can do or say that will stop me."

St. Owen swore softly.

"Let me out, Jules. I'll hire a cabriolet and get there on my own. I'll tell them I did it by myself. There's no reason to involve you—you've done enough already— more than enough. From here on, it's up to me."

Jules pulled hard on the horse's rein and the small black phaeton rolled to a stop. "Do you really believe I will let you go there alone?"

"Please, Jules. I have to do this."

The blond man looked at her hard. A long sigh whispered past his lips. "Telling them the truth is not the answer. They would probably kill both of you anyway, just to be certain the information did not somehow escape."

"What else can I do?"

"Try to get him out of there."

Hope flared in her heart. "Is there a chance we could succeed?"

"A slim one, but it is better than no chance at all."

"How? How do we go about it?"

Jules turned the horse down a side street, heading away from the Hotel Marboeuf. "There is an entrance to the catacombs on the Place Denfert-Rochereau near the north end of the Rue de la Tombe-Issoire. The place will not be heavily guarded—there is usually very little need. We can make our way to the tunnel that intersects the one beneath the Prefect of Police."

"Have you been there?"

"Once. They use the tunnel fairly often. We tried to get one of our people out a few months back."

"Did you?"

"No. They heard us coming. One of our men was captured, one was killed. Two of us were able to escape."

Alexa nervously wet her lips. "I'm sorry."

He shrugged into the darkness. "Perhaps this time our luck will be better."

"Yes . . . we must pray that it is." But she wondered what would happen, and if the catacombs might not add three more corpses to the thousands already entombed in the grotesque grave.

Victor Lafon stood behind the door at the top of the stairs.

"She is gone," Lieutenant Colbert said. "Run off with Jules St. Owen."

"Sacre bleu!" Victor slammed a fist against the door. "He must have known we were coming for her."

"Perhaps it is merely coincidence. Or she sent word that her husband had been called away. Perhaps she had simply been waiting for the chance to leave with her lover."

"Perhaps, but it is doubtful. Close off the city as best you can. Do not let anyone leave who appears in any way suspicious."

"And Falon? Shall we press him for the plans?"

"Not yet. He has no way of knowing the attempt was successful, and I am not yet ready to give him that satisfaction. Besides, there are other questions I need answered." A muscle tightened in his jaw, then relaxed. "Perhaps we have been given the perfect weapon. When your tasks are completed, you may join me and we will see."

The lieutenant saluted smartly. "I will not be gone long."

In the meantime, Victor returned downstairs. Falon was unconscious, the ropes cutting into the muscles across his chest, his head hanging forward, locks of his thick black hair falling haphazardly into his face.

"Wake him up," Victor told the sergeant.

The burly man grunted and reached for a tin pail half full of water. He tossed the contents into the major's bloody face, then cast the bucket noisily away. Falon groaned and his piercing blue eyes came open.

"So you are still among the living. That is good, Major, since I have some interesting news."

"There is very little of interest you could say to me, Victor." Damien eyed his captors through eyes he fought to keep open. Every bone in his body ached, every rib, muscle, and joint. He refused to look at the walls around him; he knew what was out there, and if he let it, the horror would only help to break him. It was all part of the game.

And in the contest of acquiring information, the sergeant knew exactly what he was about.

"So you think I know nothing of interest," Lafon said. "Perhaps you might be interested to know that while you have been . . . occupied here, your wife has run away with her lover."

Damien's brow arched up. "Oh, really? And just which lover is that?"

"Jules St. Owen." Lafon let him ponder the news. "I am sure you recall him—handsome, blond, extremely wealthy and powerful. She has been seeing the man for quite sometime."

"You're crazy if you think I'd believe that."

"No? St. Owen was seen more than once in front of your house, and we followed your wife to a rendezvous with him at the Café de Valois on two separate occasions." The colonel moved into the light of the flickering torches. "Think about it, Falon. Perhaps you will recall the way he danced with her at the Emperor's ball . . . the way his eyes always found her in the general's château. If I noticed, surely you must have. Remember . . . and perhaps you will hear the ring of truth in what I say."

Something shifted inside him, at first just a small, unobtrusive thread of doubt, nothing more than the merest ribbon. At least part of what Lafon said was true. St. Owen had been more than a little bit interested in Alexa, and there was a time he had believed that she had been interested in him.

The doubt seemed to swell, to grow into menacing proportions, forcing its unwanted presence into the front of his mind.

"Why are you telling me this? Even if it were the truth, what do you hope to gain?"

"The answer to some of our questions. Now that you

know where your wife's loyalties lay, perhaps you will tell us the truth of yours. We want to know how long you have been spying on us."

"I work for you, Victor. I have for the past eight years. If you believe anything else, then you are a fool."

"We are willing to make a deal. The woman has betrayed you for the second time. Forget about her and begin to think of yourself. Answer our questions and we will consider letting you go."

Damien spat on the floor at Lafon's feet. "Go to hell, Lafon."

"Sergeant Piquerel. Perhaps you can convince the major to answer our questions."

But Damien's mind was no longer on the round of brutal blows he was about to take. It was on Alexa and the fact that Victor Lafon was telling the truth. He had known the man for the past eight years. He wasn't a liar, and certainly not a convincing one. Alexa had left with St. Owen. The question remained: Why had she done it?

Damien took the first blow to the stomach and his head reeled with nauseating pain. Still, all he could think of was his wife and Jules St. Owen. Had St. Owen discovered his arrest, realized the threat to Alexa, and gone to her aid? It was possible, though it seemed unlikely he could have found out in such a short time. Even if he had meant to help, why would he do it? Why would he risk his life for a woman he barely knew?

And what about the meetings Lafon had mentioned? Why would she have gone to the café? What other reason could she have besides the conclusion Lafon had drawn?

Piquerel slammed a fist into his jaw, and his head snapped back. Consciousness faded then returned, and with it, an image of Alexa. She was smiling at him, a soft smile of thanks for agreeing to help Jean-Paul. Why had she gone to St. Owen? Had she really become the man's lover? The questions haunted him, made his insides twist, made him want to let the black swirls overwhelm him.

Instead came the answer, swift and hard. Because she still didn't trust him. Because, though he craved that trust, he had never really placed his trust in her.

She had wanted to go home. Perhaps St. Owen had promised to help her. He owned a number of ships; he could see it done, if he knew that was what Alexa wanted. Jules was known for his skills at seduction, he would know only too well exactly what to say and do. And for all her bravado, his wife was still naive.

He thought of Alexa with Jules and felt as though a knife had pierced his chest. Perhaps St. Owen would take her back to England. Perhaps he meant to stay there with her. Perhaps he merely meant to seduce her, make love to her until he grew tired of her, then send her on her way.

Damien took a blow to the stomach that doubled him over, but it couldn't match the pain he felt in his heart. The bitter ache swelled, nearly squeezing the breath from his lungs, making a hard knot tighten in his throat.

What happened to him no longer mattered. It was Alexa he feared for. Alexa. He had no way of knowing where she was or if she would ever get back home.

He had no way of knowing what went on between her and St. Owen, yet somehow it no longer mattered. He only knew that he was responsible, that more than anything in this world, he wanted her to be safe.

He only knew that no matter how much he wished he could change things, he would never see his beautiful wife again.

Chapter Twenty-Two

"**G**IVE ME YOUR HAND."

ALEXA REACHED OUT AND HER TREMBLING FINGERS were clasped in Jules's strong, comforting grip. She could feel his strength seeping into her, and in the light of the small brass lantern they had taken from the side of the carriage, she smiled her thanks into his handsome face.

"Better?" he asked, his blond hair gleaming in the light reflected off the walls.

"Much better. I'll be fine now. Thank you."

"My pleasure." But he didn't let go of her hand, and Alexa felt grateful.

They descended the last of the stairs leading into the tunnel, and darkness closed around them. It was damp and musty and there was an odd smell she finally identified as sodden, rotting fabric. She shivered to think what that other decaying smell was, and yet it was not putrid as she had expected. A number of years had passed since they had used this end of the quarry, Jules had told her. What bodies they would see had long ago shriveled up, or the bones been stripped bare of flesh altogether.

As they rounded a corner of the tunnel and the light from the lantern cast its eerie glow against the walls, she saw that he had spoken the truth.

Stacks of shriveled corpses, many of them headless, their skulls detached and staring sightlessly in their direction, caught her eye and held her in a terrifying macabre spell. Her stomach clenched violently and the bile rose up in her throat.

"Dear God in heaven." Her fingers bit into the skin on Jules's hand.

"It is all right, *chérie*. They can hurt no one now."

She forced down her horror. "I—I know. I'm sorry. It's just that—"

"There is no need to explain. I myself am not immune. I do not believe it is a sight a sane man could ever get used to. Try to look only in front of you. Come, we must hurry."

She forced herself to move, careful to keep her eyes straight ahead, never straying from the small yellow circle of light. Her heart beat frantically as she forced the dank air into her lungs.

"What—What is that sound?" She paused at a high-pitched chattering that echoed against the tunnel walls.

"It does not matter. Just keep moving and watch where you step."

"Tell me, Jules."

"Rats." He tightened his grip and urged her forward, forcing her to ignore the odious creatures and the icy shiver that slid through her body.

"We are close now," he whispered, pulling her to a halt where the tunnel split again. "The sound of our footfalls will carry. We must go quietly; watch very carefully where you step."

She nodded, but he didn't move forward. "Stay here for a moment. I will see what lies ahead."

He left her in the small round circle of light. She wondered how he could see where he was going in the suffocating blackness. She barely heard his footsteps receding in the distance, then she heard nothing at all.

Alexa shivered and pulled her cloak more tightly around her. In the silence of the cavern, water dripped from the ceiling and crumbled earth muddied the ground at her feet. The rats had stopped their chatter, but still there were odd sounds in the darkness; she was glad she didn't know what they were. She waited for Jules in nervous silence, all the while wondering about her husband. Damien was down here . . . somewhere. She prayed they would be able to reach him before it was too late.

A pebble glanced off the wall in the nearby darkness. Alexa jerked and spun toward the sound, then let out a breath of relief as Jules's golden head appeared in the lamplight.

"I saw him," he said, and her heart speeded up even more. "There is a guard posted where the tunnel divides again. I will have to dispense with the man if we are to free him."

"Was he all right?"

"I only caught a glimpse. He is farther down the tunnel near the end."

"Were there other men with him?"

"I saw only one. I will try to distract him, once I have finished with the guard. While I see to him, you must go in and free your husband."

She swallowed hard and nodded.

"If anything should happen, it is not difficult to find your way back out. Just keep taking the tunnel to the left. There are only four turns before you reach the stairs leading up to the street."

"Nothing is going to happen," she said firmly. "We're going to get Damien and then we're going to leave."

"Bien sûr, chérie. There is no doubt that we will, but just in case . . . remember to stay to your left."

She wouldn't even consider the possibility that Jules might not leave with them. Instead she fixed her mind on the task ahead and carefully began to place one foot quietly in front of the other.

They turned into the last passage before the split, and Jules stopped her halfway down the corridor.

"We must leave the lantern here. Once the tunnel branches, we will be able to see by the light at the guard's station."

"All right." She handed the lamp to Jules and he set it near the side of the tunnel. A gaping, open-mouth skull fell into the light's yellow rays. Bodies were stacked like cordwood above it, ten high up to the ceiling. The skin of the corpses stretched like jerked beef over the fleshless bones, and the long scraggly hair on some of the skulls fell into the eyeless sockets.

Alexa swallowed back a second wave of nausea. "We must go."

"There is one more thing."

"Yes?"

"Your husband. It appears he has been beaten very badly. But I believe he will still be able to walk."

"Dear God."

"He is a hard man. He has probably suffered far worse."

Alexa thought about that and prayed he would never have to face such circumstances again. Moving through the darkness, they made the last few feet to the split in the tunnel, and the soft glow of the guard's lantern began to ease their way. Jules pulled her into the shadows and handed her a short-bladed knife.

"He appears to be tied very tightly. You will need this to cut the ropes. I will see to the guard. Stay here till I return."

He crept forward in silence, pausing when a pebble crunched underfoot and the guard turned searching eyes into the shadows. Satisfied that there was nothing wrong, the man started walking away and Jules slipped up behind him. Wrapping a strong arm around the smaller man's neck, he slowly began to squeeze.

Alexa bit her lip as the soldier struggled and tried to kick out, but in seconds Jules had silenced him. He dragged the guard back into the shadows and dumped his unconscious body into the dirt.

A noise sounded in the passageway ahead of them.

"Eh, Henri—is that you?" It was the voice of the soldier who had been standing in the tunnel next to Damien. Jules quickly urged Alexa to the opposite side of the tunnel while the burly man slowly began making his way back toward his friend.

"Eh, Henri!" he called out, and Jules mumbled something in return. *"Nom de Dieu,* you better not be off swilling that rotten *patis* your uncle brews."

The moment the man stepped into the darkness, Alexa slipped behind him, leaving the soldier's fate to Jules. She heard the sounds of scuffling behind her, heard the grunts and groans of men landing blows, but wasted no time in considering the outcome.

Instead she raced on toward the second wall of light at the end of the passage, straight toward the dark-haired man slumped forward in his chair.

"Damien?" Her voice shook as she knelt beside him. "Damien, my love, it's Alexa." She said the words softly, soothingly, smoothing back damp black locks of his hair. He stirred as her fingers touched his forehead, roused himself and slowly lifted his head. Fear for him sliced through her, and pity and a well of love unlike anything she had ever known.

"Alexa?" Damien repeated the name in a voice thick with pain and fatigue. His head spun and dizziness beckoned him back toward the safety of unconsciousness. He tried to open his eyes, but the world looked hazy and dim, and time seemed to have slowed to immeasurable moments even more sluggish than the unsteady thudding of his heart. Perhaps that was why he thought he had heard her call his name.

Cool fingers ran along his cheek. "Yes, darling, I'm right beside you. I've come to take you out of here."

He tried to moisten his lips, to make sense of what he was hearing, but something held him back from the nightmare he would face once his eyes came open. He mumbled something instead and heard a soft response, then he felt a tugging on the ropes around his chest and realized someone worked at cutting through his bonds.

The knife that flashed in the lamplight moved frantically. The first rope slackened, and without its support he sagged forward and would have fallen if a slim arm hadn't caught his shoulders and propped him back in his chair.

"It's all right, darling," the woman said in a voice on the edge of tears. "You're going to be fine just as soon as we get you out of here."

"Alexa . . . ?" The word came out on a soft breath of air, yet he knew it could not be. He swallowed against the trembling that had suddenly seized his body. This time he opened his eyes and they came to rest on her face.

Ruby red lips, fiery-dark auburn hair . . . the prettiest green eyes he had ever seen. "You . . . came . . . back," he said, his mind still refusing to function, knowing she could not possibly have come.

Her teeth clamped down on her trembling bottom lip. "Dear God, did you think that I would leave you?"

"St. . . . Owen. You left with . . . St. Owen." He felt foolish saying the words aloud. Alexa couldn't be there. He was talking to an illusion. He glanced at the stacks of grisly cadavers, at the severed skulls and headless corpses. It wasn't any wonder he was losing his mind—he was trapped in the bowels of hell.

"No, my love," the soft voice soothed as the knife sawed fiercely at the rope around his legs. "I didn't leave with Jules. I would never leave you. Never."

"Alexa . . ." He couldn't seem to stop saying her name, couldn't drag his gaze from the image so like her. It made a pain slice into his heart.

He thought of the night she had come to him at the inn, at the feelings she had held for him and the way he had hurt her. It made an ache well up inside him, made him want to curse himself for the things he had done.

"Everything is going to be all right," the soft voice said, the knife still moving, the lovely specter haunting in the eerie glow of the lamp.

Insanely, he found himself believing it might be so.

"Damien, can you hear me?"

She caught his chin with her soft slender fingers and forced him to look at her. He nodded, wondering how the whole thing could possibly seem so real.

"Damien—I love you." The words brought a swift, hard lump to his throat.

He stared into the illusion of her lovely green eyes, wishing he could slip into the arms of the beautiful vision that spoke the words he had wanted to hear for so long. How few people in his life had ever said them? Fewer still were the ones who really meant them.

"Did you hear me?" the voice said, giving his shoulder a gentle shake. The last words came out broken. "I said . . . I . . . love you."

Tears burned the backs of his eyes. He tried to stop

them from falling, tried to will them away, but they
formed in great droplets and began to slide into the
hollows of his cheeks. "Say it again," he whispered.
"Say it one more time before you leave."

"I'm not leaving! Not without you! I love you," she
said on a sob. "So much it hurts. So much, I think I'll
die of it. Dear God, Damien, please—tell me you understand what I'm trying to say."

The image grew more vivid, and she looked as
though she meant it. Deep lines of worry etched her
face, and he saw her terrible fear for him. She loved
him. And she had not left with Jules.

"You . . . didn't go," he whispered. "You didn't
leave."

"We're leaving here together," she said as the last
rope tying him down broke free. "Dammit, we're leaving this place together!" She shook him again, but he
still couldn't rouse himself.

"You're better off . . . with St. Owen," he said to
the vision, words he had thought before but refused to
admit. "I'm . . . no good for you. All I ever do is hurt
you. I don't even know who I am anymore."

He hadn't meant to say it. He didn't even know
where the words had come from, only that they were
the truth. Too many lies. Too many games. Too many
years of deception. In the end he had only deceived
himself.

A slender hand gently touched his cheek. "I know
who you are," the vision said. "You're the sum of all of
the parts you have played. You're everything I ever
wanted, everything I ever needed in a man, and I love
all that you are."

He saw her tear-filled expression and the love for him
reflected in her eyes. The pain in his heart seemed to
ease, and for the first time the darkness in his mind
began to fade. The room swam erratically then came
sharply into focus. The buzzing had stopped in his ears.

Time, and the rhythm of his heart, had both returned to normal.

"Alexa . . ." he whispered, astonished to discover that her image still remained—that Alexa was really there. "Sweet God, what are you doing here?"

She cupped his face in her trembling hands and pressed a soft kiss on his swollen lips. "There isn't time to explain. We have to get out of here." Sliding an arm beneath his shoulders, she helped him to his feet and he leaned heavily against her.

"You shouldn't have come. You should have left with St. Owen, gotten safely away. You should have—"

"There are a lot of things I should have done. But this was the most important. Now it's time for us to leave."

His mind just beginning to function, Damien nodded and together they stumbled off down the tunnel. Alexa's arm beneath his shoulders propped him up, and by the time they reached the light from the perimeter guard's station, his steps had begun to grow more steady.

She picked up the lamp resting on a scarred wooden table along one wall and they continued along the passage. When they reached a fork in the tunnel, she paused.

"Jules came with me. He knew they had brought you here. He knew a way to get in. He is the one who took care of the guards." He glanced around but saw nothing. "Dear Lord, something must have happened. He should be waiting for us here."

Damien straightened away from her. It took all of his will just to let her go. "Stay back in the shadows."

"But you aren't strong enough—"

"Now that you're here, I'll be fine." He took the lamp and moved away from her, a bit clumsily at first, then with more certainty and grim determination. Alexa had risked her life for him. She had told him she loved him, and he damned well knew how much he loved her.

Someone groaned in the darkness, and he went still as he strained to hear. Another low groan. Damien moved toward the sound and so did Alexa.

"Over here," he called out to her softly, a rough note rising in his voice as he peered at the man in the shadows. St. Owen lay unmoving in a growing circle of blood. A bone-handled knife reflected silver in the lamplight. A few feet away Sergeant Piquerel was sprawled in a heap, his thick neck bent at an unnatural angle.

Damien heard the rustle of skirts as Alexa knelt beside him.

"Dear God—oh, dear God—not Jules."

At the sound of his name, the blond man opened his light blue eyes. He smiled when he saw Alexa and that Damien was standing there beside her.

"So . . . *chérie* . . . this has not all been in vain . . . after all. You have found . . . your man . . . now you must . . . go."

Alexa bit her lip. "Jules . . ."

Damien heard the pain in her voice as she reached for the blond man's hand. In the past he would have been jealous, now he felt only a fleeting regret that his wife had lost such a good and loyal friend.

St. Owen squeezed her hand. "Do . . . as I say, *chérie*. Take your husband . . . and make good your escape."

"I can't leave you, Jules. I won't. Damien, tell him we aren't leaving him here."

It was the smart thing to do. He knew it and so did St. Owen. Every minute was crucial, every second wasted could mean certain death. But one look at Alexa's tortured expression and he knew he would give up his life before he would ever disappoint her again.

"You aren't getting off that easy, St. Owen. The three

of us are getting the hell out of here." Swaying unsteadily on his feet, Damien bent forward and so did
Alexa.

"There is . . . not time," protested the Frenchman,
but neither of them paid him any heed. Together they
forced him to stand, then Alexa tore a wad of fabric
from her underskirt and stuffed it into the wound in his
chest.

Jules groaned weakly and his head slumped forward.
Damien slid an arm beneath one shoulder and Alexa
the other. The three of them staggered off down the
passage.

"Stay to the left," Alexa instructed when they
reached a split in the tunnel. They stumbled off again,
but had to stop a number of times to rest and steady
their shaking limbs. When they reached the stairs leading up to the street, he couldn't believe they had actually made it this far.

"This won't be easy," he said between labored
breaths.

"We can do it," said Alexa, and he remembered
when she had said much the same to Jean-Paul. Shoring
up his strength, he roused St. Owen and they started
up the stairs. Alexa put all her weight against the
Frenchman's shoulder and the three of them staggered
upward, one foot unsteadily in front of the next, each
step painful and uncertain, yet he was filled with a
growing hope that they might actually make it.

Noises sounded in the tunnel behind them and fear
clenched his stomach.

Had Lafon returned and discovered him gone? Were
the colonel and his men racing after them even now,
running through the grisly passages, deadly in their intent? He fought down his fears and the bile in his throat
at the fate they would suffer should they fail. At last
they stepped out onto the street.

The cool night air revived him. He drew great heaving breaths into his lungs.

"The carriage is just round the corner," Alexa said, her breath coming nearly as fast as his own.

He nodded, hoarding every ounce of his strength. He glanced right and then left and quickly back over his shoulder. There was no one on the street except a stray yellow cat and a drunk passed out in the gutter.

They reached the carriage and St. Owen roused himself enough to speak. "Go . . . to the . . . Hotel Marboeuf. Safe . . . there. Bernard can . . . help." As they boosted him into the carriage, he groaned, then lapsed once more into unconsciousness.

Damien propped him carefully up on the seat of the small black phaeton, held his aching ribs as Alexa helped him climb in, then fell back heavily against the seat. He barely noticed when Alexa climbed in, picked up the reins and swung the small conveyance out into the street.

Damien closed his eyes for a moment, trying to summon more of his strength. He must have passed out, for when he looked around him again, the phaeton was pulling into the stableyard at the rear of the Hotel Marboeuf and a huge bearded man was walking along beside it, peering worriedly into the seat.

"It's Jules," Alexa explained to the man who could only be St. Owen's man, Bernard. "He has been gravely injured, and my husband needs help too."

The bearded man reached up and carefully lifted Jules into his arms. The stout man cradled him like a baby against his barrel chest. "I will see to him. What about you, m'sieur? You are certain you can make it on your own?"

"I'll make it," Damien said. He had never been more determined.

Alexa reached toward him. "I'll help you." She

swung down first from the carriage, then let him lean on her for support as he made his own way down.

She was there to help, Damien realized, just as she said. The truth was, she had always been there for him. Tonight—undeterred by the horrors of the catacombs. In the castle, defending him against his sister and mother, even that night on the beach when Bewicke had come and she had believed he was a traitor. Still, she had risked herself to save him.

She had stood by him as no woman ever had, and very few men. No matter what happened, he would never forget it . . . or the tender words she had spoken.

Now it was time for him to stand by her.

He meant to see her safe, and nothing—no one—not even Napoleon's Grande Armée, was going to stop him.

Alexa barely noticed her husband's heavy weight as she helped him across the courtyard toward the tall stone building soon to be their refuge. All she could think of was how he had looked in that hell that was his prison, at the expression on his face when she had told him she loved him.

He had stared at her for long, heartbreaking moments, then his beautiful blue eyes had filled with tears. She could hardly believe it. Such a hard man, so afraid to show his feelings, yet glistening drops of wetness spilled over onto his cheeks.

Say it again he'd said, a fierce look of yearning sweeping into his battered face. *I've got to hear you say it one more time.*

Alexa's heart twisted at the memory. She could never have guessed how badly he had longed to hear the words; she only wished she had said them long ago. He had looked at her and said she should have left with Jules St. Owen, had believed she had betrayed him, yet thought only of her safety. Even now tears welled just to think of it. Alexa blinked them away.

"How are you doing?" she asked gently. She could feel his muscles straining as she guided him through the door, but with every step he took, he seemed to be getting stronger. "Are you feeling any better?"

"Better than I expected." He turned and lightly kissed her lips. "Thanks to you." Alexa's heart turned over. They made their way into the kitchen and he paused.

"What is it?" she asked, concern for him returning, riding heavy inside her breast.

"I need something to bind my ribs."

"Stay here. I'll be right back." As he leaned against a chopping block, she turned to leave, but a voice from the corner stayed the move.

"I will get you something." A gray-haired woman finished hefting a heavy kettle onto the fire, and a little of the water slopped over then rose upward in a burst of steam. She turned away from the fire and silently left the kitchen, returning a few moments later with a fresh-washed bed linen, which she began to tear into strips.

"Merci beaucoup," Alexa said softly, accepting the makeshift bandage as Damien peeled off his bloody shirt. Her stomach tightened at the mass of bruises covering his ribs, at the dried blood matting the curly black hair on his chest.

"Sit down," she instructed a little more fiercely than she had intended. "I need to clean those cuts and bruises." She took a sharp breath to steady herself, knowing she was close to falling apart and determined it would not happen.

The woman magically appeared again, providing rags and a pan of boiling water. Alexa's hands shook as she worked over Damien's torn and bloodied flesh. He must have sensed her concern, for he caught her hand, raised it gently and pressed his lips against the palm.

Neither of them spoke; the woman was there, after all, and there was such a tender look on his face it seemed no words were needed. It made her insides flutter and a softness steal into her heart. When she finished washing the abrasions, she wrapped the linen bandage around his ribs, trying to ignore his sharp hiss of pain and the answering pain she felt for him inside her.

"I—I'm sorry. I didn't mean to hurt you."

He only shook his head. "You didn't do it. None of this has been your fault—none of it."

An ache rose up in her chest for she knew it wasn't the truth. "I wish that was true, but unfortunately it is not. Everything that has happened has been my fault." She glanced up to see the old woman leaving the room, the door closing quietly behind her. "Jules and I . . . we were the ones who stole the plans."

The breath escaped softly from his lungs. "That is what this is about? They discovered the theft of the plans?"

She nodded, barely able to meet his eyes. "Surely they told you."

"No. They were baiting me, trying to find out how much I knew."

Alexa bit her lip.

"When did you do it?"

"The night Moreau called you to his office."

"Where are the documents now?"

"We sent them north. Jules has a boat leaving for England. The plans are being delivered to General Wilcox."

Damien only nodded. "I had heard St. Owen was opposed to the Emperor's policies. I never would have guessed how strongly he felt."

"Wilcox asked him to help me. I wanted to tell you but . . ."

"But you were afraid to trust me."

"Yes."

"And now?" he asked.

"Now I . . . I realize that none of it matters. I love you. I don't care what you've done or why. I don't care what you believe in. And if you meant what you said that night beside the Seine . . . if you love me a tenth as much as I love you, it doesn't matter where we go, as long as we are together."

He pulled her into his arms and buried his face in her hair. Beneath her hands she could feel the steady beating of his heart.

"I meant it," he whispered. "I meant every word. I love you, Alexa. More than life itself. I love you and I never want to risk losing you again."

Her heart swelled with joy at his words. She slid her arms around his neck and held him close against her. Only the concern she felt for his cracked and bruised ribs convinced her to release him. She started to say something more, but the gray-haired woman pushed open the door.

"M'sieur St. Owen—'e is asking for you. You must follow me upstairs."

Her stomach twisted with a fresh bout of worry. Dear God, he had been such a dear and loyal friend.

"He's conscious at least," Damien said. "That's a good sign."

Alexa took his hand and together they left the kitchen, heading for the stairs. Damien grimaced with each upward step, but finally they made it to the landing at the top.

"This way, m'sieur." The old woman led them down the hall to a large room with heavy silk draperies and molded ceilings.

"Jules . . ." Alexa hurried toward him and knelt

worriedly at his bedside. His face was ashen, his lips thinned in a silent grimace of pain. She glanced up at Bernard.

"Is he . . . ?"

" 'E is going to live—no thanks to 'is recklessness. *Mon Dieu,* but the man 'as a death wish."

"Will he be able to travel? He cannot stay here. They'll be looking for him. He'll have to leave the city."

"I will see it done," said Bernard, "just as I will do the same for you."

She turned to look at Jules and saw that his eyes were open. "Oh, Jules, I'm so sorry." Tears spilled onto her cheeks.

"Do not be sorry . . . *chérie.* Were it not for you and the major . . . I would not still be alive."

"You'll have to leave, Jules. They're bound to discover your part in this. Dear God, you've lost everything."

His lips curved faintly in a smile. "I am a man of the sea . . . remember? There are a dozen ports I can call home. And money . . . is not a problem."

"Oh, Jules, how can I ever repay you?"

"One of your beautiful smiles, *chérie* . . . is more than payment enough." He turned to look at Damien, his pain-filled gaze searching, trying to decipher the truth. "You are . . . a very lucky man . . . Major Falon." His glance strayed toward Alexa. "Your beautiful wife . . . loves you very much."

Damien met his intense gaze squarely. "Not nearly as much as I love her."

Jules's light eyes held his. "If that is so . . . then I hope you will do as I say."

"Which is?"

"Travel north. Bernard can get you . . . out of the city. I own ships in Le Havre. One will soon be sailing for America. I have been there. It is a good . . . strong country with . . . many opportunities. Your past . . .

will not matter. I will lend you some money . . . help
you get started—''

Damien cut him off. "You're a good man, St. Owen. I
hope one day you will call me friend, as you have be-
friended Alexa. As far as the other, north to Le Havre is
fine, but the ship we'll be catching will be taking us to
a neutral port so that we may go back to England. I'm
returning my wife to her home."

Alexa came to her feet, uncertainty piercing her
heart. "But we can't go back there. If they catch you,
they'll kill you—and if you leave—I don't want to stay.
Not without you. I want to go with you."

Damien only smiled. "Someday, my love, you're going to learn to trust me. We'll be returning home together—back to Castle Falon. Everything I told you was
the truth."

Her knees nearly buckled with the wave of relief that
swept through her. "Thank God."

"God and Jules St. Owen," he said, reaching out to
clasp the blond man's hand.

Another brief smile touched Jules's lips. "Perhaps
one day we shall meet again. In the meantime . . .
you should go. Bernard will see you to the edge of the
city. There will be someone there to take you north. If
you hurry . . . you can still catch the small boat sailing for England." He turned and looked at Alexa. "It
might be nice . . . *chérie* . . . to deliver those plans
yourself."

There was a flurry of movement after that. Before
she knew it, she was kissing Jules's cheek in farewell,
being swept from the room, down the stairs, and into
the flatbed of a wagon. The small traveling bag she had
taken from the house was tossed in with her, as well as
some blankets and food. Damien climbed in and a tarp
was thrown over them, then a thick layer of straw. Several bleating sheep were set atop it, the odor of their
damp wool seeping through the canvas.

Bernard climbed up on the wagon and the heavy conveyance rolled from the stable and onto the paving stones leading out of the city.

Surprisingly, inside their uncomfortable quarters, Damien fell asleep. Exhaustion and pain had taken their toll, leaving him weakened and vulnerable as she had rarely seen him.

Tears touched her eyes when she realized how tightly he still clutched her hand. And that his battered lips were gently pressed against it.

Chapter Twenty-Three

DAMIEN LAY ATOP THE BED IN THEIR SMALL ATTIC CHAMBER IN LES DEUX POISSON, AN INN CALLED THE TWO FISH THAT sat on the quay in Le Havre, overlooking the Seine. Across the cobbled street below, the tall masts of sailing ships swayed gently in the afternoon breeze, their rigging like brass chimes clattering in the salty air blowing in from the sea.

He loved the smell. It reminded him of Falon, and that with luck they would soon be home.

He couldn't wait to get there, had never wanted to see England so badly. But he had never had a wife he loved or a future that looked bright instead of barren.

Alexa stood there now, staring out the window, her slender shoulders squared against the worry that had weighed them down since she had come for him in the tunnel. She was wearing only her chemise, her long silky hair brushed out and hanging nearly to her hips.

She had bathed while he'd been sleeping; now she fretted at the window, scanning the street below for soldiers who might arrive to search the inn.

"Alexa, love, come here," he said softly. He had been watching her for some time, caught up in the gentle rise and fall of her breasts, the tempting movements of her hips beneath the thin white lawn fabric.

She turned and a soft smile curved her lips. "I thought you were sleeping."

"Not for some time." He smiled. "I've been enjoying the chance to watch you. I only wish you wouldn't worry so." His eyes ran over her lovely face as she walked toward him, noting the slight purple smudges beneath her eyes, the faint lines marring her forehead. "Joseph is a capable man. He's keeping watch outside near the front."

St. Owen's man had taken them north out of Paris, and his skill and cunning had gotten them safely this far. "He'll let us know if there is any sign of trouble."

Damien hoped his words eased her mind. In truth, he was worried enough for them both, as he had been for the last three days, the length of their grueling trek across the country. It did neither of them any good, and as soon as it was dark—if their luck continued to hold—they would be leaving Le Havre and heading north to the tiny village of Etretat, where their small sailing vessel would be waiting.

Alexa approached him beside the bed. "How are you feeling?"

His head ached and so did his ribs. He was a mass of purple bruises from the top of his head to the soles of his feet. Still, one look at her big green eyes, those pouty rose lips, one glance at the points of her breasts pushing up against the thin white fabric, and his body went hard with wanting.

He smiled at her warmly. "At the moment, I'm feeling lonesome." He ran a finger up the smooth white skin on the inside of her arm. "Why don't you join me?" He was naked beneath the bedcovers, and already his shaft pressed hard against the quilt.

"I'm afraid I'm not very sleepy."

He smiled wickedly. "Neither am I."

Her eyes went wide. "Surely you can't mean to . . ." A flush rose into her cheeks. "Sweet God, Damien, you're injured. Your poor ribs couldn't possibly stand that sort of . . . exertion." The blush grew deeper and she glanced away.

Damien chuckled softly. "It wouldn't be easy, I'll grant you. Perhaps just kissing you would be enough."

She hesitated only a moment. Leaning forward, she pressed a soft kiss on his lips, and the scent of roses drifted up from her freshly washed hair. He caught the back of her neck and pulled her mouth down to his in a kiss that was a whole lot less gentle. He ran his tongue across her bottom lip, teased the corners of her mouth until she opened to him, then tasted the sweet dark cavern inside. He didn't miss her soft moan of pleasure.

"I think, my love, that perhaps you are just as lonely as I am." He framed her face between his hands and deepened the kiss, sucking her tongue into his mouth before his hands strayed down to her breasts. He cupped them, teased the small buds at the crests into stiff upthrusting peaks and felt her tremble, then lowered his head and took one into his mouth.

"Damien . . ." Lacing her fingers in his hair, she arched her back so that he might take more of her.

The chemise grew damp from his attentions, turned translucent and even more seductive as it plastered itself against her tempting curves. He continued with an even greater fervor, and had Alexa squirming by the time he reached for the hem of the garment and lifted it over her head.

A low groan came from his throat at the sight of her

lovely bare breasts with their small pink aureoles. He
suckled her there and felt her slender body tremble.

"We . . . we can't do this." She eased a little away
from him. "Your poor bruised ribs will never—"

"Perhaps I can think of a way." He leaned forward,
circled her nipple with his tongue, then gently bit the
end. "If I stayed right here and you climbed up beside
me . . ." He eased aside the bedding, revealing his
hardened arousal, and heard her soft intake of breath.

"What . . . if I hurt you?"

"I'm willing to take the risk."

Alexa gazed down at her husband's powerful body,
admiring his solid, thickly muscled shoulders, hair-cov-
ered chest, flat stomach, and narrow hips. "I have a
better idea," she said.

Climbing carefully up on the mattress, she leaned forward and kissed him, not the gentle, soft kiss she was
sure he expected, but a hot, fiery kiss that made the
muscles of his stomach clench and his shaft rise up and
harden even more. She rained warm kisses along his
jaw, then continued down the side of his neck, across
his shoulders, and onto his chest. She paused at his flat
copper nipples, enjoying the masculine feel of them,
rough and hard beneath her tongue, then moved lower,
past his navel, pausing there to kiss it, then teasing him
with her lips as her mouth trailed relentlessly lower.

"Alexa, what in God's name . . . ?" But he needn't
have asked, for just then her hand wrapped around his
hardness and her tongue flicked over the long, hot
length of him.

She heard his low groan of pleasure when she began
to stroke him. The long muscles in his thighs went taut
and a tiny thrill shot through her. Since that night in
the library, she had wondered if she could do to him
what he had done to her, and this night she wanted to
please him.

They were still not out of danger, and both of them

knew it. If something were to happen, if, God forbid, they were caught or even killed, she wanted these last moments to remember, to carry with her through the time and beyond.

She licked his hard length slowly then opened her mouth and took him as deeply as she could, her tongue doing wicked things to his hot, tightly stretched skin. He felt like satin over steel, and his musky male taste made the dampness pool between her legs.

"Sweet Christ," he whispered, his tone rough and husky, "I can't . . . I won't be able to . . . Alexa, I can't stand much more."

Still, she did not falter, her mouth and tongue relentless. She meant to bring him release, to give him pleasure without pain, to show him how much she loved him in a way he would not soon forget, but as she bent over him on her hands and knees, he moved a little, adjusting her thighs apart as he settled himself beneath her, his head propped on a pillow between her legs.

"Two can play at this game," he said softly before his tongue ran over her thigh and his lips pressed warm kisses against her flesh.

Dear God, what was he doing? She realized his intention even as he gripped her hips and his mouth closed over the hard-soft bud that throbbed with heat at the core of her. A tiny cry escaped at the fires he stirred and the darkly erotic sensations that were burgeoning inside her. She tried to renew her efforts to bring him pleasure, to ignore the shameless things he was doing and the heat that roared through her body, but when his warm tongue gently began to lave her, when his fingers slid inside and began to stroke her with the same relentless rhythm as his mouth, white heat roared through her veins.

Tendrils of flame raced through her body, making her insides quiver and tighten. Pinpricks of sweetness burst inside her, shattered her into a thousand pieces.

"Damien, dear God!" She arched her back and gave herself up to the fiery sensations, to the spasms of pleasure engulfing her body, the bursts of red and gold in the eye of her mind, and the delicious sweetness washing through her limbs. When it was over, she felt weakened and shaky, barely able to move. Finally, she eased herself away from him, but she still did not leave.

Instead she turned and pressed a soft kiss on his lips. "That wasn't exactly the way I had it planned." Another warm kiss and then she smiled. "Now it's your turn."

"But—"

"Promise me you won't move—I don't want to hurt your ribs."

Bright blue eyes came to rest on her face. "That, my sweet wife, is a whole lot easier than it sounds."

She kissed him again, and Damien kissed her back, deeply, thoroughly, until he had her trembling. Forcing herself under control, she positioned herself astride his hips and with gentle determination carefully eased his hard length inside her. Damien hissed in a breath but did not move.

Alexa rose slowly, drawing his hardened length out then sinking down until he filled her again. She came up on her knees and sank back down, came up and sank down. She could feel the tightening of his muscles, feel his body begin to tremble beneath her. Desire blazed in his eyes as he watched her, and love for him swirled through her with the same growing fierceness as her need.

She leaned forward and increased the rhythm.

"Alexa . . . love," he whispered. He clenched his teeth, and his eyes slid closed against the tension gripping his body. He arched upward once, forgetting his promise, then hissed against the pain that shot through his ribs.

Alexa instantly froze.

"Good Christ, don't stop."

"But you're injured. I knew we shouldn't—"

"The pain I'm suffering now hurts far more than my ribs."

She laughed softly and began to move again, arching her back to take all of him, thrusting her breasts out then shivering as Damien filled his hands with them and began to stroke their fullness.

This time he almost kept his promise not to move. It wasn't until the very end that he gripped her hips and drove himself deep and hard inside her. A sheen of perspiration covered the straining muscles across his chest as he pounded into her again and again.

She hadn't expected to be caught up in the pleasure so fiercely, but it raced through her body and she joined him in a rippling burst of sweetness that left her feeling limp and replete, sated and warmly content.

She nestled at his side, and he wrapped his arms around her. In time she fell asleep, only to be awakened when he gently shook her shoulder.

"What is it?" Coming fully awake, she sat up in the bed. At the worry etched on his face, her heart began to thud erratically.

"Soldiers. A troop of Napoleon's *Chausseurs* have entered the city. They're searching every inn and tavern. We have to get away."

"Dear God . . ." But she said no more, just hurriedly climbed out of bed and pulled on her simple clothes. Quickly braiding her hair in a single long braid, she slipped on her shoes and grabbed up her cloak. Damien wrapped it around her shoulders as he led her from the room.

Out in the hallway, Joseph stood waiting, a darkhaired man, short but solidly built, his flat felt cap pulled low across a too-wide forehead. He was a homely man, some would say, yet there was a certain charm about him, and a loyalty to Jules St. Owen that boarded on the fanatic.

"How much time do we have?" Damien asked him.

"Not much, I am afraid. The wagon awaits us in the alley."

"Take her. I'll check the front then join you through the kitchen at the rear."

Joseph complied without hesitation, taking Alexa's arm and firmly guiding her off toward the back stairs leading to the alley. She glanced over her shoulder as she began her descent, then cried out at the sight of four uniformed soldiers bursting through the door at the bottom of the stairs.

"Run for the wagon!" Joseph commanded, the scowl on his homely face making him look even more fierce.

Alexa glanced back up the stairs, but they were blocked by Damien's rapid descent into the fray. She flattened herself against the wall and her husband rushed past her. Joseph took the first soldier out with a blow to the stomach, doubling him over, and a punch to the jaw that sent him sprawling. He swung a brutal right hand at the second man's nose, blood splattered, and the two began to trade hard, resounding punches.

Descending the last of the stairs two at a time, Damien clashed with the third man, landing a blow that must have tortured his ribs, for a grimace of pain twisted his features. He ducked the fourth man's blow and turned back to the third, who drew his sword with a whoosh from the scabbard at his waist.

"Damien!" Alexa screamed as he lifted a booted foot and kicked the tall soldier backward on the stairs. The man hit the ground with a harsh grunt of pain then lay unmoving, his red and navy-blue uniform soiled by the dirt off Damien's boot.

Reaching toward the fallen sword, Damien grabbed the handle, turned and blocked a cutting blow from the blade of the fourth *Chausseur,* the sound of metal clanging in the air.

"Get to the wagon!" Damien ordered. "Head out of town—we'll catch up to you later!" She only shook her head. "Dammit, do as I say!" Steel rang hard against steel as the men fought back and forth inside the narrow confining passage.

Joseph swung a fist and the battle-toughened soldier he fought went to his knees. The soldier quickly regained his feet and fought on. Both men were covered with blood. Joseph's shirt was ripped from chest to waist, the soldier's uniform dirty and torn up the side.

Off to her right Damien parried the fourth man's attack, bringing his sword down in an arching blow aimed at the tall soldier's head, but the man blocked the blade and his own sword sang out, slicing through Damien's shirtsleeve. A thin line of blood appeared where the blade had nicked his arm, and Alexa's hand flew to her mouth to stifle a scream.

Damien fought on, but his strength was beginning to ebb. The pain in his ribs ached unbearably and his breath was coming hard and fast. Fear for Alexa drove him on. He glanced toward the place she had been, saw that she had moved, and turned just in time to see her bringing a huge earthenware jar down over his attacker's head. The man dropped his sword and his eyes rolled back in his head. He staggered backward several feet, then crumpled into a pile of dusty red and brass-buttoned blue at Damien's feet.

Joseph swung a last hard blow that sent his attacker sprawling. The soldier groaned but his eyes fluttered closed and he did not get up.

Joseph flashed Damien a cocky grin and boldly winked at Alexa. "I believe, *mon amis,* it is time for us to leave."

Damien didn't hesitate, just grabbed his wife's arm

and hauled her out of there. Half of him was furious she hadn't obeyed him, and the other half was damned glad she hadn't.

"You little vixen," he whispered as he followed her under the tarp and into the back of the wagon. The sheep were now gone, but the straw remained, along with the scent of manure and soggy wool. "When will you learn to do as I say?" But he kissed the back of her neck where she nestled spoon fashion in front of him.

"You're welcome," she whispered as Joseph climbed up in the seat and the wagon began to roll away. He could feel the smile tugging at her cheeks, and his own lips curved too.

Their smiles slowly faded. Neither of them spoke, just listened to the churning wheels of the wagon, felt the jarring of their bones as the heavy conveyance moved along the rutted road. The tension had returned; he could feel Alexa's heart pounding hard beneath his hand. It matched his own.

Dozens of French soldiers still prowled the city. They had to get north before time for the boat's departure, and now they could not follow the road. So much could still go wrong, yet somehow he felt that with Alexa at his side he could overcome nearly any obstacle.

Perhaps it was just such faith that brought them to the small sheltered cove outside Etretat without further incident. It was twenty minutes till midnight. Twenty minutes before the boat was to sail.

Just twenty minutes more and it would have been too late.

"We made it," Alexa whispered softly. They stood on the beach in front of the small sailing vessel that would carry them back to England. "I can hardly believe it."

He bent and kissed her lips. "Let's go home."

Alexa said a teary good-bye to Joseph, who grinned

and tipped his flat felt cap. Damien shook the man's thick hand then helped his wife into the boat.

Only three men manned it. They handed over the set of plans Alexa and Jules had stolen, and she clutched them against her breast. Then the men pushed the small craft into the water, the oars were thrust in, and they began to row through the surf, their thick muscles straining. The sea splashed noisily against the hull as they broke through to the quiet waters beyond and the safety of darkness.

By morning they would be home.

Damien slid an arm around Alexa's waist and she leaned her head on his shoulder.

"You're quite a prize, Lady Falon," he whispered against her hair. "One I promise to treasure all the days of my life."

She turned and he caught the shimmer of tears. "I love you," she said softly.

He kissed her with all the love he felt in his heart and no small amount of possession. She was his now, and he would never let her go.

"I've loved you since the night you came to me at the inn. I'll never forget your courage or the fire in your lovely green eyes."

Alexa leaned over and kissed him. He wondered if perhaps she had loved him that long too. Perhaps it was the reason she had agreed to marry him. It made him happy to think so, whether or not it was the truth. He pulled his cloak around them both and drew her back against his chest.

Gazing out at the water, he smiled into the darkness and let his mind wander ahead to thoughts of home.

Epilogue

Castle Falon, England
October 25, 1809

A LEX FELT HER HUSBAND'S WARM BREATH AGAINST THE SIDE
OF HER NECK. HE NIBBLED HER EAR THEN ROLLED HER
onto her back and kissed her fully on the lips. She was
lying beneath a satin comforter on top of their big four-
poster bed, resting after a late morning ride into the
village. Damien had been gone these four days past,
taking care of business in the city.

It appeared that he had returned.

She smiled into his darkly handsome face. "Welcome
home, darling."

He kissed her again, this time more soundly. "I've
been missing you for days. Now that I'm here, I've a far
more interesting welcome in mind." A long finger ran

over the curve of her breast, bare beneath the quilted blue satin.

Reaching up, he unfastened his cravat and tugged it free, then slid the froth of lace from around his dark throat. He paused, his blue eyes suddenly concerned. "That is, unless you're not feeling up to it."

Alexa merely smiled. "I'm fine . . . now that you're home." They had been back in England for nearly two months, back at Falon for only a fortnight. She had discovered she carried his babe just this past week.

Damien nuzzled her neck. "Well, I am far from fine at the moment, but I very soon will be." Alexa laughed, and Damien bent over and kissed her. "You're certain it won't hurt the babe."

"Very certain." She had been a little bit tired of late, but thus far had no morning sickness. Her stomach was only gently rounded but her breasts had begun to swell. The thought of Damien's mouth moving over them made them feel heavy and achy. Her nipples grew hard and distended where they rubbed against the cool, smooth satin quilt.

"I wish I had taken you with me." Unbuttoning his shirt, he tugged it free of his breeches and stripped it away. "I missed you more than I could have imagined."

"Next time I shall insist."

"Next time, you won't have to." He had been worried about her, she knew, concerned for the babe she carried. When he'd been told, Damien was ecstatic, and the love she saw in his face every time he looked at her made her own heart swell with gladness.

He kissed her one last time, then with swift, efficient movements, stripped off his black leather boots and breeches. He was fully aroused by the time he joined her on the bed, and she was damp with desire just from watching him prowl the room without his clothes.

He's so beautiful, she thought, as she had a hundred

times, so sleek and dark and male. And so incredibly virile. He took her mouth in a blazing kiss, sifting his fingers through her hair, fanning it out across the pillow.

He tossed back the comforter and paused for a moment just to look at her.

"God, but you are lovely."

Then he was kissing her, making her burn with desire for him. The plunder of his tongue wrung a cry of pleasure from her throat, then his mouth claimed the heavy weight of her breast. He drew on the tip then began to suckle gently, sending waves of heat through her body, tugging low in her belly. Alexa writhed on the bed until he gripped her wrists and held them at the sides of the pillow beneath her head.

Another fiery kiss and he was rising above her, spreading her thighs with his knee and positioning his hard length at her core. With a single hard stroke he filled her to the hilt, and Alexa nearly swooned at the incredible fullness.

"I had to be inside you," he whispered as he nibbled the side of her neck, "I couldn't wait a moment more."

She arched beneath him. "I wanted to feel you inside."

Damien kissed her long and deep, let go of her wrists, and she slid them around his neck. Again and again he filled her with his dominating length, claiming her, it seemed, possessing her as if only she could keep away the darkness and bring him into the light.

It would always be that way, she knew, and she was thankful for it. He needed her, and there was no doubt that she needed him. She responded with a blazing desire for him, arching upward, taking him deeper, urging him on.

"Alexa . . ." he whispered, burying his face in her hair, his body going rigid, her own flaming out of control. Then she was surging upward, flying among the clouds, blinded by the brightness of the sun.

She laced her fingers in his thick black hair and cried out his name. Damien followed her to release a few moments later.

Dear God, would it always be this way between them? But she knew it was more than just the union of their bodies that made it so. It was the loving they shared, the deep, abiding respect they felt for each other, their faith in God and in the future.

They slept for a time, nestled in each other's arms, then she rose from the bed, washed, and began to dress for supper. Damien pulled on his breeches and boots, and had just shrugged into his shirt when her little maid, Sarah, began to beat madly on the door.

"For heaven's sake, Sarah, what is it?" Wearing only her chemise, Alexa pulled open the door.

"It's ye brother, luv. 'E's downstairs pacin', ranting and raving somethin' fierce. The man's in a tither, 'e is. Why, 'twas all I could do to keep 'im from comin' upstairs."

"Dear Lord in heaven." She grabbed up her plum velvet wrapper and hurriedly pulled it on. "I had hoped he would get my letter as soon as he arrived in London. Apparently he did not."

"Mistress Jo is with 'im . . . and lit'le Andrew Augustus, though that one's been takin' to the nursery. 'Er ladyship's been tryin' to make the man see reason, but 'e don't seem to pay 'er no mind. 'E just says he's come for ye husband."

"Oh, dear. I was afraid this would happen."

Damien strode past her toward the door, buttoning up his shirt along the way. "Your brother has a right to be angry. I only hope he doesn't shoot me before I get the chance to explain."

Alexa caught his arm. "Let me speak to him first. Surely I can—"

"This is my doing. I'm the one who has to straighten things out."

"But—"

Damien silenced her with a quick hard kiss, turned and strode off toward the stairs. Alexa fastened the buttons up the front of her wrapper, checked the mirror to be certain she was at least somewhat presentable, then ran after him. When she arrived in the great hall, Damien wasn't there and neither was Rayne.

Instead it was Jocelyn who paced beneath the heavy timbers, a worried look on her face. She glanced up at Alexa's approach.

"Thank heavens." Jo hurried toward her and the two of them hugged. "Are you all right?"

"I'm fine. Where are they?" A loud crash answered her question.

"The study," they said in unison. "But the door is locked," Jo added.

"Dear God, poor Damien. He's barely recovered from his last ordeal. I hope Rayne doesn't hurt him." She looked at Jo, who nervously twisted a strand of her long black hair, and suddenly she wasn't so sure. "I take it you didn't get my message."

"Oh, we got it. Mr. Nelson, Rayne's solicitor, was very explicit about everything that occurred while we were in Jamaica. Rayne checked with his friend, General Strickland, for the balance of the details, and then met with General Fieldhurst. Your brother knows the whole unfortunate story."

"And?"

"I'm afraid, dear, he also knows you were shot and spent nearly a month recovering in a brothel."

"Oh."

"Rayne isn't very happy with your husband at the moment." Another thundering crash.

"So it would seem." Alexa made her way to the

study and began to pound on the door. To her surprise, it swung open almost immediately.

Rayne was standing there with his fists clenched, a black scowl marring his handsome face. A broken Oriental vase lay on the floor at his feet and a chair had been upended and tossed across the room to land on the thick Persian carpet. He glanced from Alexa to the mess he had made. The dark scowl lifted and flashed her an unrepentant grin.

"Sorry, little sister. I meant to do that to your husband, but from the story Fieldhurst told me, he's been battered and beaten quite enough already."

Alexa went into his arms. "Oh, Rayne, I'm so glad to see you." She looked into his beloved features and immediately burst into tears. She hadn't meant to. In fact, she felt like a fool. But Rayne was the closest thing she had to a father, and since he'd been gone, she had suffered so much.

"I—I knew you would come back just as soon as you heard," she said through her tears. "There was no way to reach you once you left Jamaica." She sniffed and drew back to look at him. "I'm sorry I put you to so much trouble."

Rayne hugged her fiercely. "I'm just glad you're safe."

"It wasn't all Damien's fault." She blotted her eyes with the handkerchief Jo gave her. "When I discovered he was involved with the French, I went to see your friend General Strickland. Unfortunately, Strickland was out of the country. Colonel Bewicke . . . well, he was another matter entirely."

"That bloody little worm has tendered his resignation, thanks to Fieldhurst. He is also nursing a broken jaw—thanks to me."

Damien laughed at that. He walked toward Alexa and she gratefully went into his arms.

"I'm sorry, Lord Stoneleigh, for everything that's

happened. Your sister deserves a far better man than I am, but you may rest assured there is no one on this earth who will ever love her more."

Rayne gruffly cleared his throat. "Yes, well . . . that is all that matters. Welcome to the family, Falon." Her brother extended a broad-fingered hand and her husband clasped it firmly.

"Damien," he corrected.

Rayne smiled. "And it's time you called me Rayne."

Damien nodded, and Alexa went up on her toes to kiss him. Rayne pulled his wife into his arms and gave her a resounding kiss too.

"There is one more thing," Alexa said softly, a hint of color rising in her cheeks. "Damien and I . . . we're going to have a baby."

"Oh, Alexa," Jo said, reaching over to hug her, "that's wonderful."

Rayne grinned even broader. "Congratulations, little sister. Now that Falon and I have settled our differences, I couldn't be happier. Little Andrew Augustus will finally have someone to play with . . . two some-ones, in fact, since Jocelyn is also with child." Pride and love shown in his eyes, and an answering warmth flashed in Jo's.

Smiles of joy lit the wood-paneled study, and laughter and hugs and good wishes.

Wreathed in happiness, they left the study, and Alexa and Damien returned upstairs to finish dressing for sup-per. Her husband finished ahead of her, impossibly handsome in his black tailcoat and dove-gray breeches.

When she joined him downstairs in the small salon off the dining room, he and Rayne were discussing the war, and Jocelyn was playing with little Andrew Augus-tus.

"You remember your aunt Alex, don't you, Andy?" Jo smiled at her, and the little boy gripped her hand, his fat cheeks grinning.

"Of course he does." Alexa pulled the two-year-old onto her hip and jostled him lightly up and down. The round-faced child merely grinned, reached up and grabbed a handful of her hair, eliciting a yelp of pain.

"Serves you right," her brother teased, coming up beside her and lifting the child into his thick-muscled arms. "You've had me pulling my hair out for years."

Damien smiled. "I believe that may be only a sample of what I have in store." Alexa playfully punched him.

Little Andy was taken upstairs and the four of them walked toward the dining room. They had almost reached the doorway when the butler, thin, stately Wesley Montague, stepped into the room.

"Might I have a moment, my lord?"

"What is it, Monty?"

"Your sister, my lord. She arrived just a few moments ago."

"Melissa? For godsakes, what is she doing here?" Following Monty, Damien strode off toward the entry. It was dark outside and no word had come preparing him for her arrival. He was gone for so long Alexa began to worry that some new tragedy had befallen them.

Just when she thought to find out, Damien and Melissa walked into the great hall. Her husband stood a full foot taller than the shorter, blond-haired girl—and nearly as rigid as the suit of armor standing against the wall beside him. His face was a dark cloud of foreboding.

"Damien, dear God, what is it?"

"My sister has something to say to you, Alexa. She has come a very long way to do so. I would ask that you hear her out. As for the rest of you, I only ask that nothing you hear leaves this room."

"Of course," Rayne said.

"What is it, Melissa?" Alexa asked, her unease growing by the moment.

The young woman started to speak, stumbled,

stopped and started over. "First, I should like to say that I am thankful that you and my brother are safely returned from France. The newspapers say that you are heroes, and I am proud of you both."

Alexa said nothing, but she was more than a little surprised.

"I would also like to apologize." Melissa Melford straightened. She looked older than she had the last time Alexa had seen her, wiser somehow, more self-assured. She had lost a little weight and her curves seemed more pronounced. With her pale blue eyes and light blond hair, Melissa actually looked pretty.

"Apologize?" Alexa repeated. "I'm afraid I don't understand."

Melissa nervously wet her lips and her hands began to tremble. "As you may recall, when last we spoke, my mother mentioned that she had dismissed our tutor, Graham Tyler. He had been with us since we were children."

"Yes, I remember. Peter always spoke of Mr. Tyler with the greatest admiration."

"He was kind and intelligent, and he and Peter had always been close. At the time, I was sorry to see him go, but it never occurred to me that . . . I never had the slightest idea . . ."

Alexa took an involuntary step forward. "What is it Melissa? What are you trying to say?"

The girl took a steadying breath. "After he left Waitley, Mr. Tyler took a position with the Clarendon family, my mother and Lady Clarendon being quite good friends. It was almost by accident that his secret was discovered. If Lord Clarendon hadn't come home early . . . if he hadn't walked in on them . . ."

"Melissa, please—tell me what has happened!"

"Mr. Tyler was found in a compromising position with Lord Clarendon's fifteen-year-old son. When the marquess confronted him, Graham broke down. He admitted that he had taken advantage of the boy's youth and trust and . . . and . . . that he had tried to do the same thing . . . to Peter." Melissa's voice broke on this last, and Damien moved toward her. She accepted the comfort of his arms and he pressed her head against his shoulder.

"It's all right, Lissa. It's all over now."

Melissa turned tear-filled eyes to Alexa. "Peter was distraught over losing you. He turned to Graham for comfort. What happened between them was the reason he killed himself—Graham Tyler said so. It wasn't your fault, Alexa. I have been so cruel, and it was never your fault."

Three quick steps and the two women were hugging. Damien stood close by, his face closed up, the strain of Melissa's words riding hard on his shoulders. He was clamping down on the anger he felt at what he'd learned, yet there was something oddly tender in the way he watched his wife and his sister.

"What happened to Tyler?" he finally asked, a hard note rising in his voice.

Melissa shook her head. "Lord Clarendon believes he has fled the country."

"He had better hope that he has," Damien said with soft menace. Just then Rayne moved forward. He rested a wide hand on her husband's broad shoulders.

"Let it go, my friend. We've both learned hard lessons about the cost of revenge. Your brother is gone. You've a wife and family to think of now."

Damien said nothing for a long, tense moment, then very slowly he nodded. The hands he fisted at his sides began to relax. "I hope he rots in hell."

"I'm sure he will," Rayne said.

Damien turned to his sister. "What about Mother? How is she taking the news?"

"You know Rachael. Now that she knows the truth, she hates Graham Tyler with a vengeance, but she isn't about to admit she's been wrong about Alexa. Perhaps one day, but not yet.''

"I guess it doesn't really matter." Damien smiled. "What matters is that you came and set things right. It took a great deal of courage for you to do that, Lissa. I'm proud of you.''

"And I'm proud that you are my brother . . . and happy that Alexa is still willing to be my friend.''

"Of course I am," Alexa said. "I'm sorry for what happened to Peter, but I'm grateful to finally know the truth.''

The rest of the evening was a little subdued, each of them caught up in private thoughts. They all retired early, looking forward to a brighter day on the morrow. Walking beside her husband, Alexa climbed the stairs. When they closed the door to their bedchamber, he turned her into his arms, bent and softly kissed her lips.

"All right?" he asked.

"I'm fine, what about you?"

"I'm sorry for what happened to Peter. Perhaps if I had been here, if he'd had someone to talk to . . . still, there is no way to know, and the time has come for us to put it behind us."

She nodded.

Damien ran a finger along her jaw and lifted her chin. "I know how hard all of this has been for you, yet I cannot say that I am sorry. If none of this had happened, I never would have met you. I never would have gambled with you that night at the duke's. I never would have beaten you at cards, I never would have convinced you to come to the inn, and I never would have fallen in love with you."

Alexa smiled at him impishly. "You didn't beat me at cards. You cheated."

Damien flashed her the most devastating grin she had ever seen. "I didn't have to. You kept looking at me instead of your cards—your playing that night was atrocious.''

Alexa laughed, then she arched a seductive brow. ''Or perhaps it was I who cheated. Perhaps I lost the game on purpose.''

Damien laughed too. ''You little minx—you probably did.'' He lowered his head and kissed her. ''Whatever the truth, in the end it was I who won the game. And never have the stakes been more worth winning.''

Alexa looked into his beautiful blue eyes and handsome dark features, felt her heart swell to bursting with love for him, and knew without doubt it was she who had won the game.